s to be returned on or b
stamp

The Cuckoo Wood

The Cuckoo Wood

Jenny Glanfield

VICTOR GOLLANCZ
LONDON

EAST LOTHIAN COUNCIL LIBRARY SERVICE	
0343958	
Morley Books	14.9.98
F	£15.99

First published in Great Britain 1998
by Victor Gollancz
An imprint of the Cassell Group
Wellington House, 125 Strand, London WC2R 0BB

Copyright © Jenny Glanfield 1998

The right of Jenny Glanfield to be identified as author of
this work has been asserted by her in accordance with
the Copyright, Designs and Patents Act, 1988.

A catalogue record for this book is
available from the British Library.

ISBN 0 575 064986

Typeset by Rowland Phototypesetting Ltd
Bury St Edmunds, Suffolk
Printed and bound in Great Britain by
St Edmundsbury Press Ltd, Bury St Edmunds, Suffolk

All rights reserved. No part of this publication may be
reproduced or transmitted in any form or by any means,
electronic or mechanical including photocopying,
recording or any information storage or retrieval system,
without prior permission in writing from the publishers.

This book is sold subject to the condition that it shall not, by way
of trade or otherwise, be lent, resold, hired out, or otherwise
circulated without the publisher's prior consent in any form of
binding or cover other than that in which it is published and
without a similar condition including this condition being imposed
on the subsequent purchaser.

98 99 5 4 3 2 1

For my dearest friend Julie Rose

with love

Prologue

Imagine that you have grown up believing yourself to be an orphan.

This much you know about the circumstances of your birth.

On an autumn day in 1945 your father turned up, unannounced, at his sister Biddie's house in Avonford, in the heart of England. In his arms he was carrying a five-month-old baby girl. He was exhausted after a long and harrowing journey across ravaged, post-war Europe, and the baby was crying from hunger.

It was ten years since Biddie had last seen her brother, for most of his adult life had been spent on the continental mainland and, after the outbreak of war, she had lost touch with him. He explained that he had remarried in 1940, since when he had been living in Italy. On V-E Day, his daughter had been born, but her mother had perished in childbirth.

Somehow or other, he had managed to look after the baby since then. Now he could cope no longer and so he was asking Biddie and her husband Stephen to look after her for the time being, while he sorted himself out. A kind-hearted couple, with a seven-year-old daughter of their own, they unhesitatingly agreed.

Early next morning, your father was gone again. The following day, the front page of the morning papers announced a tragic accident in the English Channel, when a ferry had hit an unexploded mine, killing most of the passengers and crew. A few days later, Biddie received a telephone call from the police at Dover, saying that her brother was among the victims.

In due course, Biddie and Stephen legally adopted you and you were issued with a birth certificate showing your name to be Cara Trowbridge – Cara being the name by which your father had called you and Trowbridge being your aunt and uncle's surname. Your date of birth was shown as 8 May 1945 and your place of birth described simply as Italy.

Chapter 1

As I made my way home from work on the evening of Friday, 18 January 1980, I had far more immediate matters on my mind than my natural parents. The very last thing I was imagining was that, before the day was finally through, my entire perception of them and myself would have been turned topsy-turvy – and that, from then on, nothing in my world was going to be the same again.

One way and another, it had been a long old week.

January was always a particularly hectic time at the head office of the Goodchild Group, where I worked for the chairman and managing director, Miles Goodchild. The year end accounts were flooding in from the Group's subsidiaries, increasing all our workloads and making everyone tense.

Miles had exacting standards and did not tolerate fools or failure. Employees of the Goodchild Group were exceptionally well paid for doing their jobs exceptionally well. But several companies had not met – let alone exceeded – their forecasted profits, and Miles was making it clear that heads were about to roll.

The first casualty would be the managing director of Crispy Crisps and the 'trial' was taking place at the Food Division's monthly board meeting on the coming Monday. Since I would, as usual, be taking the minutes of that meeting, I wasn't looking forward to it. Although I realized that there could be little place for sentiment in business, my instinct was always to give someone a second chance. Which was why Miles was a multi-millionaire captain of industry and I was merely his secretary.

Trying to put work behind me, I crossed Trafalgar Square and went down into the underground station, only to find the platform solid with people and to hear an almost unintelligible voice explaining over a loud-speaker that a train had broken down further up the Northern Line and all services were subject to delay. When a train did finally arrive, we were crammed in like sardines and everyone in my carriage seemed to have a stinking cold.

It was about half past seven when I eventually reached Kentish Town station. On the street, I looked to see if there was a bus in sight but, as usual, there wasn't. So, telling myself, as always, that the exercise would do me good, I set off to walk the half mile or so to Highgate West Hill. Mid-way, three buses in convoy overtook me, which did nothing to improve my humour.

Remembering suddenly that I had again forgotten to take an evening meal out of the freezer that morning and that I had eaten the last egg and tin of baked beans the previous evening, I stopped at the parade of shops opposite the drive leading up to Linden Mansions and bought a ready-made meal for one.

If Nigel had been home, I would have been better organized, but Nigel was currently away on a Caribbean island art directing a campaign for suntan oil. There didn't seem much point in going to a lot of effort just for me – and on that particular grey and cold January evening, I wanted nothing more than to curl up with an instant supper.

I also bought a bottle of wine to buck myself up, then trudged up the narrow drive leading alongside the red-brick, Victorian apartment block which was Linden Mansions. On the fifth floor, I let myself into the empty flat, turned on the light, dumped my coat, briefcase and handbag on a chair in the hall, went into the kitchen, put the lasagne in the oven and opened the wine.

As I did so, I thought of Nigel on his tropical island, which he had explained over the phone was hell on earth, not only because the airline had mislaid one of his suitcases but because the island was in the throes of an unseasonable rainstorm. I sighed and poured myself a glass.

It was nothing new for me to come home to an empty flat or spend the weekend alone. But being accustomed to something disagreeable doesn't make you like it any more.

This had been the pattern of our life since Nigel joined the up-and-coming West End advertising agency, Massey Gault & Lucasz, four years earlier. When he wasn't abroad, visiting clients or working on exotic locations, he was catching up with paperwork and colleagues at the agency. He was seldom in before eight in the evening and often had to work weekends.

Although he was always assuring me that, once the pressure eased, we would spend more time together, there was little sign of that happening in the foreseeable future. In any case, from my own experience of business life at the Goodchild Group, I recognized that the higher one rose up the ladder of success, the harder one had to work to hold on to one's position.

Besides, Nigel loved every aspect of his job. He might pretend to me that all his globe-trotting was exhausting, and that trips, like his present one to the Caribbean, weren't a holiday, but I knew he enjoyed every minute of them.

He couldn't have stood a nine-to-five existence and certainly not being desk-bound. After anything more than a month in the office, he started to get fidgety and irritable. He and Miles were not dissimilar in that respect. Fresh fields and pastures new were always beckoning and, if I was totally honest with myself, that was what had originally attracted me to both of them – in their different ways, of course – one as a husband, one as a boss. I admired their restless energy, their get-up-and-go, their inability to resist a challenge.

As I ate my lonely meal, I reflected on the irony of my situation. What had initially attracted me to Nigel now kept us apart.

We had met in Italy, in Rimini, where I was working as a courier for Jacksons Travel. The year was 1966 and I was twenty-one.

After its unusual beginning, my life had been relatively uneventful until then. I had spent a happy childhood at The Willows in Avonford with Aunt Biddie, Uncle Stephen and my cousin Miranda. Upon leaving school, I had taken a two-year, trilingual secretarial course in French and Italian at Birmingham Technical College, after which I had spread my wings and worked for a few months in Paris.

When Paris had not worked out quite as planned – mainly due to Michel, a French student, with whom I had believed myself to be in love – I had returned to Avonford and taken a dead-end job at a glasshouse crops research institute. There, on the rebound, I had met Graham, to whom I had become engaged. Then Anne, a college friend, who worked for Jacksons Tours in London, had mentioned that they were looking for Italian speakers to work as couriers in Italy during the summer season.

Italy, the country of my birth, had exercised an irresistible pull. Explaining to Graham that I needed thinking time and separation would not necessarily mean the end of our engagement, I had applied for the job with Jacksons and, rather to my surprise, was successful. Graham wasn't prepared to share me, even with another country, and after several emotional scenes, our engagement was broken off.

Rimini itself turned out to be rather disappointing. Despite its history and ancient monuments, it lacked the romantic image conjured up by the tragic story of Francesca da Rimini, immortalized in Dante's *Inferno* and Tchaikovsky's symphonic fantasy. It was a big, ultra-modern resort, with deckchairs regimented on the long sandy beach, and the holidaymakers for whom I was responsible were for the most part middle-aged couples, less interested in Italian culture than cooking themselves lobster red, going to barbecues and drinking 'tea like mother makes'. Still, I had a lot of fun. The Jacksons representatives at the other hotels were a great bunch, and several young, handsome Italian men flirted with me, which helped me forget Graham.

Then the team from the *Style on Sunday* colour supplement arrived to do a fashion shoot.

The moment they came through the door from customs and passport control at the airport, I recognized them, because they looked so different from all my other clients. The photographer and his assistant were self-evident because of the aluminium camera cases they were carrying. The two models were very tall and slim, with waist-length blond hair, and wearing the shortest miniskirts ever seen in Rimini. The make-up artist and stylist were older and more practically dressed in slacks and blouses.

Nigel was the art editor. He was tall and quite well built, broad-shouldered and narrow-hipped, with shoulder-length fair hair and blue eyes. Wearing a pink lace shirt, maroon, flared trousers and Italianate shoes, he looked incredibly trendy. I introduced myself, whereupon he took my hand in his, smiled in a way that made my insides melt, and said, 'Hello, Cara, nice to meet you. I'm Nigel Sinclair from *Style on Sunday*. This is Terry, our photographer, and Ray, his assistant. These are Mandy and Jill, our two models, Nina, the make-up artist, and Pauline, the stylist.'

I led them, with the rest of my new arrivals, out to the coach waiting to take us to the hotel, telling myself not to be a fool and that Nigel Sinclair undoubtedly smiled that way at every woman he met.

During their stay, my local knowledge and ability to speak Italian came in extremely useful to them. I organized hire cars, directed them to the most scenic locations, suggested indoor venues when the weather suddenly turned bad and obtained the necessary permits from bureaucratic officials.

Their worst problems were the inevitable packs of marauding young Italian men, who made an instant beeline for Mandy and Jill. It must have been about three days after their arrival that I went down to the beach to find a group of half a dozen bronzed, would-be Lotharios, clad in skimpy swimming trunks, creating havoc on the shoot and totally ignoring Nigel and Terry's angry requests – in English – to get out of the way of the camera. Mandy and Jill were trying the smiling, pleading approach, which was only making matters worse.

One of the first lessons I had been taught after my own arrival – by a tough courier on her fifth season – was how to deal with such a situation. Liz's strategy was that adopted by Italian girls and their mothers. If a withering look didn't work, you let fly with a few choice sentences regarding the masculinity and parentage of the troublemakers. If that failed, then a flailing shoulderbag, already securely zipped shut to guard against pickpockets (another common little hazard), threatening their beauty and their pride, always did the trick.

If the pests tried the same ploy when you were in a car, you did not allow yourself to be slowed down and brought to a halt, but steered towards them. Liz had a VW Beetle, which had taken on a good few Fiats in its time and always emerged the victor. It seemed that Italian men were as proud of the appearance of their cars as they were of themselves.

Now, wrapping the strap of my bag firmly round my hand and, assuming my severest school-mistressy expression, I advanced down the sand. Nigel threw me a distraught glance and muttered, 'They're like bloody wasps. How the hell does one get rid of them?'

I let fly in a tone worthy of any Italian mamma protecting her little chicks, explaining that the two models were doing a job and ending with the threat that, if the young boys did not immediately remove their offending, pale and puny little bodies to another part of the beach, I would summon the police.

That was sufficient, especially when some Italians in nearby deckchairs added their vociferous support for me. With slightly abashed but still cheeky smiles, the pack moved off in search of an easier target.

'Thanks very much indeed,' Nigel said. 'That was most impressive.'

I shrugged with attempted nonchalance and replied, 'It's all part of my job.'

By way of thanks, Nigel asked me to join them for dinner at the hotel. That was my first real glimpse of the world he inhabited. Listening to the conversation round that dinner table was to be filled with a kind of awe, as they all spoke familiarly of people who were only names to me: models like Jean Shrimpton and Twiggy; photographers like Snowdon and Bailey; fashion designers like Mary Quant and Barbara Hulanicki; pop stars like The Beatles and The Rolling Stones, Sandie Shaw, Cilla Black and Marianne Faithful.

My own life seemed very ordinary in comparison, but since they were less interested in me than in having an audience to show off to, my shyness was quite well hidden.

Nigel, however, seemed different. He did try to bring me into the conversation by asking me questions, like where I had learned to speak Italian so well and how I had become a courier.

The following evening – to my utmost surprise and great joy – he invited me out to dinner on my own. We went to a restaurant on the way up to San Marino, eating outside on the terrace, looking across the plain towards the lights of Rimini. Fireflies danced in the night sky and the air was full of the sound of crickets, playing their miniature violins.

We talked about all the usual things people talk about when they are getting to know each other: our families, our jobs, our friends, our homes. Feeling less intimidated away from the rest of them, I told him a bit about my father and my arrival in Avonford, as well as about my childhood. But I skated over it all very quickly, bearing in mind the lesson which had been instilled into me almost since birth – that the best way to a man's heart is to be a good listener.

So, encouraged by my questions, Nigel did most of the talking. I heard about his upbringing in south London, his father who was an art teacher, and his mother, who was a housewife. I learned that he was twenty-six, five years older than me, and unmarried. Both he and his sister had inherited their father's artistic ability and gone to art college after leaving school. His sister had followed in her father's footsteps and was teaching art at a school in Hastings on the south coast. She was married to another teacher and they had two children, but although he was extremely fond of them, his busy way of life meant he didn't get down to Hastings as often as he would like.

After a short stint as a layout artist on a motoring magazine – Nigel was mad about cars and his dream was to own a Porsche – he had been taken on by the newly formed *Style on Sunday* as junior art director. Then the art editor had moved on and Nigel had been promoted. That was, as he described it with an appealing mixture of pride and modesty, his lucky break.

Financially, it had enabled him to leave home and buy a one-bedroom flat in Islington. Living at home had become claustrophobic, he explained. Refusing to recognize that he was grown-up, his mother was always worrying and fussing, and, while he still lived at home, had sat up waiting for him until he came in.

I nodded sympathetically, although Aunt Biddie and Uncle Stephen had always been very reasonable with Miranda and me. So long as we had told them where we were going and how late we were coming home, they had never laid down the law – trusting us to be responsible. And, when I had applied for this job with Jacksons, they had actively encouraged me, just as they had about going to Paris. 'See as much of the world as you can, while you are able to,' Aunt Biddie had said. 'Such opportunities didn't exist when I was young.'

Freedom was very important, Nigel went on. Everyone needed a space of their own, where they could flop out and be themselves. Also, he found living out of a suitcase so much of the time quite stressful. Not that he was complaining, but it was great to go back to his own pad in Islington – even if he did have to do his own washing, he added with a laugh.

It was very late when we finished dinner. On the way back down the Strada Panoramica, he stopped the car in a lay-by and kissed me. When I came to after this breath-stopping experience, Graham was nothing but a name. This was love with a capital L. This was the real thing. All my other experiences, such as they were, had been leading up to this night, preparing me for meeting Nigel.

Back in my little hotel room, however, where he had left me at the door with a last passionate kiss, I underwent a moment of crushing doubt. It was obvious why I should be falling in love with him, but what could he possibly see in a nobody like me? He was so suave, so sophisticated, so self-assured. Why, when he was surrounded by women far more beautiful – models like Mandy and Jill – should he be attracted to me?

Next evening, however, he took me out to dinner again, to a fish restaurant overlooking the harbour in Cesanatico. We found we shared a number of interests in common. We both had the travel bug, as he described it. We were both voracious readers, loved music, liked art and enjoyed going to the cinema. True, our tastes differed. Nigel liked Harold

Robbins, The Doors, Salvador Dali and Fellini, while I preferred Françoise Sagan, Joan Baez, Renoir and David Lean. But, fundamentally, we seemed to be on the same wavelength.

That night, on the way back to our hotel, he kissed me again, his hands travelling lightly and expertly over my body. I was terribly attracted to him but somehow managed to push his hands away. Nigel did not persist and, as a result, rose even higher in my estimation.

The following evening, at a ranch-style restaurant just behind Rimini, the conversation became more intimate. He confessed that he had recently ended a two-year affair with a model called Edwina, who was now embarking upon a career as an actress. 'I hope she makes it,' he said, with a beguiling generosity of spirit, 'though, personally, I don't think she's got what it takes. On the other hand, she's a stunning-looking bird and it's quite possible that some film director will fancy her, which is what I think she's really hoping for.'

Jealousy stabbed my heart and, although I realized that it would be stupid to expect him not to have had girlfriends, his words about freedom and needing a space of one's own suddenly took on a different weight. Feeling a bit outdone, I toyed with the idea of telling him about my engagement, but dull old Graham seemed hardly to enter the same category as the fabulous Edwina.

So, for the rest of the meal, I left the talking to Nigel. Then, as we were about to leave the restaurant, he said, 'There isn't any chance of you being able to take next weekend off, I suppose? You see, I don't have to return to London with the others. So long as Terry takes the film back and gets it processed, I needn't be in the office until Monday. I've always wanted to visit Venice and was wondering if you'd like to come with me.'

My heart seemed to stop beating.

One of my colleagues, for whom I had done a similar favour in the past, agreed to take over my duties and Nigel and I went to Venice.

There, I sat at sunset on the terrace of the Florian café in St Mark's Square, listening to music, letting my gaze roam over the famous pigeons, up to the bronze horses on the Basilica and over the pink marbled walls of the Doges' Palace. Hand in hand we wandered along the Marzaria, window-shopping as we went, to the Rialto Bridge, where gondoliers, in sailors' jumpers and straw hats with coloured ribbons, serenaded their passengers in time-honoured fashion as they glided along the Grand Canal.

I was caught in the city's spell. How could I fail to be? When, eventually, we returned to our hotel, where Nigel had booked two single rooms, my own bed was never slept in.

He told me that night, as the canal lapped outside our window, that he loved me. He claimed I was everything he wanted in a woman, that I was not only beautiful but intelligent and spirited, and, in bed, I was super sensational.

I didn't really believe any of that. When I looked in the mirror, I actually quite liked the person who looked at back at me. I wasn't as tall and slim as Mandy and Jill, but five feet six is a good height to be and nine stone a reasonable weight. But in no way could my face be described as beautiful. Distinctive, maybe, but beautiful, no. How could it be with the thatch of curly, red hair, surrounding my square face like a halo? Well, maybe it wasn't exactly square, but it certainly wasn't heart-shaped and it didn't possess interesting angles. My nose wasn't fashionably retroussé, my lips didn't pout sexily and my eyes were a nondescript greyish-blue. But at least I didn't have the pale features which so often accompany red hair. My eyebrows and lashes were dark and my skin tanned easily, albeit with a liberal sprinkling of freckles.

As for my spirit and my intellect, I was nothing out of the ordinary. And, so far as that bit about my performance in bed was concerned, I knew Nigel was exaggerating, because I had been too nervous to relax.

However, he had continued, 'Above all, you're a genuine person. You're not like these empty-headed models, who can think of nothing beyond clothes, make-up and men. And that's what I most like about you.'

And that I believed – because it was true.

After his return to London, he wrote to me. The letter wasn't very long but it said all the right things. I immediately replied, with several pages, and his next letter arrived within a few days.

At the end of the summer season, I went back to England and, after a quick visit home to Avonford, went down to London, staying at Anne's flat in Belsize Park. When Nigel and I met again, the attraction was still there, proving that what we felt for each other was not a passing fancy but the real thing.

Abandoning my dreams of travelling the world, I impulsively handed in my notice at Jacksons and set about getting a job in London. I was fortunate enough to find one almost immediately, which was when I started working for Miles. The Goodchild Group was still expanding at that time and most of its business was with food and wine companies in France and Italy, which meant that my secretarial and language skills both finally came into their own. Furthermore, one of Anne's flatmates just having left, I was able to move in with her.

Nigel and I met each other most evenings and every weekend – when he wasn't travelling. In his own environment, Nigel was different to how he had been in Rimini, more relaxed and at ease. His flat was in a purpose-built block and furnished in a very contemporary, sixties fashion. There were no signs of Edwina, no photographs of her on the wall or overtly feminine touches about the place. It was, in fact, very much a bachelor pad.

We went out quite a lot, for Nigel had a wide social circle, people he knew from school and college, as well as those he had met during the course of his job. Most of them tended to be in the same line of work – either employed on magazines or in advertising – and, although we only had Nigel in common, I got on with them all well enough.

Nigel was actually rather proud of me and showed me off, almost as a kind of status symbol. When he introduced me, he usually repeated the story of how I had chased off the Italian yobs on the beach at Rimini and I found myself the object of unaccustomed admiration.

As well as going out, though, we would often spend the evening curled up on his sofa, watching television, listening to records or simply chatting about our dreams and ambitions. I always felt that I was seeing the real Nigel then. He admitted to a love-hate relationship with the rather superficial world he inhabited. 'It's just like show-biz,' he said. 'It appears extremely glamorous to outsiders, but it can get wearing on occasions dealing with so many neurotic and fragile egos, when all you really want to do is get on with your job and do it well. That's why I find it so refreshing to be with you. You're so solid and down-to-earth. And I mean that in the nicest way.'

I could not help but be impressed by his dedication to his work and needed no convincing that he possessed enormous talent. Not having any clear career goal in sight myself – only Aunt Biddie was aware of my secret dream, one day to try to follow in my father's footsteps and become a writer – I saw my role in life as helping Nigel achieve his ambitions and providing a stable base for him always to return to.

When I met his family, I found them to be pleasant people, touchingly proud of his success. It was obvious that Nigel was indeed the apple of his mother's eye and she did still treat him rather like a little boy. I sensed her regarding me critically, almost as a rival, and went out of my way to try and endear myself to her. In that, I never succeeded totally, but his father and sister seemed to like me, which helped counteract his mother's possessiveness.

After that, we went up to Avonford so that he could meet Aunt Biddie, Uncle Stephen and Miranda – who gave him their seal of approval. 'So long as he makes you happy, that's all that concerns me,' Aunt Biddie had declared. 'Seems to have his wits about him,' Uncle Stephen had opined. And Miranda had said, 'He's exactly the sort of guy you need – extrovert, go-ahead – and he likes travelling.'

To my disappointment, Nigel was not as enthusiastic about The Willows as I had hoped, but – I had to admit – my childhood home was lacking in modern conveniences, while Avonford itself was very much a quiet, provincial backwater.

In the spring of 1967, just before my twenty-second birthday, we were married at Camden registry office in London. Aunt Biddie would have preferred me to have had a white wedding at Avonford's abbey church – like Miranda, when she had married Jonathan Evans, back in 1960. And so, in my heart of hearts, would I.

However, Nigel was an atheist and registry office weddings were trendy. Moreover, his family and friends lived in London or the southern counties. So I gave in. Aunt Biddie, Uncle Stephen, Miranda, Jonathan and their little daughter Stevie came down and stayed in an hotel. Apart from Anne, they were the only representatives of my side. I wore a white lace trouser suit and a big floppy straw hat, and Nigel a cream suit, with a flowery shirt and shocking pink tie. We didn't have a proper reception, but went out to dinner afterwards and then on to a discothèque. In fact, it was great fun and everyone enjoyed themselves, but it was not how I had always visualized my wedding.

Our honeymoon was spent in Ibiza. Nigel, who had been to most Mediterranean countries by then, liked Spain best. As for Italy, I was the only good thing to come out of there, he claimed.

When we returned, I moved into Nigel's flat. I would rather have started my married life in a home that was new to both of us but, as he said, it was daft to move for the sake of it. The time to move would be when we started a family.

By and large, our first years together were very happy. Of course, we experienced our ups and downs. What couple doesn't? For instance, every now and again, Edwina would appear on the television in a commercial or a minor role in a play and Nigel would go very quiet, while I would be seized with an almost insane jealousy. I discovered that he still kept photographs of her in his portfolio, which he claimed were necessary because she had featured in some of his best work, but I wasn't convinced and, for a long while, believed he was still in love with her.

When he went away on trips like the one to Rimini during which we had met, leaving me alone for a week or a fortnight, I worked myself up into a dreadful state of jealousy and self-doubt, positive that he was having an affair with one of the models. On his return, I would make a scene, which was not what I intended, and, instead of being reassuring, he became angry and impatient. Realizing I was going the best way about driving him away into another woman's arms, I tried – not always successfully – to keep my fears and insecurities to myself.

But, apart from those sorts of incidents, I can't remember any major rows and must assume that any storm clouds swiftly blew over. We were in love, we had hopes and plans and dreams. On the strength of our combined salaries, we could afford to buy a new car, all the clothes we wanted and the occasional piece of new furniture, as well as go abroad on holiday every summer.

Yes, looking back to our courtship and the early years of our marriage, it was easy to see why Nigel and I had fallen for each other. It wasn't just that I had been flattered by his attentions and dazzled by his handsome appearance, charming manners and glamorous lifestyle. I had glimpsed the inner man and, even before we were married, sensed his underlying insecurities. Like most women, I had needed to be needed. And Nigel had needed me, every bit as much as I had needed him – albeit for different reasons. In short, we had complemented each other.

So far as he was concerned, I had posed him no threat. I wasn't the sort of wife – like Edwina would have been – who was constantly trying to steal the limelight. I listened in adoration to everything he said, never attempting to outdo him and cap his stories with my own successes. Even my jealousy was a factor to the good, because it proved how much I loved him, boosting his ego and self-confidence.

For my part, I had provided the stability in his life – like his mother had before me. I was the one constant element in his constantly changing universe. Colleagues came, colleagues went, as did clients and campaigns.

But Cara was always faithful, always true, always waiting for him at home – whether it was at the end of a busy day or on his return from the other side of the world. He could be sure that I would be there, with open arms and dinner in the oven, ready to listen and understand, to approve and applaud, to congratulate or commiserate.

Until 1973, when I suddenly failed him. Yes, 1973 had been the turning point, after which nothing had ever been quite the same again.

During the early years of our married life, there had been only one major disappointment: I didn't seem able to get pregnant. We both wanted children, though I wanted them more than Nigel did. As an orphan, I longed for the experience of having a family of my own and enjoying that unique bond of mother, father and child.

I rush to stress that this was no reflection whatsoever on Aunt Biddie and Uncle Stephen. People who don't know me well sometimes assume that, because I always refer to them as aunt and uncle, I never considered them as parents but nothing could be further from the truth.

Although I was understandably curious about my natural mother and entertained a highly romantic image of my father, Aunt Biddie and Uncle Stephen were the people who provided the solid anchor in my life and the safe harbour to which I could always return.

In fact, Aunt Biddie and I were very similar in appearance, more so than her and Miranda, and strangers frequently mistook us for mother and daughter. We were the same height and had the same colouring. Before Aunt Biddie's hair turned white, it was red like mine, darkening almost to a deep copper in winter and bleaching nearly blond in summer. Miranda, in contrast, is shorter and has inherited her father's colouring, his brown eyes and straight dark brown hair, with only a slight chestnut tint.

I was on the whole a very normal, well-adjusted, cheerful girl. Occasionally, particularly in my teens, I used to indulge in fantasies about a chance encounter with a member of my natural mother's family, with whom I would feel an instant empathy. But these dreams fell into the same category as those in which the boy down the road fell madly in love with me, or a film producer saw me and offered me a star role in a film, or the pop star of the moment asked me to become lead singer in his group.

When I was in the fourth year at school, I acquired an Italian penfriend in Bologna, and, the first time I went to stay with her, I did make enquiries about trying to trace my natural mother. However, being Italy, everything was incredibly complicated and not made any easier by the fact that I didn't know in which region I had been born, let alone which town. So Pia's parents suggested that I should regard them as my Italian family and, from then on, I addressed them as Mamma and Papà.

Because I would have hated to say or do anything to hurt Aunt Biddie and Uncle Stephen, or do something that they might have interpreted as ingratitude or unhappiness, I never mentioned that to them. Nor did I tell them about my fantasies – nor about my nightmare.

In my nightmare, I was with my father. I know it was him, because he looked as he did in the photographs in Aunt Biddie's old albums: very tall, with a shock of red, curly hair, like my own. There was also a woman, whose features I never saw, because she was always in front of us. She was running and we were trying to catch up with her. When I was little, we would be in the river meadows, down by the old ford after which Avonford was named. But when I was older and had travelled further afield, my nightmare could take place on a hillside or a cliff top. The ending, however, was always the same. My father would go ahead and, just as he was about to catch up with her, the ground gave way beneath my feet . . .

Then, in January 1973, when I was twenty-seven and Nigel and I had been married nearly six years, the long dreamed of moment arrived. Scarcely daring to hope, I went to the doctor and tests confirmed that I was three months pregnant. I was ecstatic and Nigel was thrilled, too.

About the same time, Nigel changed jobs, leaving *Style on Sunday* for Quantum Design, where he was responsible for designing the record covers and publicity material for many well-known pop singers and groups. With his new job came an increase in salary and, at the beginning of April, we were able to move up-market, into the flat in Linden Mansions, overlooking Parliament Hill Fields. Our cup of happiness seemed full to overflowing.

But I lost the baby and then Uncle Stephen died.

I sucked in my breath and drank some more wine, then went along to the bedroom to change.

What Nigel didn't realize was the loneliness of my existence when he was away. Sure, I had friends of my own. There were Aunt Biddie, Miranda, Jonathan and Stevie up at Avonford. There was Juliette at the office. And, here at Linden Mansions, I had Sherry and Roly Pearson. But there were limits to how often I could inflict myself upon their company and, in any case, that wasn't the point: it was Nigel's company I wanted.

Although I had known, well before we were married, that he would frequently spend periods away from home because of his job, I had no idea that I would end up missing him so much – or so often. Who, at the age of twenty-one, has the sagacity to think ahead and visualize oneself thirteen years on, coming home on a gloomy January night to an empty flat and the prospect of a solitary meal of ready-made lasagne, followed by the weekend's chores?

Nor had I foreseen the long-term consequences when I blithely gave up my job at Jacksons, allowing my dreams of travelling the world to be eclipsed by my ambition to become the perfect wife and, hopefully soon, the perfect mother. Nigel hadn't forced me to leave Jacksons. I was the one who had decided that a job in the travel business was incompatible with a steady relationship – and certainly with marriage.

It hadn't occurred to me to demand an equal sacrifice from Nigel, principally because it didn't feel like a sacrifice then. Anyway, the circumstances were different. Travel was an adjunct to his job, a necessary evil, according to him, not its whole *raison d'être*.

In my secret heart, I had hoped that, especially when he progressed up the career ladder, there would be opportunities for me to accompany him on some of his foreign assignments. As time went by, though, it became clear that this wasn't on the agenda, and I had to content myself with our annual holiday. Except that those holidays didn't turn out quite as I had hoped either. While I spent fifty weeks of the year waiting to scratch my itchy feet, Nigel said he did enough gadding about the rest of the year and needed a rest when he was on holiday. His ideal holiday was to get up late, lie on a beach all day, and go to a good restaurant or nightclub in the evening.

So, instead of visiting a different country each year, hiring a car and seeing all the sights, we had kept going back to the Balearics, to Ibiza and Majorca. It sounds feeble to me now, but the conviction with which Nigel expressed his needs nearly always left me feeling selfish and cross with myself. And by the time I realized this wasn't entirely reasonable, the habit had formed and I couldn't, frankly, be bothered to make a stand.

The knowledge that I was responsible for my own destiny, however, was scant consolation as I returned to the kitchen, refilled my glass and took the foil dish containing my unappetizing-looking meal from the oven. It's one thing to identify your problem and quite another to resolve it, especially if you've spent years looking the other way for a quiet life. There was no easy solution.

I finished my lasagne, washing down the cardboard aftertaste with some more wine. That was quite enough introspection. With a stubbornly heavy heart, I tried to think positively.

What would cheer me up? If Sherry wasn't working tomorrow, maybe she'd like to go to Oxford Street with me and we could see what was left in the sales. Alternatively, Juliette might be free. Her husband worked for the electricity generating board and did peculiar shifts in various parts of the country, often leaving her a grass widow, like me. I should have thought of that before I left the office. Still, I could always give her a ring.

At that very moment, the telephone rang. I jumped up and ran into the hall, hoping it would be Nigel, but actually expecting it to be one of his friends, probably someone like Brian Turner who, not realizing Nigel was abroad, would be asking if he was playing golf the next day.

Instead of which, it was Aunt Biddie.

'Cara, thank heavens you're home!' she exclaimed. 'Go and switch the television on to BBC2 immediately. Oliver Lyon's interviewing a Russian princess who was apparently married to your father.'

She put the phone down before I could ask any questions.

Chapter 2

I turned on the television just as the broadcaster, Oliver Lyon, was saying, 'Connor Moran was a poet whose potential for greatness was never realized. He was a close friend of El Toro and in 1936 they went to Spain together to fight in the Civil War. The poems he wrote during that period are remarkable for their lyrical and narrative power.'

A black and white photograph flashed up on the screen, showing two men. One was the Spanish artist, El Toro, unmistakable with his leonine head, thrust back between his broad shoulders, and wearing baggy, knee-length shorts. The other, dressed in an open-necked shirt and slacks, stood a full head taller and had a mop of curly hair. It was Connor Moran – my father.

The snapshot faded and the camera moved to a woman reclining against the arm of a *chaise-longue*. She was very slim and dressed entirely in black, the severity of her attire offset by a gold necklace in which sparkled a single, large solitaire, and a gold bracelet on her wrist.

The camera closed in on her face, which was strikingly handsome. Her hair was thick and straight, cut to just above the shoulders, covering her ears and turning under at the ends. Presumably it owed its colour to a hairdresser's skill but the soft blond tint looked completely natural. Despite her skin being criss-crossed with a network of fine lines, her face had a strong bone structure, with pronounced high cheek bones. Her eyes were quite deep set and green, their colour emphasized by a discreet application of matching eyeshadow.

'You seem remarkably well informed about him,' she said, in a voice that was deep and gutteral, with a markedly foreign accent.

Oliver Lyon gave an urbane smile. 'My father was the art critic, Stanley Lyon, who was well acquainted with El Toro and, through him, met many of his friends. It was he who first drew my attention to Connor Moran's poetry.'

'Ah, I see.'

She took a sip of coffee, leaving Oliver Lyon to continue.

'Connor Moran suffered a chest injury during the final months of the Spanish Civil War and, after being treated in hospital, he and El Toro returned to Paris. By that time, the Second World War had, of course, broken out. The Germans were occupying much of France. They were marching on Paris . . .'

She nodded. 'It was a very anxious, frightening time. The government had fled the capital and gone south to Bordeaux. Many Parisians were following them. Friends asked me to go with them. But I could not believe that I would be in any personal danger if I remained. Then Connor arrived back. He had been invited to Italy to recuperate from his injuries by friends of his who had a villa in the country and he convinced me to go with him.'

'Not only to go with him but to marry him.'

'Yes, indeed.'

'Why did you marry him?'

'I consider that an extraordinary question. For love, of course.'

'You have to admit that it seems an unlikely match. You were a Russian princess, descended from the boyars, and your previous husband had been a member of the French aristocracy. Connor Moran, however, was merely the son of a poor Irish schoolmaster. In my experience of human relationships a princess may sometimes fall in love with a pauper, but she seldom marries him.'

She studied him haughtily. 'I did not realize that you were such a snob.'

He acknowledged the rebuke with an inclination of his head and continued, 'So you were married and went to live in Italy. Whereabouts?'

'The house where we lived was up in the mountains, surrounded by thick woods and overlooking a lake. It was a rather primitive place, far from civilization. My most vivid memory of it is of the cuckoos which arrived every spring. Never in my life before or since have I heard so many cuckoos. They were so loud that you could not sleep in the morning.' Her voice turned suddenly petulant. 'I grew to hate that sound.'

Oliver Lyon chuckled. 'However, you were safe there, unlike many of your Russian compatriots, who remained in Paris.'

'That is true,' she conceded. 'After the Germans broke the so-called Friendship Pact by invading the Soviet Union, the Russian *émigrés* were treated like Jews and sent to concentration camps. Many of my old friends did not survive.'

'You were unaffected by the war in your mountain retreat?'

'We were far from the air raids and bombs, yes. However, we were affected in other ways. The mountains were full of partisans and guerrilla groups, who made it unsafe to travel anywhere, certainly on one's own. And, I must confess that, having been used to living in a big city, I missed shops, restaurants, the theatre, the ballet and, above all, the company of my friends in Paris. However, for the sake of Connor's health and happiness, I was prepared to sacrifice such little luxuries. And because the air was so clear and we were seldom short of food, his health did indeed improve a lot and he was able to write.'

'He died, I believe, at the end of the war?'

'He died several months after it ended. He was drowned at sea.'

'A great tragedy,' Oliver Lyon murmured. Then, after allowing a considerate pause, he asked, 'So what did you do next?'

'I happened to meet up again with an old friend of Léon, who had often stayed with us in Paris – the Conte di Montefiore. Like Léon, Umberto was considerably older than myself but a very courteous, very cultured man. The Montefiores were one of the great old families of Genoa. Their fortune was founded in shipping, but the proceeds were spent in building beautiful palaces, embellished by the finest of artists. Umberto was a great *cognoscente* of the arts.'

We were shown a posed photograph of the Conte di Montefiore, a patrician-looking gentleman, standing behind a desk in a vast office, sumptuously decorated in rococo style.

'Since I had last seen him, Umberto's wife, like Connor, had died. She had been killed in an air raid, together with their daughter and their grandson. For a couple of years, we enjoyed a close friendship and then we decided to get married. Experience had shown us that life could end at any moment, so we both regarded the life that remained to us as a bonus. Each and every day was a gift, granted to us and not to others, and it was for us to live each day to the full.'

Oliver Lyon raised an imperceptible eyebrow. 'And did you?'

'Indeed! With Umberto, I travelled the world. He had offices in London, New York and South America. There was hardly a country we did not visit at some time or other – except the Soviet Union.'

'The *Conte* even named a ship after you.'

'Ah, yes, *La Belle Hélène*. Such a magnificent liner, with every luxury. She was described as the jewel of the oceans.'

'But wouldn't I be right in thinking that she never recouped her costs?'

She frowned. 'I never understood this. There seemed no reason. So far as I was aware, her passenger lists were always full.'

'Yet after she was built, the Montefiore fortunes suffered an irretrievable reversal, which eventually led to the closure of the entire shipping line.'

'There were other factors. For instance, the Montefiore shipyard had benefited from military contracts – after the war, there was no need for battleships.'

'How did the *Conte* react to the collapse of his business?'

'He never discussed business or financial matters with me. But I know he was deeply upset and felt it as a personal failure. Not long after that, he died.'

She took a sip of coffee, then went on, 'After Umberto's death, I did not want to remain in Italy, which held for me so many unhappy memories. So I came to London, where I had some good friends. It was through them that I met Howard.'

The camera moved to a framed photograph on the mantelpiece, showing an elderly man, dressed in sports jacket and plus fours, and holding a gun, with one foot resting on a stile and a retriever sitting beside him.

'Your late husband, the Earl of Winster,' Oliver Lyon prompted.

Her eyes hooded over. 'Dear Howard, he has been dead nearly four years now, but I still find it hard to believe that he is no longer with me. I was very lucky to meet him at an age when few women can hope to marry again and find happiness.'

'As well as your house here in Chelsea, he also had a home in Derbyshire – Kingston Kirkby Hall?'

'Ah, yes. Kingston Kirkby Hall was Howard's spiritual home, but, for myself, I must confess to having found it a very desolate place. The English have little idea of *confort*. It was an ugly building, very exposed and with no central heating, no running hot water.'

Another photograph, this time of a Palladian mansion, with classical columns, cornices and parapets, set against a background of bleak moorland and gritstone cliffs.

'I spent most of my time here in London, but Howard would go often to Kingston Kirkby Hall for the grouse shooting and so on.'

'So you led virtually separate lives?'

'That was not my wish or intention.'

Oliver Lyon allowed a little pause, then said, 'In the course of your life, Princess, you have run the full gamut of human experience. You have known revolution and war, wealth and poverty, tragedy and happiness, love and loss. Back in the carefree days of your Russian childhood, as you described it earlier, you cannot have expected your future to turn out as it has?'

A shadow flitted across her face and her features seemed to soften. 'No, I didn't. And now, in old age, I cannot help but wonder at the purpose of all the suffering I have witnessed. There are those who consider me fortunate, because I live in a degree of luxury which they are denied. But, as one approaches death, one realizes how relatively unimportant possessions are.'

'You had no children,' Oliver Lyon said in a sympathetic tone. 'Have you ever regretted that?'

The camera moved to an icon above the mantlepiece, depicting the Madonna with the Christ child, then returned to the Princess.

Her hair fell across her face like a curtain and she brushed it away with a graceful sweep of long thin fingers with long, blood-coloured nails. 'No. I have never considered that motherhood is necessary to being a complete woman. Indeed, I have few regrets, for regret is a futile emotion. One cannot undo what has been done, so I try never to look back. This interview has been an exception.'

She stopped, took a deep breath and gazed, almost challengingly, into the camera. 'As for the future now, I see only emptiness. All the people I have loved are dead. Only my enemies survive. But they say, do they not, that the good die early and the bad die late?'

And with those words, the interview ended.

The scene changed to a television studio and Oliver Lyon said, 'Today would have been the Princess Hélène Shuiska's eightieth birthday. Sadly, she passed away earlier this week, after a short illness. This programme has, therefore, been shown as a tribute to her.'

I switched off the television and sat numbly for a few moments, my heart pounding and my mind reeling. Who was she, this princess, who had been married to my father and lived with him in Italy at the time of my birth? Was she my mother? Yet how could she be if she had never had any children?

Dazedly, I went into the hall and dialled Aunt Biddie's number, my fingers automatically selecting the digits.

She answered at the first ring, sounding as shocked as I was. 'Wasn't that extraordinary? I can't get over it. I'd been watching a documentary about otters and then I looked at the *Radio Times* and saw there was an interview with Oliver Lyon, so I decided to leave the television on, because I've always liked him – he's such a charming man. Then to my absolute astonishment, he said something about her second husband and mentioned Connor's name. That's when I rang you.'

'Had you never heard of her before?'

'Good heavens, no. If I had, I'd have told you, of course. I just can't get over it all. I had absolutely no idea that your father was married to a Russian princess. Oh, I don't understand it at all. I don't understand any of it.'

She sounded so distressed that I forgot myself and asked anxiously, 'Are you all right?'

'Yes, of course. I'm just – I don't know – it came as such a shock. It was the very last thing I was expecting, although, strangely enough, I was actually thinking about Connor, because she was talking about her life in Paris and all the arty people she'd met through her first husband. And, because Connor had been living in Paris at the same time, I was wondering if their paths had ever crossed. You know how one does? Then suddenly Oliver Lyon came out with this question about when she had met Connor Moran. I was flabbergasted. Thank heavens you were in, otherwise I'd be thinking now that I'd imagined it all.'

'Who was she?' I asked.

'Of course, you didn't see the beginning of the programme. Oh, I'm all of a fluster. Hold on a moment. It's here in the *Radio Times*. Her name was Princess Hélène Romanovna Shuiska.'

'And she was Russian?'

'Yes, she grew up in St Petersburg and escaped during the Revolution with her cousin, Dmitri something or other. I can't remember his full name. It sounded a bit like saccharin. But it doesn't matter. They made their way somehow to Paris, where she married a French baron, whose name I can't remember either. Anyway, through him she met all sorts of artists and had her portrait painted by El Toro. Then she met Connor and married him, after which they went to Italy. You did see that bit, didn't you?'

'Yes, I came in when they were showing the photograph of him and

El Toro. And I heard all the rest, about the house in Italy up in the mountains.' I paused. 'Do you realize what this means? If she and my father were married at the time I was born . . .'

'I know,' Aunt Biddie said shakily, 'it must mean she was your mother, even though she denied ever having had any children.'

'She didn't exactly say that. She sort of brushed the question aside.'

'Yes, you're right, she did. Oh, I really don't know what to make of it all. If she was your mother, why did Connor tell me that she had died in childbirth? Why did he lie to me?'

'Listen,' I said. 'Why don't I come up to Avonford and we can talk it all through properly, together?'

'Well, if you wouldn't mind.'

'Mind? Of course I don't mind. It's ages since I've seen you, anyway.'

'What about Nigel?'

'He's abroad.'

'Well, in that case . . .'

'I could leave now.'

'Now? Cara, it's gone ten o'clock. No, come in the morning. After a shock like this, we both need a good night's sleep.'

'Then I'll leave early.'

'You just take your time.'

'In the meantime, don't worry.'

'And you, darling, don't you worry either.'

'I'm not worried for my own sake,' I assured her. 'I don't want you to be upset.' I paused, trying to formulate the correct words in my head. 'Listen, Aunt Biddie, can I say something now, which I should probably have said a long time ago? So far as I'm concerned, *you* are my real mother – you always have been and you always will be. If it should turn out that the Princess was my natural mother, then from what I saw of her on that programme, I am sure she would never have cared for me and brought me up as well as you did. Maybe I'm not expressing this very well, but what I'm trying to say is that I have always loved you like a mother and I always shall. I don't want any mother other than you.'

There was a little sniff at the other end of the phone and I wondered if I had said too much, achieving the opposite effect to that which I had intended. Then Aunt Biddie said, 'Thank you for saying that. And let me say in return that, from the moment Connor turned up with you, I have loved you as my own daughter. You do realize that, don't you?'

'Of course I do.'

'Excuse me one moment. I must blow my nose. All this emotion.'

I seized the opportunity to clear my own throat.

'That's better,' Aunt Biddie said, sounding more like her normal self.

'Now, you go to bed,' I instructed her. 'And I'll see you in the morning.'

'Drive carefully, won't you, dear?'

'Yes, of course. And now, good night, sleep well – and lots of love.'

After I had replaced the receiver, I went into the kitchen and poured myself another glass of wine, then made my way back to the living room, where I sank down again on to the sofa. No longer did I feel tired and depressed but incredibly awake and alert. Indeed, it was only consideration for Aunt Biddie which stopped me packing an overnight bag and driving straight up to Avonford. But, at seventy-four, she needed a good night's sleep. And, for that matter, it would do no harm for me to get my thoughts in order before I arrived at The Willows.

Over the thirty-four years of my life, I had built up an image of my father, based on the details Aunt Biddie had given me, the photographs in her albums – taken at Coralanty, their childhood home in Ireland – and the few poems of his I had found in anthologies, written during the Spanish Civil War.

These were the facts as I knew them.

My father had been born in 1902 and Aunt Biddie three years later. Their father had been a professor of Linguistics at Cork University – not a schoolteacher, as Oliver Lyon had said – and it was presumably from him that I had inherited my own ability for languages and my father his gift for words. My grandfather had been known as 'Red' Moran, on account of his red hair and violent temper.

Aunt Biddie had often described her and Connor's childhood at Coralanty, a large house not dissimilar to The Willows. The early years had been idyllic, when the two children were left free to roam the countryside, often going out first thing in the morning and not returning until nightfall. But then they were sent away to boarding school.

Unable to adjust to the discipline of school, Connor had repeatedly run away. And, on the occasions he hadn't run away, he was expelled. Needless to say, this did not endear him to his father, all the more so when Connor answered back, making excuses. Many were the thrashings he received.

Eventually, he ran away to relatives in Dublin, where an uncle obtained him a job as a clerk with a shipping company at the dockyard. My grandfather apparently said good riddance to bad rubbish and my grandmother dared not contradict him.

The next news the family received was that Connor had disappeared. Eventually, it turned out that he had stowed away on a ship to Liverpool, escaping the captain's clutches when the ship berthed. After that, they had heard nothing until 1925, when Aunt Biddie was twenty and Connor twenty-three.

He had written from London, saying that he had a job with a publishing company and was engaged to be married. After their marriage, Aunt Biddie had come to London to stay with him and his wife, Patricia.

Aunt Biddie was always rather vague when she came to describe Patricia, but I had the impression of a very serious young woman, rather a bluestocking, who had tried to take Connor in hand.

However, Aunt Biddie's vagueness was understandable, for it was during her visit to London that she had met her future husband, my Uncle Stephen, who was a friend of Patricia's brother. Theirs hadn't been the easiest or most conventional of courtships, much of it being conducted by letter, because she had to return to Coralanty, but in due course they were married and she went to live at The Willows.

Meanwhile, Patricia came into a small inheritance after her grandmother died, which provided her with a private income and enabled Connor to leave his job and attempt to become a writer himself. They had left London and moved to a village on the edge of the Black Mountains, so that Connor could better concentrate on his writing. Because they weren't living all that far from Avonford, Aunt Biddie had managed to get to see them every now and again. It was obvious to her that their marriage wasn't working out very well. Then, suddenly, a brief note had come from Connor in Paris, announcing that he and Patricia had broken up.

The next Aunt Biddie had seen of my father was in 1935. Their own father had died by then and, after his death, their mother had sold Coralanty and joined Biddie and Stephen. When it had become obvious that she wasn't going to last much longer, Aunt Biddie had written to Connor in Paris, asking him to come and see her. It was then she had learned that he and Patricia were divorced.

Following their mother's death, Connor had returned to Paris and Aunt Biddie hadn't heard from him again until 1939, just before the Second World War broke out. After that, all communication between England

and the occupied countries of western Europe being impossible throughout the war, she had no idea where he was or what he was doing. Then, five months after the end of the war, he had turned up with me.

Those, in brief, were the facts.

And this was how I had interpreted them.

In my mind, Connor Moran had been more poet than man, more soul than flesh. I visualized him as a sort of Byronic figure, possessed with the power to enthral people with his words, to exalt and inspire, driven by high, pure ideals and with little care for the material things in life.

Despite the bitter circumstances of his outward life – an unhappy boyhood, a vicious father, a domineering first wife – he had not allowed his natural spirit to be crushed, but found inspiration in the deep springs of a rich inner experience. His all-too-brief existence had been lived with a spiritual intensity that was beyond the ken of his fellow human beings.

A man not really of this world, he had been motivated more by lofty ideals than economic necessity. From Paris he had gone to Spain to fight for freedom. Then he had gone to Italy where he had discovered true love. The last years of his life had been supremely happy until the death of the one woman he had truly loved. His final lonely months had been clouded by melancholy, disillusion and despair. He had brought me to the safe keeping of his sister, then gone to his own tragically early death.

This was the image which had been ingrained in my mind and engraved on my heart. Until that evening, when I saw Oliver Lyon's interview with the Princess Hélène Shuiska.

How could the Connor Moran of my imaginings have been married to a woman like the Princess? And how could she be my mother?

She was everything I considered myself not to be – beautiful, elegant, sophisticated, self-assured – and above all, so very regal. There was no physical resemblance between us and I had no sense whatsoever of any mental or emotional affinity with her. In fact, if I was honest, although my impression had been of a rather splendid woman, whose life story was fascinating, I hadn't really liked her.

So what had been the attraction between her and my father?

Chapter 3

At half past six the following morning, I was on my way to Avonford. As I drove, my thoughts naturally kept turning to the Princess and my father. But, apart from going over and over what the Princess and Oliver Lyon had said during the course of their interview, I knew I could make no sense of it all until I saw Aunt Biddie.

At the back of my mind, though, was Nigel, like a niggling sort of headache that is uncomfortable rather than painful. It was because of him that I hadn't seen Aunt Biddie since the weekend before Christmas, for, as usual in recent years, his family had taken precedence over mine and we had spent the festive season with them.

While his parents had lived in London, we used to see them reasonably often, but after his father retired and they moved to a bungalow in Bexhill-on-Sea in Sussex, to be near his sister in Hastings, Nigel rarely made the effort to go down there. His excuse – as it was for most things – was lack of time. Nevertheless, he could have been a bit more considerate. The fact that his sister and her family were always in and out of the bungalow wasn't the point. His parents took her attentions for granted. It was Nigel who was their pride and joy.

So, at Christmas, we made up for the rest of the year and, although I would obviously have preferred to be with my own family at Avonford, we had spent a week at Bexhill. Before Christmas Day was even over, Nigel was becoming irritable, bored by the lack of activity and conversation which centred mainly around television, family and neighbours.

By the time Saturday came, he was almost impossible and I was trying to compensate like mad and failing miserably. His parents knew something was wrong, but could not believe it was them. His father took him off to the pub and his mother seized the opportunity to have a little heart to heart with me, along the lines of, 'Poor Nigel seems very on edge. Of course, he always was highly strung. Maybe you should get him some vitamin tablets.'

It was a relief for both of us to return to London.

On New Year's Eve we had gone to a party thrown by Liam Massey, the chairman of Massey Gault & Lucasz. Knowing hardly any of the other guests, I had drifted round with a glass in my hand, on the periphery of other people's conversations, trying to look as though I were enjoying myself immensely.

Nigel, meanwhile, was making up for Christmas, drinking far too much champagne, meeting up with loads of people he hadn't seen for ages, but not thinking to introduce me. The days were long past when I had been a status symbol. Now I was merely a wife.

He had ended the evening dancing in a tight clinch with an extremely drunk and scantily clad model. Somehow, I had resisted the temptation to leave and take a taxi home on my own, knowing that, to do so, would be making a mountain out of a molehill, potentially creating an embarrassing scene and inevitably leading to a row when Nigel got home.

As it was, the next day, when he had recovered from his hangover, he didn't exactly apologize, but he did admit that he thought he might have made a bit of a fool of himself. I had let it go at that.

I drove past Oxford and through the mellow Cotswold towns of Woodstock, Chipping Norton, Moreton-in-the-Marsh and Broadway, by which time the sun was out and the early morning frost was thawing.

Back in the Worcestershire countryside of my youth, as I approached the fields, market gardens and orchards of the Vale of Evesham, Nigel seemed to fade, as though I were literally returning to the time before we were married. It was with a lighter heart that I began to look forward to what lay ahead.

Built in the late eighteenth century, The Willows was a three-storey Georgian house which had originally been the home of a wool merchant. To its right were tall gates for the wool wagons to drive through and beyond them lay a cobbled courtyard, flanked by a row of stables, with a horse trough in the middle.

Some hundred years later, the house was acquired by Uncle Stephen's grandfather, Joshua Trowbridge. The Vale of Evesham is fine hop and apple growing country and Joshua Trowbridge was the owner of the thriving Trowbridge Brewery. Trowbridge Bitter and Trowbridge Cider were considered, by local connoisseurs, to be the most delectable of brews, which is how Joshua Trowbridge could afford such a fine house in the centre of the town, with, incidentally, a pub on either side – The Angel on its right and The Drover's Arms on its left.

This convenience was wasted on Joshua, who was a strict teetotaller, as were his wife and children. It was only after Robert Trowbridge, Uncle Stephen's older brother, inherited the business, that the mould was broken. Robert discovered early the delights of alcohol and it is a sad fact that, under his management, the brewery's fortunes declined and he was eventually forced to sell out to one of the brewing giants for a very poor price.

Aunt Biddie, who had lived at The Willows since her marriage in 1927, could remember the days when the stables had still housed a couple of hunters, a carriage horse and a gig. Now they merely housed her bicycle, a sturdy steed called Phoebus, named in honour of the bicycle belonging to Sir Edward Elgar, himself a Worcestershire man.

At the time I came on the scene, the occupants of the stable block were Uncle Stephen's Rover and an ancient man, known to everyone as Old Harry, who rented one of the outbuildings as a workshop, in which he wove baskets from the osiers which grew all along the river banks.

When I was a little girl, I used to spend hours watching Old Harry as he sat cross-legged on the stable floor, making shopping baskets, cutlery baskets, babies' cradles and baskets for the fruit pickers, called pecks, because they held a peck of fruit. The osiers were first soaked in the horse trough, then stripped of their bark, then deftly woven into shape. He made his work appear so easy, but my attempts to emulate him always produced weirdly shaped articles that sprang apart as soon as they were touched.

'We can't all be good at everything,' Aunt Biddie used to say. 'And you have your own special talents. Look at you, top of the class in English, French and Italian. I'd love to be able to speak to foreigners in their own language.'

But that was just Aunt Biddie, always looking on the bright side.

I wanted to be good at practical things too, to be more like Miranda.

After leaving school, Miranda had gone to work as an apprentice at the Royal Worcester porcelain factory, where she discovered an ability for hand-painting china. When she and Jonathan moved to Holly Hill Farm, a converted farmhouse in a picturesque village about twelve miles from Avonford, she set up her own pottery studio in a former barn. There she specializes in brightly coloured kitchenware – objects that are useful rather than ornamental. Like Aunt Biddie, she is essentially down-to-earth, practical and constructive. She can mend broken pottery and china, too, so that you can't see the glue.

I, in contrast, am a typical Taurean bull in a china shop. I only have to look at a fragile, long-stemmed wine glass for it to break. Neither do I possess any artistic or domestic skills. I can't draw or paint. I can't even put emulsion paint on a wall without getting it all over myself and the rest of the room. I can't knit and am hopeless at sewing. I loath ironing and my cooking is hardly inspired.

After my marriage, I developed a huge inferiority complex about my lack of practical accomplishments. There was Miranda, combining a career as a potter with being a housewife and mother: making all her own and Stevie's clothes, always having a well-stocked fridge, knocking up feather-light pastry and sauces which never went lumpy. And there was me, unable to put a button on a shirt without sewing the sleeves to the shirt front, and going completely to pieces if I had to prepare a three-course meal for any more than two people.

Looking back, much of my life was spent endeavouring to live up to the example of other people and ending up my own fiercest critic.

The Willows was a big house, with eight large bedrooms, three living rooms, a kitchen, scullery, cellars and attic quarters. The rooms on the ground and first floors were panelled in white painted wood and all the windows had inside shutters and window seats. The hall had an intricate mosaic floor and led into a south-facing conservatory, which commanded a pastoral view across the courtyard to a long garden, with sweeping lawns, fishpond and a pergolaed walkway leading down to the River Avon, fringed by the trees after which the house was named and from which Old Harry earned his meagre living. Here a flat-bottomed boat was moored in a small boathouse, with a jetty leading out into the river beside it.

Joshua Trowbridge's large Victorian family, together with the servants required to cater for their needs, must have amply filled the house. When Aunt Biddie married Uncle Stephen she, too, had found herself with a full household. In addition to her husband and Miranda's birth in 1938, Aunt Biddie had looked after Uncle Stephen's parents and two maiden aunts as well as her mother after she left Coralanty.

By the outbreak of war, Aunt Biddie's mother and the two maiden aunts had passed away. Far from easing her workload, this had merely liberated rooms, which were immediately filled with evacuees, children from London, sent to the safety of the country away from the threat of German air raids.

After the evacuees had returned to their own homes or moved on to relations, their rooms at The Willows were taken by paying guests – PGs, as Aunt Biddie called them, adults from vulnerable coastal areas, who were far more difficult to cope with than any number of children.

Add to them two cantankerous parents-in-law and a young daughter, not to mention the everyday wartime problems of generally keeping body and soul together, and you must agree that Aunt Biddie deserved a sainthood. The only help she received was a daily obliger. Uncle Stephen, a civil servant at the Ministry of Food in Worcester, had time only to offer moral support and mow the grass at weekends.

But Aunt Biddie was a coper, one of those women who take everything that life throws at them in their stride and, even more importantly, never fail to see the funny side of things.

Regarding my arrival at The Willows, she used to say that it was fortunate from my point of view, that I turned up when the war was over and the PGs all departed. 'Otherwise, we'd have had to put you in the boathouse and risk you being washed downriver in your wicker cradle, like Moses,' she would laugh.

She and Uncle Stephen had been perfect parents: affectionate, fair and strict when the situation demanded. If they did argue, it was never within earshot of Miranda or me. To us, they always presented a united front. Indeed, I think it extremely doubtful that they ever seriously quarrelled, even in private.

While Aunt Biddie was quite capable of getting cross, she was not the sort to fly off the handle or nurse a grudge – not like her father, whose furious rages had driven my father away from home. Aunt Biddie never meted out punishment in anger and the occasional good hiding which came in my direction was always forewarned and undoubtedly well deserved.

Uncle Stephen was a calm, gentle man, who never smacked Miranda or myself. If we were naughty, he used to look at us in a pained manner and say, 'I'm very disappointed in you.' A good hiding from Aunt Biddie would have been infinitely preferable to that anguish.

They had been not only the ideal parents, but the ideal married couple – loyal, faithful, devoted and, most important of all, each other's best friend. It was their example that shone before me throughout my own marriage. No matter that Nigel was a very different character from calm, gentle Uncle Stephen, with his whimsical sense of humour. That was no reason for me not to try and pattern myself on Aunt Biddie's high standards.

Gradually Aunt Biddie's household had diminished. Her parents-in-law had gone to their eternal rest, Old Harry had been forced into retirement at the age of ninety-something, Miranda and I had flown the nest, and, finally, Uncle Stephen had died. Since then, Aunt Biddie had occasionally, half-heartedly, mooted the idea that maybe the house really was too big for one person and she ought to move.

But, thank heavens, she had never got beyond thinking about it and then not with any seriousness. After all, Uncle Stephen's civil service pension paid the overheads and she had her own state pension. Miranda and I also found ways of helping her out. That year, for instance, our joint Christmas gift to her was paying for the house to be redecorated in the summer.

So why move? She had all the shops she needed within a stone's throw and a bus stop right outside her front door, so that she could easily get into Worcester or Evesham or up to the railway station for journeys further afield.

She knew everyone in the town and had a finger in every pie. She was a member of the Women's Institute and Townswomen's Guild; she belonged to the Horticultural Society and was on the rota for arranging the flowers in the abbey; a couple of mornings a week she worked in a charity shop and on Monday evenings gave piano lessons to two little girls.

Another reason for her not moving was her accumulation of a lifetime's possessions. Aunt Biddie never threw away anything that she thought might come in useful one day, with the result that most rooms in the house contained what she referred to as 'clutter' and Miranda as 'junk'. But the advantage of a big house of that era over its modern equivalent are its cupboards and storage spaces, so that The Willows never actually seemed untidy, as such, just lived in.

Neither did Aunt Biddie live completely on her own, although her fellow occupants at The Willows nowadays were not old people or children, but animals and birds in need of care.

Miranda's husband was largely responsible for this. Jonathan was a vet, with his own practice at Holly Hill Farm. In the course of his work, he often came across unwanted pets or injured wildlife, which he passed over to Aunt Biddie for fostering. Then there were wildfowl from the river and the marshes beyond, who seemed to home in on The Willows as a place of refuge.

Which brings me to Miranda, Jonathan and Stevie. The Evans family was just as happy as the Trowbridge family had been. They emanated warmth wherever they went.

In personality, Miranda was very like her mother – capable, efficient, good-humoured and unflappable. She was putting on weight as she approached middle age, and tended to conceal this by dressing in hip-length, smock-type pullovers or blouses over calf-length skirts – tweed in winter, cotton in summer. To look at Miranda, with her roundish, smiling face, was to feel comforted and comfortable.

Jonathan was not dissimilar to Uncle Stephen in appearance and character. About five feet ten in height, he was going bald and had an intelligent, sensitive face, with very clear, grey eyes. A quiet, unassuming man, he enjoyed an excellent local reputation as a vet and to watch him with an animal was to understand why. His manner – and his hands – were so gentle that his patients instinctively trusted him.

As for Stevie, if I could have had a daughter of my own, that is how I would have wished her to be. Stevie was very bright, as one would expect with Miranda and Jonathan as parents. She could paint, she was good with words and had also inherited Jonathan's scientific ability. She had no clear idea what she wanted to do with her life when she left school, but was obviously destined for university.

Just turned seventeen, she was also turning into a gorgeous-looking girl, with an engaging smile, deep brown, almond-shaped eyes beneath firm, wide eyebrows, and long, straight, silky dark brown hair cascading half-way down her back. One of the nicest things about her was her total lack of vanity. It still is, for that matter. She is quite unconscious of how lovely she is, quite unaware that she turns men's heads wherever she goes.

That was the sort of the family I had been hoping to create, back in the early years of my marriage.

It was just gone ten o'clock when I crossed the bridge over the River Avon, which had long ago replaced the ford. I drove past the river meadows, up Bridge Street and into the High Street, slowing down as I approached Priest's Lane on my left and peering to my right, to see whether Aunt Biddie had opened the tall gates for me.

Of course she had, bless her.

She had obviously been watching for me, for the conservatory door immediately burst open as I drove into the courtyard. She was wearing a thick, cable-knit sweater and slacks (she always wore trousers, except at funerals and weddings). I noticed that her white hair had been cut short in a sort of urchin style, which I wouldn't have thought would have suited her, but it did. As always, she appeared at least ten years younger than she was.

'Cara, darling, how lovely to see you here so early,' she exclaimed, after kissing me. 'I wasn't expecting you for hours yet.'

'I'd have been here earlier if I could. How are you feeling this morning?'

'Oh, I'm fine. It took me quite a while to get to sleep last night, I must admit. My brain was over-active. You know how it is? But don't let's stand out here talking. It's a chilly wind today. We don't want to catch our death of cold.'

Reassured by her manner, I took my overnight bag from the boot and followed her into the kitchen, where, back in the comfortable, familiar surroundings of my childhood home, the previous evening's events suddenly lost their immediate urgency.

My eyes fell on two tiny lambs, lying on a blanket in front of the Aga. 'I see we have some new additions to the family.'

'Quite a few, in fact. This couple are Larry and Mary.'

'Aren't they sweet! How old are they?'

'Five days. They were premature and their mother rejected them. I feed them from a bottle. When they're weaned, they'll be able go back to the farm.'

At that moment, a tabby cat uncurled himself from a chair and crossed the tiled floor. 'And this is Tiger,' Aunt Biddie announced. 'Poor little chap. He turned up here on New Year's Eve, all skin and bones, with a nasty abscess on his chest. Jonathan soon cured that, but, despite the notices I've put up in the town, nobody has come to claim him. Not that Tiger's worried, as you can see. He's made himself properly at home.'

In a birdcage, the yellow and blue budgerigar which had turned up in her garden a year or two earlier, was sitting on his perch with a bell on his head, admiring himself in the mirror and saying, 'Who's a pretty boy then? Who's a pretty boy then? Ark. Ark.'

I smiled. 'I see Joey's still as vain as ever.'

'His vocabulary has improved quite a lot. Joey what's your name?'

The budgie appeared to consider, then, in an amazingly clear accent, said, 'My name's Joey Trowbridge. I live at The Willows, Avonford.'

'That's incredible!' I exclaimed.

Aunt Biddie laughed. 'Normally, I don't approve of teaching birds and animals tricks, but he so enjoys speaking. And if he did get out, at least I'd stand a chance of getting him back.'

'How does he get on with Tiger?'

'No problems so far. But I do take the precaution of not letting Joey loose when Tiger's in the room – just in case. Now, if you'd like to go upstairs and have a wash and brush-up, I'll get you some breakfast. I take it you didn't eat before you left home?'

'You assume right,' I said. In fact, I seldom bothered with breakfast but Aunt Biddie had never allowed anyone to leave the house in the morning on an empty stomach. 'You can never be absolutely sure where your next meal's coming from,' she used to say, presumably a reference to the war years.

I carried my bag up to what was always known as 'Cara's room', where I still slept whenever I came to The Willows, except on the very rare occasions when Nigel accompanied me, in which case we had the double room which had been Uncle Stephen's parents'.

My room had not changed over the years. It was as cold as ever, in strong contrast to Linden Mansions, where the central heating was so efficient that you could wander round with nothing on.

Teddy was still sitting on the chest-of-drawers and Big and Little, two toy cats – bald as the result of excessive cuddling in my childhood – perched on the wide windowsill. There were still the same candlewick bedspread and quilted eiderdown on the same single bed (no duvets had infiltrated here), the same multi-coloured rag rug over the wooden floorboards, the same wardrobe with the mirror on the door, the silver backing of which had gone very dark and the glass distorted your image, making you look short and squat.

There was still the same bookcase with my favourite childhood books and a few reflecting my teenage, aspirationally intellectual self: Dante's *Inferno*; the Rt. Rev. Robinson's controversial *Honest to God*; the first, unexpurgated, paperback edition of *Lady Chatterley's Lover*, a book on contraception in the modern world; and Stendhal's *Le Rouge et le noir* in French. The only one I ever finished was *Lady Chatterley*.

I unpacked my bag, then washed my face and hands, brushed my hair, put on a thick pullover and returned downstairs, where the table had been laid and Aunt Biddie was putting bacon and sliced tomatoes under the grill.

'How's work?' she asked.

'Busy, as always.'

The kettle which had whistled throughout my childhood sent its piercing screech through the room. She poured the boiling water into a red teapot, decorated with bright yellow flowers – Miranda's distinctive handiwork. 'And Nigel?'

'OK, so far as I know. He's in the Caribbean at the moment.'

She frowned. But that could have been because steam from the kettle was rising into her face.

'One egg or two?'

'Goodness! Just one, thank you.'

'Oh, look, here's Nutkin come to say hello.'

A grey squirrel had appeared on the window sill. Aunt Biddie opened the window and it entered, tipping its head slightly on one side and studying me from a beady brown eye. Deciding that I threatened no danger, it hopped across the draining board to a bowl of peanuts, took one between its front paws and sat on its haunches nibbling it. 'You remember he had a broken leg?' Aunt Biddie asked. 'Well, that's completely healed. He can climb trees with the best of them, can't you, Nutkin, my pet?'

The appetizing smell of bacon filled the kitchen and hunger assailed me. Aunt Biddie poured tea, then asked, 'Do you know Gordon?'

'I don't think so.'

'I thought maybe you didn't. That's him.' She pointed past Nutkin, who was devouring nuts as though there were no tomorrow, to the garden where a handsome goose, light brown in colour, with a black crown to its head and white cheeks, was pecking at the lawn. 'He's a Canada Goose. His wing was broken, poor thing. He won't ever fly again. But he seems very content.'

She served up the by now crispy bacon, tomatoes and sizzling egg, poured us both tea, and sat down at the opposite side of the table. 'Miranda, Jonathan and Stevie are coming over for lunch. Jonathan and Stevie saw the interview as well. They'd been watching the programme on otters, but Miranda was doing something in the kitchen, so she only came in half-way through, like you. Then she suddenly realized who Connor was and immediately rang me – but, of course, I was already glued to my set.

Stevie's tremendously excited about it all. She rang me after you and I had finished talking last night, wanting to know all about how Connor had brought you to Avonford.'

I spread butter on a second slice of toast. 'As the person who knows me best in the world, do you believe the Princess was my natural mother?'

Aunt Biddie put her cup down on its saucer and studied me. Then she slowly shook her head. 'From what we learned about her yesterday night, I must admit that I can see no striking resemblance between you and her, in appearance or character. Having said that, you don't really take after Connor either, except in looks. In fact, if you take after take anyone, it's me. You and I are very similar in a lot of ways.'

'I wish that were true,' I said. 'But you're much, much nicer than I am.'

'Cara, darling, this is not the moment to start a discussion about the merits and demerits of our respective personalities.'

'All right. So let me ask you another question. Did you like her?'

'Well, put it this way, I didn't feel that she was the sort of woman with whom I could imagine ever having become friends. On the other hand, had I met her earlier in life – at the time that she was married to Connor, say – then my opinion could have been quite different. People change with their circumstances. I wasn't the same person then as I am now. And I'm sure she wasn't either. She couldn't have been, not if she was married to Connor and living in a remote Italian mountain village.'

She poured us both more tea. 'What I really can't get over is the fact that Connor didn't mention her to me. I know he was always reticent with regard to his personal affairs. Most men are in my experience. But a Russian princess. You'd think he would have said something, wouldn't you? On the other hand, I didn't ask. Let's face it, I was far more concerned about you than him. You were in such a terrible state, you poor little mite . . .'

'Do you think he was intending to return for me?'

'That was the impression he gave me, although I must confess that I've never been really sure. He couldn't have brought up a child on his own. It's a wonder to me that he managed as long as he did. No, if I'm really honest, my personal theory is that he intended all along that Stephen and I should bring you up as our daughter and that he would come back and see you from time to time. He knew me. He was fully aware that I'd never been able to resist taking in lame ducks.' Then she added hastily, 'Not that I'm comparing you to a lame duck, Cara.'

'I've been rather more of a responsibility,' I said wryly. 'And one that has continued considerably longer than most.'

In a rare gesture of physical affection, Aunt Biddie reached across the table and laid her hand over mine. 'My life would have been considerably poorer without you.'

I smiled. 'Thank you. So where was he going when he left here?'

'Back to Italy, I assume. He said he had left in a hurry and had to return to sort out various matters. Under the circumstances – if his wife had just died – that seemed perfectly feasible. I certainly had no sense of finality, no presentiment that I would never see him again. But, of course, why should I have done? Nobody could have predicted that tragic accident, when the ferry boat sank.'

'And he didn't leave you any address?'

She sighed. 'He didn't leave anything, not even your original birth certificate. Heaven alone knows what happened to that. It wasn't among his papers when his body was recovered from the sea.

'But, yes, I did have his address. But it was stolen with my handbag. I must have told you about that incident. I'd gone shopping in Worcester – ironically enough, to buy some things for you – and I was in the baby department in Viner's department store. I had put my handbag down on the counter and turned my back for just a few minutes, and when I looked next it was gone. That was one of the worst moments of my life and it could hardly have happened at a worse time.

'Everything was in that bag – my purse, my house keys, my ID card and, worst of all, the ration books and clothing coupons for the entire family. Without them, you couldn't buy anything. I reported the theft to the police, but they never found it. Then, of course, we had to go through the palaver of applying for new ration books, not to mention changing the locks on the house. It was a nightmare. I have never allowed my handbag out of my sight since.

'Also in my handbag was my address book with Connor's address. You see, he wrote to me after the war was over. Immediately after I received his letter, I entered his address in my book, then presumably I threw the letter away. It didn't say anything beyond informing me that he was still alive. Connor was never any good at writing letters. In fact, I've often wondered if that was why he wrote poetry rather than novels, because poems were so much shorter. But that's by the by.

'Naturally, I replied at once, assuring him that everything was fine –

well, as fine as it could be under the circumstances. He had my letter on him when he died, which is how the police knew how to contact me. My letter, his passport and a rail ticket to Zurich, that's all he had in his wallet. Oh, and a bit of money, I think. But because I'd written his address in my book, I made no attempt to memorize it. You know how it is?'

'And you can't remember even the name of the place?'

'No, I racked my brains at the time. Apart from anything else, I had no means of contacting anybody in Italy to let them know he was dead. All I can remember is that it was quite a complicated address, not just a number of a street and a town.'

She glanced at the clock. 'Good heavens! It's nearly twelve o'clock. The others will be here in any minute. I must put the casserole in the oven.'

'Casserole?' I groaned. 'You should have warned me before I ate all that breakfast.'

'Oh, I'm sure you'll manage to find some room. In any case, you could do with a bit of fattening up. Though you always were on the skinny side – like me. So was Connor, for that matter. Tall and gangly, in his case. We use up too much nervous energy, that's our problem.'

After that, I washed up, then went out to buy a couple of bottles of wine to go with lunch. The elders of the Trowbridge family had no more convinced Aunt Biddie to sign the pledge than they had Robert or Uncle Stephen. She, too, greatly enjoyed her little tipple. As did Miranda and I.

My progress to the off licence was slow because virtually everyone I encountered recognized me and wanted to stop and talk. I lost track of the number of times I heard, 'Come to see your auntie, have you? Looking well, isn't she? And you're not looking so bad yourself, Cara dear.'

Shortly after my return, a car horn hooted in the courtyard and Aunt Biddie announced, 'They're here!'

Chapter 4

Stevie rushed in ahead of her parents and we met in the conservatory. She threw her arms around me in a great hug, then gazed at me with shining eyes. 'Isn't it exciting, Cara! I've always thought it must be so much more interesting to be adopted than to know who your parents are. In your case, you knew your father was a poet – and that was romantic enough. But now to discover that your mother may have been a Russian princess . . . That beats everything.'

Miranda, following behind her, cautioned, 'Careful what you say. You're not so old that we couldn't give you away for adoption – always assuming anyone else would have you.'

'Cara would adopt me,' Stevie retorted confidently. 'Wouldn't you, Cara?'

'Probably,' I said lightly, 'but not today. I can't cope with acquiring a child as well as a possible mother. Sorry, Stevie, you'll have to stick with the parents you have.'

'But if you did adopt me, I'd have a princess as a mother, which would mean I could call myself Princess, too – Princess Stevie. Imagine! Are you going to call yourself Princess from now on? Princess Cara would sound really grand.'

That aspect of things hadn't even occurred to me. 'Stop rushing ahead,' I said fondly. 'I don't even know for sure that she was my mother.'

'Well, I'm convinced she must have been.'

'Stevie, could you be quiet for just one moment, please?' Miranda begged. 'Jonathan and I would also like to say hello to Cara and, what's more, Jonathan has a tortoise which needs to be put somewhere warm as soon as possible.'

'A tortoise?' Aunt Biddie asked.

'Yes, another foster-child for you, Biddie,' Jonathan explained, from the rear. 'A surveyor discovered it in an empty house and brought it in to me.'

We went into the kitchen, where he handed her a box.

'This is a surprise,' Miranda said, after kissing me. 'We weren't expecting to see you again quite so soon. Certainly not under such circumstances. I don't know about you, but it was very late last night before we got to bed. I couldn't believe my ears when I suddenly heard Oliver Lyon mention your father's name.'

'I wasn't even watching the television,' I explained. 'If Aunt Biddie hadn't rung me, I'd have missed the interview altogether.'

'Look at him, the little love,' Aunt Biddie cooed, gazing at the comatose tortoise in his box. 'Now, let's put you in the airing cupboard to continue your hibernation in peace. No, Tiger, I'm not talking to you. You stay here and be a good boy.'

'It needs a name,' Stevie declared.

'Dozey?' Aunt Biddie suggested.

'Oh, Granny, I wish you'd be more original!'

'What about Methuselah then?'

'That's better, I suppose, but it's a bit of a mouthful.'

'I'm going to look in the library,' she announced.

Aunt Biddie's so-called library was housed in what had once been the breakfast room. There was no rationale to it: Aunt Biddie acquired books, most of them second-hand, on much the same basis as she hoarded objects – because the information they contained might come in useful one day.

A few moments later, Stevie returned, bearing a large tome. 'Chukwa,' she stated.

'What sort of name is that?' Aunt Biddie demanded sceptically.

'It's the name of the tortoise at the South Pole, on which the earth rests.' Stevie consulted the book. 'And the name of the elephant between the tortoise and the world is Maha-pudma.'

'Well, I hope you're not thinking of bringing me an elephant,' Aunt Biddie laughed. 'Though I suppose it could always live in the stables.'

Another voice broke in. 'My name's Joey Trowbridge. I live at The Willows, Avonford. My name's Joey Trowbridge. I live at The Willows, Avonford.'

We all laughed.

It wasn't until we were seated round the dining table, eating lunch –

for which I found I did have a certain amount of appetite after all – that we started talking properly about the Princess and my father.

Stevie started it off. 'Surely you must have wondered, before now, who your mother was, Cara?'

'Of course I have,' I admitted. 'But I suppose because I knew – or rather, because I believed – that she was dead, there never seemed much point in thinking about her too much. It was different in my father's case. I have always known a certain amount about him and have an impression of the sort of person he must have been. But my mother has always been – well, nothing, really, not even a name.'

'What I don't understand is why your father told Granny that his wife had died in childbirth, when the Princess was still very much alive and, according to her, still married to him.'

'I've been thinking about that this morning,' Miranda said. 'The Princess didn't strike me as being a particularly maternal type. Cara could have been a mistake. If the Princess was born in 1900, she would have been forty-five when Cara was born, which is quite old to have a baby. I imagine it would be difficult, if not impossible, to have an abortion in Italy, certainly at that time. So, having given birth to Cara, maybe she didn't want to know any more about her. And that's why Connor brought her here. But he still loved the Princess, so he then returned to Italy. That would account for the Princess never trying to get in touch with Cara. After all, she must have known where she was.'

'Unless she believed Cara had drowned at the same time as Connor,' Aunt Biddie pointed out.

'Yes, that's possible as well. Oh, I do wish I could remember him. But I was only seven at the time and far more interested in Cara than in him. I'd always wanted a sister.'

'I have a different theory,' Stevie announced. 'I think the Princess was already having an affair with the Conte di Montefiore.'

'Where would that get us?'

'If their marriage was breaking up, it would explain why the Princess didn't want Cara and why Cara's father – Connor – brought her back to England.'

'In that case, why didn't my father remain here in Avonford?' I asked. 'Why did he go back to Italy?'

'If he'd lived there for six years, it would have become his home.'

There was silence for a moment, then Miranda said, 'There is yet another possibility. What if Connor was the one who was having an affair and the Princess wasn't Cara's mother at all? That would explain everything. It would explain why the Princess denied ever having had any children and why she didn't mention Cara's existence. I can't envisage her as having been exactly the forgiving type. And if Cara's natural mother – in other words, Connor's mistress – died in childbirth, it would explain why he brought her to Avonford. He couldn't cope with a small baby on his own and the Princess certainly wouldn't have wanted to take her on.'

That suggestion didn't appeal to me at all. There was no place in the image I had of my father for sordid extra-marital affairs and an illegitimate baby, whom he then abandoned to his sister's care in order to pursue his own selfish interests.

Stevie objected to Miranda's theory for other reasons. 'That still leaves us with two mysteries,' she said. 'One, why he went back to Italy, when his mistress was dead and the Princess had left him. And, two, who Cara's real mother was. Oh, why did the Princess have to die? If she was still alive, it would be so easy. We could simply contact her and ask her all these questions.'

Jonathan cleared his throat. 'Before we hypothesize any further, I'd be intrigued to know more about the sort of man Connor really was. Biddie, would you mind describing him to us?'

'I don't mind,' she said, rather hesitantly, 'but I'm not sure that there's all that much I can tell you. After he left home, there were years when I didn't see him or hear a word from him. And although I did see him quite often after my marriage, we were never as close again as we were as children in Ireland.'

'I've always imagined him as a bit of dreamer,' Jonathan prompted.

'Oh, he was certainly that. I remember my mother once saying that the main difference between Connor and me was that I made things, whereas he made things up. I don't think the real world ever really existed for him. Or, put it this way, the real world was too plebeian, it didn't live up to his expectations of what life should be, so he made up an imaginary world of his own.

'That was what most infuriated my father about him. As you may be aware, Connor hated school. He was always in trouble and more times than I can recall, he ran away or was expelled. He never attempted to put the blame on anyone else, but he never admitted the truth about what had happened either. He always had to fabricate a story to make the circumstances more dramatic than they really were. Yet they weren't lies really, not to him, because he had convinced himself by then that they were true.

'The most extraordinary thing about Connor's stories was that they always seemed quite plausible while he was telling them, yet afterwards you wondered how you could have been taken in. But, at the same time, you wanted to go on believing them for his sake, in order to please him, to make him happy. You see, he didn't do things out of malice or mischief. There wasn't any evil in him.

'And there was something else about him – an – oh, how can I explain it? – a sort of underlying melancholy. He laughed a lot, but there was a tragic quality to his laughter. Perhaps humorous sadness would be the phrase to describe what I mean – or despairing gaiety. Yes, he was a strange boy . . .'

Aunt Biddie paused, frowning.

'Let me give you an example. In the woods near Coralanty, there was a stream, in the middle of which was a big rock. Connor named this the Wizard's Stone. He told me that if I took seed from the ferns which grew on the banks of the stream and went through the water to the Wizard's Stone, with my hands above my head, and stood on the rock, with my eyes closed and my hands still above my head, and turned round three times, I would become invisible.

'You can imagine the number of times I fell into the stream before I succeeded in achieving this feat. But when I did succeed, he exclaimed, "Biddie, where are you? You've disappeared." And I believed him. Then, still pretending not to be able to see me, looking in every direction except where I was, he said, "Now you're invisible, you could go and set Mad Moraid's rabbits free."

'Mad Moraid lived in a little cottage on the edge of the wood and Connor was convinced she was a witch. She used to breed rabbits, keeping them in little hutches, which upset me, because I thought they should run loose in the fields. So, we went to her cottage and I climbed over the wall and started opening all the hutch doors and letting the rabbits out. Whereupon, of course, she spotted me from a window and started yelling blue murder.

'Needless to say, I was caught and marched home, to be given a good hiding by my father. So was Connor for egging me on. But Connor wasn't cross with me for getting caught. He just said, "You dropped some of the fern seed when you climbed over the wall, didn't you? That's why the spell was broken." You see what I mean?'

We all laughed and I asked, 'How old were you then?'

'About seven, probably. But I don't think Connor ever really lost his power to influence me. In fact – to be absolutely honest – when he brought you to Avonford he could have concocted any old story and I would still have been taken in . . .'

'So maybe my mother wasn't actually dead?'

'It's possible . . .' She looked at me ruefully. 'I'm sorry, Cara. It's only when I start talking about him, that I remember exactly what he was like . . .'

'Do you still think of yourself as Irish, Granny?' Stevie asked.

She smiled. 'After I married Stephen, I became as English to the core as an Avonford apple.'

'Did Connor retain Irish nationality?' Jonathan enquired.

'Oh, yes.'

'That explains something else which has been puzzling me,' Jonathan said. 'I couldn't understand how he was able to spend the war in Italy. If he was English, he'd have been living in enemy territory, but since Ireland was neutral, I suppose he could have lived wherever he wanted.'

After lunch, Miranda and I helped Aunt Biddie with the washing up, while Jonathan lit the fire in the drawing room and Stevie went back to Aunt Biddie's library. 'What do you think she's doing in there?' Aunt Biddie asked.

'My guess is that she's trying to find out more about some of the people who were mentioned in the interview last night,' Miranda said.

Stevie returned, clutching a pile of books but looking rather disappointed. 'I haven't been able to find anything about Connor. But I have found an old encyclopaedia, which has some famous people in it.'

When we settled in front of the fire, with Tiger on the hearthrug, she opened the encyclopaedia. 'Does anyone have any idea how the Princess spelt her name?'

'It's here,' Aunt Biddie said, handing her the *Radio Times*.

But there was nobody with the name Shuiska.

'Try El Toro,' Jonathan suggested.

He was in one of the art books. Christened Juan Maria Toro, he had been born in 1885 at Gerona and had died in 1960 in Paris, where he had moved in 1909, setting up a studio in the rue Cortot in Montmartre.

Instead of signing his paintings, he had marked them by painting a bull in the bottom right-hand corner.

There was a lot about the different artistic styles and art forms with which he had experimented, analytical discussion of the merits of his work and his influence upon other artists. He had a hatred of war and during the German occupation of France had been a member of the Resistance. After the liberation, he had joined the Communist Party. Among his most celebrated works were a set of murals depicting the Russian Revolution and a series of triptychs showing scenes from the Spanish Civil War, which was first exhibited at the 1937 Paris World Fair and now belonged to a private collection in New York.

He had a hatred of war and during the German occupation of France had been a member of the Resistance. After the liberation, he had joined the Communist Party.

'What were they fighting about in the Spanish Civil War?' Stevie asked.

'It was rather complicated,' Aunt Biddie replied. 'But basically, it started as a revolt of army commanders led by General Franco, who didn't agree with the policies of the republican government. Then it became a sort of ideological battleground so far as the rest of Europe was concerned. The Germans and Italians sided with Franco and Russia with the Republicans.'

'Which side would Connor and El Toro have been on?'

'I assume they would have belonged to one of the International Brigades, who were supporting the Republicans. They were made up mainly of communist and left-wing sympathizers from every country in Europe and further afield.'

'Does that mean Connor was a communist?'

'Idealistically, it's possible, I suppose. But I doubt very much that he was a card carrying member. Connor was not the sort to belong to any organization.'

'Is there anything about the Princess's husband after Connor?' I asked. 'His name was Monetfiore.'

Two Montefiores were mentioned. The first was Aretino di Montefiore (1470–1533), who was described as being a Genoese commander and statesman, born of an ancient princely house, who had led a highly adventurous life battling against the Turks and the French on the high seas.

Umberto di Montefiore (1891–1962) was the other. He was described as a Genoese shipyard owner, with additional interests in tractor and automobile manufacturing companies in Milan. A staunch anti-Communist, he had profited from Italy's reconstruction programme, until the construction of an overly ambitious passenger liner had brought financial downfall.

'Hmm,' Miranda murmured dryly, 'thus Helen did lead to Troy's destruction.'

Stevie consulted her list. 'Now for the Earl of Winster.' She flicked through the encyclopaedia to the Ws. 'Winslow. Winsor. Winter. No, he's not here.'

'You really need a *Who's Who*,' Aunt Biddie said. 'But I don't have one, I'm afraid. Now, who's for a cup of tea?'

I volunteered to make it, but she refused. 'No, thank you, dear. You stay here and go through those books with Stevie. It's time for me to feed the lambs.'

'Let me give you a hand with them,' Jonathan said.

In their absence, Stevie went through the other books, finding out more about El Toro and facts about the Spanish Civil War, the Second World War and Italian history, then starting to hypothesize wildly about what the various people had been like and their relationships with the Princess and each other.

That was when reaction began to set in on my part. I understood why Stevie was finding it all so exciting. For her, my father's past represented an exciting mystery, complete with a cast of fantastic characters – even if they were all dead – which she longed to solve. But I could not be so dispassionate . . .

Eventually, Jonathan and Aunt Biddie returned with a laden tea trolley.

We sipped our tea in silence for a while, then Jonathan turned to me. 'It seems to me that the obvious thing for you to do is to ring Oliver Lyon. It's quite possible that he knows more about the Princess – and your father – than was shown in the interview.'

'Of course!' Miranda exclaimed. 'And if his father knew El Toro, he may well have met your father . . .'

I shook my head. 'I'm not sure that I want to know anything more. In fact, I think I already know too much.'

Stevie stared at me, aghast. 'You're not serious?'

'I'll try to explain,' I said, grappling for the right words. 'Over the years, I've built up an image of my father as a sort of Byronic figure, whose life was motivated by high ideals. Now, I realize that my picture of him could be quite wrong. But that's how he has always been for me and that's how I want him to remain. I don't want to know any of the more sordid details of his life that would bring him down to the level of other men. Perhaps I should. But I don't. It's like I used to feel about my mother. Learning the truth about him won't bring him back to life.'

Stevie was about to respond, when Miranda threw her a warning glance and she clenched her mouth shut again. I was aware of Aunt Biddie looking at me in an odd, rather disturbed fashion and realized that I had made rather a fool of myself . . .

'If I may say so,' Jonathan commented mildly, 'Byron's personal life was hardly pure and chaste, but that doesn't distract from the genius of his poetry. The same applies to many other poets.'

'But my father wasn't just a poet. He was my father.'

'Speaking from personal experience, no fathers are perfect.'

'No, I guess not . . .'

'May I say something now?' Stevie requested.

'Yes, of course, darling.'

'I do understand how you feel, honestly, Cara. And so long as you didn't have any more facts at your command, then I think you were fully entitled to make up myths about your father. But now you do know some more, you can't just shut your mind to the truth. Whatever you discover won't hurt your father – or your mother, whoever she may have been.'

Myths . . . In my heart, I knew she was right.

Her brown eyes gazed into mine, with all the intrepid fearlessness of youth. 'You have to find out, Cara. Otherwise you'll go through the whole of the rest of your life wondering who you really are.'

'I know who I am. And I know who my real mother is – and I mean my real mother. It's Aunt Biddie.'

'But the relationship between you and Granny won't change, will it, Granny?'

'Please, Stevie,' I begged, 'I need time to think.'

'But there's nothing to think about. All you've got to do is ring Oliver Lyon.'

Miranda cast me a penetrating glance. 'Stevie, that's enough!' She glanced at the clock on the mantelpiece, then turned to me. 'We have people coming to dinner, so I'm afraid we'll have to be leaving soon. If I'd known earlier that you were coming, I could have put them off.'

'It doesn't matter,' I assured her. 'It's been lovely to see you.'

Stevie's eyes opened suddenly very wide. 'I know what you must do,

Cara! When you go to bed tonight, you must put a pea under your mattress like in the fairy story. And if you can feel the pea, that will mean that you're a princess!'

This ridiculous suggestion broke the tension. For a few moments, discussion raged on whether the pea should be fresh, frozen, mushy or dried. Then Stevie returned the books to the library, while Miranda went to find their coats.

We kissed each other all round and Aunt Biddie and I went to the door to see them off. Jonathan drove into the High Street and I followed to shut the big gates behind them.

Stevie wound down the window and stuck her head out. 'If you don't ring Oliver Lyon, Cara, I will.'

Aunt Biddie was unusually silent after they were gone, stroking Tiger on her lap and gazing into the fire with a preoccupied expression. Then she roused herself and asked, 'Are you hungry? Would you like something to eat?'

I laughed. 'Not really, thanks.'

'In that case, let's have a drink. How about a G and T?'

'That sounds good.'

She went out and returned with two tumblers of gin and tonic. We clinked glasses and she said, 'Well, it's certainly been an eventful twenty-four hours. Little did any of us think, this time yesterday evening, that so much was about to happen.'

I nodded, then said ruefully, 'I think I made a bit of a fool of myself earlier.'

'In what way?'

'By saying I didn't want to know any more about my father.'

'Your reasons were quite understandable.'

'If I was twenty years younger, maybe. But not now.' I paused. 'What's your opinion? Do you think Stevie's right and that now this has happened, I should try and get to the bottom of the mystery?'

'Yes, I do, actually. In fact, it's always rather surprised me that you've never shown more curiosity about your father and your natural mother.'

'I've never felt the need. I don't know, I was so happy as a child with you and Uncle Stephen that I suppose my real parents seemed part of some kind of fairytale.'

She gave a little laugh. 'Oh, dear, dear, dear. Why do we make life so complicated for ourselves on occasions? It would be so much simpler if we all just spoke our minds. You haven't wanted to hurt me and I haven't wanted to hurt you. We have the very best of intentions, but we do it all wrong.'

'What do you mean?'

She shook her head. 'Sufficient unto the day is the evil thereof. I don't know about you, but I'm feeling tired. Let's leave the subject for the moment and talk about something else. And then, if you don't mind, I think I'll get an early night.'

Chapter 5

Later, up in my chilly bedroom, I undressed quickly – like I used to do as a child – and unwrapped my nightdress from round the hot-water bottle Aunt Biddie had put in my bed. Once in bed, I pulled the sheet, blankets and eiderdown up to my chin and huddled round the bottle. Then, in an exercise book Aunt Biddie had found for me, I wrote down every detail of the television interview and the facts uncovered by Stevie's research in Aunt Biddie's books.

When I was young, I used always to keep a diary, but after my marriage I had dropped the habit, mainly out of fear that Nigel might find it. Not that I had any secrets as such to keep from him, but I didn't want him reading my innermost thoughts.

However, this was quite different from the kind of diary I had kept in the past. This was a record of events, more an *aide-mémoire* than an analysis of my feelings.

When I fell asleep, it was to dream of the Princess, sitting on a throne in a baroque palace, with Nigel, dressed in an ornate military uniform, standing behind her, one hand resting possessively on her shoulder. I was desperately unhappy, because I knew that they were about to be married and, when the ceremony was over, they were going to sail away in the man-o-war, captained by my father, which was moored in a harbour in the lake below, and go off to wage war against the Spaniards.

Stevie was there, too, painting a picture of the scene, like artists do in law courts. She kept calling to me, demanding that I come and look at her picture. But I was utterly helpless. I wasn't even in the room, but outside, lying on a rock in the middle of a river, surrounded by thick woods, viewing the scene through a closed window. Each time I tried to get up, a heavy weight prevented me from moving.

I woke up to find Tiger spread out, full length and sound asleep, on top of the hot-water bottle on my chest. Moving him and the bottle gently to one side, I took a drink of water, then, turning on to my side, fell into a deep slumber, to be awoken next by Aunt Biddie bringing me a cup of tea and exclaiming, 'So that's where you are, Tiger!' She pulled back the shutters and morning light flooded into the room.

'How did you sleep?' she asked.

'Apart from a peculiar dream, like a log. What about you?'

'Oh, much better than the night before. Now, there's no hurry to get up. And the water's hot, if you'd like a bath.'

Having a bath at The Willows was not something you undertook on the spur of the moment, like you might a shower at Linden Mansions. First the Aga needed to be well stoked up to heat the water and then at least a quarter of an hour was required for the water to sputter and gurgle through a network of ancient pipes before filling the bath to a depth that just covered one's legs when one was sitting in it.

It was a most palatial bath, situated in the middle of the room, with an oak surround about a foot wide and oak panels on all sides to conceal the plumbing fittings. When I was a little girl, I had to climb up onto a stool in order to get into it. It was so deep and so wide, that it would have comfortably accommodated two adults lying side by side.

So I took my time drinking my tea, then putting on the thick dressing gown, hanging on the back of the door, went along to the bathroom. The single bar electric heater had scarcely taken the chill off the room, but the water was steaming hot.

I lathered myself vigorously with the loofah and Knight's Castile soap, looking all the while at the familiar wallpaper, patterned with huge white daisies with big yellow centres, which had decorated the room for as long as I could remember and must surely have inspired the floral designs on Miranda's pottery.

My ablutions completed, I hoicked the plug out with my toes – another childhood habit – and stood up, reaching perilously across for the towel on the rail. The water took almost as long to empty as it did to fill the bath and I was dressed by the time it had gone down.

Downstairs, I was greeted by the aroma of grilling kippers, a Sunday breakfast tradition. I only ever ate kippers at The Willows – Nigel could stand neither the bones nor the smell.

'Shall we go for a walk this morning?' Aunt Biddie asked, after we had eaten and fed a few scraps to Tiger. 'I know the weather's not perfect for it, but I rather fancy the idea of going to Bredon Hill.'

It was indeed a grey day beyond the windows, with lowering clouds which looked as though they could be bearing snow. But the Trowbridges were not a fair-weather family: we loved the seasons in all their guises. 'Wonderful!' I exclaimed eagerly. 'Oh, let's do that! It's ages since I was last up there.'

Suddenly, out of nowhere, the memory returned of bringing Nigel to The Willows, before we were married, and taking him up Bredon Hill. It had been a hot summer's day and Nigel's steps had dragged, like those of a child being forced to go in the opposite direction to that upon which it has set its heart. He had refused to cross a field with cows in it in case there was a bull among them and, at the summit, although he had admired the view, he had been more intent on suggesting that it might be an idea if a road were built, so that one could drive up there.

Afterwards, Aunt Biddie had said to me, 'When you've always lived in the country yourself, you forget that other people spend their lives in cities. Still, you and Nigel have lots of other things in common, so I suppose it doesn't matter that he doesn't like walking.'

If she had been trying to warn me, her words fell on deaf ears. Although I was rather disappointed myself to discover that Nigel was such a city boy, I was too much in love to read any deeper meaning into the episode. With the blithe confidence that accompanies the first months of any love affair, I was convinced that, with time and under my influence, Nigel would come to appreciate the simple pleasures of the English countryside and grow to cherish those things which were dearest to me.

Meanwhile, it was not surprising that someone so sophisticated should fail to be impressed by Bredon Hill – a mere eight hundred and something feet above sea level. It might occupy a very special place in the hearts of the Trowbridge family and the poet A.E. Housman, but it hardly ranked among England's greatest landmarks.

Of course, Nigel didn't change. Watching football and taking up golf were the nearest he ever came to enjoying the great outdoors. And he joined Highgate Golf Club more for reasons of social prestige and the benefits of the club house than pleasure in being in the open air. By that time, however, I was no longer viewing my husband and married life through rose-coloured spectacles.

So Nigel would play golf and I would walk over Hampstead Heath.

But Hampstead Heath is a poor substitute for Bredon Hill. The view it offers across London cannot be even remotely compared to that glorious panorama from Bredon Hill of what Housman describes as the 'coloured counties' – with Worcestershire, Herefordshire, Gloucestershire, Oxfordshire and Warwickshire spread out at your feet and the lark so high above you in the sky.

As we had with Nigel on that long ago day, Aunt Biddie and I drove to the pretty village of Elmsley Castle. 'Spring's coming,' Aunt Biddie murmured, as we passed thatched cottages of Cotswold stone, in the gardens of which snowdrops formed a carpet of white, and sheltered banks on which the first celandines were in flower. After that, she did not say a word, trudging along with her hands thrust deep in the pockets of her duffel coat, and her head slightly bent against the chilly wind.

I did not mind her silence. I had more than enough to occupy my mind, thoughts which had nothing to do with Nigel. Writing up the last two days' events had been therapeutic. My mind was back in gear again and my emotions under control.

Which was the greater influence on a person's character, I was wondering – environment or heredity? My heart wanted to believe that environment was stronger than heredity and my personality was the result of my close relationship with Aunt Biddie and Uncle Stephen and my childhood in Avonford. Yet my head told me that genes must play a part.

What aspects of my character, therefore, were inherited from that shadowy individual who had been my father? And which – if she were indeed my mother – from the Princess Hélène Romanovna Shuiska? And at this point, time and again, my mind balked. However hard I tried to convince myself, I found it impossible to believe I was her daughter.

The lane turned into a footpath, climbing steeply up a scarp slope, then we were at the top of Bredon Hill and a biting wind was cutting through us. Gazing across the leafless orchards and the rich loam fields of cabbages, leeks and Brussels sprouts, I felt a sudden contraction of my heart, and a sharp pang of something almost akin to fear, as though I were about to go away somewhere and would never look upon this scene again. Impulsively, I grasped Aunt Biddie's arm. She turned and smiled at me, a rather strained little smile, as though she too were prey to the same emotion.

We did not stand for long, but walked for a while along the breast of the hill, until a sleety rain began to fall. We retraced our footsteps, reaching the relative shelter of the lane as the sleet turned into snow. It was then

Aunt Biddie said, 'I have a confession to make. I haven't been entirely truthful with you. I do actually know more about your father's life than I have ever let on.'

'What sort of things?'

'More about his first marriage and why he went to Paris.'

'Not about the Princess?'

'No, nothing about her – or about you. But I'm afraid you're not going to like it all the same. It's not going to fit in with your perception of Connor.'

'Are you trying to say that he was even more like Byron?' I asked.

'You could say that.'

'Then I'd like you to tell me.'

'Last night, you said you didn't want to know any details of his life that would bring him down to the level of other men.'

'That was said on the spur of the moment.'

'It came from the heart.'

'Yes, it did. But, as I said afterwards, I was being rather pathetic. I realize now that Stevie was right when she accused me of making up myths about him.'

'It's not entirely your fault. I am mostly to blame. You see, when you were a little girl, Stephen and I agreed that it was important that you should think well of your father. So I always painted a kind picture of him.'

'Do you mean that he was nothing at all like how I've always imagined him to be?'

'Oh, he was all the things I've described to you – but other things as well.'

'Was this what you were referring to last night when you said that bit about us both not wanting to hurt each other, yet having the best of intentions?'

'Yes. And I must say I'm glad to have the opportunity to tell you the truth. I haven't liked hiding things from you. But, at the same time, I didn't want to hurt you. Well, now, let's go home and I'll fill in some of the gaps.'

When we were sitting in the drawing room, the fire blazing, Tiger on the hearthrug and a pot of coffee on the table, Aunt Biddie said, 'Would you mind refreshing my memory as to what you know about Connor's marriage to Patricia?'

I repeated the little I knew and she nodded. 'Yes, that's what I thought. Well, what actually happened was this. Connor did have a job as a proofreader for a publishing company, but immediately after his marriage he gave it up and announced that his vocation was to be a writer.

'You see, Patricia had always known her grandmother was intending to leave her some money and I'm afraid that played a part in Connor's decision to marry her. Oh, I think he must have loved her a bit – but he didn't love her nearly as much as she loved him. It wasn't an overpowering passion on his side. Essentially, he married her in order to be freed from the necessity of working for his living. And then, he took advantage.'

'In what way?'

'Oh, nothing she could do was right. Even when I stayed with them almost immediately after their marriage, he was complaining about her bourgeois outlook and penny-pinching ways. Poor woman, it wasn't as if she were in possession of a fortune. She had to make ends meet and Connor had tastes beyond his means. The house they were renting in Norbury, in south London, was all she could afford, though it wasn't such a bad little place.

'He complained that she was bossy and always organizing him and, in truth, she was rather forthright and domineering, but, with a husband like Connor, she needed to be. He complained that she confined him to a small room, looking out onto a grey suburban street, and expected inspiration to come to him, like water at the turn of a tap. How could he be creative, he demanded, in surroundings which fettered his mind and stifled his imagination, and in the company of a domestic drag who was always scurrying round with a dustpan and brush?

'What he needed, he claimed, was the freedom of the wide open spaces, such as we had known at Coralanty. Only in such surroundings could he give full rein to his poetic muse, so that the words would flow spontaneously and unbidden to his pen.'

Aunt Biddie glanced at me to gauge my reaction and I nodded encouragingly.

'This went on for a couple of years, I suppose, and then he met a young American woman called Imogen Humboldt, after which the trouble started.'

'You mean, they had an affair?'

'Rather more than that.'

'Come on, tell me,' I urged.

'Well, Imogen was as different to Patricia as it was possible to be. Patricia was attractive in her way – small and dark and tidy in her person, with never a hair out of place. But Imogen was simply beautiful, tall and slim, with blond hair and blue eyes – not unlike the photograph we saw of the Princess, in fact. That same northern, Scandinavian type of beauty, although she was actually of German origin.'

'Did you meet her?'

'Oh, yes, later on.'

'And?'

'Well, Imogen was mad about everything European. Her father was immensely rich. He was Abraham Humboldt, the oil magnate. Imogen didn't go to school when she was a girl, but was educated at home by a series of English governesses. The result was that she became an avid reader of all the great European classic writers – and, at eighteen, was sent to finishing school in Switzerland. It really was as if she'd just stepped out of a Henry James novel.

'She made friends with another young American woman – Elizabeth Webber, her name was. It's funny how some things stick in the memory and others you totally forget. I can remember her name, but I can't for the life of me remember what Patricia's maiden name was. Not that it matters, I suppose.

'Elizabeth had relatives somewhere in Germany, with whom the girls stayed during their vacations. After finishing school, they embarked upon a grand European tour. Eventually they came to London and soon after their arrival, Imogen met Connor at some literary gathering.

'Now, I should explain that, although Connor was unhappy in his suburban home, there were aspects of London life which he very much enjoyed. He could be a very sociable creature and mixed with all sorts of well-known people – the Bloomsbury set, the Sitwells, William Walton, H.G. Wells, Cecil Beaton, Sickert and – oh, you name them and he seemed to know them. Connor could be very charming and outgoing, if he chose to be. And he also had the advantage of being one of those people who transcend class, if you know what I mean.

'Imogen described her meeting with him so vividly that it has remained in my memory. She said she walked into the room and her eyes immediately settled on him, standing a head above most of the other guests and with that great mop of red hair. She asked her hostess who he was and discovered him to be a real, live poet. They were introduced and – crash, bang, wallop! – she was in love.

'It isn't difficult to imagine the effect upon Connor of having a beautiful heiress worshipping the very ground at his feet. He was bored with Patricia and restless for new experiences – ripe, basically, for a love affair. However, to give him his due, he did not attempt to conceal his married state. He introduced Imogen to Patricia and tried to get the two women to become friends.

'And, to give Imogen her due, I am still convinced to this day that she didn't set out to seduce Connor and steal him away from his wife. She was spoiled, wilful and headstrong, but there was something almost endearingly innocent about her – or maybe ingenuous would be a better word.

'Anyway, she took great pains to try and make friends with Patricia and Patricia, for her part, was courteous in return. After all, they had quite a lot in common, and not just Connor. They were both intelligent, cultured and interested in the arts. There was a lot they could talk about between them.

'Imogen loved the Romantic poets, so Connor proposed that the three of them should go on a tour to the Lake District. Unfortunately, Patricia was suffering from a minor ailment – a chest cold or suchlike – and remained in the hotel while Connor and Imogen went for long walks over the hills and round the lakes, quoting poetry to each other. He read her some of his own poems and she was tremendously impressed by them. When Connor complained to her, as he had to me, of the difficulties he encountered in trying to write poetry in London, her heart went out to him.

'Back in London again, she visited Connor and Patricia in Norbury and Connor continued to play on her heartstrings, until she eventually hit upon the idea of taking a country house for them. She found an old manor house to let near the Black Mountains – Dewfield, the place was called. I believe the owner had gone abroad, which was why the property was vacant.

'The rent on Dewfield Manor was, of course, way beyond Patricia's means, but mere pocket money for Imogen, who received an extremely generous allowance from her father. Patricia was, understandably, reluctant to live upon what she saw as Imogen's charity and, no doubt, suspicious too of Imogen's motives. Connor, however, declared himself so eager to leave London that she allowed herself to be overruled and they moved to Dewfield.'

'You mean they had a *ménage à trois*?'

'That's what it amounted to. I don't know what story Imogen spun her parents. I imagine she led them to believe that she was sharing the house with Elizabeth and I also assume that Elizabeth was privy to the affair. Who knows, maybe Elizabeth had a lover of her own and, therefore, Imogen's absence suited her purposes too.

'So, to continue, Connor found himself living with two women devoted to his needs, each vying to be of the greater service to him and with increasingly divergent views on how his future should evolve.

'That was possibly the oddest aspect of their love triangle. Connor's career as a poet was of paramount importance to both Patricia and Imogen. They believed in him totally and utterly. That's the reason why they put up with each other for as long as they did.

'However, while Patricia's desire was for him to be published and win public acclaim, with the accompanying financial reward that would allow him to continue and create works of ever higher literary quality, Imogen believed that such mundane considerations should not be allowed to impede the course of true genius. In her view, a poet should write for the sake of his art and not to gratify the public whim. His life should be lived at an altogether higher level than that of ordinary mortals.

'She saw her task to be the creation of an idyllic backdrop against which Connor could compose lyrical verses. She played the piano, made beautiful flower arrangements and made herself look as attractive as possible. As a result, the burden of running the household fell on Patricia's shoulders.

'So when Connor returned from a long tramp over the mountains or, for that matter, back from a long drinking session at the village pub – gathering local colour – it was to be confronted by Patricia, tired and harassed, after toiling all day over a hot stove, and Imogen dreaming over a rose which had just come into bloom.

'Not surprisingly, he preferred the dreamer to the drudge. The three of them had separate bedrooms and Connor took to spending his nights increasingly in Imogen's bed. He told her that he no longer loved Patricia and that he did love her. He wrote her love poems . . .'

Aunt Biddie stopped and clasped her hand to her forehead. 'Good heavens! I had completely forgotten about that! He had a book published and he gave me a copy of it . . . I can remember feeling rather disappointed and thinking that the poems weren't terribly good. Now where on earth can that be? Where would I have put it in a safe place?'

She looked at me ruefully and I gave a wry smile back.

'Well, don't worry about that now,' I said. 'Finish the story first.'

'But I shall worry about it. It must be here somewhere. I certainly wouldn't have thrown it away. How infuriating—'

'Don't worry. Tell me about Imogen and Patricia. He told Imogen that he loved her . . .'

'Yes, and he said that if he was free, he would marry her.'

'How do you know all this?'

'Because Imogen told me. She treated me as a confidante, which didn't make my position very comfortable, although I must admit that, in a way, I did feel rather sorry for her. For that matter, I felt very sorry for Patricia too.'

'Why did Patricia put up with it?'

'Because she loved him. And also, because I think she knew him well enough by then to doubt that he would ever fit the action to the words. Connor did things by default, not decision. He drifted into situations and wriggled out of them again. With Imogen, I believe it was a case of forbidden fruits tasting sweetest. He couldn't be sure that, if he left Patricia and married her, he wouldn't be jumping from the frying pan into the fire, that, once she had a wedding ring on her finger, she wouldn't turn out to be like Patricia – in other words, that she would become a wife instead of a mistress. And also, I think he took pleasure in having two women competing for his attentions.'

She paused to sip her coffee.

'You make him sound rather heartless,' I said.

'Yes, I'm afraid he was – and very selfish. But you have to remember that he had great charm.'

'So what did happen?' I asked.

'Well, after a couple of years, the strain of her unconventional relationship started to tell on Imogen. And the novelty of rural life also began to pall.'

'It lasted that long?'

'Oh, yes. They moved into Dewfield shortly after Stephen and I were married – which was in June 1927 – and they must have lived there for two or three years. Anyway, Imogen went to London for a few days and met up again with Elizabeth, who for reasons of her own was anxious to move on. When Imogen returned to Dewfield, it was with the proposal that they should all go to Paris, where Elizabeth had influential friends, who could help Connor in his career. All art was in Paris, she insisted. Everyone who was anyone was there.

'At this point, Patricia's patience finally snapped. She turned on Imogen, telling her to get out the house and out of her life. Imogen, who was paying the rent, refused to leave. If anyone should go, she said, it should be Patricia. There was apparently a huge row, screams and tears.'

Aunt Biddie pursed her lips. 'Eventually, Imogen turned to Connor and demanded that he choose between them. Patricia agreed. And Connor, of course, prevaricated. In fact, I think he actually walked out of the house. He hated rows which were not of his making.

'At which point, Patricia suggested to Imogen that he should be left alone to make up his mind. Incredible though it may sound, they agreed upon a term of forty days. They both packed their belongings and returned to London – Patricia to her parents and Imogen to whatever hotel Elizabeth was staying in – leaving Connor alone at Dewfield.

'At the end of forty days, Connor still hadn't come to any decision. Personally, I think he assumed that they would both miss him so much that they would both come running back to him, pleading for forgiveness, and so he just swept the whole matter under the carpet.

'Instead of which, he received a letter from a solicitor, informing him that Patricia was seeking a divorce, and another letter from Imogen, telling him that she and Elizabeth were leaving for Paris. Then the rent on Dewfield fell due, which, of course, he was unable to pay. At that point he came to see Stephen and me, telling us what had occurred – though not exactly as I have just told you – and asking us to lend him some money. He felt extremely hard done by and considered himself very much the injured party.'

I bent down and stroked Tiger, an absent gesture, while I tried to absorb the implications of all she had told me and create in my mind a new, flesh-and-blood image of the fallen angel into which my father had been transformed.

Yet I did not find his unconventional marriage to Patricia and relationship to Imogen nearly as disturbing as his seemingly even more unlikely marriage with the Princess, as a result of which union I had conceivably come into existence. Whereas I could vaguely picture him living at Dewfield Manor with the careworn Patricia and the exotically rich and beautiful Imogen Humboldt, I could not see him and the Princess living together in any domestic arrangement.

'I do hope I haven't upset you too much,' Aunt Biddie said anxiously.

I smiled reassuringly. 'No, honestly, you haven't.'

'You do understand that I didn't feel that all this was the sort of thing I should tell you when you were a little girl?'

'Yes, I do. And, in your position, I'd have done exactly the same thing.'

'That's all right, then. I was very concerned in case I hadn't made the right decision and that you would blame me for shattering your illusions.'

'That's all they were – illusions. But how did you feel about his way of life? I can't imagine you approving of it.'

She gave a wry smile. 'I'm broader-minded than you imagine. I didn't feel it was for me to approve or disapprove. I suppose, if anything, I was angry with Connor for playing with other people's lives. But, in the end, they turned the tables on him, so he got his just desserts.'

'One last question,' I said. 'Do you know what happened to Patricia?'

'Yes, she actually remarried and went to live in South Africa, I think it was. We lost all contact with her after she and Connor broke up, but Stephen kept in touch with her brother, who was a civil servant, like him. She died, let me see, it must have been about ten years ago. While Stephen was still alive, anyway.'

After lunch, we started hunting for my father's book of poetry. We went along every shelf in the library but our only find was a cookery book that had belonged to Aunt Biddie's mother, which contained a recipe for Fairy Pudding, which had apparently been Connor's favourite as a boy, and which she promised to make next time I came to see her, now she had the instructions.

We then went through all the other rooms, ending up in the 'glory-hole', one of the second-floor bedrooms which had gradually become a repository for clutter which did not have an obvious home elsewhere. Here, although we discovered the most extraordinary things – like carrier bags full of old Christmas cards, and the deeds to the house, which were mysteriously residing in the bottom of the wardrobe – we did not find the missing book.

At the entrance to the attic, we stopped. 'We're not even going to open that door,' Aunt Biddie announced. 'It would take a month of Sundays to go through everything in there and you have to get back to London this evening. But I promise I'll continue the search and, obviously, if I find it, you'll be the first to know.'

After feeding the menagerie, we had tea and toast in front of the fire and then it was time for me to leave. 'Are you going to try and contact Oliver Lyon?' Aunt Biddie asked, as I was getting in the car.

I grinned. 'Provided Stevie doesn't beat me to it.'

Chapter 6

As I turned off Highgate West Hill into the drive beside Linden Mansions, my mood was totally different from that of two evenings earlier. Now, I was suddenly immensely glad that Nigel was away. It would have been nice to know an audience was waiting for me, but, equally, Nigel would have been more than capable of taking over. With his contacts in the media and television, he might even already know Oliver Lyon – or almost certainly know someone who did – and, before I could say Jack Robinson, the whole matter would have been taken out of my hands. However, Nigel was not due back until Wednesday.

Parking at Linden Mansions was on a first-come first-served basis for everyone except Nigel, who had allocated himself the space right outside the entrance to our block.

He always took a taxi to the airport, so his red BMW still stood in 'his' place. Our neighbours – particularly Sherry and Roly, who were antiques dealers and constantly loading and unloading boxes and crates, must have found it infuriating, but they never complained, or, at least, not to me. I assume they had learned, as I had, that it was usually easiest when dealing with Nigel to take the line of least resistance.

That evening, however, I was lucky and squeezed my Fiesta into a space at the very end of the drive under a chestnut tree, next to Roly's Volvo estate.

Once inside the flat, I was struck – as always, when I returned from a visit to Aunt Biddie's – by the contrast between my own home and The Willows. The rooms themselves were not dissimilar, high-ceilinged, spacious, with sash windows. But there the semblance ended.

The Willows was full of atmosphere, with its hotchpotch of furniture styles, confusion of books and 'clutter', and nostalgic reminders of generations past. Aunt Biddie's personality was stamped everywhere upon it; and even the unoccupied rooms did not feel empty, but seemed to retain a lingering essence of former inhabitants.

9 Linden Mansions, in contrast, although the building which housed it had been constructed a century ago, belonged unequivocally to the 1970s.

By then, the bright colours of the sixties had given way to more sober simplicity. Our living room furniture consisted of a black leather, three-piece suite, grouped around a long, chrome-legged coffee table with a smoked glass top. The deep-piled carpet and velvet curtains were powder grey, the walls were covered with cream, laid paper. Lighting was supplied by a couple of standard lamps shaped like tall, white, spindly mushrooms and the shade over the central light fitting resembled a chrome flying saucer.

Peacock blue cushions, a blue Murano glass vase and matching ashtray – souvenirs of Venice – provided bold splashes of colour, as did prints of paintings by Lowrie, Hockney and Warhol. In pride of place, facing you as you were seated, was one of Nigel's own paintings. An abstract work, consisting of exploding blobs of oil paint, it was meant to represent inspiration.

Smoked glass and chrome made their appearance again in the dining area, where the dining table was big brother to the coffee table. The chairs were black-metal framed with leather seats. The sideboard was ebony-coloured.

The kitchen was every woman's dream, equipped with all the latest Zanussi appliances. The bathroom lacked the individuality of that at The Willows but was much more luxurious. The two bedrooms had fitted wardrobes with a dressing table area and mirror in the middle. The bedlinen was colour co-ordinated with the curtains and carpets – jade and turquoise in the master bedroom, muted reds and browns in the guest room. Nigel used the third bedroom as a study. This was done out all in white: white desk, white chair, white filing cabinets.

My feelings towards that flat and the way it was furnished had always been ambivalent. It was exceedingly stylish and always attracted admiring comments. And the furniture, despite its sombreness of colour and severity of line, was extremely comfortable. You could curl up on the sofa or in the armchairs – and you could sit for hours at the dining table, chatting long after a meal had finished.

Theoretically, the furniture and colour schemes had been the result of a mutual choice. This had, after all, been our new beginning – our first new home together when we left his flat in Islington. Essentially, though, it reflected Nigel's taste. But, back in the spring of 1973, when we had moved here, I had been pregnant and so supremely happy, the last thing I had wanted to do was to annoy him by imposing my ideas over his.

In any case, he was a designer by profession and it was mainly his money which was paying for everything.

So I had consoled myself with the idea that, once I stopped work, I would be able gradually to add little touches which would make it feel less like a show flat and more like home.

And there were bits of me dotted around the place, even if few of them were on display – like the bookcase in the spare bedroom and my bedside cupboard containing my jewellery and other personal treasures, and the bathroom cabinet. The space-age sterility of the kitchen was relieved by examples of Miranda's pottery, arrayed on shelves, and a noticeboard covered with Stevie's drawings through the years.

Beyond the kitchen was a little realm that belonged uniquely to me: a rooftop garden, measuring a mere twelve feet by twelve feet, crammed full of tubs and pots in which something was always flowering. Tomorrow, when I looked out, it would be on snowdrops and golden aconites, winter jasmine and Christmas roses.

That evening, when I went through the hall to our bedroom, it struck me suddenly that 9 Linden Mansions epitomized the difference between my and Nigel's characters. Yes, the whole flat was very elegant, very appropriate for a discerning art director working for an up-and-coming advertising agency. But it wasn't really me.

However, the initial strangeness of finding myself back there quickly wore off and, having unpacked my bag, I went into the kitchen to put the kettle on for a quick cup of tea while I sorted out my clothes for the morning.

Half an hour later, I was in bed. Next to me, on my bedside table, stood a framed photograph of Nigel, a recent black and white portrait taken for *Campaign* magazine, which he had given me at Christmas. On the back he had written: 'To keep you company when I'm not there. Love, Nigel.'

I glanced at his lean face and mobile mouth, those blue eyes that had once reduced me to jelly, smiling slightly into the camera. He was still a very handsome man, I reflected dispassionately, almost as though I were thinking about a stranger.

Then I relegated him to the back of my mind and concentrated on adding the next instalment to my notes of the previous evening, while Aunt Biddie's revelations were still clear in my memory. When I put them aside and switched off the light, it took me much longer to go to sleep than it had at The Willows. I missed the chill air on my face and the hot-water bottle and Tiger to snuggle up to . . .

Next morning I made the mistake of not getting up immediately after the alarm sounded but lay, half dozing, thinking about the weekend's events, wondering what to say when I rang Oliver Lyon and wishing I didn't have to go into work. Then I suddenly remembered the divisional board meetings and leapt out of bed.

A mad panic ensued, made worse by my not being able to find my house keys. Eventually I located them in my jeans pocket and set off at a gallop down the stairs, fortuitously coinciding with Roly just driving past the entrance. He stopped and opened his car door. 'Hop in. I'll give you a lift to the station.'

He swung the car confidently into the rush-hour traffic on West Hill. 'Did you have a good weekend?'

'Absolutely incredible,' I replied, automatically glancing up the hill to see if there was a bus in sight, but, as usual, there wasn't. 'You didn't by any chance watch Oliver Lyon on Saturday, did you?'

'Afraid not. Why?'

'It's too much to tell you now, but are you and Sherry in tonight?'

'So far as I'm aware.'

'Then I'll stop by after work and tell you all about it.'

'Is Nigel still away?'

'Yes.'

'Then why not come and have supper with us?'

'That would be great!'

We reached the tube station and he drew up at the kerb. I planted a quick kiss on his cheek and precipitated myself down into the bowels of the earth, only to have to wait fifteen minutes for a train.

Why did I do this? I wondered, an image returning of Bredon Hill, with not another soul in sight except Aunt Biddie. Why did I run this rat race? But such way madness lay. So I read the ads, which told me where to go to get a better job, which was the best company to give me life assurance, and extolled the virtues of an Indian restaurant in Morden.

Eventually, I reached Charing Cross and, dodging the traffic in Trafalgar Square, sprinted to Wolesley House in St James's Square, where the Goodchild Group's suite of offices was situated on the first floor.

'What sort of time do you call this?' Sergeant demanded, as I raced past the desk in the foyer, where the clock was showing five past nine. Sergeant had come to Wolesley House as a porter after being demobbed at the end of the war, with the result that he considered the building and all its occupants to be his personal charges. Then he called, 'It's all right, Cara. The Chairman hasn't arrived yet.'

Miles insisted that everyone call him by his first name, but Sergeant couldn't cope with that. A captain of industry should have a title, just like an officer in the services. Being only rank and file myself, I was Cara. But Miles was the Chairman and thus he was addressed, whether he liked it or not.

'Bloody trains,' I muttered, slowing down to a rather more dignified pace.

'You should try getting up earlier.'

'Huh!' I grunted, throwing him a grin.

On the first floor, I went through double swing doors on which a discreet brass plaque proclaimed: The Goodchild Group Limited. In reception, Dorothy glanced up and held out a piece of paper. 'Hello, Cara. Two messages. Will you ring Massimo Patrizzi at the Banco di Investimento e Soccorso in Milan, as soon as possible? And David Parsons at the National & Colonial Bank would like Miles to ring him urgently.'

Miles was very astute in choosing his staff, just as he was extremely shrewd in his business affairs. Only in his private life did he seem to lack judgement. After three broken marriages (which had produced seven children), he had acquired a public reputation as a womanizer: the paparazzi were always photographing him in the company of beautiful young women. The gutter press maintained that he was currently contemplating a fourth marriage, with the twenty-five-year-old daughter of a baronet, Lady Fiona Waldron.

Whether this was the case, I had absolutely no idea. The relationship between Miles and myself was strictly professional. There was a closeness between us, as must develop between two people who have worked together for thirteen years. But that was all.

Miles would certainly never have had an affair with an employee. He kept his personal and business lives totally separate and, so far as his female staff were concerned, definitely put brains and ability before beauty and youth.

Dorothy, who operated our switchboard as well as manning reception, was even less of a dolly bird than me and the other three secretaries. She had just become a grandmother.

To the left of Dorothy's desk in reception a short corridor led to the offices of Alan Warburton, the managing director of the Goodchild Food Division, Keith Despard, the managing director of the Goodchild Beverages Division, and James Warren, the Group finance director. To the right, another set of double doors led to Miles' and my own offices and the boardroom.

Four directors, their secretaries and Dorothy may appear a very small management team for such a huge concern as the Goodchild Group, with over a hundred subsidiaries throughout Europe and, increasingly, throughout the world. These ranged from Buona Gusta, the Italian company who made the tomato purée, which Miles had started importing to England back in the late 1950s – the foundation stone of his empire – to the most recent acquisition of Dandy Candy, the American chewing gum and confectionery giant.

But any more staff would have been superfluous. All the companies under Goodchild's control remained autonomous, as regarded their management and business policies, and Miles seldom intervened directly in their day-to-day practice. On his own admission, he was neither good at nor interested in running companies. His great strength lay in his vision, his ability to recognize an opportunity and grab it before anyone else did.

Most of our companies were ailing when we acquired them, either because their products had an outdated image or because their management had grown complacent. Miles detailed his henchmen to go through the organization with a fine tooth-comb, identify the cause of the rot, cut it out and then pave the way for new, profitable growth. His enemies accused him of asset-stripping, but he described this process as setting an enterprise free, which was far nearer the truth. The Goodchild Group was certainly not a charitable concern, but neither was it a predator.

Many harsh things have been said about Miles over the years. He has been accused of being a ruthless entrepreneur, a faithless husband and an absentee father, who tried to buy his children's love with expensive gifts instead of giving them his time. As someone who worked closely with him for thirteen years, I would counter these charges by saying that he always tried to be fair.

Nobody was ever sacked from any Goodchild Group company unless they deserved it. As regards his marriages, none of his ex-wives lacked for anything – I know that for sure, because I dealt with the correspondence and wrote out the cheques for Miles to sign. So far as his children were concerned, what successful businessman spends every evening and weekend at home?

Towards me, Miles was more than fair. And that applies in spite of what happened at the end of our business relationship. I may have been upset at the time, but I bear him no grudge now. Miles was fair to the end.

After acquiring a new company, Group head office only intervened if things went wrong. Then, as in a recent instance, when the newly launched range of Buona Gusta gourmet frozen foods failed to be taken up by supermarkets, despite an intense advertising and marketing campaign, Alan Warburton was sent to investigate the cause.

As a result, the packaging was changed and the price cut. When, after six months, the profit margins were still too low, the range was discontinued. Somewhere in Italy, a lot of people found themselves suddenly out of a job. But that wasn't the fault of the Goodchild Group. We had invested the funds necessary for the development of the new product and lent our expertise to try and resolve the problem. The blame lay with Buona Gusta's own management in Italy, who had failed correctly to identify consumer demand. In consequence, the marketing director was sacked and another appointed in his stead, following the approval of Alan Warburton.

Taking the piece of paper containing my messages, I went along to my office, where I prepared at high speed for the day ahead.

Then the phone rang and the day commenced in earnest.

'Signor Patrizzi for you, Cara,' Dorothy announced.

'*Pronto! Pronto!*' came Massimo Patrizzi's voice down the line. His call, which continued in a voluble stream of Italian, concerned changes to the financing structure of some of our Italian interests. As he spoke, I took notes in Italian shorthand.

Miles himself arrived some ten minutes later. 'Morning, Cara,' he said, hanging his coat and scarf on the stand just inside my office door. 'How are you today?'

'Fine, thanks. And you?'

'Extremely well, thank you.'

Miles was approaching sixty and looked his age, neither older or nor younger. He was of medium height and build, balding, his remaining hair a light brown sprinkled with grey. He had a high forehead, a strong nose, a square jaw, with a cleft chin, and triangular, hazel-coloured eyes. Needless to say, he was always immaculately dressed, although he wasn't at all vain. In fact, he was of the few people I have ever met to be completely lacking in vanity, both with regard to his appearance and his achievements. While he did not believe that apparel maketh the man, he saw no point in making life difficult for himself by dressing badly. As for his accomplishments, because his ambitions were still far from satisfied, he did not consider that he had any grounds yet for complacency.

He went into his office and I followed him, carrying the transcript of my conversation with Massimo Patrizzi. For the next half hour, we worked solidly together, going through the post and his programme for the coming weeks. Then I returned to my own office and started on the jobs needing urgent attention before the Food Division meeting commenced. But, for once, my mind wasn't on them. My mind was with my father, the Princess and Oliver Lyon.

There was a tap on the door and Juliette's small, dark-haired, intelligent head appeared round it. Juliette had joined the company five years earlier and was James Warren's secretary. She and I were great pals. Often, when Nigel was away, she and I would go to the theatre or out to dinner together after work in the evening, as well as occasionally meeting up at weekends.

'Hi,' she said. 'How was your weekend?'

'Absolutely incredible.'

Her brown eyes opened wide. 'Why? What were you up to? I thought you were going to your aunt's.'

'I did. It's what happened while I was up there.'

The brown eyes expressed anxiety. 'Is something the matter with your aunt?'

'No, she's fine. It's . . . No, I haven't got time to tell you now.'

'What about having lunch today?'

'Sorry, I can't. It's meetings day. Tomorrow should be better. Miles is off to Paris.'

'OK. I'll leave you to it and catch up with you later. Shall I bring you in a sandwich at lunchtime?'

'You're a pet. That would be useful.'

A short while later, I was in the boardroom, seated at the little desk near the door, while the executives of the Food Division sat round the table, with Miles at the head. The boardroom was like the rest of the Goodchild Group offices: tastefully, expensively and impersonally furnished. Because it was a relatively new company, there were no portraits of former chairmen to decorate the walls. Generations of Goodchilds had not sat at the head of that table. In a way, my office environment was not unlike my home at Linden Mansions. There was no sense of tradition.

Minute-taking was, at the best of times, my least favourite job. Making notes while other people talk and not being allowed to interrupt or ask questions yourself is always frustrating. Being a silent witness to a trial in which the judge has decided his verdict beforehand is even worse.

Under normal circumstances, I would have had no difficulty in concentrating on the matters in hand. That morning, however, I kept finding my thoughts straying, when I should have been noting down the salient points in the long-winded explanation by Crinkly Crisps' Managing Director as to why his company's turnover had fallen short of forecast by several hundred thousand pounds, and his proposals as to how the situation should be rectified.

While Miles was at lunch, my chance would come to ring Oliver Lyon. But what was I going to say? I rehearsed my speech in my mind.

'Hello, Mr Lyon. I wonder if you can spare me a moment. I watched your interview with the Princess Shuiska on the television on Saturday night and I wondered if you could tell me a bit more about her. You see, my father was Connor Moran and, as you know, he was married to her during the war while she was living in Italy . . .'

For heaven's sake! Waffling must be contagious. Start again. Be concise . . .

'Hello, Mr Lyon, I watched your programme on Saturday and am interested in finding out a bit more about the Princess's life while she was in Italy.'

Getting there, but . . .

But, most probably, his calls would be fielded by a secretary like myself. What should I say if asked to leave a message? I'd have to say I'd ring back. Then what if he didn't have an office at the BBC? What if he worked from home? It was unlikely that the switchboard would give me his home number, but suggest that I wrote in to him. So would it be more sensible to write him a letter in the first place? But explaining my quest in writing would be even more difficult than describing it on the phone. And it would mean putting him to the trouble of replying. Or else, of course, he might simply ignore my letter or throw it in the bin . . .

It is quite extraordinary, the obstacles which can present themselves when you're doing something of vital concern to yourself. Had Miles asked me to contact Oliver Lyon on his behalf, I'd have known exactly what to say.

A different voice, speaking my name, impinged itself upon my consciousness. Alan Warburton was saying, 'Cara, please ensure that that comment of Peter's is specifically noted in the minutes.'

I nodded, without having the slightest notion what Peter's comment had been. My pencil had been moving over my shorthand pad while my thoughts were with Oliver Lyon, but the hieroglyphics it had been forming made absolutely no sense. This was going to be a case of pretending to Alan later that I couldn't read my own shorthand.

After that, I forced myself to pay attention by dint of keeping my head down and watching my hand as it wrote instead letting my gaze wander round the room. That worked, but it was an effort and I was jolly thankful to hear Miles saying, 'Well, that's all we have time for today, gentlemen.'

I hurried out to reception and asked Dorothy to tell Hawkins, the chauffeur, to bring the car round to take Miles to the Savoy for his lunch appointment, then went along to my office and read through my shorthand notes to ascertain where the gaps were. I caught Alan just as he was preparing to go off to lunch. He grinned when I explained my dilemma. 'I'm not surprised you can't make head nor tail of what he said. I've never heard so much codswallop in my life. In case you hadn't realized, he's for the chop. Listen, simply say . . .' He dictated a couple of sentences. 'That's all that's needed.'

That potentially tricky problem was resolved. Miles was at lunch. I opened the London telephone directory and looked up BBC Television. There was just one number and before I could change my mind I dialled it. My heart was pounding in a most ridiculous manner and my throat was dry.

An operator answered and I said, 'I wonder if you could tell me how I could get in touch with Oliver Lyon.'

'Hold the line, please.'

Another voice announced, 'Duty Officer.'

'I was just wondering how I could get in touch with Oliver Lyon.'

'Can you tell me what it's about?'

'His programme on Saturday evening.'

'Do you want to make a complaint?'

'No, not at all. I, umm, er, I just wanted to ask him about someone who was mentioned in the interview – Connor Moran – he was my father, you see.'

'In that case, I'll put you through to Jessica Fletcher. She's the assistant producer. Hold on one moment, please.'

'Jessica Fletcher,' a business-like woman's voice said.

'Umm, I'm sorry to disturb you,' I stammered, 'but I'd like to ask you about Oliver Lyon's interview last night with the Princess – er . . .' For some reason, I couldn't twist my tongue around her name.

'Ah, yes. And may I ask your name?'

'My name? Oh, it's Cara Sinclair.'

'Is that Mrs or Miss Sinclair?'

'Mrs. But—'

'Well, Mrs Sinclair, what's your question?'

Every word of my rehearsed speeches totally deserted me. 'Er, well, there's a possibility that the Princess may have been my mother,' I blurted out.

There was silence at the other end of the phone. Then Jessica Fletcher said, in the cautious tone people use when dealing with nutcases, 'And why do you think that?'

It was too late now to go back. 'Because she was married to my father – Connor Moran – at the time I was born.'

'Could I ask you to hold the line for just one moment, please, Mrs Sinclair?'

There was a click and then silence. I was about to replace my receiver when another voice said, 'Mrs Sinclair? This is Oliver Lyon. Jessica says that your father was Connor Moran. Is that so?'

'Yes,' I replied.

'And how do you think I might be able to help you?'

'Well, until Saturday night, I believed my mother had died in childbirth. I had never even heard of the Princess . . .' – again, I couldn't get my tongue round the 'Sh' and the 'vksa', so I floundered on – 'let alone known that my father was married to her. You said that your father knew El Toro and met some of his friends. And I wondered if you might know, for instance, where in Italy she lived.'

So much for being concise.

He asked me a few questions about my birth and childhood, then said, 'I can't promise to be of any assistance to you, but it would be interesting to meet you.'

Meet me? That had not entered into my calculations. 'Yes, but I wouldn't want to waste your time. I mean, you must be very busy . . .'

'If what you've been telling me is true, it wouldn't be a waste of my time. On the contrary, it's my job.'

'Oh, it's true,' I assured him fervently.

'Where are you phoning me from?'

'London. I'm at work at the moment.'

'Then when shall we meet? Let me just look at my diary. Hmm, it's Monday today. What about tomorrow evening? Where do you work?'

'St James's Square,' I replied weakly.

'Couldn't be better. Do you know the Ambassador Hotel?'

I knew it well, for it was just round the corner from St James's Square and Miles retained a permanent suite there, in which he held his most confidential business meetings.

'Of course,' I said.

'I'll see you there tomorrow at about six.'

'Thank you. But only if you're sure . . .'

Ignoring my last words, he said, 'I look forward to meeting you, Mrs Sinclair.'

I put down the phone, thinking that I must have given the impression of being a complete, blithering idiot.

Chapter 7

It was half-past six before I left the office that evening, having prepared all Miles's papers for his forthcoming trip to Paris, Zurich and Milan, and with a pile of work still waiting to be done during his absence. On arriving back at Linden Mansions, I went straight up to our flat, where I changed into jeans and sweater, then gave Aunt Biddie a quick ring to thank her for a lovely weekend and tell her about my conversation with Oliver Lyon.

Next, I rang Miranda, who admitted that she had doubted whether I would have the nerve to ring Oliver Lyon.

Stevie seized the phone from her. 'You remembered my threat, didn't you? You knew that if you didn't call him I would.'

I laughed. 'Well, that may have had something to do with it.'

'I wish I could come with you to meet him.'

'It's rather a long way for you to travel. I'll ring you afterwards and let you know what happens . . .'

I had literally just put the phone down, when it rang. 'Hi, it's me,' Nigel's voice said, after that funny time-lapse which occurs on transatlantic calls. 'How are you doing?' There was a cautious edge to his voice, as though he were anticipating trouble.

'I'm fine. How are you?'

'I tried ringing you over the weekend but there was no answer.'

'I went to Avonford.'

'Oh, I see. That's all right then.'

'How's the shoot going?'

'It's turning into a total and utter bloody disaster. That's why I'm ringing you. I shan't be coming back on Wednesday.'

Ah, hence the note of apprehension . . .

'Why, what's gone wrong now?'

'I told you about the fiasco with the flight being delayed and the airline losing my suitcase, didn't I? Well, on top of that, it transpired that one of the models had been on the binge over Christmas and put on at least half a stone. Then the photographer and the make-up artist got gippy tummy and one of the models found a cockroach in her room. So we've had to change hotels. As for the weather, all it's done so far is bloody rain.

'I've just been on the blower to Liam and he's agreed that the only thing for it is to stay on and to hell with the budget. Though, God knows, that's tight enough as it is. We'll have to dream up some story for the client. But they're not going to worry so much if we come back with the goods. As it is, however, Jason's shot hardly any film.'

'So when do you think you will be home?' I asked.

'Wednesday week at the earliest. Apart from anything else, there aren't any flights until then. Because we're flying charter, we can't change airlines.'

'Oh, dear. I am sorry.'

'I'm sorry too, love. The whole thing's a bloody nightmare.' He paused and I could visualize his face and almost see his relief that I was taking it so well. Then he asked, 'What's the weather like over there?'

'Blustery.'

'Any news about anything?'

'Quite a lot, actually.'

'Such as?'

'Too much to tell you on the phone.'

'Nothing serious? Everything's OK at the flat?'

'Yes, that's fine. Forget it, it'll wait till you get back.'

'In that case, I'd better be getting a move on. It actually looks as if the sun may be coming out. That will be a bloody miracle if it is.'

'Thanks for ringing.'

'Sorry it's not better news. Still, that's advertising for you. Nothing's ever plain sailing in this bloody business.'

'No. Well, I hope things get better from now on.'

'They couldn't be much worse. Listen, I'll be in touch again soon. Take care of yourself in the meantime.'

'And you.'

As I was putting down the receiver he added, 'I miss you.'

'You, too,' I replied, but the phone at the other end had already gone click.

★ ★ ★

To misquote the old song, what a difference a weekend makes.

If that call had come on Friday evening, I would probably have said the same things but, inside, I would have been feeling very different. As it was, my immediate reaction was thankfulness for his extended absence, which would enable me to meet Oliver Lyon and pursue any leads he might give me without interference from Nigel.

Yet, at the same time, I was fully aware of the implications of that phone call. And so was Nigel. That was evident from the way he had gone on about being in contact with Liam, emphasizing that the reasons for his delay were genuine and that everything was above board. He was all but saying, 'If you don't believe me, ring Liam and check.'

Yes, Nigel was remembering Patti Roscoe. He was remembering how he had phoned me then and said, 'I'm sorry, love, I shan't be coming home this week as planned. Patti's manager has decided that, while we're in California, we may as well go on down to Mexico and shoot some footage there.'

I had believed him . . .

There had been no reason for me not to. We had been married seven years by then and he had given me no grounds to believe he had ever been unfaithful to me. He had never come home with scent on his clothes or lipstick on his collar. No gossip reached me of any affairs, however brief, and I was well enough acquainted with most of his colleagues to be fairly sure it would have done. There were no strange telephone calls, with the other person hanging up when they heard my voice. If I went through Nigel's pockets, his briefcase, his wallet and his diary – as I regret to say I did on occasions – I had found nothing suspicious.

So, although I was still plagued by jealousy, Nigel had given me no cause for distrust, which was why I had believed him when he said Patti Roscoe's manager was insisting they went to Mexico . . .

But that was seven years ago and neither of us were the same people any more.

When we moved to Linden Mansions in April 1973, I was six months pregnant. We had been there less than a fortnight when I started to get bad pains in my abdomen and kept feeling sick and dizzy. I went to the doctor, who attributed the symptoms to indigestion, brought on by the stress of the move. He gave me some medicine and told me to put my feet up and take things easy for a while.

That indigestion turned out to be acute appendicitis. Fortunately, Nigel was home when my appendix ruptured, so he was able to call an ambulance. Never have I known such extreme pain. I thought I was going to die.

For a time after that I almost wished that I had. My appendix was removed in an emergency operation but peritonitis set in and my pregnancy ended in a septic abortion. I remained in hospital for about a month and then, clinically recovered, I was allowed home to convalesce.

Physically, apart from being very weak, I was all right. Antibiotics had cured the infection and my wounds were healing satisfactorily. But my mental condition was another matter. I was deeply depressed.

Nigel was also obviously upset but, because I found it hard to talk about how I was feeling, he assumed that, in a few months, once I was strong enough, I could conceive again and forget the loss of my first baby. That was what my GP and everyone at the hospital told us. Oh, yes, they were very confident and matter-of-fact. I remember my GP saying, 'Get lots of fresh air, eat lots of fruit, make yourself attractive for your husband, and you'll soon find another little bun in the oven.'

Thinking of that still rankles.

None of them had been carrying that baby. It had not been a part of them, like it was of me. I had been feeling so fit and confident, that it had simply not occurred to me that anything could go wrong. I had planned so much for that child. It had been so ineffably important to me.

My mental condition was something with which Nigel – like most men – was, emotionally, unequipped to deal. He tried to understand but my condition was beyond his experience. So he treated me rather as though I had the 'flu, feeding me aspirin and bringing flowers and magazines. However, his flowers seemed to wilt almost as soon as they were put into water, as though contaminated by the air of the room into which they been brought. And the magazines seemed to contain only articles on sex, pregnancy, childbirth and child-rearing.

My depression deepened and the doctor prescribed tranquillizers. I took the pills and maybe they stopped me crying quite so much but that was all.

Then Uncle Stephen died, suddenly, of a heart attack. Even though Nigel and Uncle Stephen had never been particularly close, Nigel was extremely good throughout this additional crisis, doing his utmost to console me in my sorrow and driving me up to Avonford for the funeral, even though, because he was busy at work, we had to return to London immediately afterwards.

Later, I realized that was probably for the best. The last thing Aunt Biddie had needed was me weeping all over her. She was terribly brave. 'As you go through life,' she told me, 'you accept that all things move to their end. Everything that you have and hold, you must in time also let go.'

But I lacked her courage and her stoicism and mourned the passing of the dear man who had brought me up as his own daughter every bit as much as I grieved the loss of my baby.

When Nigel – never the most patient of people – realized that all his efforts were to no avail and that I was not going to snap out of my depression, his sympathy turned to irritation. He ran away from the situation, coming home later and later from work in the evening, sometimes staying away for the night, and continually working weekends.

I knew how he was feeling, but there was nothing I could do. I saw his confusion, his helplessness, his frustration. I wanted to help him, but I couldn't, for I couldn't help myself. I knew what the matter was, but I didn't know the remedy.

'It takes time to get over these things,' the doctor said, going on to prescribe more tranquillizers. 'But, believe me, you'll be fine when you're pregnant again.'

It was Sherry who came to my salvation. We had already met by then and become friendly in a casual, neighbourly sort of way. She was aware that I had been ill, but didn't know the details.

On this particular day, I was feeling even lower than usual. I was just passing her flat door when she emerged. She took one look at me and asked, 'Are you all right?'

I was in the state of mind when a single kind word could convulse me to tears. That question did it. I broke down. I just stood there on the landing, weeping uncontrollably.

She took me upstairs and stayed with me, while I tried to pull myself together. Then she asked, 'Will it help to talk about it?'

At which point, the whole story came spilling out. She was wonderful, not offering any platitudes or trite words of sympathy. On other occasions, indeed, she would say that she'd never wanted children of her own and that she'd always preferred other people's – when you got bored with them, she'd say, you could hand them back. But she was far too sensitive to say such a thing at that moment. Instead, she listened and, when I was calmer, went into the kitchen and made us both coffee.

While the kettle was boiling, she had looked out at the felted, pebble-dashed flat-roofed area beyond our kitchen, above the bathrooms of the other flats, and asked, 'Can you walk over that?'

'Yes, it leads to the fire escape.'

'Why don't you turn it into a garden?' she had suggested.

She had given up the rest of that day for me, insisting that she would otherwise only have been doing housework, which she loathed. By the time evening came, we felt we had known each other for years. She knew all about me and I knew all about her. The first happy discovery we made was that we were virtually the same age. Then it transpired that she had been born in Shrewsbury, which isn't far from Avonford.

She and Roly had both been married before. They had met while she was assistant manager of a bookshop in Chester. Roly and his brother ran a company in London, which distributed, among other things, an exclusive range of photographic greetings cards.

One of their salesmen left without warning and Roly took over his calls until a replacement was found. He went to Chester, met Sherry, took her out to dinner and that was it – love at first sight. She had walked out on her boring engineer husband, come to London and lived in a poky little flat in Pimlico, while Roly sought to extricate himself from a more complicated family situation. In the end, in order to pay off his wife and give himself enough money to start afresh with Sherry, he had sold his share in the company to his brother.

'At which point we started again,' Sherry had stated simply. 'We had a brain-storming session, in which we considered every way we could think of to make money and enjoy ourselves at the same time. Roly had been dabbling in antiques for quite a while, as a sort of paying hobby. And I have always collected books and cards – you know, postcards and old greetings cards. When I left John, my first husband, all I brought with me were my clothes, my books and my cards.

'Eventually, we hit upon the idea of dealing in antique and collectable cats. There were two advantages. One, that cats are the most popular pet in this country. And two, that they crop up everywhere – in paintings, photographs, ornaments, sculpture, jewellery, toys, needlework, books . . .

'So that's what we do. We take tables at antiques and craft fairs – and, at events like The Chelsea Flower Show – and sell cats. We are the cat people. And, while we don't make at a fortune at it, we make a reasonable living. It also accounts for our rather erratic working hours and why I'm home today. It isn't a nine-to-five, five-day-week job.'

'Do you like cats?' I had asked. 'Or does that go without saying?'

'Naturally. Though we only have two real ones of our own – Tattoo and Pinkle Purr. You know the A.A. Milne poem?'

'Of course.'

'Do you like cats?'

'Yes, but Nigel's allergic to them.' That Nigel was allergic to animal fur was something else I had only discovered after we were married. 'In any case, this flat wouldn't really be suitable for keeping a pet. Imagine, if a cat scratched the settee . . .'

She glanced round my living room and nodded without comment.

'But we had lots of animals when we were kids,' I said.

I had gone on to explain about the arrangement between Jonathan and Aunt Biddie and Sherry had laughed. 'She sounds a great character!'

Next day, we went to a garden centre, where we spent the money Nigel and I had intended for baby clothes, a cot and a pram, on containers, compost, seeds and bedding plants. Then we bought some wood, which we made up into shelves, so that my new garden should be layered, and attached trellis and bamboo poles for climbing plants to clamber up.

Up there, I felt safe – away from my memories but not exposed to other people. As my seeds grew and my plants came into flower, so the despair seemed to ebb out of me and I began to see the world and my life in their proper perspectives again. I started to go for walks with Sherry across Hampstead Heath and Parliament Hill Fields, to read, to write letters, to talk to people on the phone, to drive, to go shopping, to do – in short – all those everyday things which you take for granted until you are suddenly unable to do them.

Soon, I was also well enough to return to work. Miles was extraordinarily good to me throughout that entire episode. As soon as it had become apparent that I wouldn't be in a fit state to go back to work for some time, I had offered to hand in my notice. Miles refused point-blank to accept it. What's more, although he was employing a temporary secretary during my absence, my full salary was paid into my bank account at the end of every month.

In view of the fact that, if my pregnancy had run its full term, I would have stopped work to become a full-time mother – and he was aware of that – his response was certainly kindness beyond the call of duty. Furthermore, he knew that I was still hoping to have a child and that he, therefore, stood the risk of finding he had made a false investment. Yes, Miles was more than fair to me.

So I returned to work and Nigel and I continued trying for a baby. Six months passed and I did not get pregnant again. 'Relax,' said my GP airily, 'these things take time.'

Another six months passed and he reluctantly conceded that something might be the matter. He made an appointment for me at the hospital, where an examination and X-ray showed that my tubes were blocked – presumably as a result of the peritonitis. Nowadays, this is not an irremediable problem, but in 1974 medical science was far less advanced. There was nothing to be done.

Although I had tried to prepare myself for this news, it still left me feeling very down. I knew it was not my fault, but it felt like a personal failure. To make matters worse, Nigel had just left for America on a three-week tour with the singer Patti Roscoe, for whom Quantum were making a publicity film. A mixture of pride and an unconquerable feeling of loneliness stopped me from ringing him.

The only person I did tell was Sherry, who suggested adoption. But it was a child of my own that I had been longing for, not somebody else's. 'You were adopted,' Sherry pointed out. But the circumstances had been different. I was Aunt Biddie's own kith and kin, not a stranger introduced into the nest.

In any case, there was always Stevie . . . There was nothing to stop me showering her with the love I had hoped to devote to my own child. Indeed, as an auntie, I could spoil her as outrageously as I chose. In fact, looking back, I've had much of the fun of having a daughter without the aggravations of being a parent.

When Nigel returned from the States, there was something different about him, although I couldn't put my finger on what it was. He was almost too sympathetic and something about his words did not ring quite true. He told me I should have rung him and let him know my bad news, but I sensed he was glad that I hadn't. And I couldn't help noticing that, although he professed sorrow at our childlessness, he did not suggest adoption.

Then, one Friday evening, we went to Talk of the Town to see Patti Roscoe in a performance to coincide with the launch of her new album. Nigel had tried to conceal the event from me, but one of his colleagues had let slip that a whole party from Quantum Design were going and had a special table booked. Ironically, I was quite a fan of Patti Roscoe, who had an incredibly strong voice and sang my kind of songs. So, despite all Nigel's attempts to convince me to stay at home, I insisted upon going to watch her in concert.

And, after a mesmerizing appearance, I watched as she came to our table and threw her arms round Nigel, placing little nibbling kisses on his cheek and ear.

A woman at the next table remarked, 'So that's her new boyfriend, is it? I heard she and Mike had broken up.'

I didn't stay to hear any more. Somehow I made my way back to Highgate. Unfortunately, Sherry and Roly were away, so – unable to bear the thought of remaining at Linden Mansions – I got in my car and drove through the night to Honey Hill Farm. I spent the weekend there, feeling as though my world had come to an end. I remember Miranda breathing fire and brimstone when I told her what had happened and Jonathan, very sweetly, offering to have a man-to-man talk with Nigel.

On Sunday afternoon, he turned up. He was very pale beneath his tan and there were huge dark rings under his eyes. He told me that he was sorry to the depths of his heart for having been such a fool. If he could live the last few weeks again he would not do what he had done. He had told Patti Roscoe that he was never seeing her again and on Monday he was going to resign from Quantum Design.

He said that he loved me and had always loved me. I was his life, he said. Without me, he was nothing. He begged me to give him a second chance. If I would allow him this opportunity, he would prove to me, he vowed, that he still loved me more than anyone else in the world.

And then he had started to cry.

That was the first time I had ever seen any grown man cry – let alone Nigel – so I was totally unprepared for the sheer, harrowing, gut-wrenching horror of the experience. I was so shocked and frightened that I began to cry as well. Then we were in each other's arms and he was sobbing, 'I've been such a idiot,' and I was sobbing, too, 'So have I.'

When we had recovered, we sat and talked openly for the first time in years. He made no attempt to deny his affair with Patti. 'It just kind of started and then went out of control,' he said. She was on the rebound after a long-standing affair with a footballer had broken up. And he had been feeling so down that he had been unable to resist. After losing the baby I had changed, he said. He felt he had failed me but did not know what to do to bring us close us again.

I tried to explain my feelings since I lost the baby and he explained how he had felt excluded from my life. It was as if I had put up a barrier between us, he said, becoming closer to Sherry than I was to him, spending more time in their flat than our own, never showing any interest in his life.

We agreed that we should do more things together. He offered to help me more around the flat, so I had more time to spare at weekends. For instance, while I was doing the cleaning, he could do the shopping. We should entertain more, make new friends and, on Sundays, we could maybe drive out into the country and have lunch at a pub, like we had used to do in the early days of our marriage. Meanwhile, we should go away on holiday or at least for a long weekend – a sort of second honeymoon – so that we could rediscover each other.

He was so convincing and abjectly penitent, that I went back with him that evening to Linden Mansions, even though – as I followed him in my car – I still felt terribly confused and hurt and not entirely sure that I was doing the right thing.

On the other hand, what choice did I really have? I could have left him – I would have had grounds for divorce. But I didn't want that. I loved Nigel. And I kept telling myself that he was the only man I had ever wanted to love.

Gradually, we re-built our life together. On the Monday he not only handed in his notice at Quantum Design but left the company that same day. While I was at work, he started looking for a new job, but when I came home in the evening a tidy flat and a meal were waiting for me. The following weekend, we went to Venice and, although we failed to recapture the magic of our first ever weekend together, revisiting the scene did help to bring us closer.

He was fortunate enough quickly to obtain another job as an art director at Holleyman & Elwood, an old-established advertising agency in Holborn, with no connections to the pop music business. He rang if he was going to be so much as half an hour late home from the office and, if he was delayed, his explanation of where he had been and what he had been doing was so detailed it was almost embarrassing. About the house, he remained a reformed character, helping with the washing up, doing the shopping and ironing his own shirts.

Soon, we were leading a busy social life: most weekends found us at dinner parties or giving dinner parties ourselves – mainly with Nigel's colleagues. Still, I liked them: they were fun people, slightly unconventional, but not so outrageous as to be intimidating.

In other words, he genuinely regretted his actions and I didn't have the heart to carry a grudge against him. He made every effort to make up for Patti and I made every effort to put the incident behind me.

One day, glancing through the newspapers, on the lookout for mentions of Miles – taking press cuttings was another of my duties – my eye was caught by Patti Roscoe's name in one of the gossip columns.

> The romance between singer Patti Roscoe and footballer Mike Snoddy is back on again. Recently returned from a highly successful US tour, Patti told me that she had used her time away from Mike to do some serious thinking. 'I'm convinced now that my future lies with Mike,' she said. 'There's no other man in the world who can match him on the football pitch or in the rough and tumble of love.'

Whether Nigel saw that snippet, I don't know, for Patti's name was never mentioned by either of us again.

So, for a couple of years, our life continued in harmony. In a funny way, in fact, we were almost closer than we had been before our traumas, because we were both aware of how much we had nearly lost.

Then, in 1976, three senior employees of Holleyman & Elwood broke away to found their own agency. Liam Massey, who had been an account executive and, therefore, had contact with all Holleyman & Elwood's clients, became the Chairman of the new agency. Trevor Gault, an accountant, became the Managing Director and Finance Director, and Bron Lucasz, a copywriter, became Creative Director. They took with them several of Holleyman & Elwood's most prestigious accounts, including a couple on which Nigel worked. They invited Nigel to join the new agency and he accepted without a moment's hesitation.

This was the opportunity he had been waiting for, he informed me excitedly. At Holleyman & Elwood, office politics and bureaucracy were stifling creativity and clients were threatening to leave because of lack of service. Massey Gault & Lucasz was spearheading a new departure in advertising, the creative hotshop, whose reputation would be built on creative excellence, backed up by strong marketing and planning functions.

For his own part, he would be a much bigger fish in a much smaller pond, with excellent prospects of promotion and even a possible partnership.

After Nigel joined Massey Gault & Lucasz our marriage embarked upon its second downhill slide. It didn't happen overnight. Nigel didn't change from one day to another. No, it was a slow process of erosion.

The agency's strategy succeeded and its client base swiftly expanded to include many household and international names – tobacco, drinks and confectionery brands, a car manufacturer, fashion and cosmetics houses.

Nigel had always worked hard: at Massey Gault & Lucasz he worked even harder. If he wasn't attending meetings or dealing with last-minute panics, he was at the pub, out to dinner or off to a party. He denied – a little too emphatically – that this was all pleasure. Image, he said – and doubtless correctly – was all-important in advertising. If you couldn't project your own image, why should a potential client trust you to project theirs? You had to be seen in the right places with the right people, wear the right clothes and drive the right car, yet at the same time, you had to stand out from the crowd.

Whereas I had felt relatively comfortable in the atmosphere of Holleyman & Elwood, I felt distinctively ill at ease among the trendsetters of Massey Gault & Lucasz. Liam wasn't so bad, although if any Irishman ever kissed the Blarney Stone it was him. And Trevor was probably all right: because he was the accountant, I never had much to do with him. But I really couldn't stand Bron Lucasz, Nigel's superior.

According to Nigel, Bron was a brilliant copywriter, responsible for many of advertising's most memorable slogans, who inspired a disciple-like devotion among his fellow creatives and client companies. An inspiration, maybe, but a diplomat, no. I don't think he once called me by my name. It was clear that he thought anyone outside the advertising fraternity a complete nonentity.

Unfortunately, as so often happens, like attracted like. As Massey Gault & Lucasz, expanded, Nigel's new colleagues were from a different category than those at Holleyman & Elwood. Nigel remained scrupulous about asking me to accompany him to social functions whenever possible, but our worlds were rapidly diverging. Indeed, it was almost as though we had gone the full cycle and were back again at our beginning, when I was the outsider among a circle of people who all knew each other very well and with whom I had nothing in common except Nigel.

As a result, I gradually found excuses to stay behind, preferring to spend my evenings alone or with Sherry and Roly. After a while, I also opted out of giving dinner parties, suggesting that Nigel took his guests to a restaurant. After all, at the end of a busy day at work, I lacked the energy and enthusiasm to prepare a meal and entertain people who were as uninterested in me as I was in them.

When Nigel won a prestigious Designers' and Art Directors' Association award, his career really took off. He was duly promoted, given a salary increase and his Fiat 124 was upgraded to a bright red, sporty BMW. He won a big teddy bear, the booby prize in a raffle at some high-profile function at the Dorchester in aid of charity, and *Campaign* splashed a photograph of the two of them across its front page. He named the bear Hugh and adopted it as his mascot. He took to wearing a wide-brimmed hat and yellow scarf – even at the height of summer – and, wherever he went, he was accompanied by Hugh, wearing an identical hat and scarf.

As well as working ever longer hours, he soon became the archetypal jet-setter, constantly flying off to client meetings in cities like New York, Tokyo and Frankfurt, or off on shoots to exotic locations, like the current one in the Caribbean. Hugh always went too.

To begin with, some of my old insecurities and jealousies returned. Once a person has given you cause to distrust, it is difficult ever fully to trust them again. But after a while I became confident that Nigel was unlikely ever again to indulge in a spur of the moment affair. He still had an eye for a pretty girl and women still found him attractive, but that was as far as it went.

No, I was up against a far more powerful and seductive rival for his attentions than another woman. I was up against his career. As he gained in confidence, finding himself acknowledged as a star on a world stage, he needed me less and less.

He loved his job and he was happy. It didn't occur to him that I might be feeling neglected and excluded. He simply took it for granted that I would go on supporting him, as I had always done in the past. I don't think he was much different from many other husbands in this respect.

But rather than moping about a situation that was clearly not going to change, I had to do something to get out of this deadlock. After all, Nigel was doing nothing blameworthy. There is no sin in being hard-working and ambitious. Basically, it was up to me to make a fuller life for myself during his absences and ensure that I presented an attractive, welcoming face when he returned.

Perhaps I should have been more assertive. However, the same applied then as at the time of the Patti Roscoe episode: Nigel was my husband and I still loved him. He might have changed, but I could not forget the man who had wept such bitter tears of remorse. He might no longer need me in the same way, but I was still his stability – as he was mine. And he had managed to convince me that without my support, he would collapse.

So, while our marriage wasn't perfect, it could have been far worse. We were comfortably off and had a home that many people would envy. Nigel might be a little short-fused on occasions but the storm always passed.

In the end, it was simplest not to think about it all too much and, when I felt a bit down, count my blessings and hope that things would improve.

After Nigel's call, I went down to Sherry and Roly's flat on the first floor. The door burst open almost immediately after I had rung the bell. 'I was hoping it would be you!' Sherry exclaimed. 'Come on in and have a drink. Dinner's almost ready.'

How can I describe Sherry and do her justice? She is about the same height as I and has straight, mid-brown hair with highlights in it, bobbed to chin-length, framing a roundish, jolly face, with eyes as blue as cornflowers and a smile like a ray of sun on a cloudy day. She is more like champagne than sherry – she sparkles and effervesces.

Roly is twenty years older than Sherry and me, though one wouldn't think it, for he's one of those ageless people – rather like Aunt Biddie – abounding in energy and enthusiasm. And his name belies his physique, for he's tall and thin as a rake.

'So what's all this about Oliver Lyon?' she asked, when Roly had poured me a glass of wine.

I recounted the weekend's events, up to and including my phone call to Oliver Lyon, during which time she served up a magnificent steak pie.

'Without having seen the Princess, I simply do not believe that you're her daughter,' she stated adamantly, when I came to the end of my story. 'In fact, I find it very hard, after listening to all that, to believe that you're your father's daughter either, but your physical resemblance and the similarities in character between you and Aunt Biddie presumably don't leave much room for doubt in that respect.

'But you and the Princess are chalk and cheese. First and foremost, you would never, ever have abandoned your child. *You* wouldn't have allowed Nigel to take your baby away for his sister to bring up. No matter what the circumstances, you would have fought tooth and nail to keep it.'

Roly replied before I had a chance. 'I don't quite follow your logic, darling. If Cara isn't the Princess's daughter, then she wasn't abandoned by her.'

Sherry gave a fond, exasperated snort. 'Well, Cara knows what I mean.'

I nodded. 'Yes, I do. But if she was my mother and if she was – as one has to assume, lacking in maternal feeling, there's no reason why I should automatically turn out to be like her. On the contrary, my circumstances make it all the more likely that I should instinctively become the exact opposite. That's one of the reasons why it was so important to me to have a baby, to compensate for my own lack of real parents.'

Sherry shook her head dubiously. 'You could say the same about her, if she lost her parents in the Revolution. That must have been highly traumatic, even with the sugary Prince to look after her – being in a foreign country and not knowing what was going to happen to her.'

'Which leads me to my next point. She was obviously extremely strong-willed. I would go so far as to say selfish. Put yourself in her position. Would you have married someone merely in order to obtain the nationality of your host country? Come on, Cara, be honest.'

'No,' I admitted. 'It would have had to be for love.'

'And the same applies to her marriage to your father. There was some ulterior motive behind that, I'm absolutely convinced of it. Then the Italian count – well, obviously, he was rich. And so was the Earl of Winster, one assumes.'

Roly cleared his throat. 'If I may stick my oar in again, all this depends on whether you consider heredity or environment to be the most important factor in forming a person's character – or whether, indeed, it's a combination of both.'

'I've been thinking a hell of a lot about that, as you can imagine,' I told him. 'And I believe that, in my case, the influence of Aunt Biddie and Uncle Stephen must be stronger than any characteristics I inherited from my natural mother and father.'

'I'd go along with that. And, returning to your father, the fact that he brought you to England would seem to indicate that, although he may have been a bit of a lad in his time, he was not without compassion and moral principles. He cared sufficiently about you to make sure that you went to a good home.'

'You make Cara sound as if she was a kitten or a puppy,' Sherry remonstrated.

I laughed. 'It's all right. Aunt Biddie compared me to a lame duck.'

Roly continued, 'So, even though your illusions about your father have been shattered, he doesn't emerge from all this as a thorough-going cad. In fact, I think he sounds a most intriguing character. I wish I could have met him. It would have saved me a lot of trouble and expense if I could have run a *ménage à trois*.'

'Enough of that, too!' Sherry expostulated, slapping him affectionately on the hand.

Roly grinned, then became serious again. 'But this Princess . . . No, I have to agree with Sherry, it's difficult to believe you're her daughter. In addition to the reasons Sherry's given, you're too . . .'

'Too what?' I prompted.

'Well, you're a very homely type.'

This was too much for Sherry. 'Roly! How can say such a thing? Homely is a dreadful word to use to describe anyone, let alone Cara, who always looks so wonderful.'

He laughed. 'I knew that would get me into hot water. But I'm not talking about her looks. I'm talking about her personality.'

'And you're right,' I said. 'By nature, I am a very homely person. I'm like Judith Paris – you know the Hugh Walpole books, don't you?' I quoted from memory: "But where is my place and where are my people? Like my father before me, I have no home and yet I am truly a very domestic creature and could not live except for the affections of those of whom I am fond."'

'I don't think I know Judith Paris,' Sherry said.

'Then I must lend you the books. I've always identified with her. When you read them, you'll realize why. But I'm not really like her in personality. She was a much stronger character than I am.'

'Fictitious characters are always stronger than real-live people,' Roly observed. 'If they weren't, we wouldn't be interested in reading about them, because we'd be reading about mirror images of our mundane selves. The main attraction of fiction is the escape it offers us from reality, together with the dream that, under different circumstances, we could become like the hero or heroine.'

'I think Cara's story is a case of fact being stranger than fiction,' Sherry commented. 'I'm sure there are lots of instances when an adopted child goes in search of his or her natural parents. But I've never read a book, fact or fiction, in which that child's mother could be a princess.'

'Mind you,' I pointed out, 'there were far more Russian princesses than there are British ones.'

'Nevertheless, it's decidedly more romantic than being the daughter of Mary Jones, like I am.' She paused. 'Have you told Nigel yet?'

'It's not the sort of thing one can go into over the phone.'

'Mmm. You have heard from him since he left, haven't you?'

'Yes, he rang just before I came down here.'

'When's he due home?'

'Wednesday week.'

'It will be interesting to hear his reaction when he finds out that his wife may be the daughter of a Russian princess.'

I grunted non-committally.

Soon after that I went back to my own flat. In bed, I wrote up my diary, pondering Sherry's final comment about Nigel. He wasn't going to like it. He hated to be upstaged.

Chapter 8

Next day, I had lunch with Juliette, at Chattertons, a nearby wine bar. Juliette grabbed one of the booths, while I ordered a bottle of house white and a couple of salads.

'So, come on, tell all,' she said. 'I'm dying to know what happened to you at the weekend.'

Because we only had an hour for lunch, I gave her a shorter version of the weekend's events than I had Sherry and Roly, reflecting, as I did so, that it was good practice for Oliver Lyon that evening.

Her reaction, when I finished, was the exact opposite of Sherry's. She tipped her head on one side, leaning her elfin face on her hand, and studied me thoughtfully. 'You know, it wouldn't surprise me actually. You do have a rather imposing – yes, one could almost say regal – air about you on occasions.'

'Imposing? Regal? Me?' I asked incredulously.

She laughed. 'It's most apparent when you're talking to strangers. Then you appear very superior and aloof – very Chairman's secretary.'

'I had no idea—'

'I'm sorry. Please don't look so shocked. I didn't mean to upset you. Anyone who knows you well, knows that you're not like that at all. It's just a manner you adopt – a sort of act you put on.'

'When I'm nervous . . .'

'Probably. It could just be a defence mechanism you've developed. We all do the same thing in some form or other. When I'm nervous, I go to the opposite extreme and gabble away as if I'm demented, whereas you go all kind of cool and aloof, which is much better. But the point is that you could have inherited that characteristic from the Princess, assuming she was your mother.'

'It didn't come from Aunt Biddie or Uncle Stephen, that's for sure.'

'What did your aunt think?'

'She wouldn't commit herself.'

'Have you told anyone else?'

'Sherry and Roly.'

'And?'

'Neither of them believe I was the Princess's daughter.' I didn't go into the reasons. Juliette and I were close, but nowhere near as close as Sherry and me, so there was much in my life of which Juliette was unaware, including the reasons for my childlessness and the true state of my marriage. She assumed that Nigel and I had made a conscious decision, like she and her husband, not to have children.

'Well, it will be very interesting to hear what Oliver Lyon has to say.' She glanced at her watch. 'God, it's two o'clock. We'd better be getting back.'

Like most days, whether or not Miles was in the office, I didn't have much opportunity to think about anything other than work that afternoon. There were still the dreaded minutes from yesterday's meetings to type, arrangements to make for Miles's forthcoming trips not to mention all the correspondence he had left me. On top of that the phone never seemed to stop ringing. Every five minutes, somebody was wanting to know where Miles was, when he'd be back, and did I know about this, that or the other. All in all, it was a typical day.

It was five past six before I put the phone down after the last caller. Unlike Nigel, who was never early if he could be on time, never on time if he could be late and, needless to say, hated to be kept waiting, I was a stickler for punctuality. But I made time to dash along to the ladies and pull a comb through my hair, glance at my make-up and decide it would have to do, before charging up the road to the Ambassador.

There can have been nothing imposing, regal, cool or aloof about me as I arrived, breathless, outside the hotel. The commissionaire raised his hand as I pushed through the revolving door and the hall porter and reception clerks greeted me familiarly as I entered the foyer, for I was always in and out, leaving papers or messages for Miles, meeting visitors for him and taking them to the office.

I was about to ask if Oliver Lyon had arrived, when I spotted him, sitting in a recess at the far end of the foyer surveying the scene over the top of an evening paper. As I approached, he raised an interrogative eyebrow, then rose to his feet, a rather shorter man than I had imagined him to be, but otherwise just like his screen image. 'Mrs Sinclair?'

'Yes, I'm sorry I'm late,' I said, holding out my hand. 'A last-minute phone call . . .'

'Please don't worry. It doesn't matter. Shall we go to the bar?'

We went down the short passageway to the bar, where the bar steward recognized us both as we entered. 'Good evening, Mrs Sinclair. Good evening, Mr Lyon.'

I smiled. 'Hello, Max.'

Oliver Lyon merely nodded a greeting. I could sense his surprise, although he tried to conceal it, at finding the blithering idiot on the phone so much at home in the august surroundings of the Ambassador Hotel.

We sat down at a table in one the little bays, while Max hovered.

'What would you like to drink, Mrs Sinclair?' Oliver Lyon asked me.

'Campari and soda, please.'

'Make that two, please, Max.'

Then he said to me, with a little smile, 'Do you come here often?'

I laughed. 'Only in the course of my job. I'm Miles Goodchild's secretary and all his important contacts stay here when they're in London, so I'm often backwards and forwards from the office.'

'Miles Goodchild, eh?'

His attitude towards me was changing by the minute and my confidence was increasing at the same rate.

'How long have worked for him?'

'Thirteen years.'

'It must be an interesting job.'

'It is. There's never a dull moment.'

Max brought our drinks and Oliver Lyon signed a chit. Then he lifted his glass to me and said, 'Well, to get to the purpose of our meeting, I must admit your phone call took me totally by surprise.'

'I'm afraid I was rather incoherent. I didn't quite know how to explain myself. It came as a great shock to discover that my father had been married to a Russian princess.'

'I fully understand. It's not the sort of thing that happens every day.' He took out a packet of cigarettes and offered them to me.

Nigel and I had both given up smoking when I became pregnant, but were occasional social smokers. On this occasion, I was grateful for something to calm my nerves and occupy my hands.

Oliver Lyon lit my cigarette and then his. 'May I suggest that you start at the beginning and tell me in detail what you know about your father and the circumstances of your birth?'

I repeated my story, much as I had told it to Juliette at lunchtime, including only the facts and none of the hypotheses.

'Fascinating,' he murmured. 'I wish I'd known of your existence before I interviewed her.'

'I wish I'd known about her before as well.'

'Incidentally, you won't be aware that she insisted upon being referred to as "Princess". Never the Princess Hélène or the Princess Shuiska – nor her husband's name for that matter – but always Princess.'

'No, I had no idea. I simply find her name rather difficult to pronounce.'

'Hmm . . .' He stubbed out his cigarette and immediately lit another one. 'She wasn't the easiest of people to interview. You'd be amazed if you saw the unedited version of the programme. Time after time, I asked her questions which she simply refused to answer. She just looked past me, as though I wasn't there. Basically, she had decided beforehand what she was going to tell me – and nothing would shift her.'

'What sort of questions wouldn't she answer?'

'For a start, the personal aspects of her early life in Paris.'

'I'm afraid I didn't see the beginning of the programme,' I admitted, hoping I wouldn't offend him, and explained how Aunt Biddie had rung me half-way through.

He wasn't at all put out. 'Well, let me see. She described her family background and childhood in Russia. Her father was a Guards officer, who could trace his roots back to Boyars, and her mother was a great beauty. As a child, she used to visit Tsarskoe Selo, the Tsar's village outside St Petersburg and sometimes, as a treat, she was allowed to play with the young grand duchesses. She was extremely well educated and spoke fluent French, English and German, as well as Russian.

'When the Revolution started in 1917, her father was away with his regiment and her mother, fearing for her safety, sent her to stay with relations on one of their country estates, north of St Petersburg. After that, she never saw or heard from her parents again – nor did she ever discover what happened to them. On top of that, the Bolsheviks massacred the family she was staying with. She escaped death by a hair's breadth, thanks to a cousin, Prince Dmitri Nikolaevitch Zakharin.'

'Ah, my aunt mentioned him, though she didn't catch his name.'

He spelled the surname out for me, then continued, 'Dmitri had been an aide to a Russian general during the war and was quite a resourceful chap by the sound of it. He hid her in the forest and, eventually, they made their way through Finland to Denmark and, from there, to Paris, where his family owned a house.

'Because Dmitri came from a wealthy family, who held bank accounts in Paris and Switzerland upon which he could draw, they had no money difficulties, at least to begin with. Quite what he did when his funds ran out, I'm not sure. The Princess was decidedly vague at this point and said he became involved in various business enterprises. But it's fairly certain that he didn't have to resort to driving a taxi or working in a bar in order to earn a living, like so many other Russian *émigrés*. And he didn't do badly for himself in the long run. He ended up by marrying Imogen Humboldt – Abraham Humboldt's daughter.'

'Imogen Humboldt,' I gasped. 'How incredible!'

'Why?'

'She had an affair with my father.'

'Did she indeed? I didn't know that.'

'Neither did I until the other day.' I repeated Aunt Biddie's story.

'Well I never,' he murmured when I had finished. 'That's something else I wish I'd had been aware of before the interview.' He signalled Max to bring us more Camparis.

'What about the Princess?' I asked.

'Apparently she met up with a Russian woman, whom she had known as a girl, who took her into her family. And then she married a Frenchman – the Baron Léon de St-Léon. He was a widower, considerably older than her, and a leading political figure of the time. They were married in 1924 and the marriage lasted until his death in 1939.

'According to her, they were extremely happy. He was able to provide her with the sort of lifestyle to which she had been accustomed. He owned a town house near the Bois de Boulogne on the avenue Foch, a château at Jonquières in the Marne, and a villa at Deauville. They led a very active social life, with big house parties, dinners, balls and *soirée*s. The Baron was a great patron of the arts and, through him, she met many artists, writers and musicians.

'Various poems and pieces of music were dedicated to her and numerous artists painted her portrait, including El Toro. She had one of El Toro's portraits in her drawing room. Were you watching at that point?'

'No, I switched on just as you were saying that my father and El Toro had been great friends and gone to Spain together.'

'Right, so you saw the photograph of them?'

'Yes, and you said that your father was a friend of El Toro's.'

'Actually, that was a bit of bluff on my part,' he confessed. 'He didn't know El Toro as intimately as I made out, but it did the trick. They certainly met on a number of occasions and at the time of his death, in 1960, my father was working on Toro's biography. That photograph came from a book on El Toro to which he wrote the foreword.

'In fact, I had the devil's own job to persuade the Princess to show me any photographs. Everyone else I've interviewed for this series had their albums piled up, waiting to show me. But not her. I suppose, given the circumstances under which she left Russia, it's understandable that all she should have had was a couple of crumpled, faded snapshots of her parents, but you would have thought that such a beautiful woman would have collected more souvenirs of her later life. Instead of which, all she had were two paintings of herself – the El Toro and another by some other, lesser known artist.'

'So she had no wedding photographs, for instance?'

He shook his head. 'I think that when she said that she tried never to look back, she was telling the absolute truth. And, returning to your father, I'm fairly convinced that if I hadn't known beforehand about her marriage to him, she wouldn't have volunteered the information.'

'Why not?'

'With no disrespect to your father, I think she was ashamed of it. She was a tremendous snob. You may remember that she accused me of being one, but that was a little ruse to prevent me from probing too deeply.'

'So why did she did marry him?'

'I don't know. I find it hard to believe that it was solely for love. I can only think it must have been so that she could get out of France.'

'But why should she have needed to leave France?'

'In the early days of the war, in France even more than here in the UK, there was much fear of a communist fifth column. All Russians were suspect, Whites and Reds. That could have been a reason for her to consider it expedient to marry an obscure Irish poet and hide in the backwoods of Italy.'

'You don't have any idea where in Italy they lived?'

'No, I'm afraid not. As you know, I did ask her. It's possible she had forgotten. It's equally possible that she had chosen to forget, along with her many other convenient lapses of memory. Your aunt doesn't know either?'

I told him about the stolen handbag and he shook his head sympathetically.

'I'm in possession of all my father's notebooks and diaries, but they contain no reference to the Princess or your father. I went through them again yesterday evening, just to check, but there's nothing. I also consulted various literary encyclopaedias, but again to no avail. I can only assume that because Connor Moran had nothing published after he was wounded in Spain, he ceased to be of any interest to the chroniclers.'

'Well, thank you for looking. That was very kind.'

'Not at all. Your father interests me as much as the Princess does. It's the very lack of information regarding him – almost, one could say, the cloak of obscurity surrounding him – which most intrigues me.'

I thought of Aunt Biddie going through the glory-hole and the attic, but decided to say nothing. Instead I asked, 'What about El Toro? Do you know if he has any relations still living?'

'He had several mistresses in his time but never married, so there are no direct descendants. Having said that, there's a whole clan of Toros in Spain, to whom he's still a great revolutionary hero, but I've spoken to them in the past and none of them know anything about his Paris days. Like your father, he seems virtually to have cut himself off from his family after he left home. It's quite understandable. There weren't the communications in those days that there are now.'

'I was thinking that, because my father went to Spain with El Toro, someone there might remember him.'

'Even so, I don't see that it would get us much further forward. What we need to find out is what happened after the Civil War, when he returned to France.'

An idea occurred to me. 'Did you know the Princess before your interview?'

'Good heavens, yes. I'd known her for years. I first met her through an old friend of mine, Tobin Touchstone, who is distantly related to the Winsters. Howard, the late Earl of Winster, was the last of the true Winsters. You know how these old families suddenly die out? Howard was an only child himself and didn't have any children by his first marriage to Alice and it was obviously too late to have any with the Princess. Tobin's father was next of kin. I think I'm right in saying that he was Howard's cousin. In any event, he died before Howard, so Tobin's elder brother, Harvey, succeeded to the title upon the late Earl's death, since when he's lived at Kingston Kirkby Hall, the family seat up in Derbyshire.

'Tobin was very close to the late Earl and, after his death, he continued to keep an eye on the Princess. They had an odd sort of relationship. She didn't approve of him at all, but in a way I think she quite liked him.'

'Why didn't she approve of him?'

'Oh, because he's a commercial artist. His work appears on book covers, in advertisements, on packaging. He's very good. I've always said he's wasting his talent, but I guess we all have to earn a living.

'However, so far as the Princess was concerned, Tobin was in trade. Harvey's a barrister, which she considered a slightly more suitable employment for a gentleman. As I mentioned earlier, she was a terrible snob. But, at the same time, she was a bit of a culture vulture. She liked celebrities – nobody so vulgar as pop singers or film stars, I hasten to add – but what one could class as the cultural elite: writers, artists, musicians – the same sort of people whom she and the Baron de St-Léon used to entertain in Paris before the war.

'While Lord Winster was alive, she was a renowned hostess, although her parties and dinner parties at their house in Chelsea were on a more modest scale than I imagine those in Paris to have been. Every now and again, she would invite Tobin and me to augment the numbers.

'I had learned a certain amount about her from snippets she had let drop regarding her past and thought she would make a fascinating subject for an interview. But each time I broached the topic, she refused. However, after Howard died, she changed. There were no more dinner parties and she turned down all invitations. I hardly saw her after that until the interview, but a common acquaintance told me that she had started acting in a rather peculiar manner, that she seemed suspicious of everyone, almost as though she thought they were spying on her – or, he said, as if she believed he might have plans to make off with the family silver. Tobin said she was reluctant to let even him through the front door.'

'Do you think that had anything to do with her last sentence, when she said all the people she had loved during her life were dead and only her enemies survived?'

'I have absolutely no idea what she meant by that. When I asked her to expand on the statement, she refused.'

'So what made her change her mind about being interviewed?'

'I don't know that either. Suddenly, last summer, out of the blue, I received a telephone call from her. She asked if I was still interested in interviewing her and, naturally, I said yes. We had a meeting at Beadle Walk and discussed the form the interview would take. She stipulated that a butler should be hired in for the occasion and a make-up artist and dresser should be in attendance. Furthermore, if she chose not to answer any question I might pose, I was to respect her wishes and she was to have the right to vet the final programme before it was shown.'

'And did you agree?'

'Yes. And I kept my word.'

'Do you think she sensed, when she asked if you would interview her, that she was approaching the end of her life and that's why she changed her mind?'

'It's possible.'

I swirled the slice of orange at the bottom of my Campari glass. Then I asked, 'Did you like her?'

He inhaled thoughtfully on his cigarette. 'Did I like her? What an interesting question. Yes, I suppose basically I did, insofar as it's possible to like a person one doesn't really know. Perhaps respect would be a better word than like.

'It was almost as if she had created for herself a public persona – a set of rules even – from which she would not allow herself to be deflected. She never relaxed her guard. She never permitted herself to show any true emotion. I never saw her angry, upset or genuinely amused. If I were to make a comparison, it would be with the Queen. Distant, would be the word to sum her up.'

We were both silent for a few moments. Then I asked, 'How did she die?'

'She had a severe stroke, which completely paralysed her. She lingered for a couple of weeks, then mercifully passed away.'

'When is her funeral?'

'Tomorrow. Why? Are you thinking of coming? There's nothing to stop you. Indeed, if she was your mother, you'd have every right to attend.'

I did not reply to his question. Instead I posed another of my own. 'Having met her and now having met me, do you think she was my mother?'

He stubbed out his cigarette. 'Do you think I haven't been wondering the same thing ever since I set eyes on you? The answer is that I have absolutely no idea. In appearance, you and she are not an obvious case of like mother, like daughter. You definitely take after your father in that respect. But there is something about you – some indefinable quality – although I can't quite make up my mind what it is.'

He paused. 'Let me turn your question back on you. Do you feel that you are her daughter?'

'No, not at all. I felt no affinity with her whatsoever when I watched the interview and even less now after all you've told me. But I would like to know more about her marriage to my father, so that I could understand him better. And I am, naturally, curious as to who my real mother was.'

'Do you mean to say that the possibility of being the daughter of a Russian princess doesn't excite you at all?'

I laughed. 'Of course it does. I simply find it extremely hard to believe. I'm a very ordinary person. And she was anything but.'

'I'm going to disagree with you there. I don't think you're ordinary at all. In fact, I'll admit now that, when you entered the hotel earlier, you were not in the least bit what I was expecting.'

I felt myself blushing.

He drained his glass, glanced at his watch and said, 'I'm afraid I'll have to be making a move shortly. I have another appointment.'

'And I should be getting home, too.'

'One last thing before we part. You don't by any chance have access to a video player? Because, if you do, I could let you have a tape of the interview.'

That question sounds odd now, but, back in those days, a video player was not the household object it is nowadays. Nigel did have one at the agency, but I didn't think of that. 'No, I'm afraid I don't,' I said.

At the hotel entrance, he asked, 'Would you like to come to the funeral?'

Part of me did and part of me didn't. But, in any case, I couldn't take a day off work without having made prior arrangements, even in Miles's absence.

'No, not really,' I said.

'You're probably right. Well, if I do discover anything more, I'll let you know. And if you should learn anything, please do get in touch.'

On Thursday morning, when I had been in the office about an hour, the telephone rang and Dorothy announced, 'A Mr Touchstone for you, Cara.'

Before I could collect my thoughts, an unfamiliar man's voice was asking, 'Could I speak to Mrs Sinclair?'

'Speaking.'

'My name is Tobin Touchstone. I'm a friend of Oliver Lyon.'

'Oh, yes, of course.'

'Is it all right me ringing you at work?'

'Yes, it's fine.'

'I saw Oliver yesterday at the Princess's funeral and he told me about your meeting. Unfortunately, he didn't have your telephone number. He just remembered that you worked for Miles Goodchild. I was so intrigued by your story, I felt I simply must contact you. Oliver did tell me right? Your father was Connor Moran?'

'Yes. Yes, he was . . .'

'And you believe that the Princess may have been your mother?'

'Not exactly. Until I watched the interview, I was unaware even of her existence, let alone the fact that my father had ever been married to her.'

'That must have come as quite a shock.'

'It did rather.'

'Hmm.' He was silent for a moment or two. Then he asked, 'Did Oliver explain my connection to the Princess?'

'Well, I know she was married to the late Earl of Winster and that you are—'

'Don't even try to work out the relationship between me and Howard.' There was a slight chuckle in his voice, which was dark and warm. 'I think we were second cousins. Because he and I were quite close, I knew the Princess reasonably well – or, put it this way, as well as anyone could know her. I was not aware – and I'm sure Howard wasn't either – of her having any children.'

He paused. 'Look, I doubt that I shall be able to add much to your sum of knowledge, but if you think it might be worthwhile from your point of view, I'd be fascinated to meet you and tell you what I know about her.'

'Well, if it wouldn't put you to too much inconvenience.'

'Not at all. And I should confess to having another motive for wanting to meet you. I've always been a great admirer of your father's poetry.'

Apart from my immediate family, I had met no more than a handful of people during the entire course of my life, who had ever heard of my father. Now I was talking to two in the space of a week.

'Do you really mean that?'

'Of course.' There was genuine enthusiasm in his voice. 'When Oliver originally informed me that the Princess had been married to Connor Moran, I had hoped that she would be able to tell more about him, but she was most unforthcoming. Now, where and when would be convenient for us to meet? I believe you work in St James's Square. I could meet you there.'

'If you're sure.'

'Absolutely! Well – what about this evening when you finish work?'

My eyes scanned the diary. 'Yes, that should be all right. But I doubt that I'll be able to get away much before half past six.'

'That suits me. I'll see you outside Wolesley House at six thirty. And don't worry if you're late. I'm a patient soul. I'll wait until you turn up.'

For the rest of the day I had scant opportunity to think about Tobin Touchstone or any other aspect of my personal life. Juliette brought me in a sandwich at lunchtime, which I gulped down between phone calls, then Miles was back with a briefcase full of work. We had half an hour before he went into his meetings, which ran late, and it was a quarter to seven before he set off for his dinner appointment with Sir Utley Trusted, the Chairman of Trusted Supermarkets. Five minutes later, I followed him out of the office.

Chapter 9

In the reception area, a man was talking to Sergeant, looking away from me as I came down the stairs. My initial impression was of a tall, well-built figure, casually dressed, with an anorak slung over his shoulder. He had a shock of tousled, thick brown hair.

'Ah, here's Mrs Sinclair now, sir,' Sergeant said.

The man looked up and I saw a face that was rather long, with deep grooves leading up from a widish mouth either side of a forceful nose. He had hazel eyes beneath thick, slightly arched eyebrows, giving him a look of mild surprise. I placed him as being in his mid-forties.

It was not a conventionally handsome face but it was unique and would be hard to forget. Then he smiled and the effect upon me was the same as whenever I saw Sherry – as though the sun had come out from behind a cloud – the smile lighting up his hazel eyes, reflecting an irrepressible enthusiasm for life.

It seems crazy that I should have felt so much in such a short space of time, but that's how it was. I didn't fancy him, as such. My knees didn't exactly buckle at the sight of him but there was something about him that made a huge impression.

Tobin didn't have the sort of charisma that slays the female sex. He was nowhere near as good-looking as Nigel and his clothes made no sort of statement. Yet there was something intrinsically attractive about him – something which reached out and touched me. I instinctively felt that he was my type of person. I saw him and, immediately, liked him.

'Hello, I'm Tobin Touchstone,' he said. His voice sounded just as it had on the phone – warm and dark brown. 'How very nice to meet you.'

He took my hand in a bear-like clasp.

'It's nice to meet you, too, Mr Touchstone,' I said. 'I'm so sorry I'm late.'

'That's quite all right. I've been in excellent company. We just saw your boss depart, so we knew you couldn't be far behind. You certainly work long hours, I must say. As does our friend here.' He indicated Sergeant.

Sergeant beamed. 'Oh, I'm not usually on this late, but the night porter's been delayed.'

'I hope he turns up soon,' I said.

'It doesn't matter. My old lady will have supper for me whatever time I get in.'

We both wished him goodnight and, outside on the pavement, Tobin Touchstone asked, 'Now, where do you suggest we go? Is there a reasonable wine bar in this neighbourhood or do we have to go to the Ambassador?'

His mention of the Ambassador reminded me, with a jolt, that I had omitted to check whether Bob Drewitz, the Chief Executive of Dandy Candy, who was due for meetings with Miles the next day, had arrived safely. 'No, there's Chattertons just up the road. But would you mind awfully if we popped in to the Ambassador quickly? We have an American visitor due and I'd forgotten all about him.'

'You lead and I'll follow.'

So we went first to the Ambassador, where the reception clerk assured me that all was in order. Mr Drewitz had arrived and already gone out again.

I apologized to Tobin Touchstone. 'Sorry. I was worrying unnecessarily.'

'Are you always so conscientious?' he asked.

'I try to be.'

'I like that. So many people I come across in business have a nine-to-five mentality, which infuriates me. But I suppose that comes from being freelance.'

I warmed to the compliment, but merely said, 'If you work for someone like Miles Goodchild, you have to be on the ball.'

We left the rarefied atmosphere of the Ambassador and proceeded to Chattertons, where we were fortunate to obtain the same booth in which Juliette and I had lunched earlier in the week.

He helped me off with my coat, then asked, 'Which would you prefer? Red or white?'

'White, please.'

He returned with a bottle of Sancerre and bowls of crisps and olives. After pouring the wine, he announced, 'You know, you look exactly as I expected you to. You're just as Oliver described you. I thought he was exaggerating when he said your hair was like burnished gold. But it is. A wonderful colour – most unusual. Though I bet you hated it when you were a kid.'

'Yes, I did rather. My nickname used to be Marigold.'

'Hmm, could have been worse. You should have heard some of things they called me at school. And, on the subject of names, I'm Tobin to everyone.'

'And I'm Cara.'

'Very Italian. How old were you when your father brought you to England?'

'Five months.'

'So you have no memories of him whatsoever?'

'Only what Aunt Biddie has told me.'

'That's his sister?'

'Yes, she brought me up.'

'Is she still alive?'

'Very much so. She lives in Avonford in Worcestershire.'

'That's in the Vale of Evesham, isn't it? A beautiful part of the world. I take it you know Bredon Hill?'

'I do indeed. I was up there last weekend with Aunt Biddie.'

He quoted:

> '*In summertime on Bredon*
> *The bells they sound so clear . . .*'

I looked at him in surprise. 'Not many people know that poem.'

'I wouldn't be so sure. Housman has his following. Fewer have heard of Connor Moran, though, I suspect.'

'I was going to ask how you knew of him.'

'I'm an unashamed romantic. I love poetry. I also weep over sentimental movies, get a lump in my throat when I hear the national anthem and like books with happy endings.'

'That makes two of us.'

'And before this evening is out, I have a feeling that we're going to discover a lot more in common.'

At a loss to know how to respond to that, I sipped my wine and nibbled at an olive.

'Do you have any children of your own?' Tobin asked, in one of those swift changes of direction, to which I would gradually become accustomed.

I shook my head.

'But you are married, aren't you?'

'Yes. And you?'

'I'm divorced. And I have two offspring. The oldest one, Joss, has just started at Reading University, while Pamela's at ballet school. I don't see them as often as I'd wish, but they're great kids. And they get on well with their stepfather, which is important. What does your husband do?'

I didn't want to talk about Nigel, but knew I had to get him out of the way. 'He's in advertising. He's an art director with Massey Gault & Lucasz,' I said, remembering Oliver saying that Tobin worked in advertising and willing him not already to know Nigel.

'Hmm, yes, I've never had any dealings with them. I assume Oliver told you that I'm a commercial artist?'

I nodded and helped myself to another olive.

He took a packet of cigarettes from his pocket and offered them to me. When we were both alight, he said, 'So, come on, tell me the story of your life, how you were born in Italy and ended up in Avonford.'

'I don't want to bore you by repeating what Oliver Lyon may already have said.'

'You won't. I'd like to hear the story from your own lips.'

So, once again – I was getting quite practised now – I repeated my tale, but not feeling nearly as self-conscious and reticent as I had with Oliver Lyon.

When I came to the end, Tobin exclaimed, 'Amazing! Quite amazing!' Then, instead of making any comment, he asked, 'Do you write poetry yourself?'

'I used to, when I was younger. I used to write short stories, too. But they weren't any good.'

'What makes you so sure?'

'My teachers left me in little doubt. After I failed to win the English prize upon which I'd set my heart, I gave up any ambition to be a writer.'

'Schoolteachers! It was exactly the same with me and art. Instead of encouraging my meagre talent, they did everything they could to put me off. Mind you, in the end, they had to give in. I did so badly in every other subject that they realized the only place for me to go after I left school was art college. But back to you, after relinquishing your dreams to become a poet, you decided to become a secretary?'

'Sort of. I wasn't actually given a lot of choice. The teachers at Avonford Grammar School for Girls had led pretty cloistered existences. They were mostly spinsters and teaching was the only profession which existed for them. Girls whose "A" levels were good enough to get them accepted by Oxford or Cambridge went there and those who weren't up to Oxbridge standard went to teacher training college. Our headmistress didn't recognize new "red-brick" universities like Warwick.

'Those who weren't bright enough to get into university or teacher training college were considered beyond the pale and left to find an occupation of some sort until they were fortunate enough to find a man to marry. Not that it was put exactly like that, but that was the implication. You might say that those who could, taught; and those who couldn't, were expected to get married and have children who would need to be taught.'

Tobin grinned. 'How did you escape?'

'Fortunately, Aunt Biddie's horizons extended further than my headmistress's. I went to secretarial college, after which I worked in Paris and Italy. Then I got married and went to work for Miles Goodchild.'

'Working for the good Miles child must be extremely interesting.'

I laughed. 'The good Miles child! That's wonderful. I must remember that. But yes, it is interesting. I certainly don't have any time to get bored.'

'And no time to think about writing either.'

'Oh, I don't have my father's talent.'

'You can't be sure unless you try.'

He switched subject slightly. 'Do you speak Italian?'

'Yes, and French. I use them both a lot in the course of my work.'

'The Princess was an amazing linguist. I've sat at the dinner table with her and listened to her switching from English to French to Italian to Russian without taking a breath, depending upon the nationality of the person she was addressing.'

'I'd love to know more about her.'

'Well, I'm not sure what I can tell you that will be of any use.'

'Any information you can give me will be interesting,' I urged him. 'All I know is what I learned from the television interview and from Oliver Lyon himself.'

'Hmm . . .' He sipped his wine, appearing to ponder something in his mind. Then he said, 'First, a rather unfair question, but what impression have you gained of her so far?'

Not knowing yet how he felt towards her, I recognized the necessity of picking my words carefully. 'Well, when I watched the interview, I thought she was very beautiful, elegant, intelligent and absolutely fascinating to listen to.'

'Did you feel any kind of instant rapport with her?'

I shook my head.

'So you didn't have the immediate feeling that she was your mother?'

'Not at all.'

'What about your Aunt Biddie, who must know you better than anyone else? What did she have to say?'

'She could see no resemblance between the two of us. I don't think she could understand the attraction between her and my father either. She said that the Princess wasn't the sort of woman with whom she could envisage having been friends.'

'How very perspicacious. I can't recall the Princess having any female friends. She was definitely a man's woman. Although I'm not sure that she actually had any real friends – only acquaintances. She would pick people up and then drop them for no apparent reason. You remember her last sentence in that interview, about all the people she had loved during her life being dead and only her enemies surviving? That could well have been the case. She hardly endeared herself to people.'

'Oliver Lyon gave me the impression you were very close to her.'

'Nobody was very close to her, not even Howard. She was an extremely private individual. One conversed with her on social and intellectual planes, but there was a deeper level of her personality into which one did not attempt to probe. Or, if one tried, one found oneself rebuffed.'

'He also said that, in the last months of her life, she changed a lot. From having been very socially inclined, she suddenly shut herself off from the world.'

'Yes, that was odd. I was most surprised when she allowed Oliver to interview her. That seemed quite out of character.'

'And now may I ask you a rather unfair question?'

'Fire ahead.'

'Did you like her?'

'Do you want an honest answer?'

'Please.'

'Then, at the risk of upsetting you, I didn't.'

'Why should that upset me?'

'She may have been your mother.'

'If she was, she didn't exactly do a lot to endear herself to me,' I commented. 'Whatever our relationship and the circumstances behind my father bringing me to England, I have to assume that she was aware of my existence but didn't make any great effort to find me – even after his death.'

'That's a very good point.'

'So why didn't you like her?'

'Well, now we've cleared the air, because of what she did to Howard. I was very fond of Howard. He was a nice old boy, who deserved a far better fate than the Princess. He and his first wife, Alice, were very good to me when I was young.

'Let me start by telling you a bit about them. They were married in 1931, at the height of the Depression, when agricultural prices were falling and unemployment rising. If you saw Oliver's programme you must have seen the photograph of Kingston Kirkby Hall, so you can imagine the work and cost involved in keeping a place like that going. But Alice wasn't daunted. She was the no-nonsense, tweed and brogues sort. In fact, if you imagine a woman who was the complete opposite of the Princess in every single possible respect, then you have Alice.

'She scrimped and saved to make ends meet. She did most of the housework herself and much of the gardening. She even went shopping on a bicycle to save petrol. She was tough as any man. Often the only heating in the entire house was a small coal fire in the drawing room.

'My father was in the diplomatic service and, as a result, spent most of his life abroad. My older brother, Harvey, and I both went to boarding school and, during the holidays, we often stayed with Howard and Alice at Kingston Kirkby Hall. "If you're cold," Alice used to tell us, "go for a hike. That'll warm you up." And outside, the snow would be knee-deep!'

'She sounds very like Aunt Biddie,' I remarked, remembering the frost on the inside of the bedroom windows at The Willows in winter and how Miranda and I used to dress and undress under the bedclothes because the rooms were so cold.

Tobin smiled. 'I was thinking the very same thing myself, when you were talking about her earlier on. Anyway, to continue, in 1961, when Howard and Alice had been married for thirty years, she died from cancer.

It was a tragic end, quite, quite, tragic. And, almost as dreadful was Howard's belief that she was going to recover. After her death, he went completely to pieces, wandering round Kingston Kirkby Hall like a lost soul, as though expecting her to appear out of one of the rooms. A woman came in from the village to cook for him and keep the place as tidy as she could, but after a year or so it was obvious that he could not go on like that indefinitely.

'Harvey and I had a council of war to decide what best to do for him. Harvey and I, I should perhaps explain at this point, are like chalk and cheese. By profession, he's a barrister and he married money. Since he came into the title and inherited Kingston Kirkby Hall, he's sunk a fair chunk of Gwendolen's fortune into restoring the old place. But that's jumping ahead . . .

'As I was saying, Harvey and I had a council of war, as a result of which we agreed that Howard should have a change of scene and get away from Kingston Kirkby Hall and all its memories. Somehow or other, throughout the family's various financial calamities, Howard had managed to keep hold of a house in Beadle Walk in Chelsea, where he used to stay whenever he came to town to attend the Lords. Harvey's idea was that he should take up residence there for a while.

'I must admit to having had severe reservations. Howard was a countryman through and through. Away from his beloved moors, cooped up in a London flat, he was like a bird in a cage. But what alternative was there?

'Well, the long and short of it was that Howard came to London, but instead of living at Beadle Walk, spent most of his time with me and Dawn – my ex-wife – at our house at Blackheath, driving Dawn – never the most tolerant of people – nearly to distraction with some of his little foibles. Harvey, who lived conveniently out of town and led, of course, an extremely busy life, managed to escape fulfilling his side of the obligation – or certainly the more mundane aspects of it.

'However, it was through Harvey that Howard met the Princess. I think it must have been at Ascot, because Howard loved the races. Harvey and Gwendolen attend all the events in the social calendar – Henley, Cowes, Ascot. You name it, they go to it.

'A mutual acquaintance introduced them to the Princess and Howard was hooked. He had never met anyone like her before. She was totally outside the realm of his experience. He was in his late sixties, a bluff Derbyshire squire. And the Princess was some five years younger, extremely attractive for her age and apparently wealthy. He was totally and utterly captivated by her, like putty in her hands. He took her up to Kingston Kirkby Hall, which she pretended to admire, and he believed that, with the help of her money, they would be able to live there in a moderate degree of comfort.

'Instead of which, when they returned from their honeymoon, she announced that she had no intention whatsoever of burying herself in the depths of Derbyshire and intended to make Beadle Walk her home.'

Tobin paused and topped up our glasses.

'I must admit that I couldn't altogether blame her. I have fond memories of Kingston Kirkby Hall, but I wouldn't want to live there either. As she said in the interview with Oliver, it's an ugly building, lacking in every comfort. I certainly wouldn't be in Harvey's shoes for all the tea in China. The house may have been in the family for seven hundred years but, frankly, like all stately homes, it's a liability.

'What did upset me though, was the underhand manner in which the Princess had led Howard to believe in a promise she had no intention of fulfilling. Furthermore, if she had any money of her own, none of it came in Howard's direction. But she entertained no scruples about spending his.

'Not that I was aware of this until many years later. Shortly before he died, Howard and I had a long heart-to-heart during which he admitted to me how mistaken he had been in her and how utterly miserable she had made his life. Poor old boy. Thirteen years is a long time in which to be unhappy, as I can tell you from personal experience. My own marriage lasted exactly that long, too.' He raked his fingers through his hair. 'The trouble was, Howard had no experience of women, except Alice. The Princess just twisted him round her little finger, as I suspect she did with each of her other husbands before him.'

'So you believe she married him, not out of love, but for material reasons?' I asked.

'Without a doubt. It was a marriage of convenience, like all the others.'

He shared the remains of the bottle between us.

'Well, to return to Beadle Walk, what I think she tried to do there was to recreate, albeit on a smaller scale, the home she had been forced to leave behind when she left Russia. Virtually every item of furniture, every ornament, every *objet d'art*, was Russian, very old and very expensive. You saw it on the television . . .

'The only room Howard was allowed to furnish was his study, a gloomy little den – that was crammed full of things from Kingston Kirkby Hall – a desk, leather library chairs, a Stubbs painting and various hunting trophies. The Princess refused to have anything else from Kingston Kirkby in the house.

'Mind you, everything at Kingston Kirkby was very shabby – as well as cumbersome, and would have looked dreadfully out of place at Beadle Walk. And Howard, God bless him, had no aesthetic sense. His taste was guided entirely by sentiment – and he knew it . . .'

My heart went out to the old Earl.

'No, I think he wouldn't have objected nearly so much to the Princess indulging her own fancies in the interior decoration of Beadle Walk if she hadn't been so extravagant in every other respect as well. But she spent a fortune on clothes and jewellery. She entertained on a grand scale and travelled a lot. She wasn't prepared to give up her friends abroad on Howard's behalf and was constantly popping over to New York, Paris, Nice – you name it and she was there – naturally always staying in the best hotels.'

'Did Howard – the Earl – go with her?'

'Sometimes, but, as you can imagine, their taste in people was as different as their taste in everything else. He belonged to the huntin', shootin', fishin' set, whereas she loved to mix in cosmopolitan, fashionable circles. He was most at home on a grouse moor and she in the drawing room. Which was how they ended up spending their time. He went back to Kingston Kirkby Hall and the Princess pursued her own interests in London and abroad. Then he died, at which point Kingston Kirkby Hall passed to Harvey, along with the title, and the Princess remained at Beadle Walk. And that's about it really.'

'What happens to Beadle Walk now?' I asked.

'It goes to Harvey, too, as part of Howard's estate. The Princess only had the right to live there during her lifetime.'

'So you don't get anything?'

'There's no reason why I should. Even if Howard had been my father, Harvey, as the eldest son, would have inherited. And now, before we go any further, I'm famished. According to the blackboard over there, there are *moules marinières* on the menu tonight. How does that appeal to you?'

'It sounds great.'

'Good! I'll get another bottle at the same time. You're not driving, are you?'

'No.' I was feeling quite mellow, but not at all drunk.

I reached for my bag and my purse. 'Please let me pay for something.'

'I wouldn't dream of it. Next time, maybe, but not tonight.'

Chattertons was packed by then. I watched Tobin as he pushed his way through the crowd and wondered what Dawn was like and why their marriage had broken up.

He returned, followed by a waitress bearing a bottle of champagne, an ice bucket and two champagne flutes. 'I thought we should celebrate,' he explained.

'Celebrate what?'

'The living moment?'

I laughed.

The waitress opened the bottle with a satisfactory pop of the cork and poured the champagne.

We clinked glasses. 'To you, Cara,' Tobin said.

'To you, Tobin,' I responded. And felt extraordinarily happy.

'So, while we're waiting for the food, is there anything else you want to know about the Princess that I may be able to tell you?'

'Well, yes, there is.' I sipped my champagne, trying to combine the picture of her Tobin had painted for me with what Oliver Lyon had told me on Monday. A lot of things were starting to fall into place, but there were still things I didn't understand. 'For a start,' I said, 'why do you think she didn't keep any photographs of herself?'

'I'm not a woman,' he said, with a slight smile, 'but even I can understand how a woman, who was a great beauty in her day, feels when men no longer fall in homage at her feet and she can no longer deceive herself that the face which is reflected back from the mirror is that of a twenty- or even a forty-year old.'

He studied me across his wine glass and I wondered what thoughts were going through his mind. Then he quoted:

> *'Was this the face that launched a thousand ships,*
> *And burnt the topless towers of Ilium?*
> *Sweet Helen, make me immortal with a kiss!*

'She had been *la Belle Hélène* . . .'

'She was still beautiful,' I insisted.

'But no longer young.'

At that moment, the mussels arrived, two great bowls of them swimming in a delicious smelling creamy sauce, and a basket filled with chunks of French bread. We both set to with gusto.

Suddenly he asked, 'Have you minded growing up an orphan?'

'Not really, because I've never really considered myself to be one. But there have been occasions – more so when I was at school, I suppose – when I used to feel jealous of all the other people who had proper Mums and Dads. It would sometimes have been nice to be able to say, "My parents, my Mum, my Dad . . ."'

He nodded. 'I'm sure you've had your painful moments. I used to worry about my kids, particularly when they were younger. Because of our divorce, we'd taken away the firm foundation from beneath them. They had to explain to people that their stepfather wasn't their real father. I know divorce is common nowadays, but that doesn't make it any easier on children.'

I said nothing, waiting for him to continue, but instead he asked, 'Did you ever feel resentful of Miranda?'

'Good heavens, no. Why do you ask that?'

'Because she's older than you and her parents' real daughter.'

I shook my head. 'All I've ever wished is that I could be more like her. Why, do you resent Harvey becoming the Earl of Winster?'

'Certainly not. I'd hate to have all that responsibility. And I certainly wouldn't want to have to take a seat in the Lords – whereas Harvey and Gwendolen are in seventh heaven at finding themselves the Earl and Countess of Winster.'

We ate in silence for a while, then he said, 'Harvey's asked me to help him sort through the house at Beadle Walk and decide what to do with everything there. Not a job I'm particularly looking forward to, I must admit, but Harvey hasn't got the time or inclination to do it all on his own. You never know, we may come across something among her papers that concerns you or your father.'

'Please don't put yourself to too much trouble on my behalf.'

'It will help divert my mind from the grim task in hand. In any case, I'm so intrigued by your story, I want to find out the truth. Even if you give up along the way, I shall go on trying to get to the bottom of the mystery.'

I laughed. 'You sound like Stevie.'

'Who's Stevie?'

'Miranda's daughter. I was awfully nervous about ringing Oliver Lyon after I saw his programme. But Stevie said that if I didn't she would.'

'Quite right too. And how old is Stevie?'

'Seventeen.'

'So I have an ally. That's useful to know.' He looked at me quizzically. 'Are you a hoarder? Do you keep letters, photographs, wedding invitations, theatre programmes and other sentimentalia?'

I laughed. 'I'm an amateur compared to Aunt Biddie.' I went on to describe our search for my father's book.

'I like the sound of your Aunt Biddie more and more. Do you write a diary?'

'I always used to, then I stopped. But this weekend I started again, to keep a record of everything I learn.'

'Good. I was going to suggest just that.'

It was eleven o'clock before we left the wine bar. All I can remember about our conversation for the rest of the evening is that it was personal without being intimate. Tobin talked a certain amount about his work. His early career had, in fact, followed a path not dissimilar to Nigel's. After leaving art school, he had worked on a magazine as a layout artist and then moved to a book publishing company.

'It was an old-established firm, with some very good authors on its list,' he explained, 'but it ran into financial trouble and was taken over by an American publishing company and now it's part of a huge, international media conglomerate. I stayed on for a while, but couldn't get on with the new management. Their approach towards publishing was far too commercial for my taste. Books were merely commodities so far as they were concerned. And while I fully accept that the purpose of any business is to make a profit, I also believe that books are part of our birthright and should not be judged solely on their sales potential. So, to cut a very long story short, we parted company.

'Shortly after that my father died, leaving me sufficient money to be able to consider starting up on my own. I turned one of the rooms in the house into a studio, found myself an agent, went freelance and have remained that way ever since.'

'What sort of work do you do?'

'I work mainly in oils and tend to do nature subjects. I'm currently working on a panic job for a chocolate maker, who has belatedly woken up to the fact that Easter is approaching and needs illustrations for his packaging. Easter bunnies and primroses.' He grinned. 'Still, it's all grist to the mill.'

'Which chocolate company?' I asked curiously.

'It's a French firm, I think, but I don't know the name. Why?'

'Oh, I just wondered if it was one of ours.'

'You do take your job seriously, don't you?'

'Sorry. It's difficult not to. I spend more time at the office than I do at home.'

'Ah, yes,' he said dryly, 'I remember it well, from when I, too, belonged to the ranks of the employed. Where do you live?'

'In Highgate. And you?'

'Fulham.'

He insisted upon sending me home by taxi and paid the driver's fare in advance, which I didn't realize until we arrived at Linden Mansions and the cabby said, 'That's all right, miss, the gentleman sorted it out.'

I spent that journey in a kind of trance, trying to concentrate my thoughts on the Princess and my father, only to find them constantly returning to Tobin. As I climbed the stairs to Flat 9, my feet moved so effortlessly I did not seem to walk so much as to float. I found myself humming *What is this thing called love?* And thinking, 'You're crazy, Cara.' And then thinking, 'It must be the champagne . . .'

I woke up the next morning still feeling extremely happy and slightly hungover. A shower dispelled the hangover but not the happiness. That remained, a little warm kernel in my heart, untainted by any sense of guilt, for nothing had passed between Tobin and myself that wasn't entirely proper and I wasn't contemplating that it might. He had given me no reason to believe that he fancied me and nothing was further from my mind than having an affair – with him or with anyone.

No, what I felt towards Tobin was not love in any amorous sense, but liking. I liked him as a person and wanted him as a friend. And I believed that he liked me – as a person. That was all.

At the office, Miles, James Warren and Bob Drewitz arrived from breakfast at the Ambassador in excellent spirits, which boded well for the day ahead. Even better was that Miles did not need me to take minutes during the day's meetings, nor arrange a boardroom lunch. Instead, he asked me to book a table for three at the Ambassador. Bob Drewitz and Dandy Candy were obviously in his good books.

A short while later, the telephone rang and Dorothy announced, 'Mr Touchstone is on the line for you, Cara. Shall I put him through?'

My heart gave a flutter of pleasure. 'Oh, yes please.'

'Hello, Cara. And how are you this morning?' Tobin asked.

'I'm fine. And you?'

'Blooming. Did you get home all right?'

'Yes, and thank you so much for paying for the cab.'

'I was brought up to be a gentleman.'

'Yes, but—'

He cut me off. 'Does the good Miles child allow you to take a lunch break?'

I laughed. 'Occasionally.'

'Well, if today is one of those occasions, there's something I'd like to show you. What if I were to meet you outside your building at, say, one o'clock?'

At dead on one o'clock, I went downstairs to find Tobin, clutching a well-worn document case, and chatting again to Sergeant.

Outside the building, he rushed into the road to hail a passing cab. 'In you get,' he ordered me, then gave an inaudible instruction to the driver.

'Where are we going?' I asked.

'Wait and see.'

In the cab, he said, 'I've been worrying all morning. I think I was rather heavy-handed last night. I didn't intend to carry out a character assassination on the Princess.'

'You didn't,' I assured him.

'That's kind of you to say so but I still think I was rather tactless. In your position, I'm sure I'd be hoping to hear nice things about my mother.'

'I asked for the truth and that's what you gave me,' I said. And I thought, 'Because of who you are, you could say almost anything and I wouldn't be hurt.'

A few minutes later, the taxi pulled up outside the Tate Gallery.

Tobin took my elbow and led me up the steps, through the foyer and several galleries until we reached a room, on one wall of which hung a very large painting which, at first sight, seemed to consist of a jumble of disjointed people, buildings and objects, the sort of picture I would have instantly dismissed in the past as being more up Nigel's street than mine. Tobin turned to me, one eyebrow arched questioningly.

In the right hand corner was El Toro's trademark – a graphically drawn bull.

'It's an El Toro,' I said.

'Spot on.'

'I cheated. I saw the bull.'

'Then ten out of ten for observation.'

I moved towards it.

'Begin at the middle,' he instructed.

At the centre of the picture was an eye. I concentrated my attention on that and then allowed my gaze slowly to travel upwards and outwards. To the right was a paintbrush on an artist's palette. To the left was a naked woman and behind her a window, through which one could see a street, lined with terraced houses, a café-bar, a shop. Then the perspective changed. One of the houses was bigger than the others and had an open door. Then came a room containing a table on which a book and a pen were lying. Another room and fingers on a violin, with notes of music hanging in the air. Next, an unmade bed, with discarded garments thrown over it. Then pots, pans, a loaf of bread and a bottle of wine. After that, a child playing with a toy. A labourer taking off his boots. Then, in the distance, a horse and cart climbing a steep hill and, very small, silhouetted against the blue-white sky, a windmill.

Truly amazing was the precision of the brush strokes. The more I looked, the more detail I could identify: the grain in the wood, the texture of the clothes, each fine string on the violin, the shape of the words in the book.

The bottom half of the picture, below the eye, somehow conveyed the sense that what was taking place was happening behind one. The colours were darker and richer, as were the scenes portrayed. The houses were palatial, the rooms luxuriously furnished, the people were seated, with exaggeratedly large mouths in tiny heads.

I turned to Tobin. 'He's looking beyond the model he's painting into the city and houses beyond. Each part of the painting is a picture in itself, depicting the life which he knows is going on all around him. The top half is Montmartre, while the bottom part is the wealthy area presumably round the Étoile or the Opéra.'

Tobin grinned. 'Spot on again. Fascinating, isn't it?'

'Quite amazing. Oh, thank you so much for showing me this.'

'Now, I may be wrong, but I believe that the book and the pen represent your father.'

'Why?'

'Look at the lighting. There's a sort of amber glow which could well be your father's hair.'

'It's so strange,' I said. 'Until I saw Oliver Lyon's interview, I had no idea that my father and El Toro knew each other.'

'Unless you had made a study of El Toro's life, there was no reason why you should. The only reason I became interested in El Toro was after I saw his portrait of the Princess. Then I discovered that he and your father had been friends. And, after that, Oliver told me that the Princess had been married to your father.' He glanced at his watch. 'How long do you get for lunch?'

'An hour.'

'That doesn't leave us much time to eat. Can you make do with a snack?'

'Of course. I usually only have a sandwich.'

We went to the cafeteria and, as we started lunch he asked, 'Have you ever eaten in the restaurant here?'

I shook my head.

'Then we must make up for the omission one day when we have more time. They serve surprisingly good English food and have an excellent wine list. With El Toro thrown in for good measure, what more could one ask?'

Before I could respond, he reached into his document case and handed me a carrier bag. 'A present for you.'

Inside were two books, one on El Toro, the other a well-worn and obviously much-read Penguin paperback – *Novel on Yellow Paper* by Stevie Smith.

'The El Toro book is the one with the foreword by Oliver's father and containing the photograph of your father. And *Novel on Yellow Paper* I think you may find rather apt to yourself. Or have you already read it?'

'No, I haven't. Thank you very much. I'll look after them and make sure I return them. I can see *Novel on Yellow Paper* is one of your favourites.'

'Yes, it is, but I don't want it back. I told you, they're a present.'

He accompanied me back in a taxi to Wolesley House, where he took my hand and held it, in one of those funny, slightly awkward moments at the beginning of a relationship when you know each other too well to shake hands formally but not well enough to kiss or even to peck.

'Had a good lunch?' Sergeant enquired blandly, looking pointedly at the clock – which pointed to half past two – as I entered the lobby.

'Yes, thank you,' I replied in what I hoped was an expressionless tone.

Fortunately my absence from the office had not been missed. Dorothy had no messages and Miles was still at lunch. I resisted the temptation to look at my two books and set about making up for lost time. As I did so, I was vaguely aware that I was not being entirely honest with myself about my feelings towards Tobin. What I felt for him was not just liking. It was something more.

Shortly before I left for home, Nigel rang. 'So at long last I've managed to get hold of you,' he said, in an aggrieved voice. 'I was ringing you all yesterday evening.'

'Sorry, I was out,' I replied breezily, still in my slightly euphoric state.

'You weren't with Sherry and Roly, because I tried them.'

'No, I was having dinner with, er, a friend. Why, has something happened?'

'No, I just wanted to let you know I'll definitely be back next Wednesday.'

'Oh, I see. How's the shoot going?'

'Vastly better now that the weather's improved.'

'Good.'

'Cara, are you all right?'

'Yes. Why?'

'I don't know. There's something odd about you.'

'It must be the phone line making my voice sound funny.'

'Possibly. Do you have anything planned for the weekend?'

'I'm going to do the shopping, the washing, the cleaning – as I always do – then curl up with a good book.'

'Cara, what is the matter?'

'Absolutely nothing. I'm looking forward to the book.'

There was a sigh at the other end of the phone. Then: 'Oh, well, everyone to his own tastes. Meanwhile, I'm going to get on with some work. I'll give you another bell next week before I leave.'

'Fine. Don't work too hard. And thanks for ringing.'

I didn't wait for the weekend before starting on Tobin's presents. I went through the El Toro book while I was eating my solitary supper of sausages, instant mashed potato and frozen peas. But, although the book promised to be very interesting about the artist, it contained – in addition to the photograph of my father and El Toro – only two brief references to my father, namely, that he was a poet and that he had accompanied El Toro to Spain.

So I put El Toro to one side and went to bed with *Novel on Yellow Paper.*

It was three o'clock in the morning before I put it down and went to sleep and, when I woke up, I forgot about housework and just went straight on reading.

For anyone who has never read *Novel on Yellow Paper*, it is not a novel in the conventional sense, in that it doesn't tell a straightforward story with a beginning, middle and end. It is written in the first person and is semi-autobiographical, describing people and events in the narrator's life and revealing her thoughts and opinions on a whole host of matters. What makes it absolutely unique is its style. The sub-title is *Work it out for yourself* and that about sums it up.

It was first published in 1936, when Stevie Smith was thirty-three, and the copy Tobin had given me was the first edition Penguin published in 1951. The central character calls herself Pompey Casmilus and is private secretary to Sir Phoebus Ullwater, Bt. (as Stevie Smith was, in real life, private secretary to Sir George Newnes and Sir Neville Pearson). The title derives from the fact that Pompey is typing her novel on yellow paper. And she is writing it in her spare time at the office.

Pompey was brought up by her aunt (as Stevie Smith also was, in real life), because her papa ran away to sea, leaving his wife and his little baby daughter, Pompey. This aunt is a most wonderful character – Pompey calls her the Lion of Hull – and she reminds me tremendously of another aunt.

As if that wasn't enough, Pompey (although unmarried and with a very old-fashioned upbringing) has a very liberated attitude to life and very definite views about it. She has masses of friends, travels widely, falls in love with unsuitable men, and yet, she is still subject to all the common ills, insecurities and unhappinesses which have beset women before and after her.

And, as if all that wasn't enough, the book is a chronicle of its time, vividly depicting life in the mid-1930s, the rise of Nazism in Europe and Pompey's reactions to the reactions of all the people around her.

Now, if you add to all this the fact that Stevie Smith was also a poet and her first volume of poetry was published the year after *Novel on Yellow*

Paper was published, then I think that's sufficient for you to understand the impact her novel made on me – especially reading it at that particular moment in my life.

This may sound a strange way of putting it, but I felt like a clockwork toy whose key had long been lost and was suddenly found. By coming into my life and giving me that book, Tobin had provided the key which would set me into motion and drive me forward.

On Sunday morning, I rang Aunt Biddie and Miranda, and gave them a condensed version of my meeting with Tobin. After that, I would dearly have liked to ring Tobin himself and thank him properly for the books, but I had no telephone number for him. The directory listed several Touchstones but none with the initial T living in Fulham. Then, remembering that he was going through the Princess's belongings at Beadle Walk, I realized he probably wouldn't be at home anyway. Since he didn't have my home address or telephone number and we were ex-directory, he couldn't contact me if he wanted to.

Definitely not in the mood for cleaning and washing, and the shops being closed on Sundays in those days, putting paid to that idea, I wandered downstairs to Sherry and Roly's flat, half-expecting them to be out, working at an antiques fair. But Sherry was in. 'Roly's up in Doncaster and I've been doing the accounts, working out how much money we haven't got in the bank,' she said, ruefully. 'I don't understand how we can work so hard and have so little to show for it. Still, never mind. Come in and have a coffee. Or is time for a drink?'

We opted for coffee, then went for a brisk walk over the Heath. 'Did Nigel get hold of you all right the other day?'

'Yes, sorry he disturbed you.'

'That didn't matter at all. In fact, I found it rather amusing. "Well, where is she then?" he demanded, as though you were in purdah and not supposed to go out anywhere in his absence. It didn't seem to be urgent, so I didn't worry unduly.'

'It wasn't.'

She turned her laughing, cornflower blue eyes on me. 'So where were you then?'

I told her about Tobin and I think my voice must have given away more than I intended, because from time to time I sensed her glancing at me shrewdly.

Yet, as often happens, when you are describing events aloud to someone else, my thoughts continued in a separate undercurrent. After the elation of our first meeting at Chattertons and the visit to the Tate, I was slowly coming back down to earth and common-sense was reasserting itself.

My conversations with Aunt Biddie, Miranda and now Sherry reminded me that my reason for meeting Tobin had been to learn more about the Princess, not to meet a new man. As for Tobin, his interest in me was exactly the same as Oliver Lyon's: he had been motivated purely by curiosity and kindness. Anything else was the product of my imagination.

Later still, back in my own flat, after Sherry and I had had the drink which we now felt we deserved, I was suddenly reminded of the character in George Bernard Shaw's *Getting Married*, who says, 'I would not dare go about with an empty heart: why, the first girl I met would fly into it by mere atmospheric pressure.' With a start, I realized that was my own predicament.

Taking myself in hand, I went into the study and set up my portable typewriter on Nigel's desk. Not having any yellow paper, I put a sheet of plain old white stuff into it and began to type. Aware that any attempt to emulate Stevie Smith could end only in disaster, I began my own story at the beginning:

> My father was the poet Connor Moran and I am not, as yet, sure of the identity of my mother. I was born somewhere in Italy, but brought up in Avonford, by my father's sister, my Aunt Biddie.

As I typed that first sentence, I didn't delude myself that my first effort at writing a book would ever be published. Publication was not my prime purpose. I wanted to discover whether I could write, whether I possessed the ability to string words together in a coherent and interesting form, whether I had inherited more of my father's talent than I had hitherto believed. And, if nothing else, I would, at the end of my story – whatever the end turned out to be – possess a detailed record of everything that happened to me as a result of Oliver Lyon's interview with the Princess.

In one respect only did I allow Stevie Smith to influence me. I gave my work the provisional title: *Book with No Name*. In my mind, I called it simply The Book.

Chapter 10

On Wednesday, Nigel came home.

The evening before his return, I finally got round to cleaning and tidying the flat, knowing from experience that he wouldn't remark on how spick and span it was, but that he would comment if it wasn't. As I did so, I told myself I was glad I didn't live in a house like The Willows, or even in a flat like Sherry and Roly's, with all their ornaments and stock to be dusted. On occasions, there was a lot to commend simplicity.

I also told myself that it was all for the best that I still hadn't heard from Tobin, even though it would seem to indicate that he had found nothing about my father or myself among the Princess's papers. On the other hand, I hadn't really been counting on that anyway.

Furthermore, it was a good thing Tobin didn't have my home telephone number, for it would be just my bad luck that he would choose to ring at the very moment Nigel was stepping through the door, which would not be a good idea.

Well, that's what I said to myself, as I hoovered and dusted and polished and tried to get myself in the right mood for having Nigel back.

Experience had also taught me not to make any special preparations for the evening of his return: whether the trip had gone well or badly, he was sure to be jetlagged, tired and up-tight after a long flight and a two-week absence from home and office. So, on my way home from work, I bought some cold meat, cheese, salad, a loaf of rye bread and a good bottle of white wine. If he was hungry, there would be a quick and easy meal waiting ready and, if he wasn't, it would keep for another day.

He arrived at about nine o'clock. I heard the door to the front open and ran out into the hallway.

'Hi,' he grunted, offloading his shoulderbag and putting it next to his suitcase, duty-free carrier bags and – of course – Hugh.

He tipped his hat back on his head, gave me a quick hug, kissed me and said, 'Well, here we are again.'

'It's nice to have you back.' I responded. 'You look tired. Did you have a bad flight?'

'Oh, the flight was OK. It was the fortnight leading up to it that was bad.'

'It looks as if the weather improved at any rate. You've got an incredible tan.'

'The second week was much better than the first, thank God.' He delved into one of the carrier bags. 'Here's something for you. Sorry it's not more imaginative. I hope you like it though.'

It was perfume. 'Thank you very much darling,' I said, taking his arm, and leading him into the living room. 'Would you like a drink and something to eat?'

'I had a plastic meal on the plane. I wouldn't mind a Scotch, though.'

'I'll go and get you one.'

When I returned with a tumbler of whisky and water, he was sprawled out on the sofa. He took a long drink, then let out a deep breath. 'God, what a trip. I can't remember ever being so pleased to see the back of a place. It may be paradise so far as some people are concerned, but not me.'

'Did you get the results you wanted eventually?'

'I shan't know for sure until I see the film. Fortunately Jason's a damn good photographer and the Polaroids looked OK. But you can never tell.'

'When do you see the film?'

'Tomorrow. I just hope to God that the X-ray machines at the airport haven't fogged the film and that the lab doesn't cock up. Jason's putting a test roll through first thing in the morning and the rest will go through after we've seen that. Then, provided the trannies are OK, it'll be a matter of convincing the client that they were worth going over budget for.'

'I'm sure everything will be fine,' I said soothingly. 'In any case, nobody can blame you for all the things that went wrong.'

'Can't they, though? The trouble is I talked the client into doing this shoot on location. Until now they've always done it in a studio. I should have known that freak storms could occur in January. As for the models – what a shower.'

I clucked sympathetically and he took another large gulp of whisky. 'Ah, that's better. We were drinking ninety per cent proof rum out there. Wicked stuff. It lifted the roof off your head.'

'In that case, it's a wonder you were able to do any work at all,' I said, with a smile that I hoped concealed my irritation.

His own laugh turned into a yawn. 'God, I'm tired. I could crash out for a week.'

'Can you have a lie-in tomorrow?'

'Not a hope in hell. I've got to go the office. There's two weeks' work waiting for me to catch up on.' He yawned again. 'Well, come on, tell me what you've been up to while I was away.'

I wanted to tell him but there are few things worse, when one has something important to recount, than being confronted by an audience about to fall asleep. 'There's nothing that won't wait,' I said. 'Why don't you go to bed and I'll tell you tomorrow?'

'Well, if you don't mind . . .' He eased himself out of his chair. 'Sorry, love, but I can hardly keep my eyes open.'

'What time do you want to be woken tomorrow?'

He groaned. 'I should really get in early. About seven, I suppose.'

After he had staggered out of the room, I remained where I was, sitting very still, fighting back my disappointment, listening to his noises off, to the water running in the bathroom, to his gargle when he finished cleaning his teeth, to the wardrobe doors slamming open and shut as he searched for clean clothes for tomorrow, to the grunt he gave when he got into bed, to the click of his bedside lamp being turned off.

I went into the hall, stuck Hugh on a chair, carried Nigel's suitcase into the kitchen, shut the door and filled the washing machine with water. Two thoughts occurred to me. One, was that the reasons he had given me over the phone in respect of his extra week away had, without any doubt, been absolutely true. If they weren't, he would have been making far more effort to stay awake. And, secondly, it would be better to tell him about the Princess tomorrow, when he would hopefully be less tired and have fewer things on his mind.

When I came to bed, he was lying on his right side, facing away from me. I undressed and slid under the duvet, hoping not to disturb him. But he rolled over and flung his arm across me. 'It's good to be home,' he mumbled and went back to sleep.

* * *

Next morning, Miles informed me that he was going to the States at the end of the week and asked me to book him on Concorde to New York. Among the people he was scheduled to meet over there was Craig Vidler, the President of WWT – Worldwide Tobacco, the American tobacco giant. Because the trip followed on Bob Drewitz's visit, I attached no special significance to it and made the necessary arrangements.

I managed to get away from the office at a reasonable hour that evening and hurried home, assuming Nigel would make a similar effort. I laid the table and prepared our meal, then waited as eight o'clock, nine o'clock and then ten o'clock came and went – and no Nigel appeared.

When the phone rang, I thought it would be him, but it was Miranda. 'You're not in bed, are you?' she asked.

'Hardly. Nigel isn't home yet.'

'I thought he was due back yesterday.'

'I mean home from the office. He came back to London last night.'

'Everything OK?'

'Yes, fine.'

'What did he think of your news?'

'I haven't had a chance to tell him yet. He was so tired when he got in that we only talked for a few moments, then he went to bed and crashed out.'

'I see. Well, what about you? Any developments? Have you heard any more from Tobin Touchstone?'

'No, not a dicky-bird.'

'Oh, dear . . .'

'Never mind, it doesn't matter.' At that moment, I heard a key in the lock. 'That sounds like Nigel now. I'd better go. I'll give you a ring at the weekend. Give my love to Jonathan and Stevie – and to Aunt Biddie if you see her.'

'Of course. I'll leave you to get on. Lots of love.'

'And to you. Bye for now.'

Nigel burst through the door, all the tiredness gone from his face. 'Sorry I'm late, love. But I have just had *the* most incredible day! Macintyre have appointed a new M.D., who's giving their old agency the push and has invited Massey Gault & Lucasz to pitch for the account. What's more, Bron wants me to handle it.'

'What's Macintyre?' I asked blankly.

'Oh, come off it, Cara,' he said. 'Even you must have heard of

Macintyre. They make tyres. In fact, they're one of *the* biggest tyre manufacturers in Europe.'

The name still rang no bells. 'That's brilliant. But I'm still not sure I've ever heard of them.'

A look of exasperation flitted across his face, then he said, 'You know, that's very interesting. In fact, your reaction is probably typical of a lot car owners, who aren't interested in motoring. You don't associate the name Macintyre with glamour, speed, life in the fast lane – which is what you should be thinking. That's the image which should be conjured up in your mind. And that's Macintyre's problem. It's rested too long on its laurels, with the result that it's drastically losing market share.'

His eyes shone. 'If we get Macintyre, we'll change all that. Macintyre will become like Hoover. When someone says tyre, you'll think Macintyre. Wow! What we could do with that account! It would be a dream come true. God, this makes up for the last two weeks. What a piece of news to come home to. This could be my big break. If we do get Macintyre, we'll be made as an agency.'

'I'm sorry, I am delighted for you,' I said, injecting enthusiasm into my voice. 'It's a wonderful opportunity. But who are you up against?'

'JWT, CDP, Saatchi & Saatchi – and, guess who! – Holleyman & Elwood! If they get it, I'll shoot myself in the head. But they don't stand a chance. In fact, none of them do. There isn't a better copywriter in the business than Bron. And, though I say it myself, I'm one of the few art directors around who is capable of total concept.'

'So what happens now? When does your presentation have to be ready?'

'The eighteenth of February. Which means you're not going to see much of me during the next two and a half weeks, I'm afraid. The first thing we've got to do is have a brainstorming session, during which we must come up with a new brand image. It's all very well me saying, "Think of tyre, think of Macintyre", but we need a much stronger strap line than that. Still, Bron will come up with something brilliant. He's suggesting that he and I hole ourselves up in a hotel – and I agree. We'll never get anywhere in the bloody office. In a hotel, we can get away from the phones and all the other bloody interruptions, all those stupid faces peering round the door and asking, "What do I do about this?" They'll just have to use their brains for once.

'Then, of course, when we've decided on the concept, we've still got to produce visuals and copy and work out strategies, timings, budgets. It's a hell of a lot of work to do in very little time. But we'll manage. We'll do it.'

'Presumably the other agencies are all up against the same deadline?'

'Yes, but they've all got far more resources at their disposal – in terms of personnel and finance. We're still a relatively small agency. However, it's quality not quantity that counts and, if Macintyre comes off, we'll be up in the big league.'

'When do you start?'

'We started today. What did you think? And from now on it'll be non-stop until the eighteenth. You'd better count me out of any plans you may be making. If you want to go up to Avonford for the weekend, feel free. Bron and I will undoubtedly still be thrashing out concepts in our hotel.'

'What about the suntan oil campaign?'

'I've handed that over to Duncan for the time being. He and Liam can deal with it.'

'Did the film turn out all right?'

'Oh, I glanced through the trannies and they looked fine. I didn't really expect any problems.'

'No, of course not,' I said, finding it hard to keep up with his sudden nonchalance towards a job that, only the previous day, had been so desperately important.

'Well, what have we got for dinner?' he asked.

'Just cold, I'm afraid.'

'That suits me fine. When we've eaten, I'm going to shut myself away in the study. I've got a lot to think about.'

Fortunately, my housework the previous evening had taken me into the study, where my typewriter and first draft pages of The Book had still been on the desk. Needless to say, they were no longer there. The typewriter was back in its proper place and The Book stowed safely in my briefcase.

Throughout dinner, which Nigel bolted down at high speed, he talked of nothing but Macintyre. I listened dutifully, asking the occasional question and making the occasional comment. But my mind was elsewhere.

In *Novel on Yellow Paper*, Pompey describes her life running secretly on all the time and her aunt having no idea that it did or the way that it did. The same applied to me. While Nigel babbled on about Macintyre, I was in Paris and Italy and Beadle Walk, with my father and the Princess and Tobin.

Nigel pushed his knife and fork together, drained his glass and stood up. 'Well, I'm going to push on.'

'Yes, of course,' I said. 'What time do you want to get up in the morning?'

'Oh, seven should be fine for tomorrow. Don't let me lie in, though, will you?'

'I'll try not to.'

So off he went to the study and I washed up. As I went past the study door later, I called, 'Goodnight. Don't work too late.'

A grunt was my only reply.

And that is why Nigel remained unaware of Oliver Lyon's programme, the Princess and Tobin. It wasn't that I deliberately withheld the information. I didn't make a conscious decision not to tell him. It simply happened that way.

On Friday morning, Nigel phoned to say that he and Bron were going off to an hotel for their brainstorming session and, if I needed him urgently – 'And by that I mean in an absolute emergency,' he stressed – I should ring Bron's secretary, who was the only person who knew where they were to be found.

Moments after I had put down the phone, it rang again. 'Mr Touchstone for you, Cara,' Dorothy announced.

'Sorry I haven't been in touch sooner,' Tobin apologized. 'But for the past week I've hardly known whether I've been coming or going, what with Easter bunnies and the Princess. The reason I'm calling you, however, is not to moan, but to say that I'm going to Beadle Walk again tomorrow and I was wondering whether you'd care to come over and have a look at the place.'

I knew then what Christina Rosetti had meant when she wrote that her heart was like a singing bird. 'I'd love to,' I said, 'if you're sure I shan't be in the way.'

'That would be impossible. Harvey won't be there, if that's what you're wondering. One weekend was enough for him. I thought you might like to see where the Princess lived – and I have something else to tell you about – a rather disturbing little can of worms, which may or may not turn out to be connected with you.'

'How do you mean?'

'I'll explain all when I see you. What time shall we say? Ten o'clock?'

'That would be perfect.'

'Right, the address is number seven, Beadle Walk.'

I was still sitting there at my desk, with an inane grin on my face, when Miles entered my office. 'You're looking remarkably like a cat who has just stolen the cream, Cara. What are you up to?'

'Oh, I'm just feeling happy,' I replied.

'It suits you,' he commented. And, to my further surprise, he walked straight out of the office again without asking me to do anything.

Next morning, when I arrived at 7, Beadle Walk, that bird in my heart was still chirruping away. Then the front door was opened by a pretty, smiling, dark-haired woman of about thirty and the bird fell silent.

A succession of thoughts raced through my head. The first was that maybe I had come to the wrong house, but I knew I hadn't. Then, that it should have occurred to me that Tobin might have a girlfriend. Then, that he could have warned me. Then, that there was no reason why he should have done. And, finally, to wonder at the strength of my reaction.

At that moment, Tobin himself appeared in the hallway and hurried towards me with a welcoming smile. 'Cara! Come along in! And let me introduce you. This is Consuela. Consuela, this is my friend, Mrs Sinclair.'

We shook hands and she beamed at me.

'Consuela used to keep house for the Princess,' Tobin explained. 'And she's come in today to pack some of the kitchen things.' He turned to her. 'Would you mind getting us some coffee, Consuela?'

She nodded eagerly and beamed even more broadly.

'She's Spanish and doesn't speak much English,' Tobin told me, as Consuela disappeared down the hall. 'And now, come into the drawing room, which is where Oliver interviewed the Princess.'

Somewhat shakily, I followed him through a door and then I forgot, for the time being at least, about the emotions Consuela had aroused in me.

It was as though I had been transported into another country. Outside, the weather was dull and the room was illuminated by a chandelier, with crystals shaped like brittle icicles, two or three inches long, which were never quite still, sending iridescent shafts of light darting about the room, like sun glinting on snow. The walls were panelled in a rich, dark wood and on them hung two paintings in gilt frames. At the windows were burgundy-coloured brocade curtains in which gold threads sparkled. The furniture was upholstered in velvet, matching the colour of the curtains, and the floor was covered by a magnificent Chinese carpet. In one corner stood a gleaming ebony grand piano and, in another, was a triangular glass-fronted cabinet containing gold ornaments glittering with jewels. An ornately framed tapestry screen hid the fireplace and over the mantelpiece hung the icon of the Madonna and Christ child, of which I had caught a quick glimpse at the end of Oliver Lyon's interview.

'Extraordinary, isn't it?' Tobin said. 'You could almost forget you were in Chelsea and imagine you were in old St Petersburg.'

Even the smell was foreign. A mixture of incense, pine and a lingering waft of what I think was tuberose seemed to hang in the air, as though the Princess had recently left the room and was still elsewhere in the building.

'That icon was one of the Princess's most treasured possessions,' Tobin continued. 'Apparently, she came across it in a Paris antiques shop during the twenties. According to her, it used to hang in her mother's bedroom at their palace in St Petersburg and when she was a little girl she would imagine that the Madonna was her mother and she was the baby in her arms.'

'How incredible.'

'Yes. Goodness alone knows how it reached Paris, but she took it as final proof that her parents were dead.' He glanced towards the other side of the room. 'Over there are the two portraits of her, which I think you missed seeing during Oliver's interview. But we'll talk about them later. First, come and look at the rest of the house.'

He crossed the hall and opened a door. The room beyond was furnished with a long, highly polished mahogany table, around which stood dining chairs. There was a sideboard, on which a magnificently decorated silver samovar stood in pride of place.

'That samovar was another of her most precious possessions, which she found in Paris at the same time as the icon. It certainly used to lend a great sense of occasion to taking tea with her. You can't preside over a brown china teapot in quite the same way as you can over a samovar like that.'

The next room we entered had been Howard's study. It was very small, gloomy and totally bare, with not even a carpet on the floor. 'Harvey's had everything from here taken back to Kingston Kirkby Hall,' Tobin explained.

After that came the kitchen where Consuela was pouring boiling water from a kettle into a cafetière, surrounded by packing cases, old newspapers and piles of crockery. Compared to my own kitchen, it was very out-of-date, indicating it to be a room in which the Princess had seldom set foot.

Tobin led me upstairs and opened the door to a room furnished merely with an unmade-up bed, carpet and utilitarian wardrobe and chest-of-drawers. 'This used to be Howard's bedroom.'

He went down the landing. 'And this was the Princess's room.' He stood back to let me enter. It had the same lived-in feeling to it – and the same elusive perfume – as the drawing room. The bed was covered with a quilted, cream satin counterpane. A black, lace-trimmed negligé hung on the back of the door. On the dressing table, ornate hairbrushes, combs and jars of cosmetics were laid out on a crystal tray.

To the right of the mirror stood a photograph in an elaborate gilt frame, showing a young man, leaning back in a chair on a café terrace, with an air of graceful, casual ease. He was dark-haired, with a daredevilish glint in his eye and a rakish smile on his lips.

I looked questioningly at Tobin and he gave a wry laugh. 'Yes, that's an eye-opener.'

'Who is it?'

'Her cousin, Prince Dmitri Nikolaevitch Zakharin. According to the photographer's stamp on the back, it was taken in Paris in 1921.'

She had been married four times, yet it was Dmitri's picture on which she had gazed every evening when she went to bed and every morning when she awoke . . .

Leading off the bedroom was another room, part dressing room, part boudoir, furnished with wardrobes, a chest of drawers, a delightful escritoire and a tapestry-covered chair. Tobin opened one of the wardrobes to reveal a row of dresses, with shoes along the bottom. Inside the next wardrobe were coats and more shoes. He went over to the chest of drawers and pulled out a drawer in which lay neatly folded lingerie.

'However . . .' he then said, his voice suddenly grim, picking up a large, ornate casket and opening it. The interior was divided into little, velvet-lined compartments, one of which contained a gold necklace with a single solitaire, and another a bracelet. The only other occupant of the jewellery box was a silver pendant, resembling a two-headed horse, with six small bells hanging from it on silver chains.

'The necklace and the bracelet are what she wore for the television interview, aren't they?' I asked.

'Yes, and they, together with the rings she was wearing when she had her stroke, are that all that remain of her collection,' Tobin stated. 'She used to have so much jewellery – every time you saw her she would be wearing something different.'

'Maybe she put the rest in the bank for safe-keeping.'

'No, we've checked. The deposit box was empty, apart from papers.'

I picked up the pendant and the little bells tinkled.

'That's another mystery,' Tobin said. 'I'd never seen that before. She never wore silver – only gold.'

'It's most unusual. Do you think it has some symbolic meaning?'

'I've no idea.' Tobin sucked in his breath. 'Well, let's go downstairs again and I'll explain what's happened so far as we can make out.'

We went back down to the drawing room. Consuela came in and set down a tray on the one remaining occasional table. She poured out the coffee and asked me, 'You want cream, Señora?'

'*Si, por favor.*' I replied.

'*Usted entiende español*?' she exclaimed delightedly.

'*Un poco*,' I told her.

'I wasn't aware that you spoke Spanish,' Tobin said.

'Oh, I don't speak it very well – I've sort of picked it up along the way from holidays in Spain. I understand better than I speak.'

'How many other lights do you have hidden under bushels?'

'Being able to put together a few words of Spanish is hardly a great achievement,' I demurred.

'Hmm. I disagree. But we'll leave that discussion for another time.'

Consuela left the room and Tobin said, 'The Princess's jewellery isn't the only thing to be missing. Howard's cuff-links and tie-pins have all gone, too, and his medals, which is particularly horrid. There's quite a lot of glass and porcelain disappeared from the dining room and some of the ornaments from the cabinet over there. It's difficult to be sure exactly how many, but I particularly remember a collection of Louis Quinze type scent bottles by Fabergé – she must have had at least a dozen of them. Now there are none at all.'

'But surely Consuela must have been aware . . . ?' I said hesitantly.

'I regret to say that our suspicions immediately fell on her. However, we then went through the escritoire in the Princess's boudoir and I'm glad to say that Consuela was in the clear.'

'So what had happened?'

'It would appear that the Princess was being blackmailed. We don't know for how long or by whom, but we found some letters. I can't show them to you, unfortunately, because Harvey took them away with him. But the earliest one was dated July 1976, just after Howard's death, and it said something like, "Now he's dead, you can afford to be a bit more generous." And then, something about the Princess's "secret remaining safe". The others were all in a similar vein.'

'Her secret remaining safe?' I echoed.

'Yes, naturally I had the same thought. Needless to say, when we went through the rest of her papers, we kept you in mind. But we didn't come across anything remotely connected with you or your father. In fact, there was very little that dated back before Howard's death. One would almost have said that she had deliberately set out to eradicate every last trace of her past. Even her address book was new.

'However, we did find bank statements and cheque books stubs. After Howard's death, she started drawing a cash sum at the end of every month. The amount steadily increased and at the time she died, she was taking out two thousand pounds a month.'

I let out a low whistle. To put this in perspective, my salary, before tax, was about ten thousand pounds a year.

'That was in addition to all her other expenditure, the household bills, credit card payments and the accounts she held at Harrods, Harvey Nicholls, Aspreys and so on – most of which hadn't been paid for months. We discovered a whole pile of threatening letters and summonses. Harvey had a fit when he saw them.'

'Do you have any idea who the blackmailer was?'

'Absolutely none.'

'You've presumably talked to Consuela?'

'That was one of the first things we did, when we had worked out what had been happening. But she wasn't any help. She couldn't remember anything out of the ordinary taking place – no strange telephone calls or visitors, though, of course, her hours were only between ten in the morning and three in the afternoon, during which she also used to go out to shop for groceries and suchlike. And, of course, her English isn't at all good.'

'You don't think Consuela herself . . . ?' Then I stopped, realizing the Princess was hardly likely to employ her blackmailer.

Tobin shook his head. 'Again, the same thought occurred to us. But Consuela's only been working for the Princess for a couple of years and the blackmail started before that. In any case, I'm convinced she's trustworthy. You can tell by little things. She's the sort who finds a five pound note under the sofa and hands it to you. And if she was being paid two thousand pounds a month for keeping quiet, she wouldn't have needed to work.'

'And since the Princess's death, there have been no demands?'

'Nothing, but if the blackmailer watched Oliver Lyon's programme – or if they read the newspapers – he or she presumably knows she's dead.'

'Yes, of course. That was a stupid question.'

'Not really. It depends what the Princess's secret was and whether its significance died with her or whether it had an ongoing relevance. It could be that the blackmailer knew about you, but it could, equally, have been something quite different. After all, if the Princess was capable of denying your existence, she was capable of other deceits . . .'

His voice tailed off and we sat in a pensive silence for a few moments.

Then he said, 'Well, no doubt all will be revealed in the fullness of time. Something or somebody will crawl out of the woodwork and we'll learn the answer. Meanwhile, I thought you should know.'

'Thank you. It's rather horrid, isn't it?'

'Yes, it leaves a nasty taste.'

'I wonder if it was to the blackmailer that she was referring at the end of the interview, when she said, "Only my enemies survive."?'

'It could well have been . . .' He glanced towards the two portraits of the Princess. 'However, let's leave that for the moment and talk about something slightly different. Harvey takes the view, and rightly so in my opinion, that nothing here at Beadle Walk relates to the Winster family, although most of it was bought out of Winster money. So, once probate has been granted, he's going to sell the house and put the contents up for auction. The proceeds – or what remains after he's settled the Princess's debts – will go towards refurbishing Kingston Kirkby Hall.

'But he is very kindly giving me those portraits.' He paused. 'Now, it strikes me that if you are the Princess's daughter, they really belong to you.'

I stared at him, flabbergasted.

'So I'd like you to have them.'

I shook my head. 'No, that's very kind, but I couldn't possibly take them.'

'Please, no spur-of-the-minute decision.'

'I may not be her daughter.'

'Even so, your father was married to her, whereas I had no real relationship with her at all.'

'You knew her and I didn't.'

'That's immaterial. I'd like you to have them.'

I was deeply touched by his offer but couldn't possibly have accepted. 'It's extremely generous of you and I really appreciate it,' I assured him, 'but I can't accept. I'm sorry, I just can't.'

He studied me assessingly. 'Well, at least come and have a closer look at them.'

We went and stood in front of the El Toro, signed with that unmistakable bull. In it the Princess was recognizable, but only just, for resemblance to the natural model had been sacrificed in favour of bold shape and daring use of colour.

'Even these pictures contain a mystery,' Tobin said. 'The Princess claimed that Baron Léon de St-Léon commissioned El Toro to paint this one. But if you look at the date, it was painted in 1922 and she didn't marry de St-Léon until 1924. So why the lie? On the other hand, there's no doubt that it's her. Look at the eyes. They were cold, even when she was young.'

The other painting was totally different in style. It was a formal portrait, showing the Princess wearing a simple, white, low-cut gown, with a tiara in her hair, diamonds in her ears and round her swanlike neck. It was exquisitely delicate in its execution, giving the Princess an air of almost ethereal radiance.

'This is lovely,' I breathed, trying to decipher the signature in the right-hand corner. 'Who was the artist?'

'Someone called Angelini. I've found his name in a couple of my art books but no details about him. The Princess had a very ambivalent attitude towards it. She had it on show, but would never talk about it. In fact, I always had the impression that she disliked it, but kept it because it showed off her great beauty and her jewels. Quite a contrast between the two styles, eh?'

'I know which I prefer. The Angelini has such a luminous quality to it. It seems to shimmer. It's iridescent – almost as though you're looking through a thin veil with light shining through it. Somebody must know about the artist.'

'Oh, yes. No doubt there will be various experts round from Sotheby's and Christie's to value the rest of the contents and I'll ask one of them.' He paused. 'Listen, why don't we compromise? You have the Angelini and I'll have the El Toro. But no, damn it, that's not fair either. The El Toro is undoubtedly worth far more.'

'Please,' I begged, 'believe me, I don't want either of them.' Then I suddenly thought of a reason which might convince him – and which also happened to be true. 'I wouldn't want to be reminded every day of a woman who didn't want me.'

'OK, I'll accept that,' he said. 'I'll keep them for the time being but, if anything happens to make you change your mind, you must let me know – and then they're yours. Agreed?'

I nodded, knowing I never would.

'And now, what are your plans for the rest of the day? Do you have time to stay for a bite of lunch? I'm sure Consuela can rustle something up.'

'Well . . .'

'Or is your husband expecting you back?'

'No, he's working.'

'On a Saturday?'

'He's putting together a pitch for a new account.'

'In that case, I'll go and have a word with Consuela.'

While he was gone, I wandered across to the icon. It was very small, only about a foot by eighteen inches, and obviously very old, for in places the paint was peeling away to reveal the wood on which it had been painted. The artist had done a remarkable job in capturing in the Madonna's expression a mother's tenderness for her child.

Then it suddenly struck me as strange that the Princess should have been so attached to it. Such a sentiment didn't seem to fit in with everything else I had learned about her – or with a woman who had abandoned her own child.

Tobin and I ate in the dining room, sitting opposite each other at the centre of the long mahogany table. 'According to the Princess, in a Russian household, the parents sat in the middle, with the children at either end,' Tobin explained, as a beaming Consuela served up a magnificent Spanish omelette.

'In fact, that's rather interesting,' he continued, when we were alone again. 'Although the Princess didn't generally talk about her past, she did occasionally reminisce about her childhood. It was her married life she was reluctant to speak about. Ah well, we'll probably never get to the bottom of it all. And now, let's talk about something completely different. Tell me how you're enjoying *Novel on Yellow Paper*.'

I laughed. 'I read it right through from beginning to end in one night and then read it all the way through again.'

'And you can understand why I thought it might appeal to you?'

'Not only that, but . . .' I stopped.

'But what? Come on, out with it.'

'No, I'm not going to say any more.'

But he had guessed. 'You're following Pompey's example?'

My expression gave me away.

'Wonderful!' he exclaimed. 'That's what I hoped.'

'It's not easy – particularly writing about myself.'

'I'm sure it isn't.'

'But Stevie Smith does it so well. She isn't at all self-conscious.'

'Then forget yourself. Don't think about what you're writing. Don't try too hard. Let the story tell itself. Just get the words – any words – down on paper. You can always change any bits you don't like later on, when you've finished.'

'It sounds silly, but I feel as I'm giving away too much of myself.'

'Does that matter?

'But if it's not interesting?'

'What makes you think it's not interesting?'

'Because it's me.'

'You should never do yourself down. People believe what you tell them about yourself, they take you at your own reckoning.'

'Yes, I guess so.' I picked at my food.

'What you're actually trying to say is that some of it hurts, aren't you?'

I nodded.

'Then lance the boil.'

'I'm not sure that I have the courage.'

'Of course you do. And once you've done it, you'll feel much better.'

'I suppose so.'

'What do you have to lose?'

'Nothing.'

'Well, there you are.'

We finished our meal in silence, then he said, 'I wonder if I could ask you a big favour? I'm totally out of my depth when it comes to female garments and I was wondering if you'd mind going through the Princess's wardrobe with Consuela. Harvey says her clothes will be too small and the wrong style for Gwendolen. Not that she needs them anyway. But it seems a shame to waste them. I was thinking that a charity shop . . .'

'Of course I don't mind. I'm glad you asked. Though I must stress that I'm no fashion expert.'

So Consuela and I went up to the Princess's dressing room and started on the gruesome task of sorting through the dead woman's clothes. Not that Consuela seemed to find the job distressing. She chattered away in a mixture of Spanish and English, vastly over-estimating my comprehension of her mother-tongue, but obviously so delighted to have someone to talk to that I didn't have the heart to disillusion her.

She mourned the Princess's passing, saying how much she had enjoyed working for such a great lady. The hours here had been so convenient, meaning she could take her young child to school in the morning and pick him up in the afternoon. Then she asked whether I had known the Princess personally.

Unfortunately not, I admitted.

Ah, that accounted for why she had never seen me before. But, that said, the Princess had not had many friends. Acquaintances, yes, but not friends. In fact, at the end of her life, there had been only one friend, an old lady – *una rusa* – who had still come occasionally to the house. Consuela had the impression they had known each other for many years. This friend was quite different from the Princess. She lacked the Princess's refinement. She did not wear beautiful clothes like these of the Princess. But she was still *muy aristocrática* in her manner, *bien que un poco excéntrica.* Sometimes, the Princess would give this friend a present. Consuela knew this, because after the friend had gone, she would notice that a piece of jewellery or an ornament was missing.

As casually as I could – wishing desperately that I spoke better Spanish – I asked, '*Cómo se llama esta Señora?*'

Consuela spread her hands expressively. '*No sé.*'

'*Y sus señas?*

'*No sé.*'

Later, when Consuela had left, I repeated this conversation to Tobin.

He shook his head. 'An old, aristocratic Russian woman, rather eccentric and fallen on hard times? How extraordinary! Not exactly the sort of character immediately to spring to mind when you think of a blackmailer. And Consuela didn't know her name or address? Damn!'

'I know. Isn't it infuriating? I tried to get more out of her, but that was all she knew. Perhaps she really was a friend.'

Tobin pursed his lips. 'It doesn't add up.'

'Well, we've sorted out the clothes anyway,' I said. 'Some of them have never been worn and a lot have well-known labels in them. I think they could possibly be worth quite a lot of money. There are shops which deal in second-hand designer clothes. Would you like me to make enquiries for you?'

'I think you've done more than enough already.'

'It would only take me a few moments.'

'Well, if you wouldn't mind.'

'I'll see to it on Monday. But there is one problem. I can't get in touch with you. I don't have your telephone number.'

'That's easily remedied.' He reached in his back trouser pocket and pulled out a small wallet, from which he extracted a visiting card. 'And now I think the very least I can do is buy you a drink. I don't know about you, but I've seen enough of this place for the day.'

'It's not a happy house, is it?'

'No, it isn't. Harvey's doing the right thing in selling it.' He laid his hand lightly on my shoulder. 'Come on, put your coat on and let's get out of here.'

We ended up having dinner together at a bistro in King's Road. I was slightly apprehensive in case Nigel should come home early from his brainstorming session, but decided it was just bad luck if he did.

During our meal we discussed more possible motives for the Princess being blackmailed, some of which were so absurd that we totally forgot the seriousness of the subject and had a fit of the giggles.

As I was wiping the tears from my eyes, I tried to recall when anyone had last made me laugh so much. Nigel must presumably have been fun once, when we first met, otherwise I wouldn't have fallen in love with him. But a lot of things had come to an end after we were married – quite how many I was only just starting to appreciate.

'What's up?' Tobin asked. 'Why are you looking so pensive?'

'I'm sorry, I didn't mean to— I just thought of something and—'

'What? Tell me. Please.'

I smiled. 'No, it was nothing. Honestly.'

He nodded and leaned back in his chair, pinching his lower lip thoughtfully between his thumb and forefinger. Then he said, 'You know, you have the most fascinating face. I have never known anyone with such a range of expressions. I could watch you for hours and never grow bored.'

I felt the colour rush to my cheeks and he laughed, not cruelly, not unkindly, but with affectionate amusement. 'In fact, if you weren't so transparently genuine, you could have been an actress,' he said. 'But I don't believe you're capable of subterfuge, even to order.'

Then he picked up the menu and asked, 'And now, what would you like for dessert? I rather fancy vanilla ice cream with lashings of chocolate sauce.'

Chapter 11

Nigel did not come home on Saturday night, nor on Sunday night either. On Sunday morning, I caught up with my family telephone calls and found Aunt Biddie distressed at her failure still to find my father's book of poetry. 'I've turned up no end of other long-lost treasures,' she said, 'but no sign of it. Yet, it must be here somewhere . . .'

I told both her and Miranda about my visit to Beadle Walk and about the blackmailer, but did not mention how Tobin had wanted to give me the portraits of the Princess, nor my strange feelings regarding the icon. Both matters were too close to my heart to speak about over the phone.

At the end of my conversation with Miranda, she asked, 'Have you told Nigel about the Princess yet?'

'No, there still hasn't been any opportunity.' I explained about Macintyre. 'So, you see, with all that on his mind, he wouldn't be interested.'

'You're very long-suffering,' she remarked.

'Not really. It's Nigel's job. I can't argue with that, can I?'

'No, I suppose not, but—'

'Don't worry, Miranda. I'm fine, honestly.'

'Well, if you say so.'

After that, I went through the pages I had so far written of The Book and, by the end of the afternoon, had completed another six pages. Then I turned to my hand-written notebook diary and entered in the previous day's events, finding that a considerably easier task.

On Monday, Juliette – much more of a shopping person than I – gave me the names of a couple of next-to-new clothes shops and, while Miles was at lunch, I rang Tobin to give him the details.

He thanked me and I asked how the Easter bunnies were progressing.

'Oh, I'm having great fun,' he chuckled. 'The client keeps adding extra little bits to the job, with the result that my family of rabbits keeps increasing.

Incest is rife in Fulham. At the latest count, I'm up to three adults, one male and two females, with forty-odd children between them . . .'

I laughed and we chatted for a few moments, until my other phone rang. 'I'm sorry, I have to go.'

'Yes and I must get back to the drawing board – or should I say my warren . . . ?'

That evening, Nigel came home, unshaven and in clothes which looked as if they had been slept in, to announce that he and Bron had agreed upon their concept. Whereupon he had a shower, set the alarm for six thirty and collapsed into bed.

That set the pattern for the next fortnight. We were going through a particularly hectic period at Goodchild, while the previous year's end management accounts kept piling in. Miles was in what was secretly referred to within the company as his 'speculative mode' which always seem to attack him around this time of year and often ended with a new company acquisition. It was as if, having seen the results of what he had achieved during the past twelve months, he became bored and had to prowl in search of new prey. Nobody could tell what direction he was heading off in – possibly he didn't even know himself. He simply sent out exploratory feelers, which led to meetings, the outcome of which I only became privy to when something concrete emerged from them.

More often than not, the first indication I received of what was going on was from rumours in the financial press, which usually proved to be wrong. Part of the fun for Miles was laying a trail of red herrings to divert the attention of his competitors and those eagle eyed manipulators on the stock exchange.

Every evening, when I came home – seldom before seven – I put in an hour or two on The Book. Nigel got in around midnight, absolutely exhausted and showing no curiosity whatsoever about my life. I think I could have dyed my hair purple and he wouldn't have noticed. When I asked how things were progressing, I usually received little more than a grunt in response.

He worked straight through the next weekend again and I took advantage of his absence to continue with The Book. From Tobin I heard nothing and had to assume that he was still up to his ears in Easter bunnies.

It was just as I was finishing the ironing on the Thursday of the following week – it was Valentine's Day, although that escaped Nigel's notice – that

Aunt Biddie rang me. 'I've found it!' she announced triumphantly. 'And you'll never guess where it was!'

'I'm sure I shan't,' I laughed. 'So you'd better tell me.'

'The most obvious place, of course, and the one and only place I hadn't bothered to look. In Stephen's collar box.'

'Well, of course! Where else would it have been?'

'Now don't be sarcastic, Cara. When I die, you and Miranda will need Stephen's collar box. It contains all my documents – my medical card, my birth and wedding certificates, my premium bonds, will and so on. My parents' birth, marriage and death certificates are in there as well, though I don't suppose you'll need them.'

'Before you pop off, would you mind telling us where to find Uncle Stephen's collar box?' I requested wryly.

'That's a very good point. It was in the glory-hole, which isn't really a very sensible place. I'll have to think of somewhere better.'

'Better still, stay alive.'

'Yes, that's by far the best idea. Anyway, to come back to Connor's book, I found a few letters as well. They contain rather more than I remembered. There's even an address on one of them – an address in Paris, I hasten to add, not in Italy, I'm afraid. Now, I could post them to you, which I'm rather reluctant to do, in case the Post Office loses them. You know Jessie, don't you, Mrs Ashton, my friend in Clun? Well, she sent me something by registered mail the other day and it's disappeared into thin air. Completely disappeared. Nobody has the slightest idea where it can have got to. Fortunately, it wasn't all that important, but it could have been. So, what I was wondering was, if Nigel's still working on his project, whether you'd like to come up and spend another weekend with me?'

'That sounds like an excellent idea.'

'I know it's a long way to travel and you've only just been here . . .'

'That doesn't matter. You know how much I love coming to Avonford and I'm dying to see that book and those letters.'

'If I may make a suggestion, instead of driving up here in the dark on Friday night, why not come on Saturday again?'

'In view of the hours I seem to be working at the moment, that would probably be sensible,' I agreed rather reluctantly, impatient to see her finds.

Aunt Biddie sighed. 'You and Nigel are a right pair, aren't you?'

Since there seemed no suitable response to this comment, I said I'd be with her on Saturday morning, wished her goodnight and rang off.

I had to share her news. Putting away the ironing board, I went downstairs to Sherry and Roly's, but finding them not in, I rang Tobin.

'How extraordinary, I was just thinking about you,' he said.

'Something nice, I hope.'

'Naturally. Where are you? At home?'

'Good heavens, yes. The good Miles child may be a bit of a slave-driver, but he's not that bad.'

He chuckled. 'I was expecting you to be out, celebrating the feast of the patron saint of lovers.'

That explained where Sherry and Roly were, I reflected fleetingly. 'No,' I said, 'us staid old married couples are past that.'

'Staid is not a word I would apply to you.'

'Thank you.'

'Now you'd better tell me to what I owe the honour of this call.'

'Well, I had to talk to someone. Aunt Biddie's just rung me and she's found my father's book of poetry and some letters.'

It was half an hour later before I eventually put down the phone. I can't remember exactly what else we talked about. It was just general chit-chat about Aunt Biddie and Avonford and his work and my job and that sort of thing – nothing significant – much the same sort of conversation, in fact, that I could well have had with Miranda or Sherry or Juliette.

Except that Miranda, Sherry and Juliette, fond though I was of them, didn't make little birds sing in my heart.

It rained most of the way to Avonford on Saturday. When I arrived, it was still raining, but, nevertheless, Aunt Biddie was on the front doorstep, chatting to a neighbour. I tooted my horn, waved and drove through the tall gates into the courtyard.

Seconds later, she was beside me, her face brimming with indignation. 'You'll never guess what Mrs Tilsley was just telling me! It's the abbey's eight hundredth anniversary next year and they – whoever "they" may be – are apparently planning to give the building a face-lift.' She paused dramatically. 'And they are proposing putting a face on the clock.'

Avonford abbey clock had been a source of endless fascination to Miranda and me when we were children and doubtless to countless generations before and after us. The clock did not have a visible face to show the people the time, but chimed the quarter hours and played a carillon of songs to celebrate the hour. Whoever originally set it up had possessed a rather irreverent sense of humour, for at six o'clock in the morning, it played 'Early one morning'; at pub opening times it played *Drink to me only with thine eyes;* and during funerals it always seemed either to play 'Barbara Allen' or 'Clementine'. 'The Vicar of Bray', 'The Lincolnshire Poacher' and 'Oh! Dear! What Can the Matter Be?' were also among its repertoire.

'This means war,' Aunt Biddie declared. 'Mrs Tilsley and I have already decided to start a petition – which I hope you'll sign, Cara – and if that doesn't have any effect, we'll take our case to our MP and, if necessary, to the highest court in the land. Put a face on the clock! Who ever heard anything so ridiculous?'

I couldn't help laughing and she turned on me suspiciously. 'What's so amusing?'

'I'm sorry, but it is funny when you think about it. Most clocks have a face.'

'But not ours! You know who's behind it, don't you? It's that new vicar. I've always been suspicious of men with beards who wear sandals. He's introducing all these new services, where everyone's supposed to hold hands and kiss each other. All the words have changed, too. You wouldn't recognize the twenty-third psalm. I don't understand why people can't leave well alone. And then he wonders why his congregation is dwindling. It's enough to make me join the Baptists. What Stephen would say if he was still alive, I do not know.'

'I didn't know you were such a regular church-goer.'

'I'm not. But it's the principle that counts.'

I shivered in the chilly rain. 'May I suggest that we continue this discussion indoors before we're both soaked to the skin?'

She looked up at the sky with an air of astonishment. 'How extraordinary. I didn't realize it was raining. That just goes to show how cross I am. Yes, of course, do come along in.' When we were in the kitchen, her motherly self took over from the battle-axe. 'Now, would you like breakfast or shall we have an early lunch? I thought we'd have a mixed grill today. I don't know about you, but that's something I can never be bothered to cook for myself.'

'A cup of tea and an early lunch will suit me fine.'

'Oh, look, here's Tiger come to see you.'

In front of the Aga were three little lambs. 'Your family's grown again,' I remarked.

'These are new ones. Larry and Mary have gone back to the farm. Stevie keeps telling me that I should be more imaginative with my names, so I've called them collectively the three Graces. Not very suitable, perhaps, but more classical.'

'Since they're identical, it seems a good idea to me.'

'They're not identical,' she objected. 'Grace One has bigger ears than the others. Grace Two has a little black mark by her nose. And Grace Three is the runt of the litter. Dear little thing.'

'My name's Joey Trowbridge and I live at The Willows Avonford. Who's a pretty boy, then? Ark. Ark.'

I fed him a piece of millet, then admired Gordon, marching up and down the garden like a sentry outside Buckingham Palace. 'And Chukwa?' I enquired.

'Still sleeping the sleep of the just.'

When we were both comfortably seated at the kitchen table with a cup of tea each, she handed me a manila envelope. 'Well, here they are, for what they're worth. But you'll see that I was telling the truth when I said he was a poor correspondent.'

There were just five letters inside the envelope, all written on squared paper, rather like graph paper, the kind which French school children have in their exercise books.

My father's handwriting was, as I expected, large and flamboyant, with exaggerated loops. Yet it could not decide which direction it was going and the characters were sometimes upright and other times sloping to the right or the left.

The first letter was headed simply: Paris, April 1929.

Dear Biddie,
It's all over now. From having been a cause celèbre, *I am now a* cause célibataire. *Patricia is getting her divorce, and Imogen, having enticed me here to Paris, has announced that she now realises she has been missing out on life and intends to make up for lost time by enjoying herself – which means she and Elizabeth are engaged in an endless round of parties, balls and night clubs.*

Fortunately, Imogen feels guilty at having broken up my

marriage and is paying the rent on a small apartment for me, as well as helping with my living expenses, until such time as I find a suitable occupation. I indulge in the occasional sardonic chuckle at the thought of what old Abraham would say if he were aware of how his darling daughter disposes of his hard-earned income.

She continues to believe in my great talent and assures me that she will do everything in her power to help further my career. Every now and again, I am exhibited before some literary doyen or doyenne, whose acquaintance she has cultivated. 'This is my pet poet,' she says, and I sit up and beg like a good lap-dog and perform all my party tricks.

Hey-ho! There are worse ways to exist and Paris is considerably more entertaining than Dewfield.

Much love,

Connor.

84bis, rue des Châtaigniers,
Montparnasse,
Paris 14ième.

18th December 1930

Dear Biddie,

A short note to wish you and Stephen a 'joyeux Noël et une bonne nouvelle année' – or perhaps I should say 'felice Natale e buon Capodanno', for since I last wrote I have joined the Italian fraternity. I'm lodging at the house of an Italian artist, Amadore Angelini, whom I met through a Spanish artist. See what a cosmopolitan city this is!

My Italians look after me as though I were a member of their own family. In fact, I think the Italians and the Irish have more than just an initial in common. Or perhaps it is that I am really Latin by temperament – maybe I was an Italian in a former life.

Papa Angelini paints the portraits of the rich bourgeois, making them look like angels, while Mama Angelini cooks like an angel. They have three children, two young men and a very much younger girl, though we see little of the eldest son, Benedetto, who lives in Italy, working at a family business there. The girl reminds me in a strange way of you at the same age. Remember mad Moraid?

Papa Angelini and the two sons are full of the great achievements of Mussolini and we have some grand arguments.

I get out and about a lot and have made many interesting acquaintances. Imogen still keeps me under her wing. Last summer, a party of us spent a long vacation on the Côte d'Azur and, in February, we are all going skiing in St. Moritz.

In other words, I am in the pink.

Hoping all is well with you and yours,

Your loving brother,

Connor.

'Angelini!' I gasped. 'That must be the same artist who painted the portrait of the Princess. You know, the one of her in tiara and jewels? And presumably the Spanish artist was El Toro.'

'Yes, it was,' Aunt Biddie said. 'Read on.'

rue des Châtaigniers, Paris
20th December, 1935

Dear Biddie,

It seems a life-time since I was in Avonford, and now poor mother is in her grave.

My happy household is no longer as happy as it was, because there has been much hostility towards the Italians in Paris since Mussolini invaded Abyssinia. Who are the British and the French to denounce Mussolini for wanting his own empire? Hypocrites, the lot of them. Mama Angelini keeps trying to persuade Papa to return to Italy, but he's too much of a Francophile to leave – to my great relief. After four years, I have become very established in my garret.

I need the Angelinis all the more now, since Imogen has returned to America. Her departure was not without drama, for she eloped with a Russian prince. Goodbye to the goose who laid the golden eggs. However, there are more where she came from, some of whom are even more attractive. Being a single man has much to commend it. Vive la liberté!

Life here is never dull. More anon . . .

Affectionately,

Connor.

'The Russian prince was presumably Dmitri,' I murmured. 'But does that mean Imogen Humboldt continued to support him all that time?'

Aunt Biddie sucked in her breath. 'I rather fear so.'

'He doesn't mention working or having a job.'

'I know. I have a nasty feeling he was a kept man. And I also have a nasty feeling that the Angelinis didn't always receive their rent.'

rue des Châtaigniers, Paris
December, 1936

Dear Biddie,

I am off to war! Like Don Quixote, this Knight of the Doleful Countenance is going to tilt at windmills. God knows why I'm going. In theory, it is because my Spanish artist friend, Juan Maria Toro, has convinced me to fight for freedom against mutinous Spanish generals and their fascist allies. I don't mean that we are intending to take up arms: I shall fight with the pen and Toro with paints.

In practice, I am going because Paris has become rather uncomfortable for me. A little amourette is turning sour. The good lady's husband is threatening to have me expelled. Discretion seems the better part of valour . . .

Having said that, I am, in fact, like most working people here in Paris, greatly sympathetic with the Spanish Loyalists, mainly because I am against dictators, be they Spanish, German or Italian. And this has been getting me into trouble with Angelini, with whom my arguments have of late become very heated.

Poor Amadore, his star is on the wane. The French middle classes do not want their portraits painted by an

Italian. I am sorry for him. He is a simple, decent soul, who loves France and, at the same time, believes Mussolini to be a great man, because he has restored order in Italy and saved it from communism. For the same reason, he believes Hitler to be good for Germany – although he does not like the Germans as a race and does not trust the friendship between Italy and Germany.

You see, your brother is developing, if not a political conscience, at least a political awareness.

On that note, I shall leave you. Adiós!

Much love,

Connor

I turned to the last letter.

Perpignan, May 1939

Dear Biddie,

There is much too much to write in a letter, so this must suffice until I see you next. I am alive, if only just. Having survived over two years virtually intact, I was shot up in the last of the fighting outside Barcelona. A butcher of a surgeon extricated a bullet which narrowly missed my heart. That is, if I still have a heart. Little did I think when I set off to Spain that I was going to come back so changed in spirit. And now I cannot help but fear that the whole of Europe will soon find itself plunged into a war, for which Spain will prove merely to have been a rehearsal.

This camp is hell on earth, literally hundreds of thousands of refugees and the French not at all sympathetic. Toro is taking me to friends of his at Roquebrune to convalesce until I am fit enough to return to Paris.

My fondest love to you and your family,

Connor.

I read all the letters through again, then shook my head in perplexity. 'I'm even more confused now than I was before. His attitude's so cynical at times, certainly in the first letters. Yet this last one is quite different. And he obviously did fight after all – not just with the pen.'

Aunt Biddie pursed her lips. 'Who knows? I find it very difficult to imagine Connor as a soldier. It isn't that he was lacking in courage, but he was not the sort of man to be able to kill in cold blood, which is what being a soldier amounts to. It's one thing hating a regime and quite another killing the individual men who serve under it.'

'What I still don't understand at all is why, if he was against dictators, he spent the war in Italy of all places? We're back to that same question again.'

'To learn the answer, I think you're going to have to try and track down Amadore Angelini – or, if he's dead, which could well be the case – his children. And since we don't know where Angelini lived in Italy, that would seem to indicate a trip to Paris. You're still in touch with Ginette, aren't you?'

Ginette was my French penfriend, with whom I had made a couple of exchange visits while I was at school and who had helped me get my job in Paris after I left college. She had also been responsible for introducing me to Michel – not that I held that against her.

'Of course.'

'And where's she living now?'

'In Paris.'

Aunt Biddie said no more, but handed me another envelope, inside which was a very thin book, the cover of which seemed to be made from cartridge paper. The title read:

Selected Poems
by
Connor Moran

Carefully, I opened it. On the flyleaf, my father had inscribed in his flamboyant hand: *To Biddie, from your loving but errant brother, Connor.*

On the next page, the publisher's details appeared: Helicon Press, Ltd., London. On the following page, it said: 'First published, 1928'. I turned the pages of poor quality paper. The poems appeared mostly to be quite short.

'Don't read it now,' Aunt Biddie said. 'Read it later, when you're on your own. And then, I'd like you to keep it. You'll appreciate it more than me. And I think you should keep the letters as well.'

In the evening, Miranda, Jonathan and Stevie came over and, after they had heard the drama of the abbey clock, we went through the letters again.

I read my father's poems, sitting up in bed that night, with Tiger on my lap and the hot-water bottle warming my feet.

And by the time I reached the end, I was starting to feel closer to that enigmatic figure. In the literary sense, even I was aware that those verses were not terribly good. Most were love poems, verging sometimes on the sentimental, and lacking the polish, the linguistic dexterity and, above all, the intensity of those he had written during the Spanish Civil War.

Yet, to me, their importance lay not in their literary merit but in what they revealed of his true personality, the hidden depths beneath the cynical outer shell. I might not have known the man who walked and talked and went abroad among other men. But, at long last, my thoughts had touched his thoughts. Our minds had finally met.

Chapter 12

Until I reached the chimney stacks of London on Sunday evening, my mind remained with my father, but upon entering the suburbs at Uxbridge, I switched mental channels, forcing myself back to the present day, to Nigel and Macintyre.

Nigel came in very shortly after me. There was a couple of days' growth of stubble on his chin, his eyes were bloodshot and his face was grey with tiredness. 'Ah, you're here. Good weekend?'

'Lovely, thank you. How about you? All ready for the big day?'

'As ready as we can be.'

'What time's your meeting?'

'Not until two o'clock, thank God. We're catching the ten o'clock shuttle.'

'Who's going with you?'

'Bron and Liam. Do I have any clean shirts?'

'I hope so. I ironed a whole pile on Thursday.'

'Thank the Lord for that.'

Don't thank Him, I thought, thank me. But I held my tongue. This was not the time to start a row.

'And my suit went to the cleaners recently, didn't it?'

I nodded, thinking, yes, it walked there and back all by itself.

'Right, well, I'm going to bed. I'm knackered. And, for God's sake, don't let me oversleep in the morning.'

Neither of us slept well. Nigel tossed and turned all night, then, having thoroughly woken me, fell into a deep sleep just before the alarm sounded. I switched it off, got out of bed, put on my dressing gown and went into the kitchen, where I made us both coffee.

At a quarter past seven, he appeared in the kitchen doorway, where I was keeping out of his way. He was not, I noticed, wearing his usual hat, nor did he take Hugh with him. 'Right, I'm off now. See you tonight.'

'I hope everything goes well,' I said. 'I'll keep my fingers crossed.'

In the office, I seized the first opportunity to ring Tobin.

'Well, I'll be blowed, Amadore Angelini,' he exclaimed. 'I'd love to see those letters and the book. Any chance of meeting for a drink after work tonight?'

Very reluctantly, I replied, 'No, I'm sorry, I can't, not tonight.'

'Going out?'

I hesitated, then, deciding the subject of Nigel could not be skirted round for ever, told the truth. 'It's just that Nigel has an important appointment today up in Glasgow and I ought to be home when he gets back.'

'I see. Fair enough.'

'Maybe tomorrow evening?'

'No, I'm afraid tomorrow's out the question for me,' he said, and offered no explanation.

I felt the same irrational pang of something almost akin to jealousy as I had when first confronted by Consuela at Beadle Walk.

'But any time later in the week,' he continued. 'I'll leave it to you to get in touch.'

After putting the phone down I attacked my typewriter keys with unusual ferocity.

Nigel did not arrive home until after nine, which meant I could have met Tobin for a quick drink and still been home before him. But I wasn't to know that, and when he came in, looking totally drained, I was glad I was there. Returning to an empty flat could, as I well knew, be very dispiriting.

'How did it all go?' I asked.

'Oh, all right, I think.'

'Only all right?'

'It was impossible to know what they were thinking. They asked all the right questions and hopefully we gave all the right answers. Now it's just a matter of patience and prayer.'

'When will you know if you've got it?'

'A couple of weeks.'

'That long?'

'Remember, it's a major decision on their part. We're talking about huge sums of money. I've got the storyboards here, if you're interested in seeing what I've been doing for the last two and a half weeks.'

He went into the hall and returned with a large portfolio case, which he placed on the dining table and opened to reveal a stack of about fifteen white boards covered with detailed drawings. 'There are seven TV commercials and the press campaign,' he explained.

'*Seven* commercials?'

'People get tired of seeing the same ad coming up time after time on the screen. Well, this is the first one, which is the most dramatic and therefore has the strongest initial impact.'

He pointed to the first frame. 'We start here with a giant earthmover, in the desert, pushing a mountain of sand. The background music, incidentally, is "Wheels of Fire". You know the rock song?'

I nodded.

'There are clouds of dust and sand blowing up.' His finger moved across the frames. 'The sun's setting, so there's a glorious blood-red sky, giving loads of atmosphere. Then we have a close-up of a huge tyre showing the Macintyre logo. The dust clears and a figure gets out of the earthmover. Now we have a long shot of a four-wheel-drive vehicle coming towards us. It pulls up beside the earthmover and a bloke gets out and goes across to the driver of the earthmover, who's in the throes of taking off all the protective gear. Off comes the helmet and – lo and behold! – the driver of the earthmover is revealed as a girl. And up comes the copy line: "Macintyre for when the going gets tough".'

It would have required a total lack of generosity of spirit not to be impressed. 'It's going to look quite incredible,' I breathed. 'Where would you shoot it?'

'America probably.'

The rest of the storyboards – each commercial set on completely different, foreign locations – were just as impressive. The amount of work he had put in – and the quality of it – was staggering. 'Thank you for showing me,' I said. 'After seeing those, I simply can't believe that Macintyre won't give you the account.'

He shrugged. 'Let's hope you're right. But you win some and you lose some. And now, if you'll forgive me, love, I'm going to catch up on some beauty sleep.'

'Do you have to go in to work tomorrow?'

'If you could see my desk, you wouldn't ask that. It's groaning under the weight of paper. There's a month's backlog waiting for me.'

'What will happen if you do get Macintyre? You'll hardly have much time to work on other accounts as well, will you?'

'I wouldn't have time for anything else at all. But one thing at a time. We'll worry about that if and when it happens. And, if it does, it's the sort of problem I'll be more than happy to deal with.'

The stress of waiting, together with catching up on his backlog of work, told increasingly on Nigel as the fortnight progressed. Dealing with him was like trying to cross a minefield. The most innocuous comment and my head was bitten off. Even the simplest question, such as what he'd like for dinner that evening, brought a sharp retort. He continued to come home late and, when he was home, glued himself in front of the television set, venting his nervous tension on politicians, programme producers and commercials. I'd have had to have been a complete nincompoop to mention Oliver Lyon and introduce the subject of the Princess and my father.

I didn't ring Tobin either, although several times I had picked up the phone, then put it down again. I didn't want to inflict myself upon him, particularly if he was busy. Nor did I want to appear over-eager. Ours was only a friendship – and only a burgeoning one at that. It was much better that he should contact me. Yet, if I had put him off by my mention of Nigel, I wanted to set the matter straight – though quite how to do that I had no idea.

I wasn't the only one to suffer as a result Nigel's edginess. One evening, he burst in to announce, 'Some bastard's parked in my space.'

Peering out of the window, I recognized Roly's car and said, 'I'll go down and ask him to move it.'

Nigel was out of the door before I had chance to act. I could hear his voice coming up the stairwell, calling Roly a selfish sod, with no thought or consideration for others. And I could hear Roly saying, 'Steady on, mate. I'm just about to go out again. I'm sorry . . .'

The following evening, I called in on Sherry on my way home from work. 'I'm sorry about last night. Will you apologize to Roly, please?'

'Oh, it's OK, don't worry. Roly should have known better.'

'Nevertheless, Nigel was extremely rude. But, without wanting to sound as if I'm making excuses for him, he does have rather a lot on his mind at the moment.'

'Forget it. Roly will. Do you have time for a quick drink?'

'I'd love one.'

'Good. Any news about your Princess?'

'No, but I have learned more about my father.' I told her about the portrait at Beadle Walk and the letter mentioning the Angelinis.

'Sounds like you ought to go to Paris,' she said.

'I can't go haring off to Paris with Nigel in the state he's in,' I objected.

'I'm not suggesting you should. But if he does get the Macintyre account and goes to America . . .'

As the end of the second week of waiting approached, Nigel became increasingly hard to live with and my own patience started to give way. As always, it was a straw which broke the camel's back.

On the Thursday evening, when Nigel arrived home, I happened to be on the phone to Aunt Biddie, who was telling me the latest in the saga of the abbey clock. 'Basically, the whole town's divided,' she was saying. 'It's ancient versus modern. There are us conservationists against the vicar and his acolytes. I must admit I'm rather enjoying myself. Our side has decided that if our petition fails, we'll picket the church. Oh, and I meant to tell you earlier, the decorator's started on The Willows. He's such a nice young man. His name is Tom and I've won him on to our side . . .'

Nigel dumped his briefcase, threw his coat on to the floor and stomped into the living room, where he crashed about in evident protest. As soon as I could interrupt Aunt Biddie's flow, I explained that I had to go and went into the living room. 'Sorry, darling, that was Aunt Biddie.'

He didn't give me chance to continue. 'So I gathered. And I fail to understand why, when you've had all day to talk to her, you have to choose the very time when I come home.'

It occurred to me that he was like a spoiled child, who threw a tantrum whenever he failed to get his own way or found himself no longer the centre of attention. And, all these years, I had been pandering to his moods. As his mother had before me. 'It's his creative temperament,' I heard her saying, during one of her sentimental tête-à-têtes. 'One has to make allowances, dear.' I suddenly thought that what she should have done was given him a damn good hiding.

My patience snapped. 'For one thing, Aunt Biddie rang me. And for another, I haven't had all day to talk to her. I also work for my living, if you recall. As for *the very time* you come home, anyone would think that you came home at the same time every day. This is the first time you've been home before nine o'clock for as long I can remember.'

'There is a reason.'

'Yes, I'm aware of that and I've been making allowances. But there's a limit to how long I can go on doing so. I'm fed up to the back teeth with living like this. What's the point of being married when I never see you?'

One of the most infuriating things about losing your temper is that you are aware, even as your voice rises to a screech, that you're losing control of the situation.

Nigel's mouth hardened into a tight, thin line. 'Cara, I am extremely uptight and I can do without you picking a fight.'

I compounded the felony. 'I'm not picking a fight.'

'You are.'

'I'm not. You're the one who started it by coming home in a filthy mood. But there's nothing new in that. So you're uptight. Well, I, too, have things on my mind. But are you interested in them? No, there's one person and one person only in this world that matters to you and that's Nigel Sinclair. It's me, me, me, all the time with you. A marriage is supposed to be give and take, Nigel – and you're doing far too much taking for granted.'

He let out a drawn-out, long-suffering sigh. 'Macintyre just happens to be the most important thing ever to happen to me in my whole career.'

'And your career is more important than your wife?'

'Frankly – at this precise moment – yes, it is.'

I slammed out of the room and came to a halt in the hall. When you're a child, under such circumstances, you can seek refuge in your bedroom, but when you're married even that sanctuary is denied you. I thought of going down to Sherry and Roly's but my pride forbade me.

Finally, I kicked his briefcase and went into the kitchen, again slamming the door behind me. Then I forced myself to calm down and put together a meal, which we ate in stony silence and at the end of which Nigel got up from the table and went off to the study.

We spent that night sleeping back to back.

The following morning, Tobin rang me.

'I've just heard some quite incredible news,' he said. 'Any chance of meeting up in the near future?'

I wasn't going to make the same mistake as last time and the likelihood of Nigel being home early that evening, after our row the previous night, seemed extremely remote. 'This evening?' I suggested.

'Great! I'll see you outside your office at about half past six.'

At twenty-five past six, Sergeant rang to announce, 'Mrs Sinclair, it's Sergeant here. Mr Touchstone has just arrived. He says he's early, but I thought you'd want to know. Shall I send him up?'

'No, thank you, Sergeant, I'll be down in a few moments,' I replied, making a mental note to arrange to meet Tobin at Chattertons in the future.

'Poor old Sergeant,' Tobin said, when I came down the stairs. 'The night porter's late yet again. I hope you put in for overtime, Sergeant.'

'I certainly do,' Sergeant informed him. 'It's double pay after five o'clock. Well, have a nice evening – both of you.'

Feeling like wringing his neck, I gave him a sweet smile.

When we were settled in Chattertons, Tobin said, 'Before I give you my news, you don't have those letters with you by any chance?'

I took them and the book from my briefcase. After reading through the letters several times, he opened the book, turning the pages almost reverently, his eyes scanning the lines of verse. 'Amazing,' he murmured. Then he looked up at me. 'You know, whenever I read poetry like this – so intensely personal – I always wonder at the courage of the poet in baring his soul to the public view. Emily Dickinson once wrote, "Publication is not the business of poets." I can't help wondering if your father agreed with that sentiment, which was why he never had anything more published.'

'You think he may have written more which he never showed anyone?'

'He must have been doing something all the time he was in Paris. Writing poetry – like any other creative art form – is a compulsion, not something to be switched on or off at will.'

He handed the book and letters back to me. 'Now let me tell you what I've been up to. Last Tuesday, when I was unable to meet you, I was actually at Beadle Walk with some experts from Christie's . . .'

Imagination, I reflected wrily, could be more of a curse than a blessing.

'Probate, incidentally, has finally been granted and the house is on the market. All the contents have been cleared and everything of any value, which Harvey doesn't want at Kingston Kirkby Hall, is in safe storage at Christie's. It's due to come up for auction in the late summer.

'Well, one of the experts was a Mr Ffolkes, who specializes in contemporary art and I showed him the two portraits. They were "interesting", he said, very much looking down his nose at them. Angelini he dismissed as a traditional portraitist, hardly known in England, though with a certain "cult" following on the continent. Rather reluctantly, he admitted that the Angelini portrait was, technically, better executed than the El Toro. On the other hand, because El Toro has achieved universal recognition, if I did want to sell that portrait in London, there should be no great difficulty in finding a buyer. I think he might have been a bit more enthusiastic if I'd been disposing of them. As it was, he didn't have anything to gain.

'There was a marked difference between his attitude to those two paintings and that of the Russian expert, when he saw the icon. He was incredibly excited about that – well, as far as those sort of people get excited about anything. It appears to be fifteenth century from the Novgorod school and worth far more than the El Toro and the Angelini put together. Which pleased Harvey no end, when I told him. I think he was having second thoughts about giving me the portraits.'

Tobin took his cigarettes from his pocket, glancing at me with a mischievous glint in his eyes.

'Did Mr Ffolkes know anything more about Angelini? You did explain . . . ?'

When he had lit us both cigarettes, he said, with exaggerated casualness, 'Oh, yes, I explained that I was interested in learning more about the artist's life and Mr Ffolkes was able to tell me that he lived in Paris between the wars and apparently returned to Italy at the outbreak of World War Two. Unfortunately, he didn't know where in Italy. Neither did he know what happened to him after that.'

He paused deliberately.

'And?' I asked, sensing there was more.

'Well, he suggested that if I really wanted to find out more, I should contact a certain art expert in Paris. However, he would have to come back to me with the relevant details as he didn't have them on him at the time. He rang me this morning. And the expert's name is . . .' He stopped and grinned. 'Come on, have a guess.'

'I can't.'

'Go on, try.'

'I've no idea.'

'OK. It's Prince Ludo Zakharin.'

My mouth fell open and Tobin burst into a great hoot of laughter.

'Prince Ludo Zakharin?' I eventually managed to stutter.

'He's Dmitri's son. Presumably his mother was Imogen Humboldt.'

I shook my head. 'But that's – that's such an extraordinary coincidence.'

'Not really, not when you think about it carefully. The Princess, Dmitri, the Baron de St-Léon, Imogen Humboldt, El Toro, Angelini and your father were all in Paris at the same time and, even if they didn't move in exactly the same circles, they all knew each other.'

'But all the same—'

'Any coincidence lies in the fact that Mr Ffolkes should know Ludo Zakharin and even that isn't really a coincidence. It's to be expected that someone in Mr Ffolkes's position should be acquainted with all the main art experts in all the major cities of the world.'

'Yes, I suppose so.'

'Anyway, I telephoned Ludo Zakharin in Paris this morning, before I rang you, and was fortunate enough to get straight through to him. I didn't go into detail, but merely told him about my connection with the Princess, that I had inherited the two portraits and that Mr Ffolkes had given me his name.

'He actually knew exactly who I was. Apparently he had met Howard on a couple of occasions in Paris. He claimed he would have attended the Princess's funeral, if he had not been on vacation in Mauritius. It would have saved us a lot of time and speculation if he had.

'But to get to the point, he owns a gallery on the rue du Faubourg St Honoré – the Galerie Zakharin. Since he can hardly be short of a few bob, I assume it is a business interest rather than a full-time occupation. Nevertheless, he clearly knows his onions, for he asked a number of very pertinent questions about the two portraits. He was much more complimentary about Angelini's work than Mr Ffolkes had been, describing him as an extremely capable and versatile portraitist.

'Most of Angelini's paintings were commissioned by private individuals – as your father mentions in one of his letters. So it wasn't until the sitters started to die off, and the next generation didn't want a portrait of Grandpère Henri hanging in the drawing room, that his paintings began to find their way on to the market. When it transpired that many French celebrities of the time – Zakharin mentioned Giraudoux, Eric Satie and Georges Auric among others – had sat for him, Angelini's works began to gather increasing interest in France.

'He even went so far as to inform me that, should I decide to part with the portraits, he had a customer who would almost certainly offer a very good price.'

'Did he know anything about Angelini himself?'

'Very little, by the sound of it. He confirmed Mr Ffolkes's belief that Angelini returned to Italy upon the outbreak of the Second World War, after which he apparently gave up painting on a commercial basis. He died either during or just after the war.'

'He didn't know where Angelini lived in Italy?'

'He said that he'd never had any reason to try and find out.'

'Dmitri isn't still alive, is he?'

'It didn't sound like it, but there was a limit to the number of questions I could decently ask over the phone.'

For a few moments, we sat in silence, sipping our wine. Then he said, 'Other members of the Angelini family must still be alive. Do you know what I'd do in your position? I'd go and talk to Ludo Zakharin in person. I'd go to Paris.'

'Mmm. You're the third person in a week to say that. First Aunt Biddie, then Sherry – and now you.'

'Clearly a case of great minds thinking alike. So, why don't you? The good Miles child can't object to you taking a few days' holiday.'

'No, of course not.'

Tobin rubbed his hand over his chin, studying me across the table, in such a way that I was certain he could read my mind and knew that Nigel was the potential fly in the ointment. Sure enough, he said, 'And presumably your husband would let you off the leash for a few days as well, wouldn't he?'

I gave a non-committal shrug.

'You have told him about the Princess?'

I stared down at the table.

'You mean, he doesn't know?'

'No.'

'Why ever not?'

'Well, it may sound stupid, but I haven't had an opportunity to talk to him properly since Oliver Lyon's interview. He was in the Caribbean when that was shown and, immediately upon his return, his agency was asked to pitch for a big new account – Macintyre – they make tyres. That was the meeting he had to go to last week, when I couldn't meet you. He went up to Glasgow to make the presentation.'

'Yes, I see. And when does he know the outcome of that?'

'At the beginning of next week.'

'Hmm. And hasn't he shown any interest in what might have been happening to you while he's been beavering away?'

'Under normal circumstances, he would have done,' I said, leaping in on the defensive, the same as I did with Aunt Biddie, Miranda and Sherry. It was the result of years of habit: a mixture of ingrained loyalty towards Nigel and a reluctance to appear a fool or an object of pity myself. 'It's just that he's extremely uptight at the moment. There's a lot at stake for him. This could make or break his career. Which is why I haven't bothered him with something that's relatively unimportant. After all, my father's been dead a long time.'

Again, Tobin went, 'Hmm.'

'Which is one of the reasons why I wouldn't want to bother him about, say, going to Paris,' I floundered on.

'Yes, of course, that's perfectly understandable in the circumstances. Well, let's hope he wins the account. I'm sure he deserves it.'

'Oh, he does,' I assured him, while, at the same time, a little voice inside me was asking, 'Why are you doing this? Who are you trying to convince? Why are you going to such lengths to justify Nigel – and to Tobin of all people? If you had set out to put Tobin off, you couldn't be making a better job of it.'

My fears seemed confirmed when Tobin glanced at his watch and said, 'Well, I'd better not keep you any longer. I don't want you getting into trouble for being late.'

'There's no hurry,' I protested, but the joy had already gone out of the evening. I had driven it away.

'Come on. I've been married myself and know what it's like. Drink up and I'll drive you home. My car's parked just outside on a meter.'

'Oh, please don't bother, I can go by tube.'

'No, no, I insist.'

Something about his expression told me not to argue.

Tobin had a Fiesta as did I. He was the kind of driver I liked best, pulling into the traffic with quiet confidence, changing gears smoothly and braking gently, unlike Nigel, who always drove as though he were on a Grand Prix circuit.

'How are the Easter bunnies?' I asked, for want of any other neutral subject of conversation, as he drove down Piccadilly to Hyde Park Corner.

'All scampered away. I'm on my next job now – illustrating a brochure for an oil company, in which I'm supposed to make petrol appear environmentally friendly. Maybe your Nigel and I should pool our ideas . . .'

I didn't respond and, after that, neither of us said anything until we reached a complicated road junction at Camden, whereupon Tobin asked, 'Which way now?' Which way indeed?

'Oh, sorry, left, where it's signposted to Kentish Town.'

Once we were through the traffic lights, Tobin glanced at me. 'A penny for them.'

I stared straight ahead through the windscreen and shook my head. 'They're not worth it.'

When we reached Linden Mansions, I asked him to stop at the end of the drive. Leaving the engine running, he turned to me. 'Think about Paris, won't you?'

I nodded. 'Yes, I will. And thank you for everything.'

He took my face between his hands and kissed me, lightly and tenderly, on the lips, not at all as though it were the first time, but as if it had happened before and was, therefore, the most natural thing on earth.

Then he said, 'Don't worry. I understand.'

When I opened the door to the flat, it was to find all the lights were on. From the living room came the sound of a man's voice shouting excitedly against the cheering roar of a football crowd. I could still feel the touch of Tobin's hands on my face and his lips on my mouth. I took off my coat and went into the kitchen, not wanting to lose that sense of Tobin . . .

The living room door opened. Nigel's voice yelled, 'Cara, is that you?'

'Yes,' I replied reluctantly.

Heavy footsteps in the hall. A looming presence in the kitchen doorway. Then, 'Where the hell have you been?'

'Out for a drink,' I said, with a calmness I didn't feel, sure he must be able to see the imprint of Tobin's kiss.

'Great. That's really great,' he exclaimed, puffed up with self-righteous indignation. 'I was supposed to be going to a meeting this evening, instead of which I made a special effort to get home early. And what do I find? An empty flat. I wait and what happens? No telephone call. Nothing. So I get myself something to eat and watch the bloody television. And then you calmly walk in and announce you've been out having a drink. It didn't occur to you, I suppose, to inform me of your plans this morning?'

'If you'd warned me that you were coming home early, I'd have made other arrangements,' I replied.

'Arrangements! What arrangements? You just went out deliberately to annoy me, didn't you – to make a point?'

At that moment, from the living room, came shouts, cheers and boos, while the voice of the sports commentator rose to a frenzied pitch of excitement. 'No, it can't be! Yes, it is! I don't believe it! I really don't believe it.'

Nigel spun on his heel and went to find out what earth-shattering event had occurred. And he would doubtless blame me for making him miss the crucial moment in the game . . .

So much for making a special effort, for wasting his evening, for cancelling a meeting. I would have put money on it that the meeting he claimed to have missed was at a West End pub, watching this football match. It was infuriating, though, inadvertently to have played into his hands.

In the distance, there was more cheering, shouting and strains of song, then the television went quiet. When Nigel didn't reappear in the kitchen doorway, I realized it was being left to me to make the next move.

I thought of Tobin. I thought of Aunt Biddie. And I thought of the Princess. Taking a deep breath, I went into the living room, where Nigel was stretched out full-length on the settee, reading a magazine.

'Would you like a drink?' I asked.

'I've got a beer.' He didn't look up.

'Who won the match?'

'Why ask, when you don't even know who was playing?'

'What sort of day have you had?'

'For God's sake, can't you see I'm trying to read?'

'Sorry. I didn't mean to disturb you.'

He flung the magazine down on the carpet and sat upright on the settee. 'OK, so now you've made your point, you'd better to tell me about these important things that have been happening in your life. Come on, I'm all ears.'

'I wasn't making a point,' I said evenly.

At that moment, the telephone rang. As I went to answer it, I prayed the call wouldn't be for me. It wasn't. When Nigel came back from taking it, he said, 'That was Brian Turner. I'm playing golf tomorrow.'

Not trusting myself to speak, I simply nodded. Very soon after that, I went to bed.

After the golf match on Saturday, Brian came back with Nigel and stayed for dinner, during which they talked about cars the entire time, while I retired into my secret world. By the time I had washed up, they were both well lubricated and Nigel was talking about Macintyre. I went to bed and left them to it.

Sunday passed without incident. Nigel washed and polished his car, then went off to the pub for a game of darts with Brian. In the afternoon, he buried himself in the Sunday papers, while I – unable to get on with The Book, and on the basis that if you're going to have a bad day you may as well have a thoroughly awful one – cleaned the oven, which kept me out of Nigel's hair and accomplished one of my most hated jobs.

While I was up to my elbows in grease, I tried to decide whether or not I wanted him to win the Macintyre account. If he did get it, his mood would hopefully improve, but I wouldn't see him for months. And if Macintyre went to another agency, he would be even more impossible to live with, and his existing accounts would still take him away from home. On balance, the first alternative seemed preferable . . .

Chapter 13

I spent Monday tense as a coiled-up spring, finding it difficult to concentrate on anything. Fortunately, apart from my early morning session with Miles, sorting out his programme for the coming weeks, most of my tasks required only routine typing.

Eventually, at about four o'clock, my nerve gave out and I telephoned Nigel. The switchboard operator at Massey Gault & Lucasz asked who was calling, then said, 'I'm not sure if he's back from lunch yet. Hold on please.'

I waited for what seemed an interminable age before the switchboard operator said, 'I'm putting you through now.'

'Hello,' Nigel almost shouted against a background hubbub of excited voices.

'It's only me,' I said. 'I wondered if you had any news yet.'

'Yes, we learned this morning. We've got it!'

I sank back limply in my chair. 'Congratulations!'

'Yeah, it's great. I thought we probably would. But you can never be sure.'

'You could have let me know.'

'Sorry, events sort of took over. Liam wheeled in the champagne and we started celebrating.'

'Yes, it does sound rather as if there's a party going on. Well, I'd better leave you to your celebrations.'

'OK. Thanks for ringing, love. See you later.'

I put down the phone and sat very still, attempting to work up enthusiasm on his behalf, exhorting myself not to be selfish, reminding myself of all the effort he had put into the pitch and trying to convince myself that if anyone deserved success he did. As for not ringing me, well, it was possible that, in his position and the excitement of the moment, I too might have neglected to ring him and pass on the good news . . .

In a spirit of appeasement, I went into Fortnum and Mason's after work and bought Nigel's favourite food – Parma ham, melon, smoked salmon and fresh asparagus – together with some strawberries, cream and a bottle of champagne. When I reached home, I put the champagne in the fridge and prepared the meal, cutting the melon into fancy shapes and arranging it on a dish with the Parma ham; rolling the smoked salmon round the cooked asparagus tips and putting these on another plate; quartering the strawberries and marinating them in Port and sugar. Then, after laying the table complete with candles and the two remaining lead crystal champagne flutes from the set of wine glasses Aunt Biddie had given us as a wedding present, I sat down to wait.

By eleven o'clock, I had to conclude that the party had continued, cleared the table, made myself a smoked salmon and salad sandwich, and put the rest of the food in the fridge. When he still hadn't come home at midnight, I began to worry. At one in the morning and still no word from him, I had become convinced that he must have had an accident.

At half past one, I heard the diesel throb of a black cab in the drive. Peering out of the window, I could see Nigel reeling out of the back seat and staggering against the vehicle. Taking a deep breath I went downstairs to the main entrance.

'Hello, darling,' he mumbled, 'shorry I'm sho late. We've been shelebrating.'

'I think he's going to need a hand getting to bed, love,' the cabby informed me with a grin, handing Nigel back some change, which he promptly dropped on the ground and then proceeded to crawl around on his hands and knees trying to pick up.

Things like that just don't seem amusing when you are stone cold sober. 'Nigel, leave it,' I said irritatedly, pulling him to his feet. 'We'll find it in the morning.'

'Can you manage, love?' the cabby asked.

'I think so, thank you,' I replied stiffly.

Somehow or other we made it up the stairs and into the living room, where Nigel slumped onto the sofa. 'We've got Macintyre,' he announced. 'Good old Macintyre'sh come up trumpsh. God blesh Macintyre and all who shail in her. And I'm shmashed – totally shmashed. I'sh been drinking champagne shince ten o'clock thish morning.'

'Good for you.'

'Cara, don't be an old mishery. It'sh been the besht day of my life.'

Whereupon his head lolled back on the sofa and his eyes closed. I attempted to wake him but he was dead to the world, so I took off his shoes, lifted his legs up, fetched the duvet from the spare bed and laid it over him.

When I woke him in the morning with a mug of black of black coffee and a glass of Alka-Seltzer, he was in a very sorry shape. I went to work, leaving him to recover on his own, though when I reached the office, I did ring the agency to warn them that he would probably be late. Apparently, nobody in the art studio was in yet and the switchboard operator eventually put me through to Liam's secretary, who laughed. 'Oh, I'm not in the least surprised. When I left the pub last night Nigel was dancing on the table. It's fabulous news about Macintyre, isn't it?

'Yes,' I agreed, trying to infuse warmth into my voice, 'fabulous.'

The following evening, he came home early, still suffering from a hangover but contrite about having been so drunk. 'I didn't mean to,' he said. 'In fact, I was intending to come home and take you out to dinner. But Liam insisted on taking everyone to the pub and, you know how it is, one drink led to another.'

I nodded.

'I will still take you out, though. It's the very least I can do, after the way you've put up with me through all this. I am aware that I haven't been easy to live with.'

'You can say that again.'

He attempted a penitent smile. 'Cara, I'm sorry. I know I've been a selfish sod, but I'd put my absolute all into that presentation and, though I kept trying to reconcile myself to the possibility of losing, I simply couldn't bear the thought.'

'Yes, I do understand.'

'So, can we let bygones be bygones?'

'I suppose so.'

'Kiss and make up?'

We fitted the action to the words, though perfunctorily, without passion.

Then he said, 'I'm afraid I'm going to be really tied up for the rest of this week, so would you mind if we put our dinner off until Saturday? That way I won't have to worry about being late and we'll be able to relax properly and enjoy it.'

'Sure. Whenever you like.'

'I tell you what. You choose the restaurant. And don't worry about cost. This is your special treat. But if you wouldn't mind booking the table while you're at it . . .'

By the time Saturday came, Nigel had not only recovered from his hangover but all the tensions of the past weeks had left him. He whistled while he was getting up in the morning and did not return from the office like a bear with a sore head. It was almost as if the years had fallen away and he was once again the man I had married.

As Aunt Biddie was always saying, you should be thankful for small mercies. At least he had apologized and was trying to make amends. It would be petty-minded to continue to bear a grudge because of hasty words spoken in anger. Everyone said things in the heat of the moment which they later regretted, myself included. So I reserved a table at a French restaurant in Highgate Village, which was within walking distance and where the cuisine was sufficiently creative and the prices high enough to satisfy Nigel's criteria of a special evening out.

It might have been my special treat, but Macintyre dominated the conversation. Nigel described the verbal tussles he and Bron had had during their brain-storming sessions, laughing about some of the outlandish copy lines Bron had come up with, which would have been quite impossible to depict visually, before he had finally hit upon "for when the going gets tough".

'To use 'Wheels of Fire' as the theme music was my brainwave though,' Nigel bragged. 'Bron was really pissed off that he didn't think of that himself. I love getting one up on him.'

So it went on, until the opportunity finally arose for me to ask, 'So what happens next? When do you start making the commercials?'

'As soon as possible. First priority is to choose a production company. We've already started calling in showreels. There will probably be about thirty of them, each fifteen to thirty minutes long, which will mean sitting glued to a television set for two or three days. Tedious but necessary. Obviously, it's vital to get the right producer.

'Then we make a short list, pull in the favourite and hope they can work to our budget and timetable. That's going to be the main problem, I fear. We've only got three months until launch date at the beginning of July. The media department's already started buying space.

'Having found a producer, it will be all systems go – oh, you know, all the usual stuff, just on a much, much larger scale – finding the right locations, casting for models, making sure we can get the right vehicles in the right places, organizing flights, accommodation, location trucks and so on and so forth. Virtually as soon as we finish shooting the first one, we'll be starting on the second. You see what I mean when I say it's the biggest thing that's ever happened to me in my life?

'And, simultaneously, we'll be starting work on the press campaign, which will also be launched at the beginning of July. In between watching showreels next week, I'll be interviewing for a junior art director to do layouts and paste-ups, as well as looking at photographers' portfolios. Then Bron has to decide whether we should take on a new copywriter or assign one from elsewhere in the agency . . .'

'It doesn't sound as if I'll be seeing much of you,' I remarked.

He had the grace to look remorseful. 'No, I'm afraid not.'

'Oh, well . . .'

'Though, having said that,' he continued hurriedly, 'it shouldn't be all that much different from now. I mean, the next few weeks are going to be pretty fraught, but for most of the time, I'll be here in London. Though I'll probably have to go and look at the location before we shoot the first commercial and then I guess filming will take two to three weeks. However, the second one – the bikes – will be shot in Holland, so a bit nearer to home.'

'I see.'

'Oh, come on, cheer up.'

'I'm not uncheerful.'

'It's not going to be exactly a holiday for me, remember. It's going to be damned hard work. But it will be worth it in the long run.'

'I hope so.'

We lapsed into silence as a waiter cleared our plates. Then I said evenly, 'Since you're going to be so busy, I may go to Paris for a few days.'

'To Paris? What on earth for?'

'I thought I'd go and see Ginette.'

'I didn't realize you were still in touch with her.'

'Of course I am. She's one of my oldest friends.'

'Well, I suppose there's no reason why you shouldn't, if it makes you happy. I must confess that I've always considered Paris to be highly overrated. The art galleries and museums are great, but the rest of it . . . Give me New York any day.'

That night, Nigel made love to me for the first time since before

Christmas. It was over with before my body was even half-way prepared, leaving me with not even a lingering sense of dissatisfaction. Nigel let out a sigh, presumably intended to express pleasure but which sounded more like relief at a job over and done with. Then he rolled over and fell sound asleep.

The next few weeks were somewhat easier than those which had gone before and our personal life returned to something like normality. Despite being under considerable pressure and still keeping late hours, Nigel was much more relaxed. His group quickly came together. His new junior art director was a fellow car enthusiast, called Peter, while the junior copywriter, Gary, was already employed by the agency and merely had to change desks.

By the end of the week, the production company had also been selected. 'Talk about luck,' Nigel breathed. 'I never dreamed we'd be able to get BoCo – or, at least, I thought we might be able to get one of her colleagues, but not Bo Eriksson herself. She's very picky about what she works on – and ever since she won a Gold Award at Cannes a couple of years back, she can afford to be. But she loved the storyboards and came up with some great touches of her own.

'You know who Bo Eriksson is, don't you? Her grandfather was Willi Eriksson, one of the great pre-war Hollywood film directors. Her father was a scriptwriter and her mother an actress. I think she has a sister who's an actress, too. She runs BoCo with her twin brother, Sven. Bo's the creative one, the director, and he's the organizational brain, the producer. She's a quite amazing woman – simply bursting with energy and ideas. Personally, I think she's wasted making commercials. But who am I to argue? Hollywood's loss is my gain.'

After that, I heard so much about Bo Eriksson that I became as fed up with the sound of her name as I did with that of Macintyre and with hearing 'Wheels of Fire', which Nigel played incessantly whenever he was home.

Meanwhile, I wrote to Ginette, and when Aunt Biddie, Miranda and Sherry in turn asked if I had done anything about Paris, knew the satisfaction of telling them that I had set things in motion. Ginette replied by return of post, proposing that I came over at Easter, so that we could spend the maximum amount of time together.

To make sure there could be no turning back, I also rang Tobin.

'Congratulations,' he said. 'I'll give Ludo Zakharin a call and fix an appointment for you.' He paused. 'How are things otherwise? Did your husband win the Macintyre account?'

'Yes, he did.'

'Well, that is good news.'

'Yes, it is, very,' I said and then wondered why I was sounding so much more enthusiastic than I really felt.

Perhaps that was why Tobin did not suggest meeting for a drink. Or maybe he was busy trying to meet a deadline with his oil company brochure.

'Only one slight problem,' he said, when he called me back. 'Ludo Zakharin's intending to be out of Paris for the Easter weekend. But he could be available at three o'clock on the Thursday before. The good Miles child will give you the Thursday off, won't he?'

When, at the next suitable opportunity, I asked Miles if I could tag an extra day on to the Easter weekend, he readily agreed, telling me that my timing couldn't be better, because he was taking a long weekend himself at his house in Monte Carlo. 'I shall be coming back on Tuesday morning,' he added, 'so, if you want to do likewise, that's fine by me.'

A bit later in the day, Sir Utley Trusted's secretary rang to speak to Miles, explaining that it was in connection with Sir Utley's trip to Monte Carlo that weekend. I was not surprised. Miles seldom holidayed alone and he usually combined business with pleasure.

That same evening, Nigel came home bearing a bottle of champagne and exultant with the news that, in recognition for winning the Macintyre account, he had been promoted to senior art director and offered a partnership in the agency. 'From now on, it will be Massey Gault Lucasz *and Sinclair*,' he proclaimed. 'What's more, guess what car I'm going to be given!'

I shook my head, trying to adjust my mood to his.

'A Porsche 911 Sports Coupé!'

'Oh, how wonderful!' I exclaimed, wondering when he was going to have the opportunity to drive it, since he was going to be away so much. Then, for want of anything more intelligent to ask about it, I enquired, 'What colour will it be?'

The champagne must already have been flowing again during the day, for he did not take characteristic umbrage at this typically female question.

'Silver, of course,' he replied and popped the cork out of the bottle, so that it hit the ceiling.

'What's more,' he went on, when we had drunk to his success, 'I'm being given equity in the company and a bloody great pay rise. If you want to give up your job and become a lady of leisure, you can.'

The blood rose up in me – but I merely said sweetly, 'Thank you, darling. I don't think so.'

'Still, the offer's there. Oh, and incidentally, while I think of it, we're taking Bo and Sven out to dinner next Saturday. I thought we'd go to the Ivy. It's the sort of place Bo will love.'

On Friday, the red BMW drove away in the morning and, in the evening, a brand-new silver Porsche returned home in its place. The next day was bitterly cold, with flurries of snow in the air, but when I chanced to glance out of the window, there was Nigel holding court to a number of the male inhabitants of Linden Mansions – all of them apparently oblivious to the weather. Several had their heads in the engine compartment, while Roly was in the driver's seat, a blissful expression on his face.

A little later, I encountered Sherry. 'Aren't men the most extraordinary creatures?' she commented. 'Roly isn't normally the slightest bit interested in cars and he's certainly the first to complain about the cold. But take a look at him when you go out.'

'I've already seen.'

'Nigel's obviously doing very well for himself.'

'Mmm. He's just been promoted and given a partnership.'

'The next thing is you'll be moving,' she prophesied. 'Linden Mansions won't be grand enough for you.'

She was very perspicacious. At lunchtime, Nigel said, 'Maybe we should think about moving. The Porsche shouldn't live outside. We need somewhere with a garage. I wouldn't mind going back to Islington or Camden. That area's becoming very trendy. Bo's buying a flat overlooking the Regent's Canal . . .'

I was not looking forward to dinner with Bo and, determined not to let my side down, took extra special care with my appearance. During the week, I had gone to Oxford Street and bought a classically simple black dress – knee-length, sleeveless, with a high neck and quite tight-fitting, like the one Audrey Hepburn wore in *Breakfast at Tiffany's* – and a pair of new black shoes.

My hair was in need of a trim, which meant it was just long enough to pin up in a top-knot, which added an edge of elegance. Once I had put on the drop pearl earrings and matching brooch Aunt Biddie had given me for my twenty-first birthday, the image which was reflected back at me reminded me very vaguely of the Princess.

'God, you're looking very smart,' Nigel remarked, when I entered the living room. 'I suppose that means I'd better go and change as well.'

We were late leaving home, because he couldn't make up his mind which wide-brimmed hat to wear or whether Hugh should come with us. In the end, Hugh came too. 'You never know who we might bump into,' Nigel explained. Upon reaching the West End, we had problems finding a suitable parking place for the precious Porsche, but we still reached the Ivy before Bo and Sven, who turned up a quarter of an hour after us. Unusually, though, Nigel was quite calm about being kept waiting. Indeed, I sensed an unfamiliar nervousness about him.

It was difficult to tell what age Bo and Sven were but, during the course of the evening I worked out that they must be a couple of years older than me. They were as identical as twins of different sexes can be: tall, fair-haired, blue-eyed and good-looking in a Scandinavian sort of way.

Having said that, Bo was by no means a blond bombshell. She wasn't wearing much make-up and you could see she had spent a lot of time in the sun, for there were little wrinkles round her eyes. She was dressed simply in a blouse and skirt and her only jewellery was a sturdy, practical-looking watch. Her handshake was firm and she spoke in a strong American accent.

It was soon obvious that she was the more dominant of the pair. She took charge of the conversation from the very beginning, taking advantage of the Ivy's theatrical associations to launch into a string of anecdotes about her family and their Hollywood connections. Under different circumstances, I might have found her stories quite interesting, despite the name-dropping. As it was, I kept thinking, 'Just who are you trying to impress?'

That was actually quite difficult to tell, for, although Nigel was hanging on her every word, she seemed mainly to be addressing me. And each time he tried to guide the conversation back towards himself and work, she would say something along the lines of, 'Don't let's talk shop tonight. It's not fair on Cara.'

She had been married to a stuntman. 'His name was Jan and, like most Poles, he had a real mad streak,' she said. 'I don't think he knew what fear was, so he'd take the craziest risks, just for the sake of it, just to prove that he could do something. He was killed jumping from a plane. His parachute was supposed to open once he was out of camera, but something went wrong. The accident was hushed up and I was paid compensation, but all the money in the world couldn't make up for Jan's death. You know, I still miss that guy like crazy, even after all this time.

'I didn't want to stay in America after that. Sven had just gotten divorced, so we decided to come to London and start a new life for ourselves. And it's panning out just great.'

I couldn't help but feel impressed by her courage.

She expressed concern about me being left at home while Nigel was away filming. 'That's how Sven's marriage broke up,' she explained. 'His wife got tired of never seeing him and I don't blame her. Nigel, you got to look after Cara real good before we start filming. How about you take her away somewhere for a long weekend? Easter's coming up. You could drive up to Scotland in that new car of yours.'

'Well, I suppose so,' Nigel said doubtfully. 'But it would be cutting things a bit fine. If we're intending to leave on the ninth to look at locations, I can't really afford to take time off immediately before.'

'It's all right,' I told Bo. 'Knowing Nigel was so busy, I've already made arrangements to go to Paris for the Easter break.'

She cast me an appraising glance. 'You got friends in Paris?'

'Yes, I'm meeting up with an old girlfriend. We haven't seen each other for years. I'm really looking forward to it.

'Well, that's OK then.'

'Have you decided where you'll be shooting the commercials?' I asked her.

'We don't know the exact locations yet, but the first one will probably be shot somewhere in the Mojave or Colorado Desert, behind Los Angeles. That's wild country. Do you know California?'

'No, I've never been to the States.'

'Nigel should take you some time.'

I left the Ivy feeling better than when I had arrived. Bo was a strange mixture. But whatever had gone on in her past, she had emerged as one tough cookie, with Career Woman written large all over her. Nigel was finally meeting his match.

When we were in the Porsche, Nigel, having manoeuvred his way through the Theatreland traffic round Shaftesbury Avenue, turned to me accusingly. 'You didn't tell me you'd arranged to go to Paris.'

'You didn't tell me you'd arranged to go to America.'

'You knew it was likely to happen.'

'Indeed. That's why I went ahead and made my own plans.'

We completed the rest of our journey home in silence.

The evening before I went to Paris – just over a month since our last meeting – I saw Tobin again. At my suggestion, without going into any explanation, we met at Chattertons. Sod's law, of course, Sergeant wasn't on duty that evening.

What's more, my initial nervousness, in case there was any awkwardness between Tobin and myself, also proved quite unnecessary.

'All set and raring to go?' he asked, after pouring our wine.

'Yes, and I'm looking forward to it tremendously.'

'Excellent. I've put together some bits for you to take with you.' He reached into his battered old document case and took out a hard-backed envelope. 'In here are some photographs of the two portraits, so that you'll have something to show our friend Ludo – I beg your pardon, Prince Zakharin. And also the address and telephone number of the gallery. It's in the rue du Faubourg St Honoré, so it should be easy enough to find.'

'Are you thinking of selling the portraits?'

'I promised you I'd keep them, in case you changed your mind.'

'No,' I said firmly. 'It was very kind of you to offer them to me, but I don't want them. And, if you don't want them either, then I think you should sell them.'

He looked at me searchingly, then nodded. 'Well, let's see what Ludo Zakharin has to say. Now, I've also put the portrait of Dmitri from the Princess's dressing table in with this envelope. It's up to you whether you show it to Ludo Zakharin or not. If you do and he expresses a desire to keep it, then, so far as I'm concerned, he can have it. It will be most intriguing to see how he reacts to your story. I do hope he's helpful.'

'If not, I can still have a nice weekend. It's ages since I've seen Ginette.'

'What does she do for a living?'

'She's a secretary like me. She works for a pharmaceutical company.'

'Is she married?'

'No, though I don't know why not, because she's a very attractive girl.'

'There is a life outside marriage,' Tobin pointed out with a grin.

I could have kicked myself.

He changed the subject. 'I've been meaning to ask you for some time how your attempt to emulate Stevie Smith is progressing. You are still writing, aren't you?'

'When I get the opportunity.' I was, in fact, up to something like page sixty and finding it increasingly difficult. Writing about my youth had been hard enough, but describing my married life, which contained so much that was uncomfortable, was proving almost impossible. Yet I was persevering, for I knew he had been right when he told me to lance the boil.

'Does it have a title yet?'

'No and I don't think it ever will.'

'Are you going to let me read it?'

'I don't know.'

'I'd like to, very much. I have a feeling it's better than you think.' He glanced at his watch. 'And now, I'm not rushing you, but I expect you still have to pack and presumably prepare a meal for your husband. Or is he abroad again?'

'Not until next month. He's going to America a couple of days after I return from Paris.'

'Sounds like a bit of bad timing somewhere.'

'Oh, he's only going on a recce for a few days,' I said without really thinking. Then I realized I had done it again, making it sound as if I was going to miss Nigel.

Tobin didn't pick up on my remark this time. Instead, he delved again into his document case and took out a little box. 'Before you depart, there is one last thing.'

Nestling inside the box on a bed of cotton wool lay the silver pendant of the two-headed horse with the little bells.

'I've been doing a bit of homework on this,' he continued. 'I assumed it was Russian, but it's not. It's a copy of an ancient, traditional Finnish design, which dates back to the time of the Crusades. I imagine it originally had some kind of symbolic purpose, but I haven't been able to find out what.'

'Finnish? That's rather odd, isn't it?'

'Probably not as odd as it sounds. Finland was a Russian grand duchy until the Revolution, after which it gained its independence.'

He closed the box and handed it across the table to me. 'I'd like you to have it. It's not much, I know, but the mere fact that the Princess kept it indicates that it must have been important to her.'

'Are you sure?'

His eyes twinkled. 'I can't visualize myself or Harvey ever wearing it.'

'Thank you. That's very kind. I shall treasure it.'

He stood up. 'I'm sorry, I don't have the car with me today, so I can't give you a lift home. But I will see you to the tube.'

Outside the station, he stopped and cupped my face in his hands. 'Enjoy yourself in Paris – and no falling for the charms of Ludo Zakharin, eh?'

As he had done before, he kissed me on the lips, gently and briefly. Then, with a smile, he turned and walked away down the road.

CHAPTER 14

Travelling on your own is quite, quite different from going with someone else. Just how different I had forgotten until I reached Heathrow Airport. After booking in, I mingled with the cosmopolitan crowd on the concourse, revelling in the sense of being footloose and carefree, and immensely glad Nigel wasn't with me, chafing impatiently at the waste of time, finding no pleasure in the anticipation of the journey ahead, wanting only to arrive as quickly as possible.

I studied the departures board. There was such a lot of world, so why did one spend so much of one's life in one little patch? Or, more properly, why did *I* spend it in one little patch? Why was Nigel always flying off somewhere, while I stayed at home – apart from two weeks' holiday each year, spent on a beach of Nigel's choosing – when it was I, as a girl, who had longed to travel?

Oh, there were plenty of reasons: duty, responsibility, the need to earn a living and amass possessions; even that besetting need of mine to belong somewhere and be part of the main. But, looking at that departures board and all the other passengers in the airport, none of those reasons seemed quite good enough.

A line from one of my father's poems sprang to my mind:

Others are young and dance: oh, why can't I?

I tried to imagine myself as a free and independent spirit, unfettered by any ties, at liberty to go wherever I liked and do whatever I chose. Imagine not having to return to the Goodchild Group. Imagine not having to return to Linden Mansions . . .

The beginning of another of my father's poems sprang to my mind:

Birds of passage belong to no real land:
They settle, rest, fly further on their way;
And who's to miss them if they never do come back?

Miles would soon find a another secretary to replace me. After all, nobody was indispensable. Nigel, too, would survive without me. He would be inconvenienced with nobody to do his washing, ironing, cleaning and cooking, but beyond that he wouldn't really miss me . . .

So where would I go? Rio de Janeiro? Hong Kong? Cairo? Athens? Mexico City? Vladivostok? Johannesburg? Melbourne? Or Paris? I smiled to myself as my own flight details appeared on the board. One step at a time . . . And Paris, though it might not be far away, promised excitement enough for the immediate future.

I was lucky on the plane to be allocated a window seat, just in front of a wing, with a middle-aged businessman beside me, who took a large file from his briefcase, which he proceeded to study intently. Out of habit, I glanced at the heading at the top of the typed sheet. It was the name of a company, but not one of which I had ever heard. Then, aware that my idle curiosity could be misconstrued as nosiness, I turned my head to look out of the window, reflecting how very odd it was that things important to each of us individually meant nothing to others.

The plane's engines revved, we set off down the runway and eventually rose into the sky. Air hostesses served coffee and croissants, then wheeled round trolleys of duty-free goods.

My trouble was that I was stuck in a rut – a well-paid, comfortable rut, to be sure – but a rut nevertheless. Come to that, I was stuck in two ruts – that of my job and that of my marriage.

My marriage was an insoluble problem, so I thought about my job. Did I really enjoy it? Did it fulfil some deep inner need? Come on, be honest. No, not really. I created nothing. I did nothing in which to take pride or that benefitted mankind. So why did I go on doing it? My chances of promotion were absolutely zilch. I had reached the top of my particular career ladder.

Then why, when Nigel had suggested the other day that I could give up work, had I not even stopped to consider becoming a lady of leisure?

Was it the money? I had always placed great importance on being independent, financially and in every other respect. When I was pregnant, the prospect of being totally dependent upon Nigel had worried me a lot. That was one of the little legacies of being an adopted child. Having been beholden to other people throughout my childhood, I wanted to stand on my own two feet once I was an adult.

So, yes, money did play a role. But not in the mercenary sense. Money and possessions weren't essential to me in the same way as they were to Miles or even to Nigel. Then why did I stay at Goodchild? Because I had become part of the organization. Because I felt secure there. Because I felt needed. Because my colleagues were also my friends . . .

Oh, it was such a little world that I inhabitated – Avonford, Linden Mansions and Wolesley House – peopled by so few close friends – Aunt Biddie, Miranda, Sherry, Juliette and, now, Tobin.

Take Tobin. Wasn't his the ideal existence? He lived on his own, answerable to no one, and did the work he enjoyed best. His pictures probably weren't great works of art – not having seen any, I couldn't be sure, of course – but they had the merit of being original and therefore unique, as did Miranda's pottery, as did my father's poems.

Take my father, for that matter. He wouldn't have put up with my sort of life. He had been a rebel, going against the tide, refusing to conform to the conventions of society. He had broken free, time and time again, to follow the dictates of his own heart.

So I made myself think positively. If I left Goodchild, where would I go? Back to somewhere like Jacksons, where I would have the opportunity to travel more and meet more people of my own age and younger? Or what about advertising – on the principle of if you can't beat 'em, join 'em? No, that really wasn't my scene. I couldn't stand working all day with people like Bron and Bo – or even Nigel. What about PR? I should be able to write press releases – and I'd meet stacks of people. But would they be my kind of people – or more phonies?

Then there was publishing. Imagine working for a publisher, like Stevie Smith had done. But would I be any happier working in publishing than my father had been? He had found the work depressing, Aunt Biddie had said, because he wanted to write himself and not spend his days reading what other people had written.

I could understand that. Reading books for pleasure must be quite different to reading them as a profession. And it must be very dispiriting for a would-be unpublished author to be confronted daily by the works of successfully published authors. I wouldn't be able to work for a publishing company and continue writing The Book, even in my own time. Comparison would not inspire but demoralize me.

Did I have to work for someone else? Couldn't I, too, be self-employed? Doing what, though? I couldn't paint or pot. Apart from my languages, I had no specialist area of expertise. Translating was the only obvious option open to me and for that I lacked the formal qualifications. In any case, I didn't want to spend all day and every day translating somebody else's words from one language to another. That was not the solution to my problem.

We were crossing the Channel by then and, moments later, flew over the French coastline. I relegated my problems to the back of my mind, to return to when I arrived back in England, and thought instead of the huge adventure of my first-ever trip to France, by train. Plane travel in those days had been the province of only the very rich.

Gazing down on the flat countryside of northern France, interspersed by the wide rivers after which so many battles of the First World War had been named, I remembered my excitement and nervousness as the train had headed towards Paris. Horses had still worked the fields then and, on the approach to Paris, I had been struck by the long rows of poplar trees.

Ginette, her parents and younger brother had been waiting for me at the Gare du Nord. They had recognized me from my photograph, although I hadn't recognized them. Her father had rushed up to me, cried, 'Bonjour, Cara', taken me in an embrace, kissed me on both cheeks, and then burst into a virtually incomprehensible volley of French. The Krystals had been so kind to me – like Pia's family in Bologna had been kind to me. How fortunate I had been over the years to meet so many kind people, who had taken me to their hearts.

I wondered whether Ginette would still look the same and how we would get on after not seeing each other for so long. In my last letter, I had warned her that I had an appointment that afternoon, but not gone into detail. She was taking the day off work, too, and meeting me at the airport. Since my plane was due to land at eleven o'clock French time, that would allow us four hours to catch up with each other before going to the Galerie Zakharin.

The air hostesses cleared away our plastic plates and cups. The pilot's voice asked us to extinguish all cigarettes and re-fasten our seat-belts. The plane turned slightly and began its descent towards Charles de Gaulle

Airport, and through my window appeared the outskirts of Paris. In the far distance I could just distinguish Sacré Coeur.

The businessman beside me packed his papers back in his briefcase, then sat, drumming his fingers on the lid, and I was reminded of Nigel. But he wasn't Nigel. Nigel was in London. For five whole days, I could forget him.

Once off the plane, I felt none of the leisurely detachment I had experienced at Heathrow. All I wanted was to be reunited with my suitcase, get through customs and passport control, and find Ginette.

We recognized each other simultaneously. She had changed, but only for the better. The rather gauche awkwardness of her younger years was gone, replaced by a very Parisian poise and chic. Her light brown hair was dressed in a soft, upswept style and her make-up was immaculate. She had lost weight too, and looked extremely svelte in a beautifully tailored calf-length black skirt with a cream jacket, a scarf draped elegantly round her neck, and high-heeled, black boots.

I was wearing one of my favourite outfits, which was casually smart and easy for travelling: a beige jersey trouser suit and low-heeled brown suede ankle boots, with a three-quarter length camel coat, but in comparison to Ginette, I felt suddenly scruffy and rather down at heel.

Exclaiming in French, 'Cara! How marvellous to see you again!', she flung her arms round me, as her father had done, twenty years earlier on the platform at the Gare du Nord, and kissed me twice on each cheek. Then, holding me by the arms, she said, 'I have been looking forward to this weekend so much. How many years is it since we last met? You have not changed at all.'

'*Toi non plus*,' I assured her.

Our arms linked, we went through the ultra-modern circular airport to the departure point for buses to the Porte Maillot terminal. 'You wrote that you have an appointment this afternoon,' she said, as the bus sped us towards the city centre. 'So, what would you like to do? Shall we go to my apartment first and leave your suitcase and then have some lunch?'

'That's fine by me.'

'Where is your appointment?'

'In the rue du Faubourg St Honoré.'

'Ah, in the centre of town – that is easy.'

For the rest of the bus ride, we caught up on each other's family news.

At Porte Maillot, we dived down into the metro and took the underground to Villiers. Up on the street again, the indefinable atmosphere of Paris assailed me. That smell which is a mixture of dust and petrol fumes and horse chestnut blooms and garlic and freshly baked baguettes. That sound which is a mixture of voluble French tongues, the screeching of car tyres, the clamour of car horns. The suburban houses and shops which bear no resemblance at all to the houses and shops of suburban London.

Ginette lived in an old building, with a small courtyard in the middle, guarded over by an elderly, sharp-eyed concierge, to whom Ginette introduced me. 'We call her Madame Guillotine,' she giggled, as we went up the stairs and I felt reassured. Beneath Ginette's sophisticated exterior still lurked the friend of my youth.

Her first-floor flat was much smaller and cosier than mine at Linden Mansions, but, as she said, ample for her needs. My room was comfortable, with a double divan, a heavy wooden wardrobe and chest-of-drawers. Hanging the wall was a brightly coloured woven rug and a Buffet print.

'I'm afraid I don't have a car,' Ginette said, as I unpacked my few things. 'Shall we walk down to St Honoré or would you rather take the metro?'

'Oh, let's walk.' Then I glanced at her boots.

She correctly interpreted my look. 'Don't worry, they're very comfortable. There's a little restaurant in the rue Rennequin, which serves the most delicious fish. We could eat there . . .'

She was right about the fish. We had sole with a mouth-watering white butter sauce, *pomme frites* such as only the French can cook, and a mixed salad in which lettuce was far from the staple ingredient. It was all washed down with a white wine that was twice as good and a quarter the price of any you could find in London.

We continued our conversation from where we had left off earlier. Having dealt with our families, we moved to our jobs. I hinted at my thoughts on the plane flying over and Ginette laughed. 'I know exactly what you mean. My life too often seems to consist of just *metro, boulot, dodo*.'

Underground, work, sleep summed up my existence pretty succinctly.

'But today there is no *boulot*,' she said. 'So, tell me who you are going to see on the rue du Faubourg St Honoré.'

'It's a long story,' I warned her.

'I like long stories, so long as they have a happy ending.'

'I'm not sure of that yet.'

Once again, but for the first time in a foreign language, I told her all about the Princess and my father. As I spoke, doubtless helped by the wine, my French became increasingly fluent, words that I had all but forgotten springing suddenly to memory.

When I had finished and shown her my father's letters, Ginette exclaimed, '*Mais c'est incroyable, tout ça!*' She studied me thoughtfully, then said, 'It's possible, I suppose, that you could be the daughter of a princess – you have the composure, the *sang-froid*. But the daughter of a Russian princess – no. You are too English – you do not have the temperament to be a Russian.'

'The Princess Shuiska was very cool and collected.'

'How old was she?'

'Eighty.'

'And near to death. But in her youth, she had been wild. *Ma chère Cara*, you have never been wild.'

'My father was.'

'All the more reason then why this Princess was not your mother.'

I didn't argue with her.

'May I come with you to meet the Prince Zakharin?' she asked.

'I sincerely hope you will. I think I'll need some moral support.'

At just before three that afternoon we were in that most select of all Parisian streets, the rue du Faubourg St Honoré, with the President's residence, the Palais de l'Élysée, at one end and lined with the great fashion houses.

The Galerie Zakharin had canopies over its two windows and central entrance. A single painting stood in one window, against a draped background of blue satin threaded with gold. In the other, against more of the same material, was a statue of a girl dancer in an intricately detailed costume, on a marble plinth.

I looked at Ginette, took a deep breath and opened the door. Inside, an ornately uniformed French equivalent of Sergeant – almost a double for General de Gaulle – rose majestically from behind a desk and peered superciliously at us. '*Bonjour, Mesdames.*'

Resisting the feeling he gave me that I was something the cat had dragged in, I stated, '*J'ai un rendezvous avec le Prince Zakharin.*'

'*Comment vous appelez-vous?*'

'*Madame Sinclair.*'

'Oui, madame. Un instant.'

He picked up a phone and communicated our presence to another person. Then he indicated the door to our left and said, '*On vous attend par là.*'

That door opened and a middle-aged man bowed us in, very distinguished looking and more respectful in his manner than the commissionaire. '*Bonjour, Mesdames. Entrez, s'il vous plaît. Monsieur le Prince sera à vous dans un moment.*'

As I stepped forward, my feet sank into a deeply piled carpet and my nostrils were greeted with an aroma that, if it could have been bottled, would have been named 'Opulence'.

The room ahead was probably a hundred feet long. The walls were hung with pictures, each individually lit by a lamp with a porcelain shade, and interspersed with columns, some purely decorative, others bearing statuettes and sculptures. At the centre was a table and some chairs.

An ornamental door at the far end of the room opened and another man approached, whose resemblance to Prince Dmitri in the photograph which had stood on the Princess's dressing table and was now in my shoulder bag, was so strong that he could only be Ludo Zakharin. He had the same thick black hair, dark eyes and features not regular enough to be described as handsome, yet which conveyed the overall impression of an extremely attractive man – one, moreover, who was fully aware of his attractiveness.

About six feet tall, he was slimly built and moved with a supple grace, his figure enhanced by a dark grey suit of excellent cut. His skin was tanned an expensive olive brown, intensified by the blue of his shirt. I couldn't help noticing his feet, which were very neat and small for his height, yet did not seem out of proportion with the rest of his body.

His smile revealed even white teeth but did not extend to his eyes, as his glance moved swiftly between Ginette and myself, then rested on me. 'Mrs Sinclair?'

Was it my face or my clothes or both which gave me away?

'I am Prince Zakharin.' He spoke in English, with a faint American, more a mid-Atlantic, accent, stressing the word Prince.

'Thank you very much for seeing me,' I responded in French, holding out my hand. The hand which took mine was small, like the feet, and the skin very smooth.

'The pleasure is all mine,' he claimed, lifting his chin and looking at me down his nose, so that I had a perfect view of his nostrils. His manner reminded me of the Princess. He had that same regal bearing and autocratic demeanour.

'This is my friend, Mademoiselle Krystal,' I said.

'*Enchanté, Mademoiselle,*' he said, expressionlessly, in perfectly accented French. Then, continuing in French and addressing himself to me: 'You come on a mission from Mr Touchstone?'

'Partly. I believe he has spoken to you on the telephone about two portraits in his possession of the Princess Hélène Shuiska, one by El Toro and one by Amadore Angelini. I have brought photographs of them with me, if you would be interested in seeing them.'

'Very much so. Let's go and sit down.' He led us to the table in the middle of the room. Whenever I think of Ludo Zakharin, the image of that table and those chairs returns to my mind. The chairs were extraordinarily beautiful, deep and rounded, the black-painted woodwork lacquered and painted with birds. The table consisted of a grey marble top, supported not by legs but by four birds, made out of a silvery-bronze and highly stylized in design: long and sleek, with curved tails and outstretched wings on which the table top rested. Their plumage was intricately detailed and their feet formed the claw over the ball on which the table stood. They were beautiful, but hard as the metal out of which they had been cast.

When we were seated, I reached into my bag and took out Tobin's photographs of the two portraits.

Ludo Zakharin stared at them long and hard. Then he said, 'So these are the portraits. I was aware of them, although I've never seen them. The Princess would never allow them even to be put on exhibition, let alone sell them. My father, Prince Dmitri, tried many times to persuade her to part with them, but she always refused. She claimed they were among her most precious belongings, beyond value so far as she was concerned. Mr Touchstone gave me to understand on the telephone that he was not considering selling them. Has he changed his mind?'

I hesitated, feeling my way cautiously. 'He's undecided. Before he comes to a final decision, he'd like to learn a little more about their history – and about the artists themselves, particularly Angelini. So would I, which is why I'm here.'

He looked at me in a strange manner. 'Were you acquainted with the Princess?'

'No, I saw her in a recent television interview, that's all.'

'Ah, yes, an English friend of mine told me about that programme. So your connection is not with the Princess herself but with Mr Touchstone?'

Perhaps it was only my imagination, but he seemed to be insinuating, by his tone, that my connection with Tobin was not entirely innocent. The blood rushed to my cheeks, less in embarrassment than annoyance.

'I think I should explain that my father was Connor Moran,' I said, in what I hoped was a haughty tone.

For a moment, he did not react at all. His features remained frozen. Even his eyes did not blink. Then he murmured, '*Grand Dieu!* Yes, of course, the hair. *Voilà qui explique beaucoup*. It's bizarre, I've been thinking that there was something familiar about you. I kept feeling as though we had met before, although I knew we hadn't.'

'So you know of my father?'

'*Mais bien sûr.* Connor Moran was one of my mother's protégés, whom she tried to help in his career when she lived in Paris before the war.'

'Did she often speak about him?'

'Only in passing, the same as she did about other old acquaintances.'

'She and my father were, er, very close friends.'

'That's a bit of an exaggeration. I suspect that she was more important to him than he was to her. Certainly after she returned to America and married my father, all contact between them ceased.'

It occurred to me that, just as Aunt Biddie had kept my father's affair with Imogen Humboldt secret from me, so Imogen Humboldt might well have kept it secret from her son. There seemed no point in telling him that his mother had been partly responsible for breaking up my father's first marriage. He probably wouldn't have believed me anyway.

He scrutinized me with an unfathomable expression, much as I imagine he would a painting that might turn out to be a forgery. Then he asked, 'And your mother? Who was she?'

'I don't know. I'm hoping you may be able to help me find that out.'

His lizard eyes regarded me without questioning or encouraging.

I explained that I had been born somewhere in Italy at the end of the war and how my father had brought me to England, telling my aunt that his wife had died in childbirth. 'And that was what I had believed until January this year, when I saw the television interview with the Princess. Then I discovered that she and my father had been married at the time of my birth, which makes it possible that she may have been my mother.'

There was no doubting his incredulity. 'If Hélène had had a child, I was never aware of the fact – and I'm sure my father wasn't either,' he said stiffly. From his tone, you would have thought I was claiming blood kinship with him.

'Is Prince Dmitri still alive?' I asked, determined to hold my own.

'No, he died last year.'

'I'm sorry.' And I was, though more on my own account than Ludo Zakharin's.

'Pff. He was eighty-five years old and had lived every year of them to the full.'

He stood up and paced pensively backwards and forwards across the room. Ginette glanced at me and I shrugged. The likelihood of obtaining any information from him seemed as remote as prising a pearl from a closed oyster.

Then he seemed to make up his mind about something and returned. 'You must excuse my lack of manners,' he murmured, suave and courteous again. You took me by surprise. Allow me to offer you some tea or coffee – or an apéritif?'

Ginette spoke for the only time during the entire meeting. 'Some coffee would be very welcome.'

He beckoned to the man who had let us in, who was still hovering near the entrance. '*Demandez à Marie-Claude de nous apporter du café.*'

'*Oui, monsieur le Prince.*' The man inclined his head, then disappeared through one of the doors at the far end of the gallery.

Ludo Zakharin resumed his seat. 'I suppose it's possible that Hélène could have had a child and kept its existence a secret from my father. Remind me when your father died.'

'In the autumn of 1945.'

'So you never really knew him?'

'No. I only know what my aunt has told me about him and that mainly relates to his early life before he went to Paris. Until she saw the television interview with the Princess, my aunt had never even heard of her before, let alone been aware that they were married. As you can imagine, it was a shock for both of us.'

At that moment, the door at the end of the gallery reopened and a petite young woman, in a navy-blue suit, with a crimson scarf at the neck, appeared carrying a tray. She set the tray down on the table, casting me a disdainful yet inquisitive glance, and I could sense her wondering what on earth there could be about me that was leading her employer to keep us in conversation.

After she had poured the coffee and gone away again, Ludo Zakharin glanced again at Tobin's photographs and then said, 'Now I understand why Mr Touchstone insisted upon sending his photographs with you. Unfortunately, I don't believe that I shall be able to help you much in your quest. The Princess seldom spoke about her past. My father may have known more than he let on, but . . .'

'Did he and the Princess remain in touch?'

'Oh, yes, they were extremely close. Whenever she came to Paris, she would visit him. And he helped her out financially innumerable times. I trust you will not think I am speaking ill of the dead when I say that she acquired a bad reputation in Paris. On several occasions, she ran up debts which she was unable to settle and my father paid them for her. The very last time she came to see him – just before his death – it was to ask him to lend her fifty thousand pounds.

'On that particular occasion, my father refused to let her have the money outright, but offered to play her for it in a game of two-handed chemin-de-fer. He pledged the money she required against these two portraits. Though why he should have wanted them so badly, I'm still at a loss to understand. He would not explain it to me at the time. When I asked him, he merely laughed.'

'Was the Princess a gambler?'

'Good God, yes! Was Mr Touchstone not aware of that?'

'I don't believe so.'

'She wasn't in the same league as my father. With her, it was more a means of augmenting her income. She and the late Earl of Winster often used to come to the races at Longchamps. The Earl was a far from wealthy man and Hélène had expensive tastes. After his death, she became even more spendthrift than before.'

'Did the Earl gamble too?'

'Only at the races, so far as I'm aware. I take it you're not a gambler?'

'No, apart from the odd flutter on the Grand National and then my horse always seems to fall at the first fence.'

'My father used to say lucky in love and unlucky at cards. Hopefully that applies to yourself?'

I merely smiled.

'My father was a lifelong gambler. Basically it was his profession.'

'I know very little about him,' I said, 'apart from the fact that he helped the Princess to escape from Russia during the Revolution and that he eventually married Imogen Humboldt.'

'So you are unaware that he was very largely responsible for bringing El Toro to the attention of the world?'

I shook my head.

'The Princess didn't mention his gambling or his interest in art during her interview?'

'No, she just said he was involved in various business ventures.'

Ludo Zakharin laughed and, with that laugh, suddenly became almost human. 'Various business ventures! Would you like to hear the true version?'

'Yes, of course.'

'Well, what actually happened was that when he first arrived in Paris in the early 1920s, he had a house to live in and access to funds in his family's bank accounts in Switzerland and France. Then these ran low and he had to find a means of making some money without working for a living.

'He liked to tell the story that his first bet took place when he was sixteen, at the races in Petersburg, when he placed his entire savings on three horses in an accumulator – in other words, he linked the bets. None were favourites for their particular race, but my father had a hunch about them. All three won.

'He was always a great believer in heeding instinct. There were some days, he would say, when he felt lucky and others when he sensed luck was not on his side. By and large, the devil looked after his own, and my father's winnings – at the races and at cards – enabled him to lead an extremely comfortable life.

'Then, in 1935, his luck temporarily deserted him. At the same time, the political situation in Europe was worsening. Hitler had risen to power in Germany and was showing signs of impending military aggression. France was no longer the pleasure ground it had once been. Many Americans were returning home – among them my mother – although, in her case, it was to attend her brother's wedding.

'She sailed on the *Queen Mary*, which was making its maiden voyage. My father decided to take a gamble of a different kind. He raised the money for a one-way ticket. For the week – or however long the voyage lasted – he assiduously wooed my mother. By the time they disembarked in New York, they were engaged.

'The Humboldt family celebrated a double wedding and my father then had to find a different, but again not too arduous, means of making a living. Again, luck was on his side. My grandfather had already started to follow the example of the Gettys and the Guggenheims by investing in works of art. However, he was moving in unfamiliar waters and terrified of being taken for a ride by unscrupulous dealers. The Wall Street crash in 1929 had knocked the bottom out of the art market and there were incredible bargains to be had – provided they were, indeed, real bargains.

'It was a heaven-sent opportunity for my father, who possessed a genuine feeling for art, an unerring eye and contacts in all the right places in Europe, where most art treasures were to be found – all the more so as war loomed ever closer on the horizon. Furthermore, he was personally acquainted with artists such as El Toro, whose work was not yet well known in the States and whose pictures could therefore be acquired relatively cheaply. These, he rightly forecast, would be the masterpieces of tomorrow.

'The same instinct guided him in business as in gambling – a sixth sense, a gut feeling for what was right. As a result of his foresight, the Humboldt Gallery now houses a unique collection of El Toro paintings, including his celebrated set of murals of the Russian Revolution and his triptych of the Spanish Civil War.

'My father formed an association with a New York art dealer, a fellow Russian, who – to put it bluntly – did all the hard work, while my father augmented his income playing poker and spent much of his winnings on women of whose existence my mother was unaware.

'When the long-anticipated war broke out in Europe in 1939, two things occurred. One was that the supply of works of art came to an abrupt end. The other was that America started to make preparations also to enter the fray. My father was informed by his father-in-law that his services could usefully be employed within the Humboldt Organization to help secure government contracts. He was given some kind of title – Vice President-Liaison Operations, I believe – and basically his job entailed wining and dining senators and generals, all of whom my grandfather reckoned, should be impressed by their close contact with a member of the Russian nobility.

'Well, maybe they would have been, had my father made any effort to do his job at all properly. But poker and women exercised a greater pull over him than pompous politicians and be-medalled army top brass. Time after time, he failed to keep appointments and eventually, of course, my grandfather discovered the reason.

'The fur flew. My father was given a stern lecture on husbandly responsibilities and patriotic duty, and when he showed himself to be completely unrepentant, my grandfather threatened not only to throw him out of the company but also from the family. It's almost laughable. My father was forty-five at the time and being treated like a naughty child. On the other hand, his was an extremely comfortable existence at a time when millions were dying in battle. Although he had lived for most of his life on a knife-edge, he had a healthy sense of self-preservation.

'He was saved by two events: one was my own arrival into the world – the result of a last-ditch attempt at reconciliation between my parents; the other was America's entry into the war. Both happened in the same month of the same year – December 1941 – and had the effect of deflecting my grandfather's attention from his son-in-law's peccadilloes.

'My mother, however, was another matter. She realized that she had been used and what had been love, on her part at least, turned to hatred. They lived together in a state of increasing hostility, until she could tolerate his presence no longer. A divorce settlement was agreed and, after the war ended, my father returned to Paris, free again, and considerably richer than when he had left.

'It must have been then that he acquired this gallery. I believe that the previous owner had collaborated with the Nazis during the occupation and was eager to retire to an unobtrusive life in the country. My father, who had maintained contact with his Russian colleague in New York, renewed the business he had been doing before the war intervened, only from the other side of the Atlantic, where artists who had been hungry pre-war were now starving. He even sold to the Humboldt Collection.

'And that's it, really. I was brought up by my mother until I was eighteen, when I came over here to study art – encouraged by my mother who remained a Francophile to the end of her days – and, like her, I discovered my spiritual home. For a while, I toyed with the idea of becoming an artist, until it was enforced upon me that I lacked the necessary talent but did possess an innate ability to appreciate other people's paintings. In other words, in this respect, I took after my parents.

'My mother, meanwhile, had married again – one of her father's Vice-Presidents – with whom I entertained a mutual dislike. So here I remained and, in due course, took over the gallery from my father. He never remarried. He used to say that if he had a epitaph it should be that he had never made the same mistake twice.'

Ludo Zakarin stopped and sipped his coffee, while I tried to absorb everything he had said. Then I asked, 'Do you know exactly when your father returned to Paris?'

'It must have been at the end of 1945 or the beginning of 1946.'

'So it was about the same time as my father brought me to England.'

'I don't quite see the connection.'

I bit my lip, then decided, to hell with it – I would risk offending him. 'This is very impertinent, but did your father and the Princess have an affair?'

'Why do you ask that?

I took the photograph of Prince Dmitri from my bag. 'She kept this on her dressing table.'

Ludo Zakharin nodded. 'I have seen that before. My father also had a copy of it. It was taken at a café on the Champs Élysées.' His glance returned to the portraits. 'The relationship between her and my father was a very strange one. I have never been sure what his true feelings were towards her. If he heard anyone else say a word against her, he would rise vehemently to her defence. Yet he himself could be scathingly sarcastic in her regard and mock her, to her face, almost to the point of cruelty.

'I suppose it's possible that when they left Russia, they were lovers but, if so, I don't believe the affair lasted long after they arrived in Paris. Hélène, as you are presumably aware, married the Baron Léon de St-Léon, while my father pursued his playboy existence. She was very proud – not the sort of woman to tolerate infidelity.'

'Do you know anything at all about her marriage to my father?'

'Less than you, probably. She never mentioned him in my presence.'

'So you don't know where in Italy they lived?'

'I'm afraid not.'

'And you don't know anyone who knew them at the time?'

'Nobody that immediately springs to mind. Most of her contemporaries are regrettably no longer with us.'

'I know from a couple of letters my father wrote to his sister, that he lodged for a while with the Angelini family while he was in Paris . . .'

'Ah! Hence Mr Touchstone's questions on the phone.' He spread his hands expressively. 'I'm sorry, I cannot help you. All I know is that Angelini came to Paris with his family after the First World War and shared El

Toro's studio in Montmartre for a while and then moved to Montparnasse. He was a very talented artist but overshadowed by his more innovative contemporaries. Unlike many of them, however, I imagine he made a very reasonable living from his work.

'When he returned to Italy at the outbreak of war, I believe he took up a teaching post, presumably in one of big cities, possibly Turin, Milan or Rome. He died towards the end of the war, though from what cause I do not know.'

'And you don't know what happened to his family?'

'I'm afraid not. Once he sold a picture, it ceased to be his. So even when I acquire an Angelini, the details regarding its provenance relate to the previous owners of the painting, not the artist himself – apart from the year it was painted.'

He stood up. 'However, let me show you something which, under the circumstances, may be of interest to you. We recently acquired an Angelini at auction. It's a bit of a gamble on my part. If you will wait here one moment.'

Soon he returned, holding a framed painting – a portrait of a small girl, with long dark hair and big brown eyes under straight, firm eyebrows, standing against a backdrop of sunflowers, far taller than she was. I would have known, even if Ludo Zakharin hadn't told us, who the artist was.

'A rather charming little picture, isn't it?' he remarked, handing it to me.

Despite the difference in subject, it had the same quality of light as the portrait of the Princess. A sort of inner glow seemed to radiate from the child and the sunflowers shimmered, as though they had been painted through a golden veil, iridescent as mother of pearl. The date in the bottom corner, under the artist's signature, was 1930.

'I think it's absolutely beautiful,' I breathed. 'Who's the subject?'

'The artist's daughter. Hence my gamble. My customers tend to prefer portraits of public figures and celebrities. Even the Princess has a certain notability.'

Angelini's daughter . . . The little girl of whom my father had written that she reminded him rather of Aunt Biddie at the same age.

'I suppose it's worth a lot of money?'

He shrugged. 'Not as much as Mr Touchstone's portraits of the Princess.'

'But more than I could afford on a secretary's salary?'

'I imagine so.'

Reluctantly, I handed the picture back.

'I will make some enquiries for you regarding Angelini's life after he returned to Italy,' Ludo Zakharin said. 'It's possible that one of my contacts there might be able to unearth some information which may be of use to you.'

However, he did not ask for my address or telephone number and I couldn't help but receive the impression that, courteous though he had turned out to be, soon after I left the gallery, he would forget me.

Chapter 15

Out on the rue du Faubourg St Honoré again, having received a rather more deferential '*Au revoir, Mesdames,*' from General de Gaulle than on our arrival, Ginette and I found a café, where we went over our impressions of Ludo Zakharin.

'*Quel poseur!*' Ginette exclaimed in disgust. 'I did not trust myself to speak while we were in there. I have a horror of types like him. *Prince* Zakharin! We have had no aristocracy in France since the Revolution nearly two hundred years ago, yet he still calls himself Prince. And people fall for it. They think he is something special, so they pay inflated prices for the pictures he sells. The way he spoke to you, when you asked how much that painting was worth, it was disgusting. So superior!

'What was his father? A gambler, who then married for money. Did he fight for the France who had given him sanctuary when he was forced out of Russia? Oh, no! He fled to America. And then, when it was safe to return, he came back.

'And his son is no better. He came here to study art and fell in love with Paris. *Je t'en prie.* He wanted to avoid doing his *service militaire*. That was why he came to Paris. I'm so thankful you didn't pander to him by calling him by his title. That would have made me feel really sick.

'As for little Mademoiselle Chanel . . . Serving us coffee in china from the Galeries Lafayette. I recognized it. I have exactly the same at home. Now, you're not going to tell me she uses that for their best clients. Oh, no! For them it would be Sèvres porcelain. But for plebs like us—'

I laughed. 'What does it matter, if it makes them happy? And he gave me a lot of useful information.'

She threw me a dark look. 'I hope you're not going to take their part because your mother may have been a princess. Pff! If I discovered that

I was related to him, I should prefer to deny the connection and remain an orphan.'

'I rather agree with you,' I said mildly. 'And I'm sure he would, too. If you noticed, he wasn't exactly eager to include me in the family.'

'No, that's true,' she conceded. She sipped the Pernod she had declared she needed to rid her mouth of the taste of the Galerie Zakharin. Then she asked, 'Do you think he knew about your father's affair with his mother?'

'No, I don't think so.'

'Why didn't you tell him?'

'It would have been a distraction for no useful purpose.'

'It might have shaken him up.'

'But that wasn't the reason for going to see him. I wanted to find out about my mother – not his.'

'And you know more than he does, which is good. But don't hold out any expectations about him making enquiries in Italy. He will make no effort.'

For a while longer, we discussed Prince Zakharin and the facts we had learned about the Princess and Dmitri. Then Ginette asked, 'So, what would you like do for the rest of the weekend?'

'Enjoy Paris?' I suggested.

Which is just what we did – although my father and the Princess were never far from my thoughts.

The weather that Easter could have been better but at least it didn't rain. On Friday morning, we climbed the steps to Sacré Coeur, then wandered round Montmartre, deriding the efforts of present-day artists in the place du Tertre, and I took a photograph of Ginette outside El Toro's former studio in the rue Cortot. Again, she was immaculately dressed, whereas I – regrettably – had reverted to my London weekend garb of jeans and sweater.

In the afternoon, we sauntered down the tree-lined avenue Foch, with the palatial town residences to either side, in one of which the Princess had once lived with the Baron Léon de St-Léon. It didn't really seem to matter which was the actual house – they were all so grand, representing a life of pomp and circumstance which was beyond my experience.

On Saturday, we went to Montparnasse. Before we set off, Ginette warned me that the area had changed a lot during the last decade or so. Not only did the massive, ultra modern Tour Montparnasse rival the Eiffel

Tower for domination of the Paris skyline – but many of the old buildings had been demolished.

Certainly neither my father nor Amadore Angelini would have recognized the rue des Châtaigniers. 84bis was no more. Where it had once presumably stood was a hideously functional concrete and glass office and apartment block.

'They call it progress,' Ginette commented sadly. 'They say it is necessary to bring Paris into the twenty-first century. It is the same at La Défense, where my office is situated. A showpiece of contemporary architecture they call that, with its huge skyscrapers. The building in which I work is eighty metres high and I am on the top floor. I have a marvellous view – but the Paris I look onto is no longer the Paris which once was. Perhaps I am old-fashioned, but . . .'

I squeezed her arm. 'You and me both.'

We wandered through the Cemetery of Montparnasse, where such famous people as Baudelaire, Maupassant, César Franck and those literary giants of the existentialist fifties, Simone de Beauvoir and Jean-Paul Sartre, lie buried, into the boulevard Raspail, and on into the *quartier Latin.*

We stopped for a snack lunch at a café thronged with students and tourists, where the background music consisted of hits from the sixties by Edith Piaf, Jacques Brel and Antoine. One of them brought memories flooding back of my long ago, ill-fated romance with Michel.

Because you see, little girl, when we met
we both knew it could not last . . .
You should have thought ahead, not seen yourself in white,
You knew it all the while . . .

That song of Antoine's had been a favourite of Michel's. When he had given me up he had said it epitomized our affair. Listening to the lyrics, it occurred to me that maybe I should have learned more of a lesson from it and applied it not just to my romance with Michel but also to my relationship with Nigel.

Ginette took me to the legendary second-hand bookshop, Shakespeare & Co, where I bought a 1915 Bibliothèque Miniature edition of Baudelaire's *Les Fleurs du mal* for Tobin. It was a pretty, cloth-covered book, decorated with flowers, measuring less than three inches by four. On an impulse, while I was paying for it, I showed my father's book to the assistant.

To my great surprise, he nodded in recognition, but when I asked if he knew whether Helicon Publishing was still in existence, he replied, 'No. It was a small company which started up during the twenties and published pamphlets, reviews, compilations of poetry and other rather esoteric literary works. It became defunct in the early thirties. This edition could be worth a little money. Would you like me to give a valuation?'

'Thank you, but I wouldn't dream of selling it. My father was Connor Moran.'

He seemed unimpressed. I suppose, in a shop like that, you get used to that sort of thing. But he did proffer the information that he believed my father used to live in Montparnasse.

'We've just come from there,' I told him. 'The house in which he lived no longer exists.'

He gave a Gallic shrug.

'You don't know anything more about him?'

'I regret, but no . . .'

'Well, it was worth a try,' Ginette said when we were outside again, 'but we don't seem to be having much luck, do we?'

After that, we sauntered up the boulevard Saint-Germain, stopping to gaze at the exterior of the Deux Magots café, made famous by Hemingway, and the Café de Flore, where Sartre and Simone de Beauvoir had once held court. Parts of Paris might have gone for ever, but much still remained.

While we walked, we chatted about our student days and the authors and artists who had made the greatest impression on us. As it had been since my arrival, our conversation was friendly without being intimate, containing none of the sort of confidences which I shared with Sherry and Juliette – or even with Tobin for that matter. But that was only to be expected between two people who hadn't met for a number of years. And I was happy for it to be that way. Impressions enough were crowding in on me for me not to need the added intensity of deep discussion.

That evening, Ginette relented sufficiently in her antipathy towards Ludo Zakharin to take me to a Russian restaurant in the rue de Passy, and there, after a couple of glasses of vodka from the pitcher on our table, she suddenly asked, 'Are you and Nigel happy?'

There's something liberating about being away from home, in the company of someone you feel to be sympathetic, but whom you are unlikely to meet again for a long time.

I gave a very good imitation of a Gallic shrug.

Ginette nodded. 'When you announced that you were coming here without Nigel, I thought that everything could not be well between you. And since your arrival, you have hardly mentioned him. Happily married wives talk about their husbands all the time, in the same way that mothers are always praising their children.'

I smiled.

'But, apart from your father, the only men you have talked about are Miles Goodchild and Tobin Touchstone. To begin with, I believed that you were having an affair with Miles Goodchild.'

At this, I laughed. 'I can assure you that I'm not.'

'You may laugh. But you weren't telling the complete truth when you complained about your job the other day. Anyone who is unhappy in their job finds another one. It is very simple. However, if you are in love with your boss, it is not so simple, particularly if he is married.'

Something in her voice made me look at her sharply. 'Are you . . . ?'

'Yes, Jean-Pierre and I have been lovers now for several years. But that is another matter. We are discussing you. If you are not in love with Miles Goodchild, the problem lies elsewhere. And where else can that be but in your marriage?

I picked at my *hors d'oeuvres*.

'Perhaps, after twelve years, you are understandably a little bored with your job, but that is merely an excuse you have invented to divert your mind from the truth. The problem lies in your personal life, in your marriage. Your working life is full – but your personal life is empty.'

'Possibly,' I admitted. 'Though less so, since I found out about the Princess.'

'No. Be honest. It is not merely the Princess. It is this Tobin.'

I glanced at her guardedly. 'Why do say that?'

'You give yourself away,' she announced triumphantly. 'Whenever you mentioned this Tobin to me, your face has lit up, your voice has become more vibrant, your eyes have sparkled. And when we were at the Galerie Zakharin, you blushed at something said by Monsieur le prince.'

'I didn't blush! I was angry.'

'*Quand-même* . . . Perhaps I am exaggerating a little. But tell me about him. Is he married?'

'Divorced.'

'What went wrong with his first marriage?'

'I've no idea. I don't know him well enough yet to ask.'

'*Dis donc!* How well must you know someone before you can ask them such a simple question?'

'Very well, unless they volunteer the information.'

'And you do not yet know him very well? You are not having an affair with him?'

'No, it's a totally innocent friendship.'

'Is he in love with you?'

I shrugged, then admitted honestly, 'I don't know.'

She let out a long sigh. 'Ah, you English . . . And Nigel? Is he jealous?'

'Nigel knows nothing at all about him.'

'So, a friendship which is totally innocent but clandestine. Maybe there is a chance after all.'

'A chance of what?'

'For it to develop – for you to discover happiness.'

'It doesn't sound as if your affair is making you happy.'

'*Au contraire*. When I am with Jean-Pierre, I am very happy. When we are apart, I am very unhappy. This weekend, for instance, he and his family have gone to the Provence, which is one reason why I am glad that you have come to Paris.'

'Don't you feel guilty?'

She tipped the contents of her glass down her throat and refilled it. 'No. I feel anger sometimes, but not guilt.'

'Would you like to marry him?'

She pursed her lips. 'In my weak moments, I think so. But when I am feeling strong, I think not. We have a proverb in French: Love is blind – and when you get married you get your eyesight back. Marriage takes all the romance out of love. To be a wife is quite different from being a mistress. I would not love Jean-Pierre so much if I had to wash his under-clothes and nurse him when he has a cold in the head.'

'But you work together . . .'

'That is not the same thing as being married. He does not bring his weaknesses or his dirty underwear to the office – or to my apartment.'

'Does his wife know about your affair?'

'Oh, yes.'

'Why doesn't she leave him?'

'From time to time she threatens to. But she will never carry out her threat. Why should she? She is nearly fifty and unlikely to find another husband, certainly not one who is as good to her as Jean-Pierre.'

'Aren't you jealous of her?'

'Only on weekends like this, when she has him and I don't. But in no other way. He never makes love to her. He never buys her special presents. And most of his time he spends with me. One is at work more than one is at home . . .'

For most of the rest of the evening, we talked about her affair. From various comments she made, I gained the impression that hers was a far more lonely existence than my own. Apart from Jean-Pierre, she seemed to have no close friends and I think it came as a relief to her to be able to talk about him openly, with no inhibitions. Yet, that said, she seemed happy enough. As she herself candidly summed up her situation: 'I have my own apartment, my independence, my freedom. And I also have Jean-Pierre . . .'

On Sunday, we went to Compiègne, where we stayed until Monday afternoon – a lovely couple of days, spent mainly in nostalgic reminiscences. Back in Paris, we had an early dinner, because I was returning to London first thing in the morning. 'Thank you for coming,' Ginette said, towards the end of the meal. 'I am so glad we have renewed our friendship. Beforehand, I wasn't sure if it would work out . . .'

'I felt a little apprehensive too,' I admitted. 'But I couldn't believe you would have changed very much.'

'People do, especially women. Marriage changes them more than anything. Suddenly, it is as if there are two races of women – those who have husbands and those who don't.' She smiled. 'But you fall between the two camps.'

I didn't contradict her. Nothing would have been gained by clarifying the reasons for my deeply ingrained views on fidelity – marital and otherwise. She would have thought me stupid – indeed, I was beginning to wonder if my ideas weren't just a little too entrenched . . .

'As regards your father,' she went on, 'I hope you consider your visit to have been worthwhile? I can't help feeling that you must be a little disappointed. *Monsieur le Prince* did not tell you anything you didn't already know, and the house where your father lived with Angelini no longer exists. It is such a pity . . .'

'I've learned a lot,' I assured her. 'What's more, I've had a lovely weekend.'

'I hope I didn't bore you too much with my talk of Jean-Pierre.'

'Not at all. I only wish I could have had the opportunity to meet him.'

'It is better like this.'

'Why do you say that?'

'He is not what you would expect. If you had met him, you might have been disappointed. As it is, you carry in your mind the image of him I have given you.'

During my flight back to Heathrow the following morning, these words continued to echo in my head. It occurred to me that we all present a face to the world, but, because we are multi-faceted, everyone receives a different impression of us. Nobody sees the whole in a single glance – and nobody sees what lies beneath the exterior, except what we choose to disclose or others reveal in their descriptions of us. And anything anyone else says must, of necessity, distort the truth, however slightly, like a mirror or a camera lens. None of us can ever truly understand anybody else. How can we, when we do not understand ourselves?

Thus it was with Jean-Pierre. Thus it was also with my father and the Princess. Thus it was with me, as well. Even now, as I was crossing the Channel, I was taking on a different form, turning my Paris side away from the light, so that it became concealed.

Yet, at the same time, I was aware that Paris and Ginette had left their mark upon me. There was more to life than *metro, boulot, dodo.*

The Mrs Cara Sinclair who landed at Heathrow was still the faithful wife of Nigel and loyal secretary to Miles Goodchild, but Paris had entered her bloodstream . . .

'How was gay Paree?' Sergeant enquired, with what he intended as a roguish wink, when I passed his desk. 'I hope you went to the Moulin Rouge. Cha-cha-cha.'

I had a sudden vision of General de Gaulle and smiled.

'Did you have a nice Easter?' Dorothy asked.

'Lovely, thank you. And you?'

'Wonderful. Our granddaughter came to stay. She is such a dear, sweet-natured child. She hardly cried all weekend. We've taken lots of photographs – I'll bring them in when they've been developed.'

Juliette stuck her head round my office door, just as I was finishing opening the post. 'How was Prince Charming?'

I grinned. 'He was actually.'

'Did you learn anything more?'

'Quite a lot, though not exactly the sort of thing I went over there for.'

'What does that mean?'

'It means I'm wiser than when I set out.'

'You're being very mysterious. Did he fall swooning at your feet or offer you half the family fortune or something?'

I laughed. 'Nothing like that. I simply had a very interesting time.'

'Shall we have lunch today?'

'I'd love to, but let me see how Miles is first.'

Then the phone rang and Dorothy announced, 'Massimo Patrizzi on the line.' I reached for my shorthand pad, switching my mind from English and French to Italian, as Massimo Patrizzi yelled, '*Pronto! Pronto!*' into my left ear.

Miles arrived about an hour later, wearing a little smile which managed to be simultaneously cherubic and diabolic, reminding me of a mischievous schoolboy, struggling to keep a secret. It was a smile I recognized and usually foretokened a new acquisition. Bearing in mind Sir Utley Trusted's presence among his house guests, it did not seem beyond the realms of feasibility that Trusted Supermarkets might be in line for a take-over.

'Did you have a good time in Paris?' he asked.

'Excellent, thank you. How was your Easter?'

'Very good. I won fifty thousand francs at roulette, which made it even more satisfying.'

No mention of Sir Utley Trusted, though I would have been surprised if there was. I laughed and was reminded of Prince Dmitri.

With Thursday's work still to catch up on, the morning sped by and I had no chance to ring Tobin. At one o'clock Miles went out to lunch and Juliette and I nipped down to a sandwich bar, where I described my encounter with Ludo Zakharin and she told me about her weekend with her husband in Devon. 'It was bliss,' she purred, 'four whole days together. We stayed in the most gorgeous little inn, beside a stream. You'd have loved it . . .'

Except that such a weekend could never have taken place with Nigel.

We had not long returned from lunch when Tobin rang. 'I thought I'd better allow you time to settle back in before I got in touch.'

'Thanks, the morning was pretty hectic.'

'When did you get back?'

'This morning. I came straight to the office from the airport.'

'How did it all go?'

'Brilliantly. I've got masses to tell you.'

'Did Ludo take one look at you and embrace you as a long-lost cousin?'

I laughed. 'No. He certainly didn't.'

'But you did tell him your story?'

'Of course. And he told me heaps about his father and the Princess. Did you know that she gambled?'

'Gambled? No, that's the first I've heard of it.'

'She and the Earl apparently.'

'Good grief! I had absolutely no idea.'

'Apparently they often went to the races at Longchamps.'

'Well, I'll be blowed. That just goes to show. You can know someone and not know them at all.'

I told him what Dmitri had said about the Princess running up debts in Paris and Dmitri bailing her out and about their final game of cards in which she had pledged the two portraits.

'Curiouser and curiouser,' he murmured. 'And what did he have to say about the portraits themselves?'

'He'd like to buy them. There's no doubt about that. Oh, but Tobin, I must tell you *the* most amazing thing, and then I'm afraid I'll have to go. I've just heard Miles come back. Ludo had a portrait there of Angelini's daughter, when she was a little girl. It was absolutely lovely. If I could have afforded it, I'd have bought it on the spot.'

'And he had nothing to add about Angelini's family?'

'No, he said the same thing to us as he did to you, that he had no idea what happened to them after they returned to Italy.'

'Oh, well, it was worth a try and I'm sorry it failed.'

'It wasn't a failure at all. But, listen, I'm sorry, I must go now.'

'Of course. It wouldn't do to keep the good Miles child waiting. When can I see you?'

I should have liked to say, 'Tonight?' But common sense prevailed. It was my first evening back and Nigel's last before he went to the States on his recce. 'Tonight I'd better go home,' I said reluctantly, 'but maybe tomorrow?'

'I'll give you a ring in the afternoon. How's that?'

'Wonderful! Bye for now.'

★ ★ ★

I went home that evening to a flat which looked as if a bomb had hit it and smelt like a pub the morning after the night before. There were overflowing ashtrays in the hall, the living room and in the dining area, and empty glasses, wine bottles and beer cans on every available surface. Cushions were scattered over the floor. Crisps and peanuts crunched underfoot. The kitchen was piled high with dirty dishes, cutlery and mugs. The muck bucket was overflowing. Teabags had been left on the draining board, amidst half a bottle of spilt coffee granules. It had obviously been some party.

Anger surged through me. I carried my suitcase into the bedroom, where our bed was unmade and Nigel's clothes were strewn over the carpet. In the bathroom, a soapy scum crusted the washbasin and shower, a damp towel lay in a heap on the toilet seat and the core of a used-up toilet roll had been left in the holder, while a new roll had unwound itself on the floor, looking as if the Andrex puppy had been let loose with it.

I had not expected Nigel to have vacuumed and polished. I had not expected the bedclothes to have been changed or the washing done. In other words, I had hoped for no miracles. But I had assumed, particularly since he was the one who had such a fetish about orderliness, that he would make a basic effort to ensure the flat was looking tidy for my return – just as I always did for him, whenever he returned from a trip abroad – or from the office at the end of the day, for that matter . . .

Then it occurred to me that, maybe, this was a protest against me going away: a childish 'this will show her, this will make her feel guilty'. But, in that case, he would just have left a general mess, as he had in the bedroom and bathroom. No, Nigel had decided to throw a party and simply taken it for granted that when I came home I would clear up after him. It was not a protest at being neglected, but sheer thoughtless, bloody selfishness.

With trepidation, I entered the spare bedroom, but to my relief it was as neat as I had left it. I put my suitcase on the floor and sat down on the bed.

My father's book of poetry was still in my handbag. Now I took it out and opened it at the very first poem, thinking as I did so, how little my father could have imagined that his daughter, sixty years on, would read his words and find them so apt to herself and her own marriage.

There is the long end of loving:
After sweet day draws in dull night;
Young, we loved, and now the weary end
Grows darkly over body's deep delight.
We went the way we had to:
After rich laughter, felt the weight of tears.
Words are not loving: the heart beats no more:
We sink in heavy silence to the years.

And at that moment, something in me died. It didn't snap and break, with a rending crack. It didn't explode and go up in smoke. It gave no scream of agony. Instead, like an ailing plant, whose leaves have been withering and whose roots beneath the soil have been gradually rotting over a long period of time, it suddenly relinquished the unequal battle for life. And, as it happened, I felt almost a sense of relief, as though I had been released from the responsibility of keeping that something alive, while all the time knowing, in my deep heart of hearts, that it could not be revitalized.

Eventually, I confronted the debris. I opened all the windows and put all the refuse into a bin bag. I washed and dried up, wiped down all the surfaces, mopped the kitchen floor and hoovered the carpet in the hall and living room. I made the bed and cleaned the bathroom, after which I unpacked my case and made up the bed in the spare room. Finally, I went back into the kitchen to see what, if anything, was left in the larder and fridge to eat. The bread had gone mouldy, but the fridge was still full. Obviously Nigel had relied on take-aways or eaten out.

Suddenly, despite all my rushing about, I felt very cold, so cold that I started to shiver uncontrollably. I closed the windows and poured myself a stiff tot of the whisky I had bought for Nigel in the duty-free shop at Charles de Gaulle Airport. Slowly the blood began to course again, albeit sluggishly, through my veins and I started to warm up. But my mind remained numb and the heart within me was heavy like a stone.

By the time the front door opened and Nigel came in, I had myself more or less under control. I heard him go down the hall into the kitchen and give a grunt of surprise. Then he came into the living room and saw me. 'What on earth are you doing here?' he demanded. 'You weren't due back until tomorrow.'

'No. Today. Tuesday.'

'Oh, Gawd. I'm sorry.' He made his apology sound like an accusation.

'I gather you've had a party.'

'It wasn't really a party as such. I just asked Bo and a few other people over for a drink and everyone stayed longer than I anticipated. In fact, it was four o'clock when the last ones went. I was going to clear up tonight. But I see you've already done it. Thanks.'

I simply nodded.

'So, did you have a good time in Paris?'

I nodded again.

'Cara, I honestly didn't know you were coming back today. I honestly thought it was tomorrow.'

'For one thing, I had to work today. And for another, if I had come back tomorrow, I wouldn't have seen you before you went to the States.'

'Oh, I didn't think of that. Well, come on, tell me. How was Paris?'

'Great. I really enjoyed it. And I wish I'd stayed there.'

He sucked in his breath. 'If this is the sort of mood you've come back in, it might have been better if you had stayed.'

'I didn't come back in any sort of mood. I was feeling really good until I walked into this flat.'

He shook his head irritably. 'I haven't got the time, energy or inclination to get involved in a row. I've said I'm sorry and I can't do any more. Now I'm going to get on with my packing.'

That was my homecoming from Paris. And that was the end of my love for Nigel. And that was really the beginning of the end of our marriage.

I still find it strange, looking back. I didn't stop loving Nigel and our marriage didn't start to disintegrate because of a sink full of washing-up and a toilet roll not replaced. Neither was it because he put his career in front of everything else. Or because going to Paris re-awakened a restlessness in me. Or because he went off to America with Bo Eriksson. Or because I met Tobin.

Those all contributed to the ultimate break-up of our marriage, but they were not the fundamental cause. My love died because I realized that Nigel was not only thoughtless and selfish, but that he no longer loved me. Had he loved me he would not have forgotten which day I was coming home. Had he loved me, he would have cared enough to remember. But he didn't care. And, possibly saddest of all, I no longer cared either. I had, but now I didn't. It was as swift and as simple as that.

There was no screaming match, no bitter accusations hurled between us, no open rupture, no huge schismatic rift: no outward sign, in fact, that anything had actually changed at all from one moment to the next.

While he packed, I cooked us a meal. I didn't sleep in the spare room as I had vaguely intended. Next morning, at the crack of dawn, I woke him, called the cab to take him to the airport, and gave him a wifely peck as he departed.

But, from that moment on, the sweet day of our loving ended and dull night began to draw in.

Chapter 16

In contrast to my reception from Nigel, my reunion with Tobin at Chattertons left nothing to be desired. I gave him the little book of Baudelaire poems I had bought at Shakespeare & Co., with which he was far more excited and pleased than I had anticipated.

'I've never seen anything like this before my life,' he exclaimed, handling it with almost as much reverence as he had my father's book of poetry. He even tried to translate the first poem – and did much better than I expected. 'Not bad for someone who hasn't spoken French since they left school, eh?' he laughed.

He then made me repeat every detail of my conversation with Ludo Zakharin and listened with equally rapt interest to my description of everything else Ginette and I had done during the weekend. I told him, too, about Ginette's affair – although I did not repeat her comments about Nigel, Miles and himself.

Mediterranean prawns in garlic and butter were on the menu. 'Do you have to get home early?' Tobin asked.

'No, Nigel's on his way to the States.' His flight had left Heathrow at ten that morning, which meant he would land in Los Angeles at nine o'clock in the evening British time and one o'clock in the afternoon local time. I doubted very much that he would ring me after his arrival and, if he did and received no reply, tough luck.

I made no mention to Tobin of the scene which had greeted me at Linden Mansions: that was something which concerned only Nigel and me. 'What about your weekend?' I asked.

'It was so-so. Harvey and Gwendolen were in town and I had dinner with them on Saturday. Incidentally, it looks as though there's a buyer for Beadle Walk. And Sunday I spent with my kids. I'm coming to the conclusion that children do improve with age. Joss is becoming quite human and Pamela's turning into an extremely pretty girl. She has her first serious boyfriend – a fellow ballet student. I'm taking them both out to dinner next weekend. That will be a new experience. Still, it's flattering that she wants my company.'

I felt a sharp pang of jealousy, so painful that I had to struggle not to show it in my expression. I knew it was crazy to be jealous of Tobin's brother and of his children – his brother and his children, for goodness sake! – but I couldn't help it. I told myself that I would be horrified if he were jealous of Aunt Biddie and Miranda – or even Nigel. But that didn't help either. My old tormentor was back with a vengeance and all my familiar insecurities returned to plague me. It was as if an old scar, invisible to the naked eye and therefore all but forgotten, had flared up again to remind me of its existence . . .

At the end of the evening, Tobin again drove me home to Linden Mansions.

Being a passenger in a car, particularly if it's night-time, is rather like sharing a room with someone and talking after the light has been turned off, in the sense that you feel able to say things you might not otherwise say. 'May I ask you something personal?' I said.

'Whatever you like.'

'What went wrong with your marriage?'

'Ah.' He negotiated Hyde Park Corner, then said, 'Well, that's a simple enough story. I married the wrong girl and she married the wrong man. We met at my first job. Dawn was a typist, working for the beauty editor on the magazine. She was very pretty, very sexy and had men hanging round her like bees round the honeysuckle. I was the fortunate one she favoured.

'We married and, within a year, she was pregnant with Joss. She gave up her job and played at being housewife and mother, which was fine until the novelty started to wear off. Then she became bored. She missed her freedom, she missed going out with her friends, she missed the admiration of other men. We started to have dreadful rows. Then she became pregnant again and Pamela was born.

'Joss had been a very good baby but Pamela was dreadful, crying all night and needing constant attention. To add to our problems, Alice died shortly after Joss was born and Howard moved up to London. As I told you before, he spent more time at our house than he did at Beadle Walk, which did not improve relations at all between Dawn and me. Things did ease off a bit after he married the Princess, insomuch as we saw less of him, but the rot had basically set in.

'I was working at Astra Publishing then and one of my colleagues was a lovely, bubbly girl called Penny. We went away on a business trip and ended up in bed together. Our affair continued for about six months, until a mutual acquaintance took it upon herself to inform Dawn. Needless to say, there was a huge scene and I was made to feel like a thorough-going bastard, which, of course, I was. But we kissed and made up.'

He paused as he circumnavigated Marble Arch and I sat very still.

'Penny found another job elsewhere. There was no real alternative. We couldn't go on working together. But, by that time, the affair was starting to peter out anyway. In fact, she's done extremely well for herself. She's head of the art department at Rambler Books now.'

'So you're still in touch with her?'

'Yes, indeed. In fact, we're still very good friends. Rambler publish children's non-fiction books and Penny gives me commissions from time to time.'

'Oh, I see,' I said faintly.

He laughed. 'Somebody, I don't know who, once said that it's only possible for a man and a woman to be true friends if they could have had an affair and mutually decided not to – or if they did have an affair and still liked each other afterwards.'

And what was I supposed to make of that, I wondered.

'Why did you go back to Dawn?' I asked eventually.

'Mainly for the sake of the children.'

'Did you still love her?'

'God, it's difficult looking back and trying to remember how one felt at a certain time, but I think I must have done really, otherwise I wouldn't have put up with everything I did put up with. After Penny, Dawn dictated the terms. When my father died and I went freelance, we had a sort of role reversal. Because I was working from home, Dawn decided that I should become a house-husband, while she went back to work.

'She got herself a job as secretary to the fashion editor on one of the daily newspapers. For a while everything was fine – well, from her point of view, if not from mine. I looked after the children when they came home from school and during the holidays. When Dawn returned from the office, there was a meal waiting for her. And so on.

'Then the inevitable happened. She took to coming home later and later and, more often than not, she was drunk. She would ring and say that she was delayed at the office but I could hear, from the background noise, that she was in a pub. Finally, my patience gave out. We had a huge argument, during which she accused me – among other things – of having become boring. Which I probably was, since I never seemed to get out of the damned house.

'Well, we teetered on for a few more months then she suddenly announced that she was in love with a journalist on the news desk, a guy called Mark Osborne, and wanted a divorce. Obviously, I met Mark in due course and, funnily enough, under different circumstances, I could have quite liked him. He was divorced, with a couple of kids whom he was supporting. His wife had gone off with someone else – or, at least, that's what Dawn told me.

'Our divorce was extremely unpleasant. My priority was the kids and I tried to obtain custody of them. However, Dawn used a really high-powered solicitor, from a firm who acted for the newspaper, and against whom my chap didn't stand a chance. While the squabbling was going on, the kids, of course, were getting more and more upset. In the end, rightly or wrongly, I gave in and let them go with her. And, naturally, I agreed to pay for their maintenance. She took me for everything she could get. Our house in Blackheath had to be sold – it still had a huge mortgage on it – and, one way and another, I came out with just enough to put down a deposit on a terraced cottage in Fulham. And that's about it, really.'

'What did you actually feel when she told you about Mark?' I asked in a little voice.

He let out a long breath. 'Do you want the truth?'

'Yes.'

'Well – apart from my concern for the children – the main effect was the blow to my masculine pride. Rejection always hurts. But, like all bruises, I recovered from it. Getting over losing the children took considerably longer. That was extremely painful, particularly when Dawn tried to poison their minds against me. But, now they're older, they can see things more clearly.'

'And since your divorce?' I forced myself to ask. 'Have you had a lot of girlfriends?'

He gave a dry laugh. 'Well, in the last seven years, I've had a couple of relationships which could be described as serious. The second finished about a year ago, since when I've lived a very chaste existence. Less from choice than necessity, I must confess. When you're married, the world appears to be full of attractive, unattached women. But, for some reason, when you're single, they all turn out to be married.'

Neither of us spoke again until we reached West Hill, when he pulled in at the end of the drive and switched off the car engine. There was an almost palpable tension in the atmosphere, as though we were both waiting for the other to say or do something. My heart was pounding so furiously that I was sure Tobin must be able to hear it.

Suddenly, he turned and took me in his arms, drawing me close to him, and kissed me, quite differently than he had ever kissed me before, not lightly and gently, but strong and hard and full of passion. Then, equally abruptly, he drew away, holding me by the shoulders, gazing into my eyes, his own eyes deep, unfathomable pools of darkness.

I started to tremble and he relaxed his grip. 'I'm sorry, I didn't mean to do that.'

I wanted to say, 'I'm glad you did', but the words wouldn't come out. And I wasn't altogether sure that I would have meant them if I had.

'When I found myself a bachelor again, I made a rule that married women were out. Then you came into my life.'

I froze.

'Are you all right?' he asked.

'Yes,' I whispered, 'I'm fine.'

I let myself out of the car and, without looking back, walked up the rest of the drive, past Nigel's Porsche and into Linden Mansions.

It was a very long time before I fell asleep that night. Well, there was Ginette's question answered. And where did it get me? Looked at from one angle, it made Tobin no better than Nigel. On the other hand, Dawn had hardly been an angel.

And that kiss, before I got out of the car? What had that meant? And his final words? What was I supposed to understand by them?

In the end, I gave up my vain questioning and fell into a restive sleep.

I was right about Nigel not telephoning. In fact, I didn't hear from him at all. Instead, on Thursday morning, a girl rang me at the office. 'This is Tracey at Massey Gault Lucasz & Sinclair,' she said. 'Nigel's just rung from the States and asked me to tell you that he arrived OK.'

'Oh, I see,' I said and paused. But it seemed Tracey had nothing more to add. 'Thank you for letting me know.'

'That's OK,' she replied and, her duty done, rang off.

It occurred to me that I didn't have a telephone number for him in the States and, should I need to contact him, I would therefore have to ring Tracey, whoever she might be, and either ask her for it or get her to pass on a message. But since I had nothing to say to him, it was probably for the best.

Most of my Saturday was spent writing. There were thank you letters to Ginette and Ludo Zakharin, after which there was my diary and The Book. In the evening – when Tobin was at the theatre with Pamela and her boyfriend – I had dinner with Sherry and Roly. Rather to my surprise, I found I was able to mention Tobin without my voice betraying me. Or, put it this way, Sherry and Roly didn't seem to pick up on anything unusual.

On Sunday morning, I rang Aunt Biddie, to bring her up to date with everything as well – well, again, most of everything. However, although she was interested, her mind was really on the abbey clock.

Cleaning the outside of the abbey had now commenced and Tom, the decorator, had climbed up the scaffolding on the night before Good Friday and hung banners from it, made by the Women's Institute, proclaiming SAVE OUR CLOCK. One of the popular national newspapers had picked up the story and, tickled by the notion of a clock with no face, published a photograph of the banner beneath the blank wall of the bell tower.

'Come hell or high water, we're going to win,' Aunt Biddie announced.

I laughed, grateful for her preoccupation with the abbey clock, which had made her less attentive to my frame of mind than she might otherwise have been.

After that, I went for a long walk over the Heath.

It was a lovely spring day. People were walking their dogs and flying kites and model aeroplanes with their children. I walked with my hands in my pockets and thought of Ginette. *'When I am with Jean-Pierre, I am very happy. When we are apart, I am very unhappy . . . I am not sure that I would love Jean-Pierre so much if I had to wash his underclothes and nurse him when he has a cold in the head . . . I have my own apartment, my independence, my freedom. And I also have Jean-Pierre.'*

But I wasn't made like Ginette. Being a mistress, having an affair, wasn't for me. I wasn't cut out for living a double life: not telling Nigel about the Princess and Tobin – even though I had nothing to feel guilty about – was duplicity enough.

However, there had been more than a grain of truth in what she had said regarding marriage and wives. You married for love – or, at least, what you believed was love. As she said, marriage took the romance out of love. It took away a lot of other things as well. And, in my case, it gave very little in return.

Basically, the only real advantage to me now of being married to Nigel was material. Our combined salaries enabled us to live at Linden Mansions, to go out to dinner whenever we chose, for me to run a car, buy clothes, go to Paris. If we split up, I wouldn't be able to afford the same lifestyle on my salary.

What price lifestyle? *'I have my own apartment, my independence, my freedom.'* What price freedom? And what value was freedom, if it represented emptiness, with nothing to fill the void left by the other person?

I considered Nigel. What were the advantages of marriage from his point-of-view? They had to be same. He had the benefit of owning a property with a housekeeper to look after it and him.

'She is nearly fifty and unlikely to find another husband, certainly not one who is as good to her as Jean-Pierre . . . He never makes love to her. He never buys her special presents. And most of his time he spends with me.'

Ginette could almost have been describing me. At least I was only coming up to thirty-five – in a few weeks' time, in fact. Sure, thirty-five wasn't exactly young, but fifty would be a real mid-life crisis. And Nigel's affair was with his job, not with someone like Ginette.

But this wasn't getting me very far. It was all negative, re-crossing old ground. *Tell me the old, old story.* That was the first line from a hymn, which Aunt Biddie used to sing when I was a child and going through 'one of those phases'. My whole life, it struck me, was 'one of those phases'.

What I had to do was set my emotional house in order – sort my life into compartments – and examine each one separately. If I could do that, I would not only save myself a lot of anguish, but maybe even work out what I wanted to do with the rest of my life.

Back at the flat, I put a halt to introspection, made myself a pot of tea and curled up in an armchair with *Tender is the Night.* It probably wasn't the right sort of book for me to read in the mood I was in, but it was set in the right era and the right country – in 1920s France – and if some of it was poignantly sad and the mess the characters made of their lives not at all reassuring, the writing was beautiful and F. Scott Fitzgerald's observations as relevant now as they had been then.

A couple of times during the following week, Tobin rang me, but he made no reference to our conversation on the drive back to Linden Mansions, neither did he allude to our kiss. Nor did we meet up. For his part, he had a rush job in, which was unfortunately going to occupy him fully for the next few days.

In my own case, Miles was keeping me extremely busy at the office. There was little doubt by then that Miles definitely had something up his sleeve. He was holding a lot of meetings in his suite at the Ambassador – at some of which James Warren was present. The telephone wires kept humming, among the callers Sir Utley Trusted, Oswald Jaffe of Allied Vintners and Craig Vidler, the President of WWT. But what was being discussed between them I had no idea. Neither did Juliette, although she too was aware of something in the wind.

Later, I wondered if I ought to have been able to put two and two together, but there was no reason why I should. I was thinking in terms of take-overs and mergers. And so was everyone else on the financial press and in the stock market. The result was that the value of shares in the Goodchild Group rose, as always happened when Miles was mooted to be in acquisitive mood.

On Friday, Tracey rang again, this time to inform me that Nigel was flying home the next day, and the following evening he duly arrived, very sun-burned, very tired and very preoccupied. Civil would be the word, I suppose, to describe his manner towards me and I adopted the same attitude back.

Despite his jetlag, he did not go straight to bed, but sat up, telling me about his trip: the hundreds of miles they had driven until they had come to Silurian Lake – no longer a lake, but a desert. It was about three hours' drive from Los Angeles and the nearest habitation was a one-horse town called Baker, consisting of a few houses, a couple of motels and a burger bar, strung out along the highway. 'Hardly a holiday resort, but exactly the sort of location I had in mind when I was visualizing the commercial,' he said.

He and Rick, the cameraman, seemed to have got on like a house on fire, for he mentioned him more than he did Bo. In fact, his comments regarding Bo were restricted to the likes of: 'Yeah, she's fine. Knows her stuff. Very determined.' Reading between the lines, I had the impression that he and Bo had experienced a few head-on collisions, and couldn't help feeling a malicious satisfaction.

As weekends went, I had known better, but I had also experienced far worse. It was as if, by unspoken mutual consent, we had each separately resolved not to do anything needlessly to antagonize the other.

On Sunday morning he lay in and, in the afternoon, took me for a short spin in the Porsche, informing me in passing that he would be back off to California on Friday, explaining, 'That will give us the weekend to recover from jet lag and set ourselves up before we start shooting on Monday.'

For the rest of the week, I saw him only briefly in the mornings and for an hour or so each evening, for he was heavily engaged in meetings and finalizing arrangements prior to shooting the commercial.

One evening, Tobin and I had a quick drink at Chattertons after work, but there was a constraint between us, which had never existed before. Our conversation was stilted and Tobin kept glancing at his watch. To begin with, I thought he was keeping an eye on the time for my sake, but eventually he admitted that he was having dinner with someone after he left me.

'It's actually Penny, who I was telling you about the other day,' he explained. 'She has a very exciting new project coming up – a whole series of natural history books. I'm hoping some of the illustrations will come my way.'

At half past seven we left Chattertons and went our separate ways. When I got home, I poured myself a stiff drink and tried not to think about Penny.

On Thursday, Nigel brought me a copy of the call sheet, a lengthy document, listing flights, hotel details, a day-by-day shooting schedule, camera and lighting equipment, film stock, location vehicles, as well as the names, functions, home and office telephone numbers of absolutely everybody involved in the commercial, in the UK and in America.

'This is for you,' he said. 'There's every bit of information here you can possibly require. But if you have any problems, just ring Tracey. She'll sort you out.'

'Until the other day I wasn't aware of Tracey's existence,' I commented.

'Can't think why not. She's been working for me since we got Mac-intyre. She's achieved a miracle of organization putting this lot together. She's a gem, by far the best secretary I've ever known.'

I bit my tongue and let that pass. Instead I asked, 'When will you be back?'

'It's on the call sheet,' he said, flicking through the sheets. 'Here we are. Bo and I return on the fifteenth of May – that's a Thursday, so the film can be processed on Friday and we can have a slash print to work on over the weekend. Then we're off to Amsterdam.'

'That means you'll be away for my birthday.'

'Oh, Gawd,' he groaned. 'I'd forgotten about that. Sorry, love, but I'm afraid it can't be helped.'

Early next morning, he was gone again.

Tracey rang to let me know Nigel had arrived safely in America. She was a bit chattier than before. 'He says it's really hot out there. I'd love to go to California, wouldn't you?'

A couple of days later, Tobin rang, asking if I had time for a glass of wine after work one evening. We went to Chattertons and the first thing I did was to enquire how his dinner had gone – trying to sound nonchalant.

'Oh, poor old Penny,' Tobin said. 'I feel really sorry for her. She's a lovely girl but she's going through a rough patch at the moment. However, it looks like I shall be getting quite a lot of work from her new children's series.'

'Good,' I said, rather stiffly. 'I mean, good about the books.'

'Yes, I'm really looking forward to doing them.'

Apart from that, our conversation was light and inconsequential – about subjects like Aunt Biddie and the abbey clock. At the end of it, he did not offer to drive me home and I went back on the tube

What Ginette would have said, I hated to think.

On the May Day bank holiday weekend, I went up to Avonford for a pre-birthday celebration. The Three Graces had gone to join Mary and Larry in the fields and in their place was Reynard the fox cub, who had been knocked down by a car. Tiger couldn't quite decide what to make of this newcomer.

'And Chukwa?' I asked Aunt Biddie.

'Has woken up and discovered a taste for dandelions.'

'What about Nutkin?'

'He has three babies.'

'How can *he* have three babies?'

'Oh, I'm hopeless at this sex business. I just call all animals he. And, on that subject, Gordon has laid an egg.'

I burst out laughing. 'He'll have to be renamed.'

'Yes, that's what Stevie said. But, after all, what's in a name?'

'And what about the abbey clock?'

Her face broke into a smile worthy of the Cheshire Cat. 'We've hit upon a wonderful idea. We think that any change to the appearance of the abbey should be subject to planning permission. So we've lodged a complaint with the Council. There's to be a meeting on Thursday week. I can't wait for it.'

On the Sunday, Miranda, Jonathan and Stevie came over and I treated us all to lunch at the Lygon Arms in Broadway. Aunt Biddie gave me an original copy of *The Times* published on 8 May 1945. Miranda had made me a wonderful vase, the pale blue background decorated with butterflies. And Stevie had found a delightfully illustrated, old-fashioned, pop-up book of fairy stories, including that of the Princess and the Pea.

While we were in the restaurant, Miranda asked about my plans for the day itself and I was about to say, 'I'll just treat it as any other day,' when the idea occurred to me that there was nothing to stop me giving a dinner party. 'I may invite some friends in for the evening,' I said.

Which is what I did. I gave my first ever dinner party without Nigel. There were just five of us: Sherry and Roly, Juliette, Tobin and me.

I reflected long and hard before asking Tobin, then thought, what the hell, why not? The worst he could do was refuse. On the other hand, the coolness of our last couple of meetings was entirely due to me. If I wasn't careful, I might find that by trying to keep my distance, I had shut the door on him for ever, which was the last thing I wanted. It wasn't as if I were inviting him to an intimate dinner for two, so there could be no misunderstandings on that score. And if the others chose to misconstrue his presence, that was just too bad. They all knew of him, his connection with the Princess and his kindness to me, so they should be able to accept that a friendship between us did not imply a burgeoning romance.

When I rang him, he said, 'Ah! I was wondering how you were going to celebrate. Thank you, I'd be delighted to be among the honoured guests.'

I shopped the evening before and chose a tried and trusted menu which did not require me spending most of the dinner party in the kitchen. That same evening, I made Gazpacho soup, which I put in the fridge. The main course was *coq au vin*, new potatoes and broccoli. The chicken I also cooked that evening, so it would only need heating through next day. For dessert, I made lemon syllabubs, also prepared beforehand, so that they too could be served from the fridge.

On the day itself, Miles presented me with a purple Asprey's box, tied up with a purple ribbon, containing a beautiful handbag, made of exquisitely supple black leather, with a gold shoulder chain, not only elegant but deceptively capacious. He always remembered my birthday, because of the date, but never before had he given me so generous a gift.

I had been prepared for my birthday to slip Nigel's memory completely, but he too remembered. In the morning a bouquet of flowers was delivered to the office from a florist in Charlotte Street and, in the afternoon, Nigel rang. Everything was going fine out there, he said. They'd had a couple of setbacks. The first had been when they discovered Macintyre had sent the wrong tyres. And the next had been a sudden and dramatic storm and flash flood, which had transformed the dead lake into a real one for a few hours. However, they were making up for lost time and, all being well, he'd be back this time next week, as planned.

'Apart from that, it's bloody hot,' he said. 'The beer almost evaporates before you can drink it. And that's about it except for wishing you a happy birthday. Sorry again that I can't be with you. But try and enjoy yourself all the same.'

Miles let me off the hook early and I dashed home to peel the potatoes, prepare the broccoli and make little bowls of croutons, chopped olives, cucumber, hard-boiled egg and raw onion to go with the Gazpacho. Then I laid the table with a crisp white table cloth, the best silver cutlery and Aunt Biddie's lead crystal wine glasses. I folded the napkins into fans and put a little posy of flowers in front of each person's setting. Finally, I showered, did my make-up and put on the dress I had bought to go the Ivy, with the Princess's pendant as jewellery.

Moments later, my guests arrived, all within a few minutes of each other: Sherry and Roly first, then Juliette and Tobin, all armed with bottles of champagne.

The evening was a great success. Everyone got on like a house on fire and found heaps to talk about. And to laugh about. I can't even recall what made us laugh so much, not that it matters. We just laughed a lot about funny, silly things. Even Roly, who had a slight tendency to forget that a dinner party was a social occasion and would start lecturing the other guests – which always put Nigel's nose out of joint – was in a thoroughly good humour.

As Sherry remarked when she was putting the plates into the dishwasher, while I made coffee, 'Roly is being unusually well behaved. He hasn't disagreed with a single person over anything.'

On the other hand, Nigel wasn't there to ruffle his feathers.

Yes, if Nigel had been present, it would have been a very different evening.

But not only was Nigel in California, his name wasn't mentioned once. It was as if, by tacit agreement, we had all decided to ignore him. Or perhaps that still confers upon him a greater importance than he deserved and it was only I who deliberately failed to refer to him and the others had, temporarily at least, forgotten his existence.

It was after we had eaten, that I received my shock. Tobin went out into the hall, where he had left his coat, and returned with a package, which he handed to me po-faced, saying, 'Happy birthday.'

Inside was the painting of Angelini's daughter.

Literally dumbstruck, I shook my head, as the others crowded round to admire it. My immediate reaction was to wish I had bought it when I was in Paris – or that I had kept quiet about it when I returned. Eventually, I managed to mumble, 'You shouldn't have done that. I wish I hadn't said anything.'

He grinned. 'Why not?'

'Because . . . It was very expensive.'

'Not really. In fact, it didn't cost me anything at all.'

'What do you mean?'

'I engaged in a bit of barter. I decided to take you at your word and swapped it for the El Toro portrait of the Princess.'

'But that's not . . .'

He put his forefinger against my lips. 'Stop arguing. Do you still like it now you've seen it again?'

'Of course I do. It's a beautiful picture. But—'

Sherry turned round. 'Cara, for heaven's sake! Didn't anyone ever teach you to say "thank you" graciously?'

This was not the moment to make a scene. I looked up at Tobin. 'Sorry. I am grateful. It's a wonderful present. Thank you.'

At the end of the evening, Tobin left at the same time as the others. But, for a brief moment, we were alone in the hall.

'Thank you for a lovely evening,' he said.

'I can't accept that picture,' I said. 'It's too much.'

He cupped my face between his hands. 'Please don't argue now.' Then he kissed me full on the lips, very, very tenderly.

At that moment, Sherry, Roly and Juliette emerged from the living room. Tobin let fall his hands and I hurried across to the coat rack.

On Sunday, Sherry and I walked over the Heath to Kenwood House. 'What are you going to do with the painting Tobin gave you?' she asked.

'I don't know. I wish he hadn't given it to me. It's just too much.'

'What did he mean about swapping it for the El Toro?'

I explained how he had originally offered me both portraits of the Princess and Sherry nodded. 'Roly and I liked him a lot. I think he'll be genuinely upset if you refuse to accept that picture. And if it didn't actually cost him any money . . .'

'That's not the point. It places me under an obligation.'

'Without wanting to pry, what's the relationship between you and him?'

'We're just friends. We've met for a drink a few times and that's all really.'

'Does Nigel know about him yet?'

'No. But only because he's been so immersed in Macintyre that I haven't had a chance to talk to him about anything.'

'Hmm. When's he due back?'

'This Thursday. Then he's off again to Holland.'

'And where's the picture now?'

'Still wrapped up, in the bottom of my wardrobe.'

'That's not very kind to it.'

'I know, but what else can I do?'

'I know what I'd do in your place,' Sherry said. 'I'd put it up in the living room instead of Nigel's horrible blobs of inspiration.'

I managed a laugh.

'But I can see that might lead to ructions,' Sherry continued. 'I tell you what, why don't we look after it for you temporarily? That way, you can come and look at it whenever you like and Nigel need be none the wiser.'

It seemed an elegant solution. 'Would you mind?'

'It will be a pleasure, so long as Tobin doesn't misunderstand.'

I wasn't intending that Tobin should become a frequent visitor to Linden Mansions. He no more belonged there than did the painting of Angelini's daughter.

'He need never find out.'

Suddenly, from the trees surrounding Kenwood House, came the call of a cuckoo. I heard the princess saying, 'My most vivid memory is of the cuckoos which arrived every spring. Never in my life before or since have I heard so many cuckoos. They were so loud that you could not sleep in the morning.'

'That's the first cuckoo I've heard this year,' Sherry remarked. 'That means summer's really arrived. When I was a little girl, there used to be a wood near us actually called the Cuckoo Wood.'

We walked on in companionable silence, until the cuckoo's call faded to an echo on the air.

Next day, in the middle of the afternoon, Tobin rang and, without any preamble, announced, 'I've just had Ludo Zakharin on the phone. He's managed to get in touch with Angelini's daughter and you were right in your hunch. Your father did stay with them during the war.'

I sank back in my chair. 'Angelini's daughter? The girl in the portrait?'

'I assume so. Apparently she still lives in the family house in a village called San Fortunato, in the Lombardy region.'

'What exactly did she say?'

'I don't know. Zakharin's sending me a copy of a letter he's received from her. Obviously, as soon as I get it, I'll be in touch.'

'I'm amazed that he bothered.'

'I'm not. He's an opportunist. As a result of your visit, he offloaded a picture which he knew he'd have difficulty in selling and acquired an El Toro for which he had customers waiting. And he'd still like to buy the Angelini portrait of the Princess. On top of that, Angelini's daughter might just have a house full of Amadore's paintings, in which case he'd like to be first on the scene. By doing us a small favour, he's possibly doing himself a potentially infinitely greater one. A rather cynical view, maybe, but I suspect I'm right.'

Before I could say anything beyond, 'Thank you very much for letting me know,' he was saying, 'Now, I'd better leave you to get on with your work and do some myself. I'll give you a bell as soon as I hear from Zakharin. Take care of yourself in the meantime.'

After I had put down the phone, I looked up San Fortunato in our office atlas – but it was too small to be shown. So I phoned the Italian Tourist Office, where the girl on the enquiries desk eventually located the village on the shore of Lake Lugano and offered to send me information on the area, details of package tours, hotels and flights.

The postman brought the awaited envelope on Wednesday morning, just as I was leaving for work, and in the train I flicked through the brochures.

There was only one photograph of San Fortunato, a stunningly beautiful view, taken from the lake. A few dozen houses, painted in pastel shades with terracotta roofs, were strung out along the shore, dominated by a church. Immediately behind the village, the ground rose steeply and thickly wooded to a ridge upon which a few more houses were precariously perched. On the other side of a deep cleft or ravine, another church stood in solitary splendour upon its own monticle. Beyond that, craggy mountain peaks formed a magnificent backdrop. An inverted mirror image of the entire scene was reflected in the dark foreground water.

Not long after I reached the office, Tobin rang to say he had received the letter from Ludo Zakharin and would see me at Wolesley House at one o'clock.

When I came down, Sergeant said, 'Mr Touchstone's waiting outside. I haven't seen him for some while. A very nice gentleman. The world would be a pleasanter place if there were a few more like him around.'

Tobin was leaning against the railings, watching the doorway. He hurried forward, gave me a quick kiss – unfortunately, in full view of Sergeant – then, taking my hand, led me up the road towards Chattertons. Neither of us said a word until we were inside. He saw me to a booth and reached in his pocket. 'You read these,' he said, 'while I get us something to eat and drink.'

Ludo Zakharin had sent a copy of his own letter to Angelini's daughter, as well as her original reply. Both letters were written in French. His was dated 10 April and addressed to Madame Filomena Angelini. It read:

Madame,
I have obtained your name and address from my colleague, Professore Vittorini, and am taking the liberty of writing to you on behalf of a client in London, a certain Mrs Cara Sinclair, who recently visited the Galerie Zakharin and acquired from me a portrait of yourself as a little girl, painted by your esteemed father in the year 1930.

Mrs Sinclair is the daughter of the Irish poet Connor

Moran, with whom your family was acquainted in Paris before the war. She believes that her father spent the war in Italy and wonders whether you may be able to furnish her with any information regarding where he lived, so that she can pursue her enquiries into his life.

Unfortunately, my own father, Prince Dmitri Zakharin and his cousin, Princess Hélène Shuiska, who might have been able to assist Mrs Sinclair, have both recently passed away.

May I take this opportunity of assuring you, Madame, that your father's works continue to enjoy great popularity with art connoisseurs throughout the world.

The reply was in an immaculate copperplate hand, on thick cream vellum paper, bearing the address: Villa Lontana, Granburrone, San Fortunato, Lombardia, Italia. Underneath the letter-heading was a three-digit telephone number. The letter was dated 8 May 1980 and read:

Monsieur le prince,
I thank you for your letter, which took me by great surprise. After so many years, I did not expect to receive news from Paris.

Naturally, I am pleased to learn that my father's paintings still find favour with your clients, but I have no recollection of the portrait you mention.

As regards Connor Moran, he spent the war here at the Villa Lontana. Should Mrs Sinclair wish to contact me herself, I will try to answer her questions regarding him to the best of my ability.

Agréez, monsieur le prince, mes salutations meilleurs,
Filomena Angelini.

Tobin set two glasses of wine and a plate of sandwiches on the table. 'From her name, one must assume that she never married, although he addresses her as Madame.'

'In France it's considered polite to address all woman of a certain age as Madame, whether or not they're married.'

'Did you also notice that she wrote on your birthday?'

'Yes. That's a strange coincidence, isn't it?'

'Maybe, maybe not.' He looked at me in such a way that I knew the same thought was passing through his mind as mine. If the Princess wasn't my mother, then . . .

We clinked glasses, sipped our wine and he asked, 'Have you found out yet where San Fortunato is?'

I delved into my bag, took out the tourist office envelope and unfolded the brochure containing the map. 'It's here,' I said, pointing. 'There's a photograph of it somewhere.' I flicked through the other leaflets. 'Yes, here it is.'

He studied it long and hard, then asked, 'What does Lontana mean?'

'Distant, remote.'

'I guessed as much. The Princess said the villa overlooked the lake and was surrounded by woods, which presumably means it was up on the mountainside. It could be one of those houses up there, which look as if they're imminently about to topple over the edge.'

'They do rather,' I agreed. 'And the trees look as if they're hanging on by their roots. But the mountainside can't be as steep as it appears. There must be a road going up somewhere to get to the houses – and to that church up there.'

'Hmm, especially the church. Look at the size of those churches compared to the houses. And two of them for a few hundred inhabitants. Talk about the omnipotent power of the Catholic Church . . .'

He turned to the rest of the pamphlets. 'There seems to be one hotel in the village. The Hotel del Lago. Fifteen rooms, five with shower, WC and lake view. Bed and breakfast from forty thousand Lire per night. That's very reasonable.'

Suddenly, I had a sense of events overtaking me. Everything was happening too quickly and all at once.

'Mmm,' I grunted, not looking at him.

'The nearest airport is Milan, where you could hire a car. If you left on the first morning flight, you'd probably be there by lunchtime.'

'Mmm,' I went again.

He reached across the table, put his hand under my chin and tipped my face up, forcing me to look at him. 'What's the matter?'

My reply came out involuntarily, the words speaking themselves. 'I don't know. Everything. It's all too much. I'm still not happy about accepting that portrait. And now we've found out about Filomena herself, oh, I don't know, it sounds stupid, but for some reason I'm scared.' And I didn't only mean scared about finding out the truth about my father and mother, but about Tobin and myself and where we were going from here.

His eyes bored into mine, as if trying to see inside my head. Then he let fall his hand and nodded. 'I seem to be doing everything wrong at the moment. I'd hoped to give you pleasure when I gave you the portrait of Filomena. I didn't mean to upset you. As for going to San Fortunato, you don't have to go. Nobody's forcing you. You can stop at this point.'

I nibbled at a sandwich and collected myself together. 'No, I can't stop now.'

He smiled at me with his eyes. 'Good. So will you telephone her or write to her? Or take a chance and just go out there?'

'I'm going to think about it first,' I said.

'But you will get in touch with her?'

'Yes,' I promised. 'I'll get in touch with her.'

Sergeant didn't say a single word when I returned to Wolesley House.

It had required courage enough to ring Oliver Lyon for the first time. The prospect of contacting Filomena Angelini was far more daunting. I knew nothing about her, except her approximate age and the fact that she had spent her early life in Paris, whereas with Oliver Lyon, I had at least known what he looked like and what sort of man I was dealing with.

So I prevaricated, making the excuse to myself that it would be best, in any case, to ring her from home rather than the office. But, once home, I continued to procrastinate, stopping off at Sherry and Roly's on the way upstairs. The portrait of Filomena was hanging in their living room and the little girl gazed at me from her big brown eyes while I brought Sherry and Roly up to date with the latest development.

It was a lovely picture and I knew it would break my heart to part with it.

As I was leaving, Sherry looked from me to it and suggested, 'Why don't you delay any final decision on that until you've been to Italy and met Filomena?'

I nodded, grateful to her for making my decision for me.

Up in my own flat, I rang Aunt Biddie. 'I was just about to ring you,' she said. 'We had a most exciting day yesterday. Someone from whichever ministry deals with ancient monuments came here and has stated categorically that the abbey is a preserved building. And he's taking the matter up with the Archbishop of Canterbury – well, maybe not with the Archbishop himself but with his office or whoever deals with church buildings. And tomorrow's the Council meeting. Oh, that vicar will be sorry for all the trouble he's caused.'

After a quarter of an hour or so, I was eventually allowed to get a word in edgewise and told her about the letters.

'That's wonderful,' she exclaimed. 'Why on earth didn't you say something earlier? So when are you going to Italy?'

'I don't know. First I'll have to see if I can get time off work. And I still have to talk to Filomena Angelini, to find out if she's prepared to see me.'

Shortly before I went to bed, Miranda called me. 'Mum's just been telling me about the latest developments in the Princess saga. It's Stevie's half-term at the beginning of June and she's come up with the idea that, if you do decide to go to San Fortunato, she'd love to go with you. Jonathan and I have talked it over and think it could be very good experience for her, as well as company for you. We'd pay all her expenses, of course . . .'

Events were not just overtaking me, they were taking me over . . .

Next day, fate continued to take a hand, when Miles informed me that his programme for the next two or three weeks was changing. A European trip was to be cancelled and, instead, he and James Warren were going to New York for the week beginning 2 June. He asked me to book tickets on Concorde and reserve rooms at the Waldorf Astoria, but gave me no clue as to the purpose of the trip, nor whom they were meeting over there.

'If you're away that week, would it be all right if I took a few days' holiday at the same time?' I asked.

He positively beamed. 'The timing couldn't be better. Where are you thinking of going?'

'Obviously I haven't made any arrangements yet, but possibly to Italy.'

'Do it,' he ordered. 'So long as Juliette isn't planning on being away at the same time.'

Juliette had no plans for going anywhere. Apart from Nigel and Filomena Angelini herself, there were no obstacles in my path.

Nigel came home that evening, in a remarkably expansive mood, not merely civil as he had been before his departure but unexpectedly communicative. In fact, he sat, drinking wine and talking to me for a couple of hours.

By and large everything had gone well on the shoot, he said, although – as always – until he saw the film, which Bo had taken straight from the airport to be processed, he couldn't be a hundred per cent sure.

'How did you and Bo get on this time?' I asked.

'Oh, fine. We had the odd difference of opinion but nothing serious. She's certainly got very definite ideas on things and a couple of times I had to pull rank over her. But she accepted that I was the boss. And credit where credit's due, she takes her job extremely seriously. I've come to the conclusion that she's actually rather insecure, so she puts on an act to cover up. It must be quite difficult following in the footsteps of her father and grandfather. And it can't be easy either working in what is essentially a man's world.'

'No,' I said, surprised at his unusual attempt to analyse another person's character, and trying to marry the image he was painting of her with the impression I had received at the Ivy.

He went on to tell me about the rest of the crew, the bar at the back of Denny's burger joint, where everyone congregated in the evening to slake the day's thirst. 'I've never known heat like it,' he said. 'There's this huge thermometer when you drive in to Baker – it's like a mini-Eiffel Tower – and wherever you are you can read the temperature, which is the last thing you want to know. That storm was absolutely amazing – we got some our best footage after that.'

Before we went up to bed, I asked about his plans for the next few weeks.

'Sorry, love,' he said, 'I'm afraid we're working all weekend on the slash print, chopping it up and doing a rough edit, so the editor can get on with it while we're in Amsterdam.'

'When do you go to Amsterdam?'

'Next Friday. I thought I told you that.'

'No, you just said you were going. How long will you be there?'

'About a fortnight, I think. I'll have to check with Tracey tomorrow.'

When we were in bed, a further surprise awaited me. Instead of falling immediately asleep, he drew me to him and started kissing me passionately. 'God, I want you,' he murmured. 'I've missed you a hell of a lot.'

I just lay there, totally rigid, unable to respond. It was dreadful. I wanted to push him away, to curl up in the foetal position, protecting myself against him. But I couldn't. So I allowed his lips to slobber kisses and his fingers to go to all the private places of my body, attempting to stimulate me into a desire I did not feel. To make matters worse, despite being, as he must have been, exhausted, he did not rush our love-making, and gradually, to my dismay, I found my body beginning to react.

I squeezed my eyes tight shut and did something even more dreadful. I didn't do it deliberately. It just happened. Tobin's face appeared in front of my closed eyelids and I found myself imagining that Nigel was Tobin. Instantly, my body relaxed and I began to experience pleasure where previously there had been distaste.

Afterwards, I cried, bitter, bitter tears, which Nigel misinterpreted. 'You needed that as much as I did, didn't you?' he murmured. 'God, I feel better now.'

Neither of us slept well. Nigel kept tossing and turning, while I had a recurrence of my childhood nightmare. This time, I wasn't in a marsh but on the hillside above San Fortunato. Suddenly, the cliff gave way and I was plunging down the steep bank. My scream awoke us both and Nigel muttered, 'What's the matter?'

'Just a dream,' I said, wondering where the hell my life was leading me.

The following morning, he brought me a mug of coffee in bed, then went straight off to work. Uneasy memories returned and I went into the shower, scrubbing myself hard all over, in an attempt to wash away all evidence of the previous night.

Juliette and I arrived at Wolesley House at the same moment. 'You look very pale,' she remarked. 'Are you all right?'

'Yes, I'm fine,' I said. 'I just didn't sleep very well, that's all.'

Fortunately, it was a busy day and I had no time to brood. And, to my great relief, Tobin didn't ring. That I could not have borne.

Nigel came home that evening like a bear with a sore head, which I attributed to jet lag catching up with him. The film was fine, he informed me curtly. Now it was all down to the editing, which would keep him and Bo busy throughout the weekend. He handed me the call sheet for his Amsterdam trip. After dinner, he went to bed and when I eventually joined him, he was sound asleep.

Saturday I devoted to mindless chores, at the end of which I felt more like my old self. Nigel returned from his first day's editing in a vastly improved frame of mind and, after he had put a couple of drinks inside him, I ventured to ask, 'While you're in Holland, would you mind if I took Stevie to Italy?'

He hesitated for a moment then laughed. 'Goodness, first Paris and now Italy. You are gadding about.'

'Well, it's just an idea at the moment, but it's Stevie's half-term.'

'Where are you thinking of going?'

'A village called San Fortunato on Lake Lugano.'

I waited for him to ask why that particular place. But he merely said, 'Well, if it makes you happy, I don't see why not.'

On Sunday morning, after he had gone off to the editing suite, I summoned up all my courage and dialled Filomena Angelini's number.

The telephone rang for a long time and I was about to hang up, when a female voice answered, '*Pronto*!'

'*Pronto*!' I replied. '*Vorrei parlare con la Signora Angelini, per favore*.'

'*E chi è Lei*?'

'*Mi chiamo Cara Sinclair e telefono di Londra*.'

'*Cóme*?'

I repeated my name.

The voice at the other end said, doubtfully, '*Si. Un momento*.'

I could hear footsteps receding, followed by various other noises off. Then a different woman's voice said, '*Pronto! Sono Filomena Angelini*.' The voice wavered.

'*Buon giorno, signora*.' I continued in Italian. 'My name is Cara Sinclair. Prince Zakharin wrote to you about me and you were kind enough to reply and say I could contact you to find out more about my father, Connor Moran.'

There was a very long pause, then she said, 'Yes that is so.'

'In your letter, you said my father stayed with your family during the war.'

Another pause. Then: 'That is correct. He had been a friend of my family for many years.'

'And did you also know the Princess Hélène Shuiska?'

'Yes, I knew her, too.'

I decided to plunge straight in. 'As you may be aware, my father died shortly after the war. I was just a few months old at the time of his death and so I don't remember anything about him. All I knew, until very recently, was that he spent the war somewhere in Italy and that I was born there and that he brought me to England to be looked after by his sister. He told my aunt that my mother had died in childbirth. Then, a few months ago, I learned that at the time of my birth he had been married to Princess Hélène Shuiska.'

I stopped deliberately.

At the other end of the phone there was silence for so long that I began to wonder if our connection had been broken. Then she asked faintly, 'You were not aware that he was married to the Princess?'

'No, until then, I had never even heard of her. Neither had my aunt.'

There was another silence.

This time, I broke it. 'The Princess gave a television interview, but unfortunately she died shortly before it was shown, so I didn't find out about her existence until after her death.'

'Oh, I see.' Another pause. 'And what led you to me?'

'That was a bit of a long shot. My aunt showed me some letters from my father, written from Paris before the war, when he was staying with your family. Because I knew your father had returned to Italy during the war, I thought it possible that my father might have stayed in touch with you. Prince Zakharin managed to trace you and sent me a copy of your letter to him.'

'Ah, it is becoming somewhat clearer now.'

'Did the Princess also stay with you in San Fortunato during the war?'

'Yes, for much of the time she was here at the Villa Lontana, too.'

'Was she with you at the very end of the war?'

There was another of those long silences before she said, 'It is difficult to remember everything that happened so long ago. At the end of the war so many things were taking place all at the same time. And I was still very young . . .'

'I was born on the eighth of May, nineteen forty-five,' I prompted, 'the day the war ended.'

Yet another silence. Then, 'No, towards the end of the war the Princess was away from this house.'

'But my father was still there?'

'Yes, he was still here.' I felt the words almost being dragged out of her.

'And myself? Did you ever see me? Were you aware of my existence?'

In little more than a whisper, she replied, 'Yes, I knew that you existed.'

'So, please will you tell me what happened? Was the Princess my mother? And why did my father bring me to England?'

'Oh, this is too difficult for me.' Now there was anguish in her voice. 'I cannot say any more on the telephone. They were bad times, very bad times . . .'

'If I came to San Fortunato, would you talk to me?'

At the end of yet another, even longer silence, she said, 'Yes, I would be willing to talk to you.'

'I was thinking of coming in a fortnight's time. Will you be there then?'

'So soon? But yes, I'll be here. I am always here. I seldom leave the Villa Lontana nowadays.'

'I won't just turn up unannounced. I'll telephone once I arrive,' I said, not wanting her to find any excuse to change her mind.

'Thank you,' she said weakly. 'And now, *arrivederci, Signora.*'

'*Arrivederci, Signora.*'

As I replaced the receiver, I was struck by the literal translation of the Italian word for goodbye. It meant: until we see each other again.

Chapter 17

There I was, back at Heathrow Airport, and as I had enjoyed the novelty of travelling to Paris on my own, so now I was grateful for Stevie's company. She had come to London the previous afternoon, bubbling with excitement, adding to my pleasure and boosting my courage. For her, this whole journey was an adventure: her first-ever visit to Italy, with the added thrill of not just being a holiday but having a purpose – of being a mission. She foresaw no complications and anticipated no disasters. *Che sarà, sarà* – as the Italian proverb goes – what will be, will be. Whatever its outcome, the next week would count as a never-to-be-forgotten landmark in her life.

In a way, travelling with her was like being with my younger self, in the days when I had not only travelled hopefully but been confident that some new and unforgettable experience awaited me at my journey's end.

She chattered away virtually non-stop, commenting on the other passengers in the airport, giggling about their antics, wondering where they were going to and coming from; telling me that she had brought several books with her, including *Teach Yourself Italian*, as well as a camera, so that she would have lots to do if I became involved in lengthy conversations with Filomena Angelini in which she would be unable to participate. So I didn't have to worry about her. She wouldn't get in the way, she promised. She wouldn't be a nuisance.

And she had packed all different sorts of clothes, in addition to the jeans and sweatshirt she was wearing. She had shorts, T-shirts and a bikini, in case it was hot. 'I know the hotel doesn't have a swimming pool, but we may be able to swim in the lake, although Dad says that, being Italy, it will probably be full of sewage. But we can still sunbathe. And I've brought a posh frock in case we're invited out somewhere. Filomena may still know lots of arty people – and the Italians are very fashion-conscious. I don't want to let you down, Cara.'

For the past week, the weather had been dreadful – raining almost continuously – and bitterly cold for the time of year. Nigel had rung me since his arrival in Holland to say that it was the same in Amsterdam and his first week's shoot had been literally a wash out, putting them massively behind schedule. On top of that, Macintyre had again failed to send the right tyres and one of the child models had developed chicken-pox.

Today, though, the clouds had all gone and London was bathed in warm sunshine.

Stevie said, for the umpteenth time, 'I wonder what she'll be like. I can't wait to meet her. And I wonder what the villa be like. I know the Princess said it was very primitive but I think she was being snooty and it will be really rather grand, with marble halls, high windows and stately courtyards filled with statues – oh, and lots of loggias.'

'We're not going to Venice or Rome, Stevie, but to a little mountain village. And although it's called a villa, it will probably just be an ordinary Italian house.'

I tried to enter into her mood, attempting to forget about London and work and what Miles was up to in New York; endeavouring to forget about Nigel and those strange, abrupt changes in his mood: one moment so close and the next so distant; one moment so passionate and the next so indifferent; striving to forget about Tobin and the love-making of which he was unaware.

I had spoken to Tobin, too, before our departure. He had said, 'I'm glad you're taking Stevie with you. It will be an experience for her and company for you.'

'Who do you think that woman was who first answered the phone to you when you rang?' Stevie asked.

'I've absolutely no idea, darling. We'll find out when we get there.'

Eventually, we were boarding the plane, where we again struck lucky and had window seats in front of the wing. A hostess served us coffee and a roll and another wheeled round the duty-free trolley.

'I've been thinking,' Stevie said suddenly. 'If the Princess wasn't your mother, do you think it's possible that Filomena was?'

'That thought has crossed my mind, too,' I admitted.

'It will be very strange if she is. For her as well as you.'

'Mmm,' I murmured.

'Are you nervous about meeting her?'

'A bit,' I replied, in one of the great understatements of all time.

'Oh, I do so hope she'll turn out to be nice.'

'Well, we'll soon find out.' I hoped I sounded like Aunt Biddie – cool, calm, collected and in control of the situation, as an aunt should be.

The plane gained in altitude and the earth disappeared beneath clouds.

'You have got the photographs of the portraits of the Princess with you, haven't you?' Stevie asked.

'Yes.' I had one of the Angelini's portrait of Filomena as a little girl as well, which Roly had taken for me.

'And your father's book of poetry and his letters?'

'Of course I have. They go with me wherever I go.'

'I wonder what Filomena will be like.'

At Milan airport, everything went miraculously like clockwork. Our hire car was waiting and it was even the Fiesta I had requested, so that the controls were familiar, meaning I didn't have to worry about those while coping with driving on the wrong side of the road in the terrifying Italian traffic. I was deeply thankful that the airport was situated outside Milan, so I didn't have to negotiate the city centre – the ring road was quite bad enough.

'I don't think you have any Italian blood in you,' Stevie accused me, after we had been going for half an hour or so. 'You're English through and through. You're expecting all the other drivers to look in their mirrors and give way to you when you have right-of-way.'

Memories came back of the way Liz had used to drive in Rimini, with her hand on the horn and her left foot hovering over the brake. 'You're right,' I said, 'I am English.' Though Nigel, it occurred to me, would have been entering with gusto into the fray and giving as good as he got.

I was relieved when we were on the motorway leading up towards Como, where I could stay in the slow lane and let the maniacs overtake me. Eventually, we were up into the hills and driving through a tunnel, to be greeted on the other side by a spectacular view over Lake Como. 'We have a choice now,' Stevie, who had been studying the map, informed me. 'We can either continue along the motorway or go along the lake. Can we do that? We've got time, haven't we? Or do you want to go straight to San Fortunato?'

'No, I don't want to rush there. I'd rather absorb the atmosphere . . .'

That was a lovely drive, despite the narrow roads and horrendous weekend traffic, and punctuated by Stevie's excited exhortations. 'Cara, look at that!' 'Oh, isn't that amazing!' Mountains towered to either side of the clear blue lake, on which ferries plied their way from one pretty little port to another and sailing boats tacked in a gentle breeze. The houses in the sunny picturesque villages were painted all shades of pastel colours, their balconies and terrace gardens bright with flowers. Every now and again, we caught a glimpse of a lofty castle or splendid villa. The trees were fresh and green – silvery olives mingling with tall, dark cypresses.

At Menaggio, we lunched at a lakeside restaurant, in the shade of a mulberry tree. The sun was hot, the air languid and the gabble of Italian voices around us exhilarating. London suddenly seemed a long way removed – part of another world. Almost with reluctance I asked for our bill and Stevie, who had appointed herself treasurer, revelling in the sense of being a Lire-millionaire, peeled out the banknotes.

We left Lake Como there and climbed a series of horseshoe bends onto a plateau. The mountain peaks to the north were white-capped, like those we had flown over in the plane. Then we reached Porlezza at the eastern end of Lake Lugano and commenced the final stage of our journey, along a narrow, twisting road, banked by high, wooded cliffs through which it occasionally tunnelled briefly.

'This lake's quite different from Lake Como,' Stevie remarked. 'It's much wilder, but although it's not so pretty, it's almost more beautiful.'

The traffic was even more terrifying and I was constantly being hooted at for going too slowly into the bends by drivers who seemed to regard the road as a racetrack and whose principal aim appeared to be to force everyone else either into the sheer rock face on one side or the lake on the other.

Suddenly, to our right, the cliffs gave way to a wide ravine, down which a small river cascaded. Risking a quick glance up the valley, I caught a glimpse of a large church way up the mountainside. Then we crossed a bridge, rounded a corner and a sign announced: San Fortunato.

'We're here!' Stevie cried exultantly.

A few hundred yards along the compact village street, we entered a cobbled square, flanked by houses, shops and a café-bar. Above it, loomed a church and immediately behind the church the steep, wooded hillside began.

'Stop, Cara, stop!' Stevie yelled.

Assuming an emergency, I slammed my foot down on the brake pedal causing a fanfare of car horns to erupt behind me.

'Turn left! Now!' Stevie went on. 'It's the Hotel del Lago!'

Without indicating, I slewed into the car park and drew to a halt in the one free parking space.

'Well done,' Stevie said. 'That's how to drive Italian fashion.'

'Phew!' I sighed, sinking back in my seat.

'I think you'll do very well now you've got the hang of it,' Stevie informed me.

We got out of the car. To our right was the hotel, straight ahead lay the lake, to the left a little promontory jutted out on which stood several large three-storied houses, and behind us was the square. I craned back my head but the houses huddled on the rocky eyrie overlooking San Fortunato were hidden by the rooftops, the church and the trees.

Far from being the tranquil spot it had appeared in the tourist office brochure, it was a typically Italian hubbub of noise, with an unending stream of cars, scooters and buses hurtling along the main road. Pop music blared through open windows and women shouted to each other from balconies on which washing was hanging out to dry. To add to the din, church bells were pealing and from the lake came the sound of a ship's siren, as a steamer approached the jetty.

We went into the Hotel del Lago and found ourselves in a pleasant reception area. A rather overweight, middle-aged woman – homely in the Italian style – emerged from an office and I introduced myself. Speaking in Italian, I referred to my telephone reservation and letter of confirmation.

She nodded vigorously. *'Si, Signora Sinclair.* We are expecting you. I am Signora Nebbiolo, the proprietress. Welcome to the Hotel del Lago. And I have good news for you. We have had a last-minute cancellation, so, instead of the double room you have booked, we could let you have the apartment. It's only ten thousand Lire more a night. I will show you and when you see it, I am sure you will agree it is worth it. And now where is your luggage?'

'In the car.'

She called, 'Giuseppe!' and a handsome young man in waiter's uniform appeared from somewhere.

'My son,' Signora Nebbiolo informed us proudly.

He eyed Stevie appreciatively and accompanied us with alacrity to the car to get our cases. Then we processed down a flight of stairs, along a marble-floored corridor, and into a suite of rooms.

There was a sitting room simply furnished with a couple of armchairs, a table and dining chairs, a single divan and a wardrobe. At the other end, French windows opened on to a balcony. Leading off it was a bathroom, a small alcove containing a mini-kitchen, and a bedroom also with French windows leading on to the balcony. Amazingly, we were completely cut off from the noise outside: the only sound to disturb the silence was the steamer's siren, making a different, higher-pitched note as the boat departed on the next stage of its journey down the lake.

'Oh, wow!' Stevie exclaimed. 'This is heaven!'

Signora Nebbiolo laughed in gratification. *'Le piace?'*

'*Si*,' Stevie answered emphatically.

For an extra fiver it was a bargain. 'Thank you, Signora,' I said. 'We'll take the apartment.'

Giuseppe took Stevie to the French windows, where he explained in rapid Italian how to shut them and pull the louvered shutters, fortunately accompanying his explanation with a demonstration. Stevie treated him to one of her devastating, eyelash fluttering smiles and he almost melted under the impact.

With an inward grin, I thought to myself, 'That should guarantee us good service in the restaurant.'

When we were alone, I asked, 'Shall we toss for the bedroom?'

'No,' Stevie said, 'You can have it. I want to sleep in here. And I'm not going to close the French windows either. I'm going to lie in bed and listen to the water lapping below and watch the moon over the mountains.'

'So long as Romeo can't climb up onto the balcony,' I remarked dryly.

'Oh, I hadn't thought of that.' She rushed outside, then called, 'Cara, just come and look at this view.'

We leaned our elbows on the railings. Below us was a small terrace laid out with tables and chairs, most of which were occupied. Beyond was a stone wall, with urns full of plants arranged along it until it reached a weeping willow tree, the trailing branches of which arched over the lake.

Opposite us were uninhabited wooded slopes. We followed the line of them with our eyes, westward to Switzerland, where the mountains, dominated by the distinctive peak of Monte di San Salvatore rising behind the city of Lugano, appeared as blue as the lake water.

Stevie gave a deep, contented sigh, before going inside for her camera to take some photographs. Eventually, we dragged ourselves away, found some cold drinks in the fridge in the mini-kitchen, unpacked our cases, had a wash and changed our clothes.

'So what do you want to do now?' I asked.

'Whatever you want. Whatever it is will be bliss.'

'Then let's go exploring.'

'Do you mean going to find Filomena?'

I shook my head. We had a whole week ahead of us. Having waited so long I could wait a little longer. One should look before one leaps. Fools rush in where angels fear to tread. I repeated these and other similar clichés to myself, while to Stevie, I said, 'Let's get the feel of our surroundings first.'

So we made our way back up to reception, where Signora Nebbiolo handed us registration forms and we relinquished our passports. She glanced at mine and said, 'You were born in Italy, Signora? That explains why you speak such good Italian.'

'Thank you. But I've lived for most of my life in England.'

Before she could enquire where I had been born, I asked how long she had lived in San Fortunato. Since 1956, nearly twenty-five years, she told me. She had come here to work as a chambermaid and married one of the waiters. When the previous *padrone* had retired, she and her husband had leased the hotel from him. They had four children, of whom Giuseppe was the oldest and only boy. One of her daughters also helped in the hotel and the other two were still at school.

We then chatted for a while about San Fortunato and what a lovely place it was, and so on, which neatly led me to the question, 'Do you by any chance know a house called Villa Lontana?'

She showed surprise. 'Yes, I know where it is. It is not in San Fortunato itself but beyond Granburrone, up in the mountains. Wait, I'll show you.' Going over to a rack on the wall she took out a sheaf of leaflets, one of which she opened to reveal a local map. 'Here is San Fortunato. You drive along the lake to Varone.' She indicated the next village, then traced with her finger a road snaking up the mountainside, linking various outlying farms and hamlets and eventually reaching a cluster of black dots immediately above San Fortunato. 'Here is Granburrone.' A couple more horseshoes, then a single black dot. 'And here is the Villa Lontana.'

The road continued past the Villa Lontana to the top of a valley – the ravine up which I had glanced just before we entered San Fortunato –

whereupon it doubled back on the opposite side to halt almost exactly opposite the Villa Lontana at a church. 'L'Abbazia e Convento della Madonna della Misericordia,' Signora Nebbiolo explained. Then curiosity overcame her. 'What is your interest in the Villa Lontana?'

'I have an introduction to the Signora Angelini from a friend in Paris.'

'Oh, I see.'

'Do you know her?'

'No, I don't know, but—' Then she clamped her mouth shut.

'Her father was an artist,' I prompted.

She shrugged. 'Yes, I have heard so.'

Whatever she had been going to say would appear not to have concerned Angelini. 'Does the Signora come down to the village often?' I asked.

'No, never. She keeps herself to herself.'

No more help to be gained from this source, I decided, and asked, 'Can I buy this map?'

'Please,' she said, 'take it. It is free from the Office of Tourism. Take this other information, too. There are steamer and bus timetables. And here is a brochure on San Fortunato. It tells the history of the village and gives details of local walks and places to visit, including the *Abbazia* and our own church of San Fortunato.' She indicated in the direction of the square.

'Thank you. And now can you tell us how to get on to the terrace we look down on to from our balcony?'

'But, of course!' She pointed straight ahead. 'Along that corridor are the lounge, the bar and the restaurant. Dinner, incidentally, is served from seven o'clock. Then there are stairs leading down to the terrace.'

We followed her directions and emerged into the sunshine.

'I understood a bit of that. But I didn't get it all. What did she have to say about Filomena?' Stevie asked.

'Not a lot, I'm afraid. It sounds as if she's a bit of a recluse.'

'By the time I leave here I'm going to be fluent in Italian. Well, maybe not fluent, but at least able to make some conversation.'

At that moment, Giuseppe materialized, his face wreathed in smiles. 'Would the *Signore* liked something to drink?'

I glanced at Stevie, who shook her head.

Giuseppe continued to hover, ignoring his existing customers, as we threaded our way between the tables to the stone balustrade. Beside the weeping willow tree, two swans were gliding majestically past some steps leading down to a small jetty at which a red-painted rowing boat was moored.

Stevie's eyes shone. 'Cara, look! Oh, do you think we could go out in it?'

Moments later, Giuseppe having chivalrously helped us aboard, Stevie was rowing us out into the lake. Like me, she had learned to row on the Avon.

'No need to teach yourself Italian,' I commented. 'I know someone who'll be more than happy to help you.'

Stevie laughed. 'He is rather gorgeous.'

'Uh-uh. I'm responsible for you, remember.'

'Don't worry, I'm not serious.' She sighed contentedly and pulled on her oars. 'Does the Swiss border cross the lake?'

'Yes, just past a village called Oria.'

'So it would be possible to row into Switzerland like Hemingway and Catherine did in *Farewell to Arms*?'

'Theoretically, I suppose.'

'Let's try it one day.'

'We'd probably get arrested.'

'That would be an experience.'

'Well, today, let's content ourselves with going the other way. I want to look at Granburrone.'

'OK.' She changed course slightly. 'I just can't get over how beautiful this place is. Look at the reflections in the water. And it's so clear, you can see fish. Does it say in any of those leaflets who San Fortunato was?'

Reluctantly I tore my eyes away from the view and found the answer to her question. 'He's a local saint, canonized back in the fourteenth century, and his full name is San Fortunato Rocca. He was the son of a wealthy tyrant, who owned all the land in this vicinity, including Sacro Monte where the Abbazia e Convento della Madonna della Misericordia – the Abbey and Convent of the Madonna of Mercy – now stands.

'One day, when Fortunato was up on the mountainside, the Madonna appeared before him. Shortly after that his father died, whereupon he donated the mountain site to the Augustinian order and gave the rest of the land and his possessions to the poor and needy. Thenceforth he lived a hermit's existence in a cave. At various stages along the footpath leading up to the Abbey, there are fourteen crosses, representing the stations of the cross, marking Christ's journey to Calvary. The original crosses made by Fortunato have unfortunately long since disappeared but their replacements are fascinating for the beautiful wood carving.'

I let the brochure fall on my lap and trailed my fingers in the water, gazing up towards the mountains. Granburrone was now fully in view and, beyond and above it, a house, separate from the others, was becoming visible.

Unlike them, it did not perch quite so perilously on the mountainside, but appeared to be set back, almost as though it were built into the mountain rather than on it. It stood against a backdrop of trees, including sentinel-like cypresses. Facing south, towards the lake, its front aspect was several storeys high, each floor with its own colonnaded balcony. It lay too far away for us to see distinctly, but it looked as though it might have a smallish terraced garden, before the trees began.

'That must be the Villa Lontana,' I said.

Stevie rested her oars, allowing the boat to drift slowly. 'Gosh, what a place. Hardly an ordinary house, Cara.'

'Mmm, I was wrong about that.'

And what else was I wrong about, I wondered.

The abbey confronted it from the opposite side of the ravine. 'What did you say the abbey was called?' Stevie asked.

'L'Abbazia e Convento della Madonna della Misericordia.'

Stevie slowly repeated the name. 'It's beautiful, too. It looks very old.'

I opened the brochure again and translated, 'The Abbey of the Madonna of Mercy was built in the late thirteenth century. Over the main doorway is a fresco showing the Madonna between Saint Augustine and Saint Fortunato. The convent itself was founded in the fourteenth century and is run by an Augustinian order of Sisters of Charity – a nursing order. Particularly worth visiting are the Romanesque cloisters – the Chiostro del Paradiso – the Cloisters of Paradise – remarkable for the fine austerity of their architecture and the beautiful tombs to be seen in their galleries.'

Stevie took several snapshots, then started rowing again towards the centre of the lake, always keeping the Villa Lontana and the abbey in sight.

It was very quiet out there in the middle of the lake, with only the gentle splash of the oars to disturb the silence. The nearer we approached the uninhabited opposite shore, the more we became aware of a clamour of birdsong floating towards us on the breeze. And, loudest in that chorus, was the distinctive two-note call of the cuckoo. Not just one cuckoo, but dozens of them.

Last Sunday, I had been in London, telephoning Filomena Angelini for the first time. This Sunday, I was within sight of the Villa Lontana. If she was looking out of the window, she might even be watching me.

'All right,' I said, 'I give in. Turn round and go back to the hotel. I'll telephone her.'

The following morning, I was driving up the narrow, twisting, badly surfaced road from Varone to Granburrone. To my relief, I attracted no cavalcade behind me and was able to go at my own pace, though every now and again we met a car hurtling down in the opposite direction, which seemed to take it for granted that I would squeeze into the side, stop and let it pass. When this happened, we would hear through the open window the distinctive call of the cuckoos in the surrounding woods.

Occasionally, there was a fire break, some fifty feet wide, cut through the trees – and we would catch a glimpse of the Abbazia e Convento della Madonna della Misericordia perched on the Sacro Monte, with snow-capped mountain peaks in the distance behind it. Then the road would double back upon itself and the trees would close in again and the abbey disappear from view.

Eventually, we reached Granburrone, where the houses fronted on to the street, only just wide enough for a single car. The hamlet had a strangely primitive aspect, making one feel that one had gone back in time to an earlier century. Doors stood open and, from them, impassive peasant faces watched us pass.

Beyond the houses, the road curved sharply and to our right the ground fell steeply away. A few moments later, a solitary house came into view, appearing deceptively small as one approached it from the road, its presence announced by a high wall shielding its garden from the gaze of curious passers-by. This joined a wall of the house itself, the yellow stucco of which had faded almost to white. Shutters concealed the windows. Then came steps leading up to a door, next to which was a sign: Villa Lontana. After that the wall continued for about a hundred feet before turning at a right angle. On the other side, were the cypresses we had seen from the rowing boat. After that, the woods began again, enclosing the house and its garden.

A grey Fiat was parked in a lay-by amidst the trees and I pulled in next to it. Without saying a word, we both got out of the car. The air smelled of pine resin and was loud with the pealing of bells from the abbey and the song of those birds.

There were many types of birds in those trees. There was a whole multisonorous choir and orchestra of birds: birds from whose throats poured liquid harmonies; birds that warbled and whistled and cooed and twittered. But loudest and most persistent were the cuckoos – as if the woods belonged to them and there was a cuckoo on every branch.

'*There used to be a wood near us actually called the Cuckoo Wood . . .*'

'Do I look all right?' Stevie asked.

We were both were wearing summer dresses – Stevie a loose-fitting, blue denim sundress, I a cream shirtwaister. 'You look super.'

'So do you – very cool, calm and collected.'

I wished I felt it.

We made our way towards the door and, yet again, Stevie said, 'I wonder what she'll be like.'

Taking a deep breath, I tugged on a wrought-iron bell-pull and, from deep inside the house, we had heard a jangling, followed by the sound of footsteps. A woman opened the door, older but not dissimilar to Signora Nebbiolo in looks, her comfortable figure clad in a blue-and-white checked overall.

According to my calculations, Filomena Angelini should now be in her mid-fifties and this woman looked at least ten years older. However, I could be wrong and appearances could deceive. '*Signora Angelini*?' I asked. '*Sono Cara Sinclair.*'

The woman shook her head, her eyes moving from me to Stevie. Then she said, '*Non sono Signora Angelini, ma la signora aspette Loro. Prego, entrate.*'

She stood back, ushering us into the house. The hall, with its marbled floor and only dimly lit, struck chill and gloomy after the warm sunshine outside. I was vaguely aware of several doors leading off the hall: all were shut. At the far end, the woman knocked on a door and a voice called, '*Si, entrate.*' Beside the door was a small alcove set into the wall, containing a small statue of the Virgin Mary, with a posy of flowers and a flickering candle beneath it.

We passed from darkness into a room that seemed to shimmer with the same quality of white and yellow and golden light that made an Angelini picture so quickly and easily distinguishable to my eyes. It was simply decorated and furnished. The walls and ceiling were white. The curtains were a deep rich buttercup; the armchairs and sofas were upholstered in a warm brown velveteen and had giltwood arms and legs, from which much of the gilt had worn away. The carpet was a muted beige, but the sunlight, streaming in from the French windows opening on to the balcony, fell across it in a broad beam that was pure gold.

On the walls, were a couple of portraits painted in Amadore's unmistakable style – one of an artist at an easel, the other of a youngish, dark-haired woman. The only other ornamentation was another small shrine to the Virgin Mary – again, with a lighted candle.

I have only to close my eyes and it is as if I am back there again, reliving that moment: that first ever time I stood inside the Villa Lontana and saw Filomena, sitting in her chair, gazing out across the blue lake and the blue mountains, while the bells of the Abbazia e Convento della Madonna della Misericordia echoed across the valley and the woods resounded to the calls of countless cuckoos.

Then she turned her chair and wheeled herself towards us.

Chapter 18

She stopped the wheelchair and looked up at us. She was wearing a white blouse, pinned at the collar by a cameo brooch, and a blanket concealed her lower body. Her hair, drawn back in a knot at the nape of her neck, was steel grey. Her face was strong – handsome rather than beautiful – with dark brown eyes beneath thick, dark eyebrows. Her nose was pure Roman, her mouth full lipped and to either side of it deep lines were etched in the sallow skin.

A myriad thoughts flashed across my mind, including the wish that someone could have warned me that she was an invalid, swiftly followed by the almost guilty reflection that it should make no difference to anything. And then the reflection that her ill-health could well account for the frailness of her voice and hesitancy of speech when I had telephoned her from London. And then, the realization that there was as little obvious physical resemblance between her and me as between me and the Princess.

She reached out her hand and murmured shakily, '*È incredibile.* You look so much like your father.'

Her hand, as I took it in mine, was cool, almost cold.

'Thank you so much for seeing me,' I said, more fervently than I had intended.

She looked from me to Stevie. 'Is this your daughter?'

'No, my cousin's daughter. Please allow me to introduce Stevie Evans.'

They shook hands and Stevie said, '*Buon giorno, Signora Angelini.*'

'You speak Italian, too?'

Much of the previous evening had been spent with *Teach Yourself Italian*, without the assistance of Giuseppe. Stevie said, '*Non parlo bene italiano, ma capisco un poco.*'

Signora Angelini gave a faint smile and asked how old she was.

Stevie replied, '*Ho diciasette anni.*'

'Seventeen – I remember being your age. I too was young and pretty and full of hope. I wasn't in a wheelchair then.' She shook her head and pushed her chair backwards a little. 'Please, come and sit down. Lucia will bring us some coffee. Or would you prefer tea?'

'Thank you, coffee would be very nice,' I replied.

Lucia departed and Signora Angelini expertly manoeuvred her chair back towards the window. 'It's such a beautiful day,' she said. 'Shall we go into the garden?'

'As you please,' I said. 'We don't want to put you to any trouble.'

'It's no trouble.'

While Stevie and I stood back to allow her to go ahead, we glanced at each other and I saw my own shock reflected in Stevie's face.

Signora Angelini wheeled herself on to the balcony, at the far end of which a ramp led onto a path, which in turn led through an archway into a paved courtyard, where two padded deckchairs and a small table were arranged in the semi-shade of a fig tree. Pink roses in full bloom, buzzing with bees, clambered over the arch of a loggia. Terracotta urns and ceramic pots were massed with flowers. Swallows darted in and out of a nest beneath the overhang of the balcony, uttering excited, twittering cries. At the centre was a fountain, the water spouting from the cherubic lips of a statue of Cupid on a pedestal into a sunken pond, its surface covered by waterlilies, over which a dragonfly skimmed. The splashing of the water almost – but not quite – obliterated the sound of the cuckoos.

'This is my own garden,' she explained, encompassing the courtyard with her hands. 'Lucia's husband, Cesare, looks after the rest.'

'It's lovely.' I sat down on one of the deckchairs and Stevie wandered off into the rest of the garden, which fell away in a series of terraces, until it met the woods.

Lucia appeared from another door, beside the loggia, carrying a tray. She poured our coffees then, after asking if we wanted anything else and, casting an anxious, almost maternal look at Signora Angelini, went away again.

Filomena and I were alone.

'Are you familiar with this part of Italy, *Signora*?' she asked.

'Not at all. It's the first time I've ever been here.'

'But you have been to Italy before?'

'Several times. I worked in Italy for a while before I was married.'

'What is your profession?'

'Now I'm secretary to a company chairman.'

'It must be a very good feeling to be a businesswoman. I never worked for my living. I didn't have the opportunity. When I was a girl in Paris, I once dreamed of working for one of the great *maisons de haute-couture* – for Else Schiaparelli or Coco Chanel. But, after the war broke out, we returned here to Italy and, after that, this happened,' – she indicated the wheelchair – 'and I had to give up my dreams. But that's life and one can't do anything about it.'

Naturally, I itched to ask what had happened, just as I was longing to get to the real purpose of my visit, but politeness forbade me. She must be allowed her own time to get her measure of me.

We sipped our coffee and I felt her brown eyes studying me nervously over the rim of her cup, which trembled slightly in her hand. Then she said, 'I couldn't take in everything you told me on the telephone last weekend. Would you mind explaining it all again?'

I nodded and embarked, once more, on my story, telling it in the order in which it had taken place, beginning with Oliver Lyon's interview, adding each new piece of information as it had come to me. She listened intently, interrupting only to ask the occasional question or to suggest a word when my vocabulary failed me.

'And now here I am in San Fortunato,' I ended.

She gazed out across the garden and the trees, over the red rooftops down by the lakeside and the bell-tower of the church of San Fortunato, to the blue lake and the blue mountains. 'Where is the *signorina*? Her coffee will be cold.'

'Don't worry,' I begged. 'She can take care of herself.'

'So long as she doesn't wander into the woods.'

'Why? Are the woods not safe?'

Her voice became agitated. 'The slopes are so steep and the ground can be slippery. It would be easy to fall and have an accident.'

At that moment Stevie came into view in the company of a weather-beaten, grey-haired man, pushing a wheelbarrow. 'There she is!' I exclaimed.

Signora Angelini relaxed. 'Ah, she is with Cesare. That's all right.'

Stevie gave a little wave and tilted her head questioningly. I nodded back to indicate that all was going well. She took a book from her bag and sat down on the grass, near enough to be within calling distance, far enough not to distract.

'You have no children of your own, Signora?' Filomena Angelini asked.

I shook my head. 'I would very much have liked to have a family but I lost my first baby, after which it was impossible for me to have any more.' I don't quite know why I came out with that. It was not the sort of thing I would normally say to anyone, let alone a stranger.

She murmured, 'Nature can be very cruel.'

'It doesn't matter any more. Stevie is almost like a daughter to me.'

From beneath her blanket, Signora Angelini withdrew a rosary and fingered the shiny beads. 'I know how that can be. I was six years old when your father first entered my life and he became more like a father to me than my own father was – more like a brother than my real brothers.'

She glanced timidly at me and I smiled back encouragingly.

'I loved your father – I adored him from the moment I first set eyes on him, when my father brought him to our house in the rue des Châtaigniers. He was quite unlike anyone I had ever seen before – not at all like a Frenchman or an Italian. You know what he looked like, of course – very tall and rather thin, with a shock of red hair. We used to call him Rosso and that is how I still think of him. Rosso. His hair was much redder than yours. And his skin was paler. He couldn't sit in the sun without burning, whereas I can see that the sun doesn't affect you.

'He had a personality to match his appearance. Above all, I remember his laugh. Later, he didn't laugh so much. But in those days, he seemed always to be laughing, as though life were a perpetual joke to him, something he couldn't take at all seriously. Or maybe that was only with me.

'He was very good with children. He had the gift to enter a child's world. In fact, I don't think he ever really grew up. He was like Peter Pan. He used to tell the most wonderful stories. After he came to live with us, he used to tell me a story most nights before I went to sleep. Every time the story was different. He promised me that one day he would take me to Ireland to meet a leprechaun. Because of him, for years – long after I was grown up – I believed that there really existed little people called leprechauns.

'My brothers used to scoff at me but they were very much older and had no time for a small girl. Benedetto was thirteen years older than me and Emilio ten years older. That's a big age difference. I think they were resentful of me because I was spoiled by everyone. My parents always said that I was a miracle. After my mother had Emilio, the doctors told her she would be able to have no more children – then eventually I came along. But she had a terrible confinement and never really recovered her health after my birth. She was not yet my age when she died.

'And hers was a far from easy life. She hated Paris. She never learned to speak French and made very few friends there. But my father had ambitions to become a great artist and Paris was the centre of the artistic world, so, because she was a dutiful wife she did what was expected of her.

'Had my father possessed any great talent, then maybe the sacrifices she made would have been worthwhile, but he didn't. He was a copyist. He painted what he saw. That was all he could do. And, in his heart of hearts, he was aware of that, which made him very bitter.'

I frowned and she stopped.

'I'm not an artist,' I said, 'but, to me, your father had a very distinctive style. Perhaps his work was representational and perhaps it was not as innovative as – say – El Toro's, but I like it very much more.'

'Prince Zakharin said in his letter that you had bought one of my father's paintings. I don't remember it.'

'I've brought a photograph of it with me.'

She looked at it and shrugged. 'Yes, that is me, although I don't remember the picture. If it was painted in 1930, I must have been five.'

So I hadn't been far out in my calculations.

'I think he must have done it here, at the Villa Lontana, when we came on holiday. We used to come back every summer – for my mother's health and to see my grandparents.'

'Did your grandparents live here then?'

'Yes, this house was built by my great-grandfather as a summer retreat. He was quite a wealthy man, a silk manufacturer, with a factory at Saronno, on the road between Milan and Como. You may have passed through it on your way to San Fortunato. That district is one of the major silk production centres of the world. You may have noticed the mulberry bushes?'

'I'm afraid I was concentrating more on the traffic.'

'Very wise. I should be terrified to drive a car.'

'Is the silk factory still in your family?'

'Yes, it passed from my great-grandfather to my grandfather, to my father's older brother and then to his son. Benedetto worked there too.

After the war, he was in charge of it and now he has retired his sons have taken over.' She gave a little shiver, although it was very warm. 'What are the other photographs you have there?'

'The portraits of the Princess by your father and El Toro.' I handed them to her.

The change in her mood was quite extraordinary. Her eyes narrowed and her lip curled. 'Yes, of course. I remember these. Just look at her in her tiara and jewels. Nobody could know, seeing her like that, how she started. Pfff! *La belle Hélène.*'

I recoiled at the venom in her voice. 'What do you mean, how she started?'

'Oh, so she didn't describe her entire life story in the television interview? Tell me, exactly, what did she say about her life in Paris?'

'Well, not all that much.' It was too complicated to explain that I hadn't seen the beginning of the programme, so I repeated what Oliver had told me. 'She described how she escaped from Russia with Prince Dmitri and said that, after they arrived in Paris, he provided for her financially, while she went to live with a married woman friend she had known before the war. Then she married the Baron de St-Léon.'

'Prince Zakharin looked after her! Did she explain how?'

'She said that he had a family house and access to money in Paris and that he developed various business interests. However, when I was in Paris myself, Ludo Zakharin explained that his father had actually been a gambler.'

She nodded vehemently. 'And what did the Princess have to say about her marriage to the Baron Léon de St-Léon?'

'She said that they were very happy. Oh, yes, and that, through him, she met many great artists, writers and musicians, including El Toro – and, presumably, your father and my father as well, although she did not say that as such.'

Signora Angelini's eyes glittered. 'Such a weave of truth and lies! She knew Toro and my father long before she met the Baron Léon de St-Léon. I will show you something. Stay here. I won't be long.' With a powerful thrust of her arms, she set her chair in motion across the courtyard and under the loggia to the door from which Lucia had earlier brought the coffee tray. 'Lucia! Lucia!'

I could hear Lucia's voice answering almost immediately, '*Si Signora?*' but not the words which ensued.

Stevie looked up from her book and mouthed the question, 'What's going on?'

I wandered over to her. 'Are you OK?'

'Oh, I'm fine. Getting a lovely tan and I can now say, "The girl is in the beautiful garden and the woman is in the house" in Italian. What about you?'

'We're making slow progress. I'll tell you about it later.'

Shortly after I returned to my deckchair, Signora Angelini came back, followed by Lucia carrying a portfolio case, about the same size as the one in which Nigel kept his storyboards. From the baleful look Lucia cast me, I sensed that she was not in favour of what was about to happen and that, furthermore, she blamed me.

I moved our coffee cups and Lucia placed the case on the table, then opened it. It was full of sketch pads and water colour blocks, which Lucia showed one after another to Signora Angelini, until Signora Angelini announced, '*Si, questo!*'

Lucia handed me the sketch book. I was confronted by a series of pencil studies of a young woman, a nude. She had a lovely body, small-breasted and narrow-hipped, with long, slim legs. The drawings were tastefully done, with nothing pornographic about them, but equally they left little to the imagination.

'Turn the page,' Signora Angelini instructed me and I did as I was told. There were more. 'That is the Princess Hélène,' she spat out the sentence, placing a scathing emphasis on the word 'Princess'. 'That is how she earned her living after she arrived in Paris. Prince Zakharin didn't keep her. Such money as he had, he spent. So he gambled and she took off her clothes.'

Fleetingly, I tried to imagine Ludo Zakharin's reaction, if he could see the contents of that case.

'It must have taken considerable courage to do such a thing, particularly in those days,' I ventured, less out of a desire to defend the Princess than to restore a sense of balance and perspective.

Signora Angelini was having none of that. 'Courage! She enjoyed flaunting her body. If I had been in her position, I would rather have starved.'

If the sketches offended her so much, why show them to me? I wondered. Then, glancing up and catching her eyes riveted on the Princess's naked form, it occurred to me that she was taking a perverse pleasure in looking at them.

'As for my mother,' she went on passionately, 'can you imagine how she felt, knowing that this was how my father – the great artist – was spending his days?'

I thought of the date on the El Toro portrait and asked, 'Did she model for El Toro as well?'

'Oh, yes. But look at El Toro's painting here.' She pointed to the photograph. 'That is just a jumble of shapes and colours, not a graphic image of a naked woman. In any case, El Toro was not a respectably married man with a family.'

Her logic slightly escaped me and I selected my next words carefully. 'Were these sketches just for your father's private use,' – I stopped myself in time from saying amusement – 'or did they form the basis for other works?'

'What difference does it make? But, yes, he made them into paintings which he sold and which brought him to people's attention. He changed the hair and the face, so that nobody should recognize the Princess. But still rumours spread – and she acquired notoriety. Wherever she went, people were wondering whether she was the model, although nobody except my father and Toro knew for certain that she was. And she revelled in the knowledge that every man in Paris was lusting after her – the shameless whore.

'Those paintings were how she came to marry the Baron Léon de St-Léon. He bought one of them and fell in love with the model. Can you imagine such a thing? He belonged to one of the oldest, richest and most powerful noble families in France, whose lineage could be traced back to William the Conqueror. His first wife had been dead only four or five years. He had adolescent children – children at the most impressionable age – who needed the loving influence of a mother.

Her voice rose in pitch. 'But he married *her*, who cared nothing for family happiness, with the result that the slut became mistress of a fine *hôtel* in the avenue Foch, a *chateau* in the Marne and a house at Deauville. She had servants to wait on her hand and foot. She had diamonds, furs, a tiara, an automobile with a chauffeur and her own stable of racing horses.

'Then the Baron de St-Léon commissioned my father to paint her portrait. Of all people – my father. And my father was so proud of having helped her regain her rightful position in society, so pleased at being asked to paint the portrait of one of the most celebrated of all society hostesses.

Why are men so stupid, so gullible, so credulous? There was never enough that he could do to help the Princess Hélène.'

Her voice rose to a screech, the words tumbling over each other. 'Even after what she did to the Baron de St-Léon, my father still defended her. She destroyed the Baron, but still my father refused to believe the truth about her. He even tried to make out that she was justified in acting as she did.'

A host of questions were buzzing in my head, but I was becoming deeply concerned by the state of near hysteria into which she was working herself. So too, evidently, was Lucia, for she interrupted sharply, '*Signora, basta cosí! Finiamola!*'

Signora Angelini sagged back in her chair, her eyes closed, as though she had exhausted all her strength. There was no colour in her face, no blood in her lips.

Grimly, Lucia returned the sketch pads to the case and I seized the opportunity to put the photographs back in their envelope. Lucia carried the portfolio away while I wondered what to do. I had come so far and learned so little, but to prolong the interview would be tantamount to cruelty.

Signora Angelini moved slightly in her chair and gazed at me from lacklustre eyes. 'Forgive me. I don't know what came over me.'

'There is nothing to forgive. The fault is all mine for reminding you of things you would clearly prefer to forget. I am sorry. That was not my intention.'

'No, I realize that. You wanted to hear about Rosso. Then that woman came between us.' Her voice sank to a whisper. 'In death as in life.'

At that moment, Lucia reappeared, carrying a glass of water and a bottle of pills on a small silver tray. Her expression left me in no doubt that we should depart – and swiftly.

Glancing at my watch, I said, 'Perhaps we should be leaving. I don't want to tire you. It's nearly lunch-time . . .'

'Where are you staying?'

'At the Hotel del Lago in San Fortunato.'

'Will you come and see me again?'

I could sense Lucia's eyes boring into my head, urging me not to protract my leave-taking. 'If you're sure you want me to.'

'Yes. Another day I will be better. Lucia will telephone you at the

Hotel del Lago. Today was such a very strange experience. Oh, you look so like your father.' A tear welled in the corner of her eye.

Taking her hand, I said gently, 'Goodbye, Signora Angelini – and thank you.' Despite the sun's warmth, her hand was still cold, yet its grasp on mine was surprisingly firm.

'Please do not refer to me as Signora Angelini. Call me Filomena.'

'If it pleases you. And if you will call me Cara.'

'It would make me very happy to do so – Cara.'

'You can leave by the garden gate,' Lucia informed me, pointing past the house. 'Cesare is over there. He will show you.'

I called to Stevie, who jumped to her feet. We followed the path and came across Cesare, digging a flower bed. He straightened himself, beamed at Stevie and led us to an ornamental wrought-iron gate in the wall, explaining about the flowers he was going to plant in a rough dialect I could hardly understand.

As we got into the car, his farewells were still echoing behind us: '*Arrivederci, Signore, arrivederci.*' And the cuckoos were still loud in the woods.

We said little during the drive back down to San Fortunato, I preoccupied with thoughts of Filomena and concentrating on the twisting road, Stevie respecting my silence. When we reached the Hotel del Lago, Giuseppe led us to a table on the terrace next to the lake. On the water, the swans floated majestically by, a troupe of fluffy, grey cygnets in their wake.

'I know your Italian is improving but how on earth did you and Cesare manage to converse?' I asked Stevie, after we had ordered our meal, wanting to delay the moment until I had to talk about Filomena. 'Even I found him difficult to understand. He speaks a very strong dialect.'

She laughed. 'He spoke very slowly and demonstrated things with his hands. And I did the same back. So we got along fine. He showed me all round the garden, including his vegetable patch, and we even went a short way into the wood. Incidentally, there's a path across to the abbey. Cesare tried to tell me something about it but I didn't get that, I'm afraid.'

Giuseppe brought a carafe of white wine, a bottle of mineral water and a basket of bread. Suddenly very thirsty, I drank a full glass of water.

'And now put me out me out of my misery and tell me what happened,' Stevie begged.

'I'm not quite sure,' I replied slowly.

'She seemed very upset when we were leaving.'

'I don't think she's at all well and the conversation tired her out.' It seemed simplest to attribute Filomena's state of mind to her physical condition, even though I was convinced that there was a far deeper underlying mental cause for her distress – and that her father's attitude towards the Princess was only part of the reason for it.

While we ate, I gave Stevie the gist of all Filomena had said, including telling her about the sketch pads, but I could not bring myself to myself to describe that disturbing undercurrent of raw emotion. To do so would be somehow to take advantage of Filomena's weakness and betray a trust – almost like a doctor breaking his Hippocratic oath.

When I had finished, Stevie seized the facts in much the same way as Jonathan would have done. 'There's something odd. If the Princess married the Baron Léon de St-Léon in 1924 and Filomena wasn't born until 1925, how did she know all that about her modelling in the nude and every man in Paris lusting after her?'

'Her mother could have told her – or maybe the Princess herself when she was staying at the Villa Lontana during the war.'

'If she hated the Princess so much that's rather hard to believe.'

For all her youth, Stevie was endowed with a greater sense of logic than I was. 'Yes, I suppose you're right. For that matter, it's equally difficult to imagine her and the Princess living in the same house.'

'She didn't say any more about your father?'

'No, just how much she adored him as a child.'

'Nothing at all about his marriage to the Princess?'

'We didn't get that far. She started to get agitated talking about the Baron de St-Léon.'

Stevie threw some bread over the parapet to the swans. 'So what's your gut-feeling now? Which one of them is your mother? The Princess or Filomena?

I took my time before answering. Then I said, 'There's no doubt that Filomena was in love with my father. She all but admitted it. And presumably that's why she hates the Princess so much. Because the Princess was married to the man she loved. No, I don't think there's any doubt about it. The Princess must have been my mother.'

'Well, don't sound so disappointed. I still say what I've said from the beginning. I can't think of anything more romantic than to discover your real mother was a real, live princess.'

I gave a rueful smile. 'The trouble is, the more I learn about her the less I like her.'

Stevie considered that and nodded sympathetically. 'Yes, I do see your point, but, let's face, if Filomena was in love with your father, she wasn't going to like the Princess very much, was she? I mean, even if the Princess had been the nicest person on earth, Filomena would still have seen her as a rival.'

'Yes, I guess you're right,' I said faintly.

'Well, let's hope Filomena soon feels better and can see you again. Meanwhile, can we go out in the rowing boat this afternoon?'

That evening, Stevie phoned Miranda to let her know we were all right, shortly after which Tobin rang.

'I just wanted to make sure you were all right,' he said.

His call took me by surprise and I felt stupidly flustered because Stevie was in the room. 'Yes, we're fine, thank you.'

'Have you been to see Filomena Angelini yet?'

'We went today.'

'And?'

'Well, it was a bit of shock. She's an invalid. We only stayed a little while, but hopefully we'll be able to go back on another occasion.'

'What about San Fortunato? Do you have any sense of *déjà-vu*?'

I laughed nervously. 'None at all.'

'You don't feel that you've found your spiritual home and you'll never want to return to the UK?'

'Well, it's a lovely place. I can't blame my father for liking it here.'

'I'd miss you if you didn't come back.'

I didn't know how to reply to that, so I merely laughed again.

'Who was that?' Stevie asked, when I put down the receiver a few moments later.

'Tobin Touchstone, the friend of Oliver Lyon's, who was responsible for finding Ludo Zakharin and putting me in touch with Filomena.'

'Oh, I see. That was nice of him to call, wasn't it?'

'Very,' I agreed and changed the subject.

Tuesday came and went with no news from the Villa Lontana. In the morning, we explored the village, such as it was. There was only one shop, a general store, at which we bought some postcards, then wandered along the narrow alleys leading off the main square and climbed up a steep flight of steps which brought us to the church of San Fortunato Rocca.

Inside, there were some frescos depicting the life of the saint: as a wealthy young man; on the mountainside seeing his apparition of the Madonna; as a philanthropist giving away his land to the church and his fortune the poor; as a hermit, living in a cave on the wooded mountainside.

Outside again, we wandered through the churchyard, with its ornately embellished tombs, many bearing photographs of the deceased, most decorated with flowers. Among them, we found a double grave bearing the names of Amadore and Bettina Angelini.

In the afternoon, we climbed up to the Abbazia e Convento della Madonna della Misericordia. The path was very steep but surprisingly well trodden. Every so often, it stopped at a small clearing in which stood a carved cross, carefully kept free of weeds, with a little posy of flowers at its base.

From the top, we had a clear view across to the Villa Lontana. The little courtyard where Filomena and I had sat was not visible, but we could make out the figure of Cesare working in the garden. We could also see the path which led across from the abbey to Granburrone. It was cut into the hillside and crossed the river by means of a rather hazardous-looking footbridge quite high up the ravine, over a series of waterfalls, coming out just above the Villa Lontana.

The abbey had an incredible sense of peace about it, although, since we were both wearing shorts and T-shirts, we didn't like to go in. However, we did find the Chiostro del Paradiso, which was one of the most exquisitely beautiful graveyards I have ever seen, the number of flowerbeds seeming to equal the number of graves. It was less a cemetery than a true garden of rest.

Two nuns were weeding and smiled shyly at us as we passed. From time to time, other nuns walked along the covered arcades surrounding the quadrangle.

'Being a nun must be a very strange existence,' Stevie murmured when we were out of earshot.

'Worry-free,' I suggested.

'Mmm, but having nothing to worry about means you have nothing to look forward to either.'

Stevie, it suddenly struck me, was possessed of a wisdom beyond her years.

On Wednesday, we went on the steamer to Porlezza, returning in the afternoon with a crowd of schoolchildren. We had not long been back at the hotel and were sipping cold drinks on the terrace, when Giuseppe hurried over to inform me: '*La vogliono al telèfono, Signora.*'

I took the call in reception, with Signora Nebbiolo watching me inquisitively.

It was Lucia. 'The signora has asked me to ring you and invite you and the signorina to lunch tomorrow,' she said expressionlessly.

'That's very kind of her,' I replied. 'And we'd be delighted to accept, provided she is well enough.'

'Yes, she is much recovered. If you would come at about midday.'

'You found the Villa Lontana?' Signora Nebbiolo enquired when I put down the phone.

'Thank you, yes,' I replied, but made no attempt to satisfy her curiosity.

When I returned to the terrace, Stevie was grinning impishly at Giuseppe, who was gazing at her from imploring, liquid brown eyes.

My arrival sent him away with a last beseeching look.

'He's invited me out to a night club,' she told me.

'Are you going?'

'I pretended I didn't understand.'

'You can if you like.'

'No, I think I'll pass on that one. Anyway, I couldn't leave you all on your own.'

'That's very sweet of you, but I'd probably manage for an evening.'

'I'm not so sure. I think you need looking after.'

I cast her a sardonic glance, then asked, 'It's none of my business, but do you have a boyfriend back in Holly Hill?'

'Lots of friends who are boys, but no boyfriend. Judging by my friends' experiences, boyfriends are a highly overrated commodity. They expect to take absolute possession and give nothing in return. I intend to keep my heart for myself for as long as possible.'

Out of the mouths of babes and sucklings . . .

'Far more importantly, who was your phone call from?' she asked.

'Lucia. We've been invited to lunch tomorrow at the Villa Lontana . . .'

Lucia greeted us upon our arrival slightly less suspiciously than before, while Filomena gave the impression of being more in control of her nerves. Before lunch, we sat on the balcony, sipping aperitifs, looking across to the Abbazia, to the background chorus from the cuckoo wood.

She began by asking if we were finding our hotel comfortable and how we had spent the last couple of days.

I told her that, among other things, we had been to the abbey, and she murmured, 'Ah, yes, the Via San Fortunato Rocca. It's a long time since I went that way.' Then, hurriedly, she explained, 'During the war, that was the path we took down to the village. It was hard work carrying our heavy bags back up the steep hillside to the top of the Sacro Monte.'

I could only assume that during the past couple of days she must have done a lot of thinking and, deciding to take the bull by the horns, led us straight into the subject nearest to my heart – and hers.

Not wanting to rush her, I tried to keep the conversation general within the wartime context. 'How did you manage for supplies during the war? There's only one shop in San Fortunato now.'

'We never lacked for food, but clothes were more difficult to come by. We were self-sufficient so far as we could be, growing as many of our vegetables as possible, keeping chickens and rabbits. If we needed something special we would go by steamer to Porlezza. And there were always black market goods available. We were on one of the main smuggling routes to and from Switzerland. You may be aware that smuggling used to be a way of life in this area. Now, of course, it is easy to cross into Switzerland, but during the war the border was closely guarded and, as Italians, we were not allowed through. That didn't stop the smugglers though.'

'It must have been quite exciting on occasions.'

'Yes,' she said, 'our life was very eventful.' She glanced at Stevie. 'It is unfair on the *Signorina* that we talk in Italian. I hope she won't be too bored.'

'Don't worry,' Stevie said in English. 'I'm picking up quite a lot. You're talking about smugglers. I understood *contrabbandieri* and *Svizzera*.'

'She's a very intelligent girl,' Filomena remarked.

'A gift for words and languages runs in our family.'

'That was certainly true of your father – and you.'

'Do you mind talking about my father?'

'No, today I would like to talk about him. On Monday, it was difficult. I wasn't prepared. When I last saw you, you were a few months old. And suddenly, there you were, a grown woman, looking so like Rosso. It was a shock.'

'I understand.'

She shook her head. 'No, you cannot possibly understand. But you must tell me what you want to know.'

'Everything you feel able to. What his life was like in Paris. How he came to spend the war here at the Villa Lontana.' I paused, wary of re-invoking disturbing memories by mentioning the Princess and losing my advantage. Yet there was no alternative. 'About his marriage and about my birth.'

She sipped her vermouth, looking past us over the treetops to the blue mountains on the opposite shore of the lake. Then she said, 'I shall start at the beginning, although I am unable to tell you much about his life in Paris outside our house. As I have already explained, I was only a little girl when he came to live with us. When he first arrived in Paris, he had an apartment in Montmartre, then my father took pity on him. Ours was a large house and, after my brothers returned to Italy, we had space to spare.

'I don't know where Rosso and my father met. It could have been at Toro's studio or at the mansion of the Baron de St-Leon on the avenue Foch – or maybe even at our own home on the rue des Châtaigniers. My father was very gregarious and held open house to everyone, even people who were virtually complete strangers to him. If he liked their face, he would befriend them, regardless of who or what they were. All were welcome *chez* Angelini.

'My mother used to get angry with him, for she had all the work and none of the pleasure. But for me as a child, it was very entertaining. Sometimes, my father allowed me to stay up and sit at his feet, listening to the conversation. "If you listen you will learn, Filomena," he used to say. "Even if you only learn what fools men are."

'Those evenings were marvellous – the company so cosmopolitan and diverse in their opinions. Intellectuals, philosophers, aristocrats, artists, writers, musicians – all were welcome at our humble home. Never since have I witnessed conversation so stimulating. Such passionate arguments there would be, that often the participants came close to blows. Ah, not for anything would I have missed those discussions.'

It did not escape my attention that the Amadore Angelini she seemed to be depicting now was a very different man from the father she had described with such malevolence on Monday. But I held my tongue.

'So it could be that your father was a friend of a friend and that was how he first came to our house. It may even have been through Imogen

Humboldt, the American heiress. She was in love with your father – I don't know if you are aware of that?'

Cautiously, I said, 'My aunt told me that they were friends.'

'Oh, she was passionately in love with him. Many women were. He was a very attractive man. But, although he was penniless and Imogen Humboldt was so rich, he resisted temptation.'

So that was how he had played it. He had let it be known that he had turned down Imogen Humboldt, not the other way round. And, doubtless, he had also found it expedient not to mention the wife he had left behind in England. I wondered what Aunt Biddie would have to say to this version of events.

'Nevertheless, when Rosso arrived in Paris, Imogen Humboldt was very generous towards him. Maybe she still hoped to buy his affections. That is possible. On the other hand, to give her her due, she was generous to everyone. For all that she was so wealthy, she was a very genuine, unaffected woman – unlike some that one could name.' Her eyes glinted. 'If you have met Ludo Zakharin, then you must also be aware that Imogen Humboldt later married Prince Dmitri?'

I nodded.

'The Princess was furious when she discovered that Prince Dmitri had followed Imogen Humboldt to America and married her. Pfff! Never have I seen such rage. She struck out at everyone, like a snake. Yes, that describes her very well. She was like a snake, lashing out indiscriminately with its tongue, poisoning and devouring its prey.'

'Do you think she was in love with Prince Dmitri?'

'Pfff! That woman did not know what love was. She cared for one person only – herself. No, I don't think she was in love with Prince Dmitri but she did believe that he was in love with her. And, when he married Imogen Humboldt, her pride was deeply wounded. In revenge, she turned her attentions to your father.'

Remembering Stevie's comment, I asked, 'How do you know all this? You were very young at the time.'

'Being young does not prevent one from being observant, even if one doesn't always understand,' she responded tartly. 'Then later, during the war, your father and I had a lot of time to talk, here at the Villa Lontana, and he explained to me many things which I had not fully understood before.'

At that moment, Lucia appeared in the French windows. I sensed her assessing Filomena's mood, ascertaining that her mistress was not becoming over-excited. Clearly reassured, she said, 'Lunch is ready, *Signora*.'

Filomena shook her head to bring herself back to the present day. 'Thank you, Lucia. We shall come immediately.'

She manoeuvred her chair and led the way across the drawing room, into the hall. Stevie and I followed behind. 'How much are you managing to understand?' I asked her.

'Not as much as I would like, but I'm picking up a lot from the odd words and her expression and tone of voice. Anyway, don't worry about me. I'm fine.'

Although the dining room gave out onto the same view as the drawing room, it was a much gloomier, more formal room, with walls panelled in dark wood and heavy furniture. The sole relief came from another small prie-dieu, a large mirror, reflecting light back from the outside world, and two Angelini paintings on the walls: one a portrait of a formidable looking old lady; the other a group of three young people.

The table was laid for three and Cesare was standing at the head of it. When Filomena reached him, he lifted her from the wheelchair onto the dining chair, the transfer happening so swiftly and effortlessly, that I was hardly aware of it being accomplished. Stevie and I took our places to either side of her. Cesare left as Lucia entered, bearing bowls of steaming soup. She poured us wine and water in separate glasses, wished us, '*Buon appetito, Signore*,' and also took her departure.

When Filomena didn't lift her spoon, I thought she might be going to say grace. Instead, she said, 'It is an unusual experience for us to have guests. I hope the meal is to your taste.'

'This soup smells excellent,' I assured her.

'It's home-made from vegetables grown by Cesare. Please start.'

'Mmm, *è delizioso*,' Stevie said, after a few mouthfuls.

Filomena smiled. 'You must tell Lucia. She will be pleased.'

I was facing the portrait of the old lady. She was dressed in black and posed against a sombre background, so the only opportunities for Angelini to inject his unique quality of shimmering light had been in her white hair – and her eyes. Those eyes were quite extraordinary: even when I bent my head to my soup, I felt them gazing at me – benign they were not.

'Who is the old lady?' I asked Filomena.

'My grandmother, my father's mother.'

'She looks very severe.'

'She was,' Filomena answered grimly.

I found myself wondering how often my father had eaten in this room, sitting maybe on this very chair, confronted by that same portrait.

Stevie was facing the portrait of the three young people. 'And that one?' she enquired, in hesitant Italian. She was certainly learning very quickly. 'Is it you and your brothers?'

'Yes. My father painted that shortly before we left Paris, so I was about fifteen, Emilio twenty-five and Benedetto twenty-eight. Emilio is to my right and Benedetto behind me.'

I turned to study it properly. They say a picture speaks a thousand words and that one said them all. A whole family relationship was expressed there.

Filomena, at fifteen, her hair cut short and her face filled out, still radiated that kind of inner glow which distinguished the sunflowers portrait Tobin had given me. There was a vibrant quality about her, so that she seemed to be stepping forward, as though trying to break loose from the confines of the picture.

Her brothers, in contrast, were sturdy, rock-solid figures. Emilio's hand, resting on Filomena's shoulder, seemed to be restraining her, but there was affection in his smile, as though he were saying, 'I am doing this for your own good.' Benedetto, on the other hand, was intolerant of the impetuousness of youth. His eyes, like those of the old lady facing me, scorned frivolity. His broad shoulders, one sensed, already bore the weight of responsibility. Knowing nothing about him, except that he had taken over the family silk business, I took an instant and irrational dislike to him.

When we had finished our soup – or rather, Stevie and I had finished ours, but our hostess had taken merely a few spoonfuls – Filomena rang a handbell on the table beside her to summon Lucia. Stevie repeated her praise to the housekeeper, who, looking suitably gratified, took away our dishes and duly returned with the main course – stuffed red peppers, served with rice and salad.

For a few moments, we ate in silence. Then, without any prompting, Filomena picked up her story where she had left off on the balcony, as though there had been no interruption.

'As I was saying, when Prince Dmitri went to America with Imogen Humboldt, the Princess turned her attentions to your father. She knew how infatuated Imogen Humboldt had been with Rosso and that he had never reciprocated her feelings. To her, he represented the unattainable and she wanted to prove that she could conquer where her rival had failed.

'That was why she went after him. She did not love your father any more than she loved Prince Dmitri. As I said earlier, she was incapable of love. But she could not bear to be rejected, which is how she interpreted Prince Dmitri's action. She had not wanted Prince Dmitri herself – but she did not want Imogen Humboldt to have him either. Do you understand what I am trying to say?'

'Yes, I understand.'

'However, Rosso took her attentions seriously. He really believed that she was in love with him. Men are so blind. They are so easily deceived by appearances, seeing only what they choose to see.

'But one can't altogether blame him for that. If my father and Toro and the Baron de St-Léon – as well as countless others – were taken in by her, there's no reason why Rosso shouldn't have been too. She was very beautiful, even though her beauty was only skin-deep, and very cultured, very sophisticated, very accomplished, as well as being of Russian royal blood.

'However, Rosso was by nature a virtuous, honourable man. It didn't occur to him that the Princess might be amusing herself and teasing him, playing with him, like a cat with a mouse. All he saw was that the wife of a friend of his – who was also an important political figure – was trying to lead him into temptation.

'When El Toro announced that he was going to Spain to fight in the Civil War, your father seized upon this as an excuse to extricate himself from an embarrassing and potentially damaging situation for all concerned, and went with him.' She paused to take a mouthful of food. 'While your father was still away from Paris, there was a political scandal involving the Baron de St-Léon. It's so long ago I cannot remember the details, but it was to do with espionage. The Princess was having an affair with a German. He committed suicide to protect her. The Princess assumed deep mourning – less on his behalf than her own. She had thought to live in luxury for the rest of her life. Instead of which, most of his estate went to his children. Not that she was poor, in the sense that you and I understand by poor. She had all her clothes, her jewellery and other things, like the portraits and a Russian icon of the Madonna and child. That icon I remember very well. The expression of the Madonna was so tender.'

Her eyes glittered, making me aware of the emotional tightrope on which she was balancing. 'Yes, I've seen it,' I said, endeavouring to make my voice sound matter-of-fact. 'It is a lovely picture.'

Our eyes met and in her glance I encountered recognition of a mutual experience. She seemed to gain courage from that and her voice grew stronger again.

'She had no home any more and moved into the Ritz Hotel. Furthermore, she was ostracized by all her former friends. At least, that is what she told Rosso – and he believed her.'

She stopped again and picked at her food, pushing it around on the plate.

'My father had returned from Spain by then?'

'Yes, though he did not come back to Paris immediately. For several months, he was in hospital in Perpignan, after which he stayed with friends in the Midi to convalesce. It was not until the early spring of 1940 that he returned to Paris.

'He came back a changed man. He seldom spoke about his experiences in Spain but they made a deep impact on him. He had witnessed immense cruelty, courage and suffering. He had nearly lost his own life and never really recovered his health. Yes, he was a different person – more restrained, more serious – it was almost as though the laughter had been taken out of him.'

Those details, at least, coincided with my father's letters to Aunt Biddie.

'By that time, the Second World War had started, although we were still in the "phoney war" then. Hitler, having invaded Poland, had lulled us into a false state of security. We hoped the war might even be over. Then, shortly after Rosso returned to Paris, the Germans invaded Holland, Belgium and Luxembourg, and it was obvious that France must be the next target.

'It may sound strange to you, but I was never sure where my political loyalties ought to lie. By nationality I was Italian but, until then, I had spent most of my life in Paris, so I felt more French than Italian. My parents and brothers, on the other hand, experienced no such division of loyalties. They had no liking for Hitler and the Nazis, but possessed great faith in Mussolini. France and Britain were at war with Germany, but although Mussolini had formed an alliance with Hitler, Mussolini was still holding back from entering into the hostilities. Italy seemed to be a safe haven.

'When the German armies crossed into France, my parents began to prepare for departure. My father told Rosso, who was staying with us, that he could come too. It was then that he married the Princess, which enabled her to come with us, too. Ireland, as you must know, remained neutral throughout the war. Through her marriage to Rosso, the Princess acquired Irish nationality.'

'So that's why he married her,' I murmured.

'Yes, he married her out of pity,' she said, in a bitter tone. 'He had just returned from witnessing Nazi atrocities in Spain. You must have heard of what the Luftwaffe did to Guernica. And you must know how the Germans destroyed Warsaw and Rotterdam. The French government kept insisting that the French army would hold the Maginot Line and France would never fall, but people had little faith in the government. We were all terrified that Paris would be razed to the ground.

'When my mother learned that the Princess was accompanying us she was furious. I remember her screaming at my father, demanding to know if he was intending to take every rag, tag and bobtail with him. But my father just said, "They are my friends. I cannot desert them."

'As the Germans approached ever nearer to Paris, panic set in and the city was engulfed with fear. Suddenly, one Sunday in early June, rumours spread that German tanks were on the outskirts of the city and the government was abandoning the capital. My father announced that we were leaving immediately for Italy.

'Our car was crammed full, so there was no room for Rosso and the Princess. But Rosso exchanged a piece of the Princess's jewellery for a car with a woman who was unable to leave Paris because of her husband's work.

'The next day we left Paris. I shall never forget that drive. My mother sat in the front of the car with my father and I was wedged in the back between boxes and cases. Rosso and the Princess followed behind. It was one huge traffic jam. It seemed as though everyone was leaving, escaping ahead of the Germans. We crawled along. One could almost have walked quicker. We drove through the night and, when we crossed the border into Italy at Menton, we learned that Mussolini had, that same day, declared war on France and Britain. We had left France just in time.'

Stevie and I had long since finished eating by then. Filomena pushed her knife and fork together on her plate of virtually untouched food and rang the handbell. With a disapproving look at Filomena's plate, Lucia cleared away our dishes, coming back a few moments later with a bowl of fruit.

Meanwhile, Filomena had slumped back in her chair, exhaustion etched on her features. I glanced at Stevie and could see that she, too, was aware that our audience was reaching its end.

With an effort, Filomena roused herself. 'Forgive me, I feel very tired suddenly. I will finish the story quickly.' She sipped some water, looking up at the portrait of her grandmother. 'What happened then was that my father took a teaching post in Turin and my mother went with him, leaving me here at the Villa Lontana with my grandmother, Rosso and the Princess. My brothers had already been called up into the army.

'When we first arrived at San Fortunato, we had a maid, but she soon left, after which I did all the work in the house. My grandmother was difficult enough to work for – but the Princess . . . She expected to be waited on hand and foot, as she had been all her life. Nothing was ever right for her.

'Rosso enjoyed being in the country, but she hated it and regarded us all as peasants. In the mornings, Rosso tended the garden and in the afternoon he worked at his writing. He required peace and quiet in order to concentrate, but she would not leave him alone. She did not want his company as such, but she could not bear to be ignored.

'My grandmother did not make life any easier. She did nothing but complain. She was a proud woman and disliked the Princess almost as much as I did, resenting being treated by her as an inferior. Still, we survived.

'Then, in the summer of 1943, the King dismissed Mussolini and Italy made peace with the Allies.' Agitation crept into her voice. 'As the Allies fought their way up Italy, so the Germans invaded us and occupied the whole of the north of Italy. My brother Emilio was killed in the fighting at Monte Cassino. My oldest brother, Benedetto, was taken prisoner by the Germans and sent to Prussia to work in a labour camp. Then my father sent news from Turin that my mother had died. A few months later in the spring of 1944, he was himself killed in an Allied air raid. That was a particularly cruel stroke of fate. Yes, those were bad, bad days.

'Another thing also occurred. You have heard of the Conte di Montefiore?'

'The Princess's third husband?'

Filomena's eyes glittered. 'Yes, him. He had been a friend of the Baron de St-Léon and was also acquainted with my father. I believe my father once painted his portrait. He used to stay at the avenue Foch whenever he came to Paris on business, as well as visiting the Baron de St-Léon and the Princess at the Château de Jonquières. He himself had a fine *palazzo* in Genoa – and a villa on Lake Como, to which he retired after his factories were bombed.

'Once he took up residence on Como, the Princess spent a lot of time at his villa. He used to send a car to collect her and bring her back again. To begin with, it seemed providential, for her absence eased the tensions in our household and, when she returned, she was in far better humour, having mixed with other people nearer to her own class.

'Her absence also meant that Rosso and I became closer.' Her expression softened momentarily. 'I was eighteen by then and had left my childhood long behind. Your father talked to me as an adult. He told me all about his life – his childhood in Ireland and his sister. He told me how he had run away from school and from home, and how he had lived in a squalid slum in London, trying to earn a living writing poetry, until Paris had called him – as it had called to my father and countless others.

'It was such a moving story, my heart went out to him. That such a deeply sensitive man should have suffered so much hurt, seemed absolutely tragic. And now he was being made to suffer again through his marriage to a woman who cared nothing for him, who treated him like dirt under her feet.

'It was then, too, that I learned about the Princess's past, her adventures after she had arrived in Paris and how she had come to marry the Baron de St-Léon – the things I told you about the other day. It was then, too, that Rosso explained his reasons for marrying her when he had found her all alone upon his return to Paris: how he had felt sorry for her and hoped, in his humble way, to take care of her.'

She suddenly stopped again, her face grey with fatigue. I held my breath, willing her to find the strength to continue to the very end.

'Let us return to the balcony,' she said. She looked at me appealingly. 'Would you mind helping me into my chair?'

'No, of course not.'

Pity and tenderness surged through me as I lifted her body, light and fragile as a child's, into the wheelchair. Without asking, I pushed the chair out of the dining room, through the drawing room and back out onto the balcony.

Once outside, Stevie said tactfully, 'I'm going to look at the garden.'

Filomena and I sat in silence for a while and, gradually, some faint colour returned to her cheeks. Then, in little more than a whisper, she said, 'As you must surely have realized by now, I was in love with your father. I had loved him since I was a little girl and have gone on loving him. I loved him with every part of me. There was nothing I would not have done for him.'

I nodded gently.

Her hands gripped the sides of her chair. 'But that was my misfortune. He was married to Princess. Although she did not love him and he did not love her, they were still husband and wife. They spent the most intimate moments of their lives together.' She glanced at me and looked away, with what I took to be the embarrassed expression of an elderly virgin talking to an experienced, younger, married woman. 'They shared the same bed.'

So it was as I had thought. Filomena had loved him but the Princess had been his bedmate and my mother. Yet still I had to ask the question. 'So she was my mother?'

Filomena spread her hands in a despairing gesture, which could only be interpreted as assent.

'Where was I born? Was it here at the Villa Lontana?'

As on our last visit, her mood changed from one second to another. 'No. You weren't born here. Not in this house.' Her voice rose and her words stabbed the air in sharp, staccato sentences. 'She did terrible things which Rosso found out about. She had been deceiving him. It was the Conte di Montefiore. There was a big argument. It was all horrible. I can't bear to think of that time. But Rosso always believed the best of everyone. He, he . . . They, they, they . . .'

Forcing my own voice to sound calm, I asked, 'Did they make it up?'

She stared at me wildly.

'And I was the result?'

Her whole body sagged and she nodded.

'What happened then?'

'She was very angry. She went away. She left the Villa Lontana.'

'Was she angry because she didn't want to have a baby?'

Her eyes glittered. 'Oh, your poor child. You poor, poor child.'

'Please don't be upset on my behalf,' I begged. 'She wasn't the only woman in the world to have a child she didn't plan and didn't want. I haven't suffered as a result. I was well looked after by my aunt and uncle and have had a very happy life.'

Tears sprang to her eyes. 'You don't understand,' she cried. 'You weren't unwanted. Rosso wanted you. Rosso adored you. Rosso brought you back here. He carried you in his arms. And *I* wanted you. I wanted to bring you up as my own daughter. But *he* wouldn't let me. *He* wouldn't let me. *He* said I was too young, that I had to—' Her tears spilled over and her body shook with painful, rasping sobs.

I knelt beside her and put my arm round her shoulders, holding her close to me. 'Please, Filomena, please don't distress yourself.'

'Rosso took you away to England. I didn't know where you had gone. I thought you were gone for ever. And then I fell. For weeks I was in the hospital. I wanted to die. But God wouldn't let me. As if I hadn't suffered enough, He punished me by keeping me alive. And Rosso never came back.' She shook her head frenziedly and the tears poured down her cheeks. 'He never returned to this house. I never saw him again. I never saw him again. Oh, why have I had to go on living? I can only believe my life is a form of divine retribution. God is punishing me by keeping me alive.'

I sensed Lucia's presence and, glancing up, encountered her face, in which I read pity for Filomena and hostile reproach for me. In her hand she carried a glass of water and a small phial of pills. I let go of Filomena's shoulder and rose shakily to my feet.

'Please go,' Lucia ordered peremptorily. 'She needs my attention.'

I nodded and went down into the garden which my father had once tended, walking past the courtyard with its tinkling fountain, rushing blindly across the grass, running down the steps of the terraces, drawn involuntarily towards the wood.

'I was in love with your father. I had loved him since I was a little girl and have gone on loving him. I loved him with every part of me. There was nothing I would not have done for him . . .'

Vaguely, I was aware of Stevie calling, 'Cara, Cara, are you all right?' and of her footsteps hurrying after me. I charged on in among the trees, crashing through the undergrowth and stumbling over rocks, until, suddenly, the ground began to drop away and I found myself on the edge of the ravine – exactly as it had been in my nightmare.

Somehow, I stopped. I don't know how. One step further and I would have plunged down that precipitous slope towards the mountain torrent far below, cascading towards the lake.

Shaking all over, I drew back and sank to the ground.

'And then I fell. For weeks I was in the hospital. I wanted to die. But God wouldn't let me. As if I hadn't suffered enough, He punished me by keeping me alive . . .'

Across the other side of the valley, the Abbazia e Convento della Madonna della Misericordia gleamed white in the afternoon sun.

'Rosso wanted you. Rosso adored you. And I *wanted you. I wanted to bring you up as my own daughter. But he wouldn't let me . . .'*

'Cara, are you all right?'

With an effort I turned and looked up into Stevie's white, anxious face. I nodded and she sank down beside me, linking her arm through mine.

'Rosso never came back . . . He never returned to this house. I never saw him again . . .'

The birds which had fallen silent when I had disturbed the peace of their woods, resumed their muted songs. Loudest among them were the cuckoos, seeming to mock me with their repetitive, taunting, two-note call.

CHAPTER 19

When we eventually made our way out of the woods and up along the edge of the garden, there was no evidence of life about the villa. The balcony was empty. Of Cesare there was no sign. We let ourselves out through the wrought-iron gate and walked in silence to the car. Then I drove through Granburrone and down the twisting, narrow road through the cuckoo-filled woods to Varone, convinced as I did so that I would never come this way again.

Upon reaching San Fortunato, I went straight through the village and Stevie asked in a little voice, 'Where are we going?'

'Nowhere in particular.'

'What happened?'

I flashed her what I hoped was a reassuring smile. 'I'm sorry. I didn't mean to frighten you. She just got very upset – and that upset me.'

After a while we came to a café with a car park and I pulled off the road. The café terrace was occupied by sufficient people to give a sense of normality and not so many as to be crowded.

'Let's have a coffee,' I said.

I started, as Filomena had done, at the beginning. As I spoke, I began to feel calmer and, by the time I reached the part in Filomena's story where my father and the Princess had tried to make up their differences in bed, with myself as the unforeseen consequence, I could hear my voice sounding remarkably steady.

But when I said, 'Filomena was so much in love with my father that she wanted to keep me,' I couldn't stop my voice from faltering. 'But he wouldn't let her. He said she was too young. After that, she had a fall. She said she wanted to die.'

'Poor girl,' Stevie breathed. 'How awful for her. Fancy loving someone *so* much that you want to keep his child by another woman. That really is love. Oh, I find that terribly sad.'

Reason was struggling to replace emotion in my head, if not in my heart. 'What would she have been in 1945? Only twenty, not much older than you. Even if she hadn't become an invalid, it would have been difficult for her to have taken on that sort of responsibility. And unfair, too. No, I think my father did the right thing – the only possible thing really.'

'And the Princess?'

'It sounded as if he went to wherever she had gone to have me – some clinic or hospital, I assume – and brought me back to the Villa Lontana. Then, presumably, as soon as things had calmed down after the war and the transport systems were functioning, he took me to Avonford.'

Stevie regarded me from big eyes. 'Do you believe he was as much in love with Filomena as she was with him and that he was coming back to her after he left you with Granny?'

'I should like to hope so, but who knows?'

'When do you think she found out that he was no longer alive?'

'I've no idea. I couldn't ask. She was becoming almost hysterical by then. Maybe she saw it in a newspaper. Or in a book. Any book which mentions him makes it clear that he is dead.'

'It must have been horrid for her to find out like that.'

We finished our coffees and wandered along the lakeside. In my head, I kept hearing in my head the refrain from Tennyson's *Mariana*:

> *She only said, 'My life is dreary,*
> *He cometh not,' she said;*
> *She said, 'I am aweary, aweary,*
> *I would that I were dead!'*

For thirty-five years, she had been waiting and wishing she were dead. Then into her solitude I had blundered, wanting merely to satisfy my curiosity.

I felt deeply contrite. I had been wrong to make her continue in her story, causing old wounds to be reopened and spectres of the past to be revived. What did it ultimately matter who my parents had been and what they had done? They were dead. They belonged to the past. But Filomena was alive – and belonged to the present. And because of that, she was of greater importance.

That night, before I went to bed, I wrote her a short note, inadequate words to try and express my remorse:

> *Dear Filomena,*
> *I thank you with all my heart for telling me about my parents and I am truly sorry to have caused you so much pain in the process. I beg you to believe that that was not my intention. We shall be leaving San Fortunato on Sunday and I shall not disturb you again.*

I deliberated whether to include my London address then decided against it, for to do so would make it look as though I was expecting a reply, placing an onus on her, which was the opposite of my intention.

After putting the letter in an envelope and sealing it, I went out on to the balcony, leaning on the railings. The night was very quiet, the village asleep, the silence broken only by wavelets splashing gently against the wall beneath me and the occasional car passing along the main road. The moon gleamed silver on the lake and I could just make out the shape of the rowing boat bobbing at its mooring beside the weeping willow tree. The mountains on the opposite shore were featureless silhouettes.

In order that Filomena's anguish should not be in vain, I must try to make some sense of it all – for her sake even more than mine. I had to fit the pieces of the jigsaw together and form a complete picture. I might not like what I saw but that was immaterial. What was important was to confront the truth. And it had to be done here, at San Fortunato, where I had spent the first months of my life, looked after by Filomena and my father.

Somewhere, not far from here, the Princess had given birth to me.

Then what had happened?

She – or someone – must have let my father know and he had gone to claim me. Because the Princess hadn't wanted me – because she wanted to start a new life with the Conte di Montefiore – my father had taken me to the Villa Lontana. For a few months, I had been cared for by Filomena and, presumably, her grandmother. There could easily have been a wet-nurse in the village to suckle me. Then, when I was weaned and life in post-war Europe was starting to settle down, my father had taken me to Avonford. Yes, that all made sense.

Why, though, had he told Aunt Biddie that my mother had died in childbirth?

Because that had provided an irrefutable reason. If Aunt Biddie had known that my natural mother was alive, albeit living with another man, she might have been less willing to adopt me.

But what had Filomena meant when she said her life was a form of divine retribution and God was punishing her by keeping alive? If she had done nothing wrong, why should she be punished?

Except that – I thought of her rosary and those little shrines to the Virgin – she was obviously very religious. In the eyes of the Church, she had sinned. By coveting another woman's husband, she had broken one of the Ten Commandments. And who knew what else might have happened? Perhaps my father had kissed her – or maybe even gone further than that.

Which brought me to Stevie's question. Had my father been intending to return to the Villa Lontana after leaving me in Avonford?

I gazed out across the silver lake and heard again Filomena's agonized words: *'He never returned to this house. I never saw him again.'*

Had he made her a promise to return? Or – and in the light of all I had learned about him, this seemed far more likely – had he made her a promise he never intended to keep? Had he been fobbing her off, running away from a situation with which he couldn't cope, as he had run away from so many situations before?

I heard Aunt Biddie saying, 'Connor did things by default, not decision. He drifted into situations and wriggled out of them again.'

Taking me to England would have presented a heaven-sent opportunity to extricate himself from a relationship which was palling on him. He had escaped from Patricia and Imogen with equal aplomb.

In other words, he had lied to Filomena, as he had lied to her before. He had not told her about his marriage to Patricia nor about his affair with Imogen Humboldt. And, thinking about his letter to Aunt Biddie before he left for Spain – '*Paris has become rather uncomfortable for me. A little amourette is turning sour. The good lady's husband is threatening to have me expelled. Discretion seems the better part of valour*' – it would seem probable that he had indeed had an affair with the Princess back in 1935 or 1936. In which case, he had lied about that, too.

'He was by nature a virtuous, honourable man.'

He had lied, also, about his reason for marrying the Princess.

'He married her out of pity.'

Pity be damned. His experiences in the Spanish Civil War could well have affected him deeply, but it was extremely difficult to believe that the leopard had changed its spots.

My father might have remained a saint in Filomena's eyes, but not in mine. Those myths I had so long cherished about him had been well and truly destroyed. The Byronic hero was no longer even a fallen angel but a mortal man, with more than his full share of human failings.

He had married the Princess for her money, just as he had Patricia before her, and pursued Imogen Humboldt for the same reasons. The Princess might not have been rich by her own standards, but she had been rich by his. *'She had all her clothes, her jewellery and other things, like the portraits and a Russian icon.'* And Amadore Angelini had kindly provided them both with a roof over their heads.

As for the Princess, she had married my father because he had offered her a passport to freedom. Then the Conte di Montefiore had turned up on Lake Como and she had transferred her affections to him.

How much of what Filomena had said about the Princess could I believe? As Stevie had pointed out the other day, her opinion was understandably biased. Yet if you took only a quarter of what Filomena had told me as true – and added to that everything Oliver Lyon, Tobin and Ludo Zakharin had said – the Princess hardly emerged as the sort of woman you would choose as a mother, given such an impossibility.

No, she and my father had been two of a kind: both opportunists, utterly self-indulgent, not giving a damn who they hurt as they went through life, so long as they were all right.

And they were my parents – I was the fruit of their loins . . .

For a long, long time, I remained on the balcony, trying to re-establish myself as a person within the framework of the new knowledge I had gained about them; trying to convince myself that their identities did not make any difference to my fundamental personality – that, whatever scientists or psychologists might believe, environment was more important than heredity.

Yes, my original reaction after Oliver Lyon's programme had been correct. The Princess's blood might flow in my veins but there was no further relationship, mental or emotional, between us. Aunt Biddie was my real mother, Uncle Stephen my real father. The example of their goodness, their loving kindness, their unstinting generosity of nature, had counteracted the selfishness of my natural parents.

How fortunate I was. Had I been brought up by the Princess, how miserable my childhood would have been and how different my life since then – and my personality, too – what a truly mixed-up person I would be now, totally lacking in any sense of stability.

I thought I was unhappy with Nigel but, as the Princess's daughter, I would quite possibly have rushed in desperation into a far worse marriage. In fact, if I had followed my parents' lead, I might well have had several husbands by now, each progressively worse than the first. It simply didn't bear contemplating.

And if I had been brought up by Filomena?

What difference would my presence have made to Filomena? Would she have been a happier person, more complete and more balanced, if she could have spent her every day in the company of Rosso's daughter? Would affection for a fellow human being have triumphed, or would I have served as a constant, taunting, painful reminder of her hated rival and the man she had loved and lost? Would she have come to see me as a cuckoo in her nest – and would the love she had imagined herself to feel towards me eventually have turned to loathing?

As for me, what if I had grown up at the Villa Lontana? What would I be doing now? On the assumption that Filomena had gone on caring for me, she would undoubtedly have been very possessive and I, with my nature, would have found it almost impossible to leave her and go out into the world. In which case it could now be me, and not Lucia, who was looking after her. If I had married, I would be living nearby, possibly even here in San Fortunato, in order that I could visit her every day at the Villa Lontana.

Was San Fortunato my spiritual home? It was beautiful, but it was a far smaller, far more enclosed community even than Avonford. Whatever I had or had not inherited from my parents, something of their restlessness was in me. Only with great difficulty, could I have spent my life in San Fortunato.

At that point in my hypothesizing, I caught myself out. Who was I trying to kid? I had been twenty when I finally left Avonford and, within two years of that, I had exchanged one kind of permanence for another. To see myself as an adventurer was to practice self-deception on a massive scale. I was *Sweet Stay-at-Home, sweet Well-content, sweet Love-one-place.*

My current restlessness was the result not of wanderlust but a dissatisfaction with my personal circumstances – with Nigel. If my marriage had been happier, I would have been quite content to stay in one place. As I had admitted to Sherry and Roly, I was a very domestic person – the most important thing in my life was the affection of other people.

Therefore, if I had grown up with Filomena as a mother, I might not have turned out very much different to how I was now – merely more Italian. And, if I had never known any different existence and had met the right man, I might have been perfectly happy now. I might even have had a brood of children to whom Filomena would have been grandmother.

But where was all this leading me? There was no going back on the past. My father and the Princess – my parents – had been the people they were. And I was the person I had become. My parents were dead. From the participants in those far-off events, only Aunt Biddie, Filomena and I remained.

I did not need to worry about Aunt Biddie. Not for her the anguish of a broken heart, the searchings of a tormented soul, the regrets of a love unconsummated and a life frozen before it reached its zenith.

From Aunt Biddie's lips you would never hear the words: *'Oh, why have I had to go on living? I can only believe my life is a form of divine retribution. God is punishing me by keeping me alive.'* Aunt Biddie battled to save the abbey clock, but she did not have a shrine to the Virgin Mary in every room. She was not Mariana sitting by her casement, seeing old faces glimmering through the doors, hearing old footsteps treading the upper floors, hearing old voices calling her from without – and waiting for a man who would never return, lamenting,

'I am aweary, aweary,
I would that I were dead!'

I could not undo the hurts my father, the Princess and I – who had resurrected events long since buried, if never forgotten – had done Filomena. But there were a couple of things I could do, if not to make repairs, at least not to make things worse for her. I could call a halt to my quest. And I could keep my knowledge of my father's sins to myself: because my own illusions were destroyed, that did not mean I had to destroy Filomena's too.

Let her keep her dream of him – such as it was – for it was that dream, and that alone, which made her life tolerable.

And there was something else I could do, something of which she would never be aware – and neither need anybody else. I could be grateful for the husband and the home and the employment which had been withheld from her. Though, to me, they might seem lacking, they represented the kind of life she had longed for and been denied.

So, I stood in the moonlight, under the shadow of the Sacro Monte, the holy mountain, where San Fortunato had once renounced all his worldly possessions, and, for the sake of Filomena Angelini – in an attempt to compensate for the wrongs my parents had inflicted upon her – I renounced temptation.

I cringe now to read the words I wrote in my diary, when I returned inside, still gripped by an almost religious fervour of noble self-sacrifice and virtuous self-denial. Yet I can still remember how I felt and understand the reasons why.

I vowed to be tolerant and totally unselfish, to put the happiness of others before my own. I pledged myself to the continuance of my present circumstances – to my job with Miles and my marriage to Nigel, loveless though it might be. And I promised to give up Tobin.

At the thought of Tobin, my resolve faltered momentarily and then reasserted itself. Filomena's love for my father had been unrequited and her love for his child rebuffed. Yet all these years she had remained faithful to his memory.

Looked at objectively, all that had existed between Tobin and me was a friendship and there had been nothing for me to reproach myself with. But his kiss that night at the end of the drive after he had told me about his divorce, had not been platonic. And the night when Nigel and I had had sex – it could hardly be described as making love – I had thought of Tobin, I had committed adultery in spirit if not in the flesh.

So Tobin had to go. I would explain that I was a very married woman and wanted to remain that way. I would return the portrait of Filomena, yes, and also take him home a present – something expensive but not too personal – by way of honouring my debt to him. I would be firm. I would not yield to the temptations of the devil and the flesh.

For the next three days, although Filomena was never far from my mind, I devoted myself to Stevie, who was surprisingly easy company, despite the difference in our ages. On holiday with Nigel – the same as at home – I could never properly relax: I was always on edge. But I didn't have to worry about Stevie.

The weather remained kind to us. On the Thursday, we drove to Lake Como, then up through Dongo, which, the guide book told us, was the place from where Mussolini had administered German-occupied northern Italy after his enforced resignation in July 1943, until his capture by Italian partisans at the end of April 1945.

'Shall we try and find the Conte di Montefiore's villa?' Stevie asked.

'No, let's do something totally different. Enough is enough . . .'

'Mmm,' Stevie murmured doubtfully. 'So where are we going?'

'To the very top of the lake and then up to Chiavenna. Can you see that on the map?'

'Found it! Can we go on after that, right up to the Splügen Pass?'

'That's what I was intending.'

After Chiavenna we entered a region of high mountains and wild valleys which made Lugano seem tame in comparison, while the road between Campodolcina and Pianazzo must be one of the most spectacularly beautiful in the world, although it was terrifying to drive along, since it was cut into the precipitous mountainside and consisted solely of hairpin bends and tunnels.

Next day, Stevie attempted to follow Hemingway's example and row us to Switzerland, with nearly disastrous results, for when we reached the border a volley of shots was fired from the land. They came nowhere near us and it could have been coincidental. Stevie turned the boat quickly and headed back towards San Fortunato. 'Do you think those were really meant for us?' she asked excitedly, when we were definitely back in Italian waters.

I could imagine someone, somewhere peering through binoculars and laughing his head off. On the other hand, as I pointed out, we were about to enter a country illegally.

That evening, Stevie made me tell Giuseppe the story, who regaled us with accounts he had heard from his father of more serious attempts to enter Switzerland during the war, and with smuggling stories, including his favourite, about a miniature submarine which used to ply its way backwards and forwards between the Swiss and Italian parts of the lake until it was eventually captured by Swiss customs officials and found to contain a ton of salami.

On Saturday, we took the more conventional route and did a tour of the lake on a steamer, stopping off in Campione, an Italian enclave inside Switzerland, most famous for its casino. Here, we bought presents to take home. For Nigel, I was lucky enough to chance upon a handmade glass model of a Lamborghini and, for Tobin, a very expensive document case in dark brown leather.

Each carried a different, implicit message. Nigel's was to say, 'This is a peace offering. Let's try and make our marriage work.' Tobin's was to say, 'This is thank you for everything and goodbye.'

Then it was Sunday morning and, as if in sadness at our departure, the temperature fell and the sun disappeared behind clouds. After a last stroll round the village and a row on the rather choppy lake, we returned to our apartment via the terrace and started packing.

'The time's gone so quickly,' Stevie complained. 'I don't want to go home.'

'I'm glad you've enjoyed yourself.'

'Oh, I have. I only wish that things had turned out differently with Filomena. I feel as if we're leaving something unfinished.'

'Not really. There's nothing more we could have done.'

'Yes, I suppose you're right,' Stevie said dubiously, wandering out onto the balcony. 'Do you think you'll ever come back here?'

'I doubt it.'

'That's a shame.'

'Yes and no. I may not know everything about my parents, but I know far more than when I arrived. To quote your own words, because of everything I've learned from Filomena, I shan't have to go through the rest of my life wondering who I really am. I've seen where I spent the first months after I was born and met the woman who looked after me.'

At that moment, there was a knock on the door. I opened it to find Signora Nebbiolo with an envelope in her hand. 'This was delivered for you earlier, while you were out. It was brought by Cesare from the Villa Lontana.' She peered through the door, nodding in satisfaction at the evidence of our packing, then waited for me to open my letter.

She waited in vain. I merely thanked her, closed the door firmly upon her and carried the envelope out onto the balcony, my heart pounding. For a few moments, I just stared at the unmistakable copperplate handwriting, then I sat down at the wicker table and opened it.

'Who's it from? What is it, Cara?' Stevie asked.

'Filomena.'

Inside was a short letter.

Dear Cara,
Thank you for your kind note, but I assure you that any pain you caused me was far outweighed by the joy of making your acquaintance. You can have no idea how often I have thought about you over the years and wondered what had become of the little babe I once loved so dearly. Having met you, I feel as though your father is still alive, living through you, and that makes me very happy in my heart.

Wishing you a good journey back to England,
I am, yours affectionately,
Filomena Angelini.

Our packing finally completed, we bade farewell to our rooms and carried our cases down to reception. While I was settling the bill with Signora Nebbiolo, Giuseppe appeared and asked if he could take our luggage to the car. I handed Stevie the keys and they went off together to the car park.

'I hope we shall see you here again,' Signora Nebbiolo said, when our financial transactions were completed. 'Maybe you will return to visit Signora Angelini again?'

'Maybe,' I replied.

Then I went out into the sunshine. Stevie and Giuseppe were standing by the car, deeply engrossed in conversation. Poor Giuseppe, I reflected fleetingly, having to wait until we were leaving before Stevie responded to his overtures.

I walked down the main road until I came to the bridge, where I stopped and gazed up the wooded ravine towards the Abbazia e Convento della Madonna della Misericordia on the one side and the Villa Lontana on the other. I willed my thoughts to travel up the hillside to Filomena – an incoherent message of gratitude and love.

In the trees the cuckoos were still singing, their clarion calls echoing across the valley, louder even than the rushing of the water in the mountain torrent.

It was late afternoon, when we landed at Heathrow. We went by tube to Paddington Station, where I saw Stevie on to a train to Worcester, then took a taxi the rest of the way home.

I looked out of the cab window at the London streets and felt curiously alien, as though I had been away for far longer than a week and come back a different person from the one who had left.

No parties had taken place in the flat during my absence. It was exactly as I had left it, except that the air smelled slightly stale and the rooms appeared cheerless, as though sad at having been uninhabited and neglected for a week. I sifted through the mail, which I had picked up from the main lobby on the way through, but it consisted only of bills and circulars, so I carried my suitcase into the bedroom and unpacked, a feeling of anti-climax sweeping over me. After a week in Stevie's company, it was strange to be alone again, with nobody to chat to.

I opened the windows, switched on the immersion heater, put the kettle on, changed out of my travelling clothes and was starting to fill the washing machine, when the telephone rang.

'So you're back!' Tobin's voice exclaimed.

My eyes blinked shut and I was standing again on a moonlit balcony, with lake water lapping beneath me and the Sacro Monte with the Abbazia e Convento della Madonna della Misericordia looming over me.

I tried to play it cool. 'Who's that?'

'It's me – Tobin.'

'Oh, hello. What a surprise. I've only just got in.'

'How did it all go?'

'Fine, thank you. We had a lovely time.'

'Do you have anything planned for this evening?'

'Catching up with myself. Unpacking, doing the washing, getting ready to go back to work tomorrow.'

'Not any more you're not. You're going out to dinner.'

'Thank you, but— Honestly, I'd really rather . . .'

'What's the matter? Is Nigel home?'

'No.'

'So what's wrong?'

'Nothing's wrong, well, not exactly.'

He sucked in his breath. 'Listen, I'll be over there in about half-an-hour. We'll go out for a meal and you can tell me what's happened.'

'Tobin, I—'

'Are we still friends?'

'Yes, no—' I owed him an explanation. But I hadn't imagined it would have to be this swiftly forthcoming. 'Yes,' I said, 'of course we're still friends.'

'In that case, please don't let us have any misunderstandings.'

'No. You're right.'

Half an hour later, when the door bell rang, I was waiting, with my jacket on and his present in my hand: all steeled up, ready to resist temptation in whatever form it might manifest itself.

When I opened the door, he remained on the landing, looking at me with a quizzical expression. Feeling suddenly rather silly, I smiled brightly and hurried out to join him, turning away my face while I locked the door, so that he couldn't kiss me, and saying, 'Hi. It's lovely to see you again. Thank you so much for coming over.' I thrust his present at him. 'This is for you. I hope you like it. It's nothing much, but I thought it might be useful.'

Poor Tobin. He must have wondered what on earth had got into me. But he merely said, 'Thank you. I wasn't expecting anything. If you don't mind, I'll open it when we get to the restaurant. I thought we'd go to an Italian place in Hampstead Village. I haven't been there for ages, but it used to be very good.'

His car was parked next to Nigel's. I saw him glance at the Porsche, taking in its new registration number, and waited for him to pass some comment. But he didn't. He simply opened the passenger door and said, 'In you get.'

Neither of us spoke on the way to Hampstead. He drove in his usual relaxed fashion, while I sat, very tense in my seat, my hands clenched over my handbag, wondering how the hell I was going to explain myself. What had appeared simple and logical in San Fortunato, under the influence of Filomena and the village's patron saint, no longer seemed quite so straightforward.

When we were settled at our table in the restaurant, with the ubiquitous Chianti bottles as candlesticks and fishing nets on the walls, Tobin unwrapped his present.

'This is super,' he said, fingering the leather and sniffing it appreciatively. 'But it's very naughty of you. It must have cost the earth.'

'It's the very least I could do after all you've done for me.' I was going to say something about the picture of Filomena, but he cut me off.

'I shall take it with me wherever I go – and be reminded of you.' He reached across the table, took my hand from the menu, raised my fingers to his lips, then replaced my hand to where it had been.

A waiter, who could have been Giuseppe's brother, materialized at our side. 'Would you like an aperitif?'

Tobin looked at me. 'Campari and soda?'

I was tempted to order something different, just to be contrary, but that would have been stupidly childish. 'Yes, please.'

We studied our menus and, when another waiter came to take our order, it transpired that we had both decided to order the same dishes – *hors d'oeuvres* from the trolley as a starter and *fritto misto* as the main course.

And there was my problem, encapsulated in one simple thing. Tobin and I shared so many tastes in common. I didn't want to stop being friends with him. To give him up would be like losing a part of myself.

'How was the food at your hotel?'

'Excellent, thank you. Stevie captured the heart of the proprietor's son, who was one of the waiters, which meant we were very well looked after.'

'Did she enjoy herself?'

'Yes, immensely. And she was excellent company.'

We sipped our Camparis.

Then he asked, 'What's the matter? What's upset you?'

'I don't know how to explain.'

'Was it something to do with Filomena?'

'Sort of. More as a result of her.'

'Why don't you start at the beginning and tell me about her.'

'If you're interested.'

'For goodness sake, girl! What's got into you? Of course I'm interested.'

That may sound like the sort of thing Nigel would have said, but his tone was more like Aunt Biddie's – exasperated, in a fond, caring, puzzled sort of way.

I stopped being over-defensive. 'Well, we went to see her twice. The first time was on the Monday . . .' I told him everything about both visits, describing the house, Lucia, Cesare, the pictures on the walls, the little shrines, Amadore's sketchpads, Filomena's revelations – everything, including my precipitous dash down the garden at the Villa Lontana into the cuckoo wood and my miraculous halt on the edge of the ravine, in that scene so reminiscent of my previous nightmare. All I left out was my moonlit sojourn on the balcony.

By the time I finished, we were at the end of our second course and I was feeling better, more relaxed, more like I had been on the occasion of our first ever meeting – before kisses and emotions and desire and self-analysis had started to intervene.

The waiter cleared away our plates and the wine waiter refilled our glasses. 'Would you like a dessert?' Tobin asked.

'Not really, thank you.'

The waiters departed, leaving us alone.

'Poor soul,' Tobin murmured. 'What a tragic life.'

'I feel so desperately sorry for her. It seems such a waste.'

We sipped our wine and I kept my gaze averted from him, while I smoked a cigarette, nervously tapping the ash into the ashtray.

Suddenly, Tobin said, 'I think I know what's really troubling you – over and above Filomena. It started before you went away, didn't it?'

I nodded.

'It started after you came back from Paris, that night I drove you home and you asked me about my marriage.'

'Sort of, yes.'

'And I made it worse by giving you the picture of Filomena?'

'Mmm.'

'I'm sorry. I seem to have handled everything very badly. I assure you I didn't mean to.'

'No, I realize that,' I mumbled.

'Cara, will you look at me – please?'

I bit my lip and raised my head slowly.

He leaned forward, resting one elbow on the table and propping his chin on his hand, his expression very earnest. 'I don't know whether I'm doing the right thing or not by saying what I'm going to say next, but it seems to me that I can't make things much worse than they already are. And if you hear my side, at least you'll know where you stand so far as I'm concerned.

'I love you, Cara. I fell in love with you the very first moment I set eyes on you, as you were coming down the stairs in Wolesley House. And I have loved you more with every moment of every day that has passed since then. In fact, I've never felt the same about anyone as I do about you.

'I'll tell you why I love you. I love looking at you. I love your hair like burnished gold, the clear blue sincerity of your eyes and the joys and sorrows of your changing face. I love your shy and nervous ways, which you try in vain to conceal under a cloak of sophistication. I love your transparent honesty and your total lack of guile. I love your seriousness, your intensity, your intelligence, your integrity, your intrinsic goodness. I love your courage and determination. Above all, I love you when you laugh – which, unfortunately, is all too seldom.

'I love you because you are the exact opposite of everything I was expecting when I first spoke to you, even though Oliver had told me he found it difficult to believe that you were the Princess's daughter. To me, it doesn't matter whose daughter you are. You are yourself and that is sufficient for me. But I care for your sake – and that is why I have done what I could to help you.

'Having said all that, I am also very well aware that you are married. Whether your marriage is happy or not, I don't know. I hope it is, because you deserve a husband who loves and cherishes you.'

He paused and I felt a huge lump forming in my throat.

Then he continued, 'As I tried to tell you once before, I made a resolution, after my own marriage broke up, not to destroy anyone else's. Until I met you, I kept to it. If a woman was married, I did not so much as invite her for a drink. But the circumstances with you were different. We were joined in a common cause. Or so I convinced myself. But I was treading a dangerous path. And, on several occasions, I overstepped the edge and did things for which I afterwards reproached myself – although I could not regret them.

'I have been well aware that you have been feeling torn and that I have not been helping you. I realize that the decent thing for me to do would be to get the hell out of your life. I've considered it many times. You can have no idea how often I have picked up the telephone to ring you and put it back down again. No idea how often I have set off from Fulham to wait for you outside your office and turned back again. No idea how often I have driven towards Highgate, then turned round and come back home. Then, something to do with the Princess has cropped up and I have been presented with a perfectly legitimate excuse to see you again.

'During the past week, I, too, have done a lot of thinking and I've realized that there is one huge difference between what I feel for you and what I've felt for all the other women I've known. I am not only in love with you as a woman, but I like you as a person. Sure, every time I see you I want to take you in my arms and kiss you. Indeed, I'd like to do far more than that. I would like to spend every day and every night with you. I would like to be the person who sees you first thing in the morning and last thing at night.

'But it is far more important for me to keep you as my friend than to have you as a lover. Our friendship has become more valuable to me than anything else in the world. I would hate to lose it. And I would like to think that, provided I can control my feelings, it would be possible for us to remain friends.

'On the other hand, if you find the situation we have now reached impossible to continue, I shall respect your wishes. I don't want you to do anything you may regret. I don't want to hurt you in any way – ever. All I want is for you to be happy.'

If we hadn't been in a restaurant, I would have burst into tears. As it was, I swallowed at the huge lump in my throat and reached in my handbag for a tissue. My heart was thumping as if the captive bird imprisoned within it was struggling to beat down the walls of its cage.

'You're not offended?' Tobin asked.

I shook my head vehemently.

'No misunderstandings?'

I shook my head again.

'Then let's have some coffee.' He signalled to the waiter.

After the waiter had brought us espressos, Tobin asked, 'What did you do with the portrait of Filomena?'

I didn't even consider lying. 'I couldn't keep it in the flat. Nigel would have asked all sorts of questions, so Sherry and Roly are looking after it.'

'Yes, I realized afterwards that I hadn't thought that through properly. I can only say again that I meant well.'

My opportunity was there to tell him I didn't want to keep it, but I couldn't bring myself to say so.

After that, neither of us said anything more at all.

When the waiter brought the bill, I said, 'Please may I pay for this meal?' Tobin didn't attempt to argue. I paid by credit card and he said, 'Thank you.'

He drove me to my front door, stopping again beside Nigel's Porsche. 'I shan't make a nuisance of myself,' he promised. 'I'll wait to hear from you. If you don't want to talk to me or see me again after tonight, I'll understand.'

There was so much I wanted to say. Among other things, I wanted to say, 'You're mistaken. I'm not at all happy in my marriage. I don't love

Nigel and I do love you.' I wanted him to kiss me. I wanted to kiss him. I wanted to do more than that.

But the burden of my parents' sins was weighing too heavily upon me. Even more than I loved Tobin, I could not bear to follow in their footsteps.

So I simply said, 'Thank you for being so honest. And I *will* be in touch.'

Then I got out of the car and went up to the flat, where I promptly burst into tears.

Chapter 20

I had not been looking forward to returning to work, but, funnily, when I actually reached the office, it was good to be greeted by Sergeant's rendering of *Bring me Cornetto*, to hear Dorothy extolling her granddaughter's virtues, and to have Juliette saying, 'It's so nice to see you again. I've been really lonely without you.'

When she asked about Italy, I found myself able to answer matter-of-factly, saying that San Fortunato had been a beautiful place and Filomena had given me a lot of interesting detail, disclosing none of the feelings it had aroused.

After that we were down to the nitty-gritty of everyday office life, going through the previous week's letters, telexes, faxes and telephone messages, Juliette explaining which communications she had considered important enough to send over to New York and which she had merely acknowledged, pending Miles's return.

I thanked her and she said, 'No problem. It couldn't have worked out better. It was quite a quiet week, with Miles and James both away. You know, something is definitely up. James is staying in New York for another week and Miles is coming back on his own. What do you think they're playing at?'

I shrugged and she laughed. 'Yes, we'll probably be the last to find out.'

When Miles arrived, he was looking decidedly smug. 'How was Italy?' he enquired.

'Wonderful, thank you.'

'Good. You've got a bit of colour. Were you out in the fresh air a lot?'

'Yes, we were actually. Was your trip to New York successful?'

'Extremely.' With which, he went off to his own office and I followed, diary, shorthand pad and pencils in hand.

At lunchtime, Juliette and I went to the sandwich bar and I told her a bit more about Italy and felt increasingly in control of myself, more like a normal human being. Miles was still at lunch when we got back, so I seized the opportunity to ring Aunt Biddie.

'I tried calling you last night,' she said, 'but there was no answer.'

'I'm sorry, I went out to dinner.'

'Oh, I see. Is Nigel back?'

'No. I went out with – er – with a friend.'

'Well, that was nice. I was interested to hear how you got on with Filomena. I've already spoken to Stevie and heard some of what happened.'

I laughed. 'In which case I imagine you've heard most of it.'

'Put it this way, I gather she was an invalid, that Connor did spend the war at San Fortunato and it would sound as if the Princess was indeed your mother.'

'That's certainly how it would appear. But Filomena has a very idealized image of him. Some of the things she told me about him were at total odds with things you had said. For instance, she didn't know anything about Patricia and his affair with Imogen Humboldt.'

'Cara, I promise you I wasn't making all that up.'

'Yes, and I believe your version,' I assured her hurriedly. 'I was just explaining the discrepancies between her story and yours. She also seemed to think that he had gone to Spain merely in order to escape the Princess, who was apparently trying to get her hooks into him as early as 1935, when Dmitri and Imogen went to America.'

'Anything's possible. You've read his letters the same I have. I think he did have a political conscience. But, at the same time, he had absolutely no sense of conventional morality. He wouldn't have been deterred from having an affair with the Princess simply because she was already married.'

That did nothing to help me. It simply made Tobin seem more of a gentleman – even a saint.

I changed the subject. 'What's happening with the abbey clock?'

'Oh, that excitement's all over now. We won, of course. I knew we would. The vicar and church authorities backed down in the end. But now someone's come up with a hare-brained scheme for turning the High Street into a pedestrian precinct. It's quite ridiculous. They're talking about closing down the grammar school because of lack of funds yet they're fully prepared to waste money on other things nobody wants. It makes my blood boil.'

* * *

Miles left the office early that evening for a meeting in the City and I was putting the cover over my typewriter, looking forward to an early night, when the phone rang and Dorothy announced, 'Your husband's on the line, Cara.'

'At last!' Nigel exclaimed. 'I was beginning to get seriously worried. I've been ringing you all weekend and getting no reply. Where have you been?'

'In Italy.'

'Oh, yes, of course. You were taking Stevie. Enjoy yourself?'

'Very much so. How are things going over there?'

'Better since the weather improved. Only one little hiccup when the client suddenly decided he didn't like the clothes one of the kids was wearing, thought they put over too tough an image. So we had to re-shoot a couple of sequences. But apart from that, everything's hunky-dory and I should be home on Wednesday.'

'Well, I'll see you then and we can catch up on everything.'

'Yes, see you then. Take care in the meantime.'

'You, too. Bye for now.'

It wasn't until I was on the tube going home that it occurred to me to wonder why he had suddenly decided to ring me himself and not leave the job to Tracey. It seemed to indicate a spirit of *rapprochement* on his side as well as mine. And that made me feel even more mixed-up and confused.

Nigel arrived home quite early on Wednesday evening, only about an hour after me. He dumped his luggage in the hall, gave me a husbandly peck, presented me with another bottle of duty-free perfume, then went into the living room and sank down in a chair. 'Well, that's the second one in the can. Two down and four to go.'

'So everything went OK in the end?'

'Yes, fine. As always, the proof of the pudding's in the eating and I shan't really know until I see the processed film tomorrow. And then comes the editing.'

'What about Bo?'

'Bo? What do you mean?'

'Last time you were having a few problems with her. She kept trying to pull rank over you.'

'Oh, that's all in the past. She's OK now. I must say, Sven's a great guy. Very cool. I've got a lot of time for him. No, it's a good team and the crew are a great bunch of guys. The only real problem's the bloody client, who's a pain in the arse, but we're getting him tamed. We took him out to a night club one evening and got him so pissed that we literally had to carry him out to a taxi afterwards and undress him and put him to bed when we got back to the hotel. But after that we didn't have nearly so much nonsense from him.'

I laughed, my voice sounding unnaturally shrill and false even to my own ears. However, Nigel seemed to take it for genuine amusement and went on to elaborate upon the episode, and then described a subsequent visit to the red light district, where they had set the poor man up with a transvestite prostitute. 'Any trouble with him in Kenya and we'll feed him to a lion,' he went on.

'Is Kenya your next trip?'

'Yes, we're off on Monday.'

'Which commercial's that?'

'Safari saloon car rallying. That should be an experience. I'm looking forward to it, I have to admit. Although I'm sorry to be neglecting you so much. You're being very decent about it all, I must say.'

No, I thought, I simply have a conscience.

'Well, that's enough of me for the moment. Tell me about Italy. Where were you staying?'

'In a little village on Lake Lugano, right up near the Swiss border. Stevie took lots of pictures. She's promised to send me some when the film's developed.'

'Great,' he said, with a marked lack of interest. 'So what did you get up to?'

For a moment, I was tempted to tell him the whole story, right from the beginning. Then he yawned and I thought, 'What's the point? It's all over now. I shall never see Filomena again. And I shall probably never see Tobin either. Let it go.'

'Lots of things,' I said. 'We drove up into the mountains and went for a steamer trip round the lake. Oh, and I've brought you a present.'

I went over to the sideboard and fetched the box containing the hand-made glass model of a car I had bought in Campione.

He ripped the wrapping off and took out the car. 'Yes, well, umm, thank you very much,' he said in a voice totally devoid of enthusiasm.

'It's Italian, it's a Lamborghini.'

'Yes, I know exactly what it is. It's a Lamborghini Countach to be precise.'

'I thought it was the sort of car you liked.'

'Well, thanks for the thought. It's beautifully made, but – er – it's a pity you couldn't have chosen some other marque.'

'Oh. I didn't realize. I thought it looked very exotic.'

'It looks like something out of *Thunderbirds*,' Nigel stated disparagingly and put it back in its box.

Talk about the road to hell being paved with good intentions.

I found myself half-wishing that Tobin could be a fly on the wall. Then I need not explain and he would understand.

They were strange days which followed – or, to be precise – strange evenings and nights, for Nigel was out all day, either at the agency or the editing suite. There was a distance between us, but I was almost grateful for it. On the balcony at San Fortunato, I had vowed to remain faithful to my husband, which was a different thing from pretending to be in love with him again.

He made no demands on me, emotionally or physically. Each night, as though by mutual consent, we avoided any kind of situation which could be interpreted as an invitation or a prelude to sex. Every evening, one of us went to bed earlier than the other, to avoid undressing in the other's sight. I had always worn a nightie and now Nigel took to wearing a T-shirt in bed.

'It's a habit I've got into, staying in hotels,' he explained and I made no comment.

Similarly, in the mornings, we did not remain in bed after the alarm went off, but one or other of us got up, made coffees, then went off to the bathroom to wash and dress.

Possibly the strangest thing was that our actions seemed to fall into place quite naturally, although I could not help being aware of a certain sense of unreality. Indeed, often I had the feeling that we were two characters in a play acting out parts and, even when the curtain came down between us and the audience, we were keeping – by unspoken agreement – to our self-imposed roles and scripts.

On Friday evening, Nigel left work early enough to take me to the cinema – the first time in ages – and we had dinner out afterwards, when we talked mainly about the film and other films we had seen in the past.

'I've enjoyed this evening,' he said, as we were driving home. 'It made a nice change. It's a pity we can't do it more often.'

On Saturday morning, the postman brought a letter from Stevie, together with a set of prints from the photographs she had taken in San Fortunato. On and off throughout the day I looked at them and felt a stab of longing that was almost like homesickness. I wished I could show them to Tobin and, instead, when Nigel came home, showed them to him. He pretended interest, but his mind was clearly elsewhere.

After dinner, he gave me the call sheet for his forthcoming trip and asked, 'Are you planning on going away anywhere while I'm in Kenya?'

'I very much doubt it. I've done my gadding about for the time being.'

'Well, if you do want to go away with Stevie again, I don't mind at all. I'm certainly not going to be able to take any holiday this summer.'

'I realize that,' I said. 'It doesn't matter for my sake. So long as you don't make yourself ill through over-work. You ought to take a break some time.'

'Maybe, when it's all over. In any case, although I'm working hard, I'm enjoying it too. You know what they say – a change is as good as a rest.' Thereupon he yawned. 'Having said that, I wouldn't mind an early night tonight.'

Then it was Sunday evening and he was packing again. And, in the morning, he was gone and I was alone.

Tracey rang me late that afternoon, to let me know he had arrived safely in Nairobi. 'It's a shame you can't go with him to some of these places,' she said. 'I'd love to go to Kenya. I'm absolutely mad about animals. I watch all the nature programmes on TV.'

And there we were, back to Tracey's and my pally little chats again.

If those few days while Nigel was home had been strange, the next week was even odder. Until then, I hadn't realized quite how important Tobin had become in my life, how much of my time had been spent thinking about him, even if we didn't meet, even if we didn't talk. He had been there – it seemed like always now – in my subconscious – and at the end of the phone.

As the influence of San Fortunato and Filomena wore off, I found myself questioning the resolutions I had made so rashly. Was I literally cutting off my nose to spite my face by not having any more to do with him? Could we not remain friends as he suggested – and as I wanted?

For that matter, was I placing too much significance upon fidelity? Ginette was not the only one to have an extra-marital affair and while others might feel guiltier than her were they not happier and more fulfilled than I was?

I saw the years stretching ahead, with Nigel and I becoming ever more like strangers, until the time came when we would have nothing at all left to say to each other. That wasn't marriage. That wasn't companionship. That was nothing except the futile waste of two lives.

Time without number, I did what Tobin had described at the restaurant in Hampstead. I picked up the phone and put it down again. Each time it rang, I hoped it would be him. Whenever I left Wolesley House, I looked for him in St James's Square. Once I caught sight of a figure further up the street, which looked like him from the back. I ran to catch up with him, calling his name, only to discover to my intense embarrassment, that it was someone else – who looked nothing like him from the front.

When Juliette and I had a drink at Chattertons one lunchtime, the waitress said, 'It's a long seen we've seen you – or your boyfriend.'

At which, of course, Juliette pricked up her ears. 'Boyfriend? Cara, are you leading a double life?'

I could feel myself flushing scarlet. 'Don't be silly. Of course I haven't got a boyfriend.'

To make matters worse, upon our return to Wolesley House, Sergeant had some post for me. As he handed it over, he remarked, 'Haven't seen Mr Touchstone recently. I do hope he's all right. Such a well-mannered gentleman.'

Juliette threw me a meaningful look. As we went up the stairs, she said in a low voice, so that Sergeant shouldn't hear, 'It's all right, you can trust me. I shan't tell a soul. What's more, I don't blame you. I must admit, I thought Tobin was gorgeous.'

On Saturday, I took out my portable typewriter and the folder containing The Book, but I didn't get so far as opening it. There seemed no point suddenly. So I wrote up the pages of my diary from the notes I had made in Italy. Yet even this seemed a meaningless exercise. I knew who my parents were. I knew who I was. My quest had come to its end . . .

I put typewriter and diary away again and took out the vacuum cleaner, for want of something physical to do, as the flat was spotless. But just as quickly losing heart in unnecessary housework, I put it back in the cupboard and went downstairs to the car. At Hyde Park Corner, instead of continuing to Fulham, I made a complete circuit of the roundabout and returned to Linden Mansions.

On Sunday I rang Aunt Biddie and Miranda, contemplated going to have a coffee with Sherry and decided instead to potter in the roof garden, taking cuttings and dividing up plants.

It was actually a relief when Monday came round again and I was back on what I believed to be solid ground in the business world.

Shortly after I arrived at the office that Monday morning, Miles phoned and said, 'I shan't be in until the afternoon. Tell any callers that I'll ring back later.'

Juliette stuck her head round the door. 'Good weekend?'

'Fine, thanks. And you?'

'All right. You know, the usual stuff, housework, washing, cooking.'

'Is James back?'

'Sort of. He rushed in and dashed straight out again, muttering something about a meeting with Miles at the Ambassador. I'm going to make a bet with you. A bottle of wine at Chattertons. I reckon we're about to take over WWT.'

'In that case, what have the meetings with Sir Utley Trusted and Oswald Jaffe been about?'

'Red herrings. Or else they weren't prepared to be taken over.'

'OK, I'll go along with that. You're on.'

As the morning progressed, I became increasingly convinced that Juliette was right. The phone seemed never to stop ringing and many of the calls were from Craig Vidler's office at WWT in New York. Others were from Kornfeld, Wiley and Vance, the Group's solicitors in the City, and several from Miles's stockbroker.

Miles returned shortly after lunch and, after taking his list of calls, promptly closeted himself in the boardroom with James, Alan Warburton and Keith Despard. During the course of the afternoon, I saw both Alan's and Keith's secretaries. They didn't say any more than Dorothy did, but I could tell from their faces that they were as aware as Juliette and I that some major event was about to occur.

At about five o'clock the meeting dispersed and Miles summoned me into his office. 'Do you have anything scheduled for this evening?'

I shook my head.

'Good. Because I want the chief executives of all the subsidiary companies here in London at midday on Wednesday. I don't care what else they have planned. They'll have to cancel it. And I don't care what lengths you have to go to find them. Just make sure each of them gets the message personally.'

'What about accommodation?' I asked.

'I won't be keeping them long. Apart from Bob Drewitz, they should all be able to get here and back in the same day. Book Drewitz into the Ambassador.'

He looked at me in such a way that I thought he was going to add something else. But he didn't. He merely said, 'That's it for the moment.'

I was remarkably lucky. Most of them were either in the office or at home, although some were in bed and none too pleased at being disturbed. By midnight, I had contacted all but two, whose offices were closed and whose home phones went unanswered. Deciding to leave them for the morning, I took a cab home.

In the morning, those two had been tracked down and my mission was accomplished. Every single one had asked the purpose of the summons and to every single one I replied in the same way: 'I'm sorry, I don't know.'

Miles and James spent all of that day out of the office. 'The plot sickens,' Juliette said. 'But all is obviously about to be revealed. I'm looking forward to that bottle.'

All was revealed the following morning. And Juliette was wrong. The Goodchild Group wasn't taking over WWT.

As soon as I got in, I prepared the boardroom. While I was hastily putting the final touches to the table, James came in and looked around. 'A bit cramped but it will have to do,' he said. 'It would have been better to take one of the conference rooms at the Ambassador, but Miles is right. That would have attracted too much attention. Discretion and timing are of the utmost in a situation like this.'

Then he must have realized that I was still in the dark for, looking vaguely embarrassed, he went away again.

A few moments after I returned to my office, Miles buzzed. 'Will you come in, Cara, please?'

As I had goodness knows how many hundred times before, I picked up the diary, my shorthand pad and pencils and went into his office.

Miles was standing at the window, with his back to me, gazing out across St James's Square. Without turning round, he announced, 'I've sold the Goodchild Group and most of my shares in it to WWT.'

The deal was agreed in New York the week before last and, for the past ten days, the lawyers have been drawing up contracts and dotting i's and crossing t's.' He paused. 'I am also resigning as Chairman and Managing Director.'

'But why?' I eventually managed to gasp.

Miles left the window and sat down in his big, black, leather executive chair at the opposite side of the desk. 'Because WWT offered an excellent price. Because it's a good company with sound management practices. Because I'm sixty and want to do something different with my life. Because there are easier ways to make money.'

I nodded, not knowing what else to say.

He made a steeple of his hands and looked down at them. 'I am leaving on Friday, at which point Craig Vidler will take over as Chairman and James Warren as Chief Executive Officer. Craig has his own secretaries – three of them, in fact – one of whom will be permanently based over here. And James, obviously, has Juliette. Which means, Cara, that there will be no job for you any more.'

I just sat there, staring stupidly at him.

'That is why I felt I owed it to you to let you know what was happening before you learned the news from any other source. If I were planning on remaining in London, I would ask you to come and work for me in a personal capacity. But I'm afraid I'm not. I'm setting up base in Monte Carlo, which would be rather a long way for you to commute.'

He looked up. 'James and I have discussed a redundancy package for you, which I hope you will consider reasonable. In addition to the statutory redundancy pay, which I think is something like thirteen weeks' salary – one for each year of your invaluable service – you will be given three months' salary in lieu of notice and a further three months' salary in the form of a tax-free ex gratia payment.' He opened a file and studied a computation. 'According to James, that comes to about five and a half thousand pounds after the necessary deductions.'

Memories of other people whom Miles had fired flitted through my head. Dignity, I thought. Be dignified. That's all that matters for the moment. 'When will I be expected to leave?' I asked in a clipped voice.

'I would suggest we go together. That will allow us time to go through the files and for you to hand over to Juliette.'

I nodded.

'I realize that it's asking a lot of you under the circumstances, but I should be grateful if you would keep this information to yourself until tomorrow, when a formal announcement will be made.'

'Of course.'

He glanced up at the clock. 'Half past ten. I should speak to Felix Wiley. Will you get him for me, please?'

I left his office and returned to my own, where I picked up the phone and dialled Kornfeld Wiley and Vance's number, was put through to the solicitor and connected him to Miles.

Then I sat in a trance-like state, trying to work out what the hell had happened. It was funny, it didn't actually hurt. Not then, not immediately. It was like when you hit yourself hard against something. After the initial shock, the bruise doesn't become really painful until it starts to come out a day or two later.

That's how it was when I got the sack – or, rather, when I was made redundant. Either way it amounted to the same thing. After Friday, I wouldn't have a job any more. Nearly fourteen years ended, just like that.

Juliette came in for something and somehow I managed to hide my shock, found the document she needed in a file, laughed when she referred again to her bet and the bottle of wine at Chattertons. But suddenly it was as if a huge chasm – like the ravine at San Fortunato, which divided the Villa Lontana from the Abbazia e Convento della Madonna della Misericordia – had opened up between us.

At the end of this week, Juliette would still have a job – *my* job – and I would be unemployed. It wasn't her fault. She would be horrified when she found out, mortified on my behalf. Yet the fact remained that she would still be here and I would not.

Somehow I got through the rest of that day without anyone suspecting that anything untoward had occurred. I saw all the chief executives from the subsidiary companies into the boardroom and, an hour later, saw them out again. I identified with the expressions of shock on their faces and could see them all wondering, 'How will this affect me?' Then I gathered up the notepads and pens and returned all the chairs to their rightful owners.

When I reached home, I still maintained control. As I walked into the empty flat, I thought how lovely it would be to find somebody waiting there for me. For the first time in weeks, I wanted to see Nigel and have him comfort me. Not that there was anything he or anyone else could do. Nobody could wave a magic wand and give me back my job. But it would have been wonderful just to have company, not to be on my own.

I thought of going down to Sherry and Roly's but I had promised Miles to tell nobody and it didn't occur to me not to keep my word. So I forced myself to have something to eat, washing it down with a large glass of wine and tried to see things rationally.

I remembered my thoughts on the way to Paris about being stuck in a rut and looking for another job. I wondered how I would be feeling now if things were the other way round and I had just handed in my notice, instead of being given the push. But it was doubtful whether I would ever have done it. I would never have let Miles down. Which made a mockery of my pledge at San Fortunato. There had been as little likelihood of my leaving Miles as of my walking out on Nigel. I was too firmly wedded to a sense of duty.

That night, my nightmare returned, with added intensity, for it was no longer merely a dream, but a re-enactment of reality. I woke myself up screaming, as I reached the edge of the ravine, and, unable to get to sleep again, made myself a pot of tea and some toast and sat in the kitchen waiting for the dawn.

Next day, the news broke. In the afternoon, Miles and Craig Vidler held simultaneous press conferences on both sides of the Atlantic, after which Dorothy's switchboard went crazy.

So did Juliette, when she learned about me. James left it until the very end of the day to tell her, at which point she burst into my office where I was still going through files, separating Miles's personal files from the business ones.

'Cara, I'm so sorry!' she cried, her elfin face white, tears glittering in her eyes. 'You do realize that I didn't know, don't you? Of all the shitty things to do! Miles is a bastard. To treat you like that, after all you've done for him. Thirteen years in the company and then goodbye, clear your desk. It's despicable. It's worse than despicable, it's—'

'Calm down,' I said. 'I'm being given a very generous redundancy package.'

'I know exactly what you're getting. Five thousand four hundred and fifty something pounds. And how much is Miles taking away with him? Millions, Cara, literally millions.'

'It's his company, Juliette, he built it.'

'If it hadn't been for the help of people like you, he wouldn't have been able to build it.'

'Don't exaggerate. Loads of people could have done what I did.'

'That's crap! There aren't many secretaries who speak fluent French and Italian like you do. I can't, for a start, which is why it's quite ridiculous me taking over from you.'

I shook my head wearily. 'I have a feeling that you're not exactly going to be taking over from me. Craig Vidler has three secretaries, one of whom is moving over here.'

Juliette frowned. 'Does that mean that Craig Vidler is taking over Miles's position – and not James?'

'I don't know how the responsibilities will be divided up. But since Goodchild will be only a subsidiary of WWT from now on and Vidler is WWT's President, I imagine he'll make his presence felt.'

'Christ! It gets worse and worse. Oh, stuff those bloody files back in the cupboard and let's go and have a drink.'

But the thought of a maudlin session at Chattertons was more than I could bear. 'I'd rather get this over and done with.'

She nodded, suddenly contrite. 'I'm sorry about letting off steam, but I was so angry. It's so unfair.'

'It matters a lot to me that you care,' I assured her.

I reached home that evening in time to watch the nine o'clock news, but there was no mention of the take-over.

Friday came and, with it, my last day at Wolesley House. The *Financial Times* devoted two front-page columns to the takeover and the other broadsheets alluded to it in their City pages. Both Goodchild Group and WWT shares had apparently shot up in value since the announcement.

During the morning, I went through everything I could think of with Juliette, while a van driver, supervised by Hawkins and myself, took away all Miles's personal belongings, including his files. 'What's happening to you?' I asked Hawkins.

'Not a lot of change really. I'll be driving for Mr Vidler from now on.' It looked as though I was the only casualty.

At lunchtime, Juliette organized an impromptu farewell party for me in the boardroom, but essentially everyone was more excited and concerned about their own futures than mine and most of the conversation was about WWT.

Miles turned up towards the very end and made a brief speech, thanking us all for our support and unstinting effort over the years, and enthusing about the Group's prospects for growth and expansion under WWT.

After that, James called me to his office, where he asserted that the decision to make me redundant had not been arrived at easily. He tried to make out that Craig Vidler was to blame and that he and Miles had argued my cause. Perhaps that made him feel better, but I knew my fate would have been decided in less than a minute flat. When multi-million pound companies are changing hands, the fate of one secretary is neither here nor there. Vidler would possibly have remarked in passing, 'I'll be bringing my own secretary.' And Miles and James would have said, 'Fine.'

James gave me my cheque, salary slip and P45, and went into explanations about my pension scheme contributions. Then he said, 'I'm sure you won't have any difficulty finding another job. Needless to say, if you require a reference, I shall be only too pleased to give you one.'

I thanked him, we shook hands and I went back to my own office. Miles was standing the doorway, ready to depart. 'I hope this is not goodbye as such, Cara, but merely farewell, and that our paths will cross again.'

'Yes, I hope so.'

'I'm sorry, for your sake, that it had to end like this. But business is business.'

'Of course,' I said.

We shook hands and then he walked off down the corridor and disappeared out of my life.

I went through the drawers in my desk, putting my few personal possessions – fountain pen, pencil sharpener, dictionaries and a box of tissues – into a carrier bag. Finally, I put the cover over my typewriter. Like a shroud, I thought grimly. Then I rang Juliette on the internal phone and told her I was off. We agreed to meet up in the near future and she promised to keep me informed of all that happened after I was gone.

On my way through reception I wished Dorothy – and her granddaughter – well, then went downstairs to the main lobby.

Sergeant greeted me gloomily. 'I'm going to miss you, Cara. You're always cheerful, that's what I most like about you.'

'Thank you,' I said, touched. 'I shall miss you, too.' On an impulse, I leaned across the desk and gave him a quick kiss. To my surprise, he coloured up to the roots of his white hair.

Then I walked out of Wolesley House for the last time.

Chapter 21

That evening, the numbness wore off and reaction finally began to set in. I walked into the empty flat and wished again that somebody could have been there waiting for me. I poured myself a glass of wine and walked up and down the hall, going into the living room, the bedrooms, the study, the kitchen, out on to the roof garden and back indoors again, like an animal pacing restlessly to and fro in a zoo cage.

Why hadn't Miles and James done more to protect me? Why was Hawkins keeping his job while I had lost mine? Why hadn't Craig Vidler even considered keeping me on? Why hadn't I been offered an alternative position within the Group? Why had I been given no choice in the matter – no say in my own destiny?

The more I asked myself these questions, the more it seemed that the fault lay with me. Nobody wanted me because I was no good. The more wine I drank, the more sorry for myself I became. And the more I wanted to weep my sorrows on to someone else's shoulder.

Why did nobody ring me? Surely somebody must have seen the news in the papers? Even in my irrational state, I was aware that Aunt Biddie, Miranda, Jonathan and even Tobin were unlikely to read the financial pages, but I felt that some kind of sixth sense should have made them aware. But the phone remained silent.

I went on drinking and doing silly things, like moving cushions and putting vases in different positions. I tried to make myself think positively. I recalled all the really dreadful things that had happened to me during my lifetime. Like losing the baby. Uncle Stephen dying. Being told that I would never be able to have another baby. Nigel's affair with Patti Roscoe.

This was nowhere near as bad as any of those. Every day, somebody somewhere lost their job. And, with a cheque for over nearly five and a half thousand pounds in my purse, I was better off than most. In fact, some people would consider it a triumph. Five and a half thousand pounds was not to be sniffed at, whatever Juliette said about Miles's millions. Everything was relative.

But none of that stopped the pain of rejection and the humiliation of failure.

I don't know what eventually decided me to ring Nigel. Possibly the idea entered my head after I started thinking about the baby, and remembering how brave and incredibly stupid I had been about not ringing him after the doctor had told me I would never be able to have any more children. Maybe I associated that with Patti Roscoe and everything that had taken place as a result.

When you're in that sort of state you don't think rationally. What's more, by then, I had got through a whole bottle of wine and started on another one, without eating anything. Not that I felt drunk. My vision was perfectly clear, my steps completely steady. It was just my mind that wasn't focusing properly.

It couldn't have been, otherwise I would have known better than to think Nigel would care. Yet, somehow, I managed to convince myself that he would. I persuaded myself that he would want to be the first to know, that he would be deeply sympathetic, that he might even come rushing back from Kenya to comfort me.

So I took Tracey's latest call sheet from my briefcase, found the number of Nigel's hotel and dialled it. I was told to hold on and eventually Nigel's voice was grunting, 'Hello.'

'It's me,' I said, 'Cara.'

There was a pause, almost as if he was trying to remember who I was. Then he exclaimed, 'Good God! What's happened?'

'Miles has sold the Goodchild Group and I've been made redundant.' As I made that statement aloud for the first time, I was impressed by the detached calmness in my voice.

'He – what?' There was another pause. As often happens on international calls, the line was amazingly clear. I could hear the click of a switch and Nigel exclaimed, 'Do you realize what time it is? It's three o'clock in the bloody morning.'

'Oh,' I said blankly. 'Were you asleep?'

'Of course I was asleep.'

Then it happened. Quite distinctly, I heard a woman's voice, with an American accent, asking in a loud whisper, 'What is it? What's the matter?'

I recognized that voice.

There was a rustling, as Nigel must have covered the mouthpiece.

Seconds later, it can only have been seconds later, although it felt like an eternity, he asked, 'Are you still there, Cara?'

Behind him was silence. I wanted to put down the receiver but it seemed glued to my hand.

Again – 'Are you still there, Cara?'

The words emerged involuntarily from my lips. 'Bo's in the room with you, isn't she?'

I waited for him to lie. But he just gave a deep sigh. 'Cara, go to bed and don't start imagining things. I'll talk to you in the morning.'

The receiver released itself from my grasp and I replaced it on its cradle.

For a long time, I sat there staring blindly at the phone, wondering whether I was imagining things and Bo had just happened to walk into his room while he was on the phone. But at three o'clock in the morning? In any case, he had been asleep.

No, she had been in bed with him . . .

I don't remember my trains of thought after that. I suppose I must have thought back – as I certainly did later – and tried to work out when their affair had begun and how he had managed to take me in. I must have relived the previous weeks, since our dinner with Bo at the Ivy, and wondered, sickly, how long he had been deceiving me.

But the only thing I can remember clearly is an overwhelming sense of weariness, a feeling that everything was just too much effort. I remember dragging myself into the bedroom, undressing and getting into bed. I remember seeing Nigel's photograph beside the alarm clock and hurling it across the room. And after that I don't remember anything until the morning, when I was woken by the telephone ringing.

I rolled out of bed, but by the time I reached the phone it had stopped. Memories of the previous day flooded back. I no longer had a job. Nigel was having an affair with Bo.

Groggily I made my way into the bathroom. When I was showered, dressed and with a mug of coffee inside me, I felt a bit more together.

The next time the phone rang, I was there to answer it.

'How are you?' Nigel asked in a cautious voice.

'OK.'

'Did you sleep?'

'Sort of.'

'If it's any consolation, I didn't sleep at all after your call.'

I remember thinking, 'Surely he can't be expecting sympathy?'

He sucked in his breath. 'Listen, Cara. I wish you hadn't phoned. I didn't intend for you to find out that way. I'd much rather have told you to your face.'

Obviously he had forgotten the reason for my call. 'Told me what?'

'About Bo and me.'

'How long has it been going on?'

Silence, then reluctantly, 'Since Baker.'

'Are you in love with her?'

'Do you want the truth?'

'Preferably.'

'Then the answer is yes, I am. She's a very special person.'

'And is she in love with you?'

'Yes.'

'I see.'

'Listen, Cara, I don't really want to go into any more detail now. I know it's not fair on you, but I'd prefer to leave it until I get back and we can talk in person.'

'When will that be?'

'In about ten days' time. We certainly won't be finished ahead of schedule. And I can't leave in mid-shoot.'

'No, of course not. Your job must come first. And since Bo's out there with you, you don't have to hurry home for her.'

'Cara, please, don't be like that. You're not a fool. You must surely have realized that things weren't right between you and me. We've been growing steadily further and further apart. Even if I hadn't met Bo, we couldn't have continued like we were. Ours isn't a marriage.'

I couldn't take any more. I put down the phone and found myself shaking all over. I took a deep breath and counted to ten, but the shaking wouldn't stop. In the end, I went into the living room and poured myself a measure of neat vodka. Things had come to a pretty pass when I was drinking at half past nine in the morning, I reflected, as the strong alcohol caught at the back of my throat and burned its way down my oesophagus. But it did the trick. I stopped shaking.

I did something that Saturday which I had never done before. After indulging in a bout of sadness, self-pity, anger and bitterness, I pulled myself together and decided that I had to get out of Linden Mansions. The flat was too oppressive and too full of the wrong kind of memories. So I went away, on my own, with no destination in mind. I just got into the car and drove.

My first instinct was to go to Avonford, but I knew that would provide no solution. My family would be very kind, very concerned, very indignant on my behalf – as they had been at the time of the Patti Roscoe episode – but, in their secret hearts, they would be thinking that I should have learned from my past mistakes. Forewarned should be forearmed. In any case, they wouldn't be able to tell me what to do. Nobody could.

I had to go somewhere on my own, somewhere unfamiliar, where I would be on neutral territory, in a place I didn't know and where I wasn't known. Vaguely, in the back of my head, I remembered Juliette telling me about a weekend in Devon. *'We stayed in the most gorgeous little inn, beside a stream. You'd have loved it . . .'*

I packed an overnight bag and wrote a note to Sherry, saying I was going away for a few days, which I left in her letter-box. Then I got into the car and headed west, past Bath, Bristol, Watchet and Minehead, up on to Exmoor, my thoughts as incoherent and directionless as my driving.

Suddenly I saw a signpost to a village called Biddicombe and, because it seemed like an omen, I turned off the main road, down a narrow lane, leading into a sheltered wooded valley.

Biddicombe, when I reached it, turned out to be a very pretty village, with a lively little stream running through the middle of it. The main street was lined with old terraced cottages, their exteriors painted in pastel shades. There was a general store and post office, a newsagent, a baker, a butcher and a greengrocer. At the centre stood the church and, nearby, an old inn. I hesitated for a second, then drove on. At the far end of the village was a hump-backed bridge over the stream, with a thatched cottage next to it – Brook Cottage, it was called – the idyllic sort of place you see on chocolate boxes, birthday cards and calendars – with pink roses clambering up the front and a typically English cottage garden full of flowers. There was even a well. And outside was a bed and breakfast sign showing VACANCIES.

I pulled off the road and rang the bell. An attractive, middle-aged woman, with short mid-brown hair and a friendly smile, answered the door and said, yes, they had a single room available. Floral curtains hung at the windows, the wallpaper was patterned with tiny roses – miniature versions of those peeking in through the open window – a patchwork quilt covered the bed and on the dressing table was a little dish of pot-pourri. It even had its own en-suite bathroom. And, outside, was the little, babbling brook.

My hostess introduced herself as Veronica Willmott and asked if I would like some tea while I was unpacking and freshening up. She brought a tray with a teapot and a plate of home-made biscuits up to my room and told me that I was, in fact, their only guest that weekend. She was cooking roast lamb for herself and her husband Paul that evening and, if I would like to join them, I would be more than welcome. Alternatively, if I preferred, I could eat on my own in a separate room. I said I'd love to join them.

After she had gone again, I burst into tears. It was her kindness that did it. That and her lack of inquisitiveness. I had arrived out of the blue and she had taken me in, given me exactly the sort of room I needed to suit my mood, and not fussed, not flapped, not asked any questions – just been kind.

I felt better for having cried and better still when I had blown my nose, drunk some tea, eaten some biscuits, washed my face and hands. I went downstairs, taking my tray with me, and found Veronica in the kitchen, peeling potatoes. We chatted for a few moments about the cottage and what a lovely part of the world this was, then I left her to her cooking and wandered into the garden.

It was a character in Tennessee Williams' *A Streetcar Named Desire* who said, 'I have always depended on the kindness of strangers.' The same applied to me, especially during the days immediately following my redundancy and finding out about Nigel and Bo. Veronica and Paul were exactly the kind of strangers I needed at that time.

By the end of my first evening there I had learned a lot about them and they had learned very little about me, except that I lived in London and had recently lost my job. They had also lived in London and Paul, too, had been made redundant. It had happened five years ago, when he was fifty. He had been a metal trader and the firm he had worked for had been taken over by a German company. Three months after the takeover, he and several other colleagues of a similar age had been informed that their services were no longer needed. 'Basically, we were too old,' he said, still with a tinge of bitterness.

His age had continued to count against him with every job he had applied for. 'Employers refused to accept that experience was worth more than youthful energy. And that hurt. It's not amusing to discover that you're considered over the hill when you believe you are in the prime of life.'

As a result, their marriage had gone through a bad patch and, in an attempt to re-discover themselves, they had come to Devon for a short holiday. While they were driving round, they had passed through Biddicombe and seen Brook Cottage with a FOR SALE sign outside.

They smiled at each other. 'And that was it,' Veronica said. 'We fell in love with it on the spot. We sold our flat in London and gave up the rat-race. The cottage was in a pretty awful state when we moved in, but we did most of the work ourselves – except for the thatching. Paul was always very good with his hands and I had always wanted to have a proper garden.

'Sure, we're not as well off as we used to be, which is one of the reasons why we decided to do B & B, though that's not the only reason. It's nice meeting new people like yourself. We've made so many new friends since we've been here. We have guests who come back every year. They're almost like family.'

Next morning, with a rucksack on my back – which they lent me – packed with sandwiches, chocolate, a big bottle of water and a large-scale Ordnance Survey map – I set off up on to the moors. All day, I tramped amidst gorse, heather and scrub, stopping only to regain my breath from time to time and look at the view. The sky was overcast – grey clouds parted only occasionally to allow peeks of blue – which suited my mood better than hot sunshine would have done.

Every now and again, I encountered fellow hikers, but for the most part my only company was shaggy-coated sheep and shaggy-coated wild ponies. Leg muscles which I had forgotten existed started to ache, and my feet were hot and sore in my trainers. But that was all to the good. It was something different to think about – something other than Goodchild and Nigel.

I was exhausted by the time I returned to Brook Cottage. But it was a different kind of tiredness and after a hot bath, a good meal, more philosophical conversation with Veronica and Paul, I went to bed and slept like a baby.

Next day, I walked again at a slightly more leisurely pace, mainly because my leg muscles were making themselves well and truly felt. And, as I walked, I forced myself to consider my position. To begin with, my thoughts were negative, running along the same kind of lines as they had on the Friday evening after I had left Goodchild.

Two rejections in almost as many days are hard to come to terms with. I felt a failure twice over – a failure as a secretary and a failure as a wife. I was as much at fault as Nigel. I had given up on our marriage. I had stopped making any effort. I had excluded him from my search into my parents' lives. I hadn't told him about Tobin. I hadn't told him the truth about going to Paris and Italy. When he had made love to me after he had come from Baker, I had frozen – and then I had deceived him by thinking of another man. If I had acted differently, perhaps he would have been less attracted to Bo.

But what was done was done. It was the future I had to consider now. I had to decide whether I wanted him back, whether I wanted to attempt a reconciliation or whether I should simply let him go.

Up on Exmoor, striding towards Dunkery Beacon, I could see for miles. But the inside of my head was filled with fog. I could see only in my immediate vicinity and had lost sight of the milestones which had marked the thirteen years of my marriage. So while my feet marched steadily forwards, in my mind I was stumbling about, going round in circles.

The third day was a bit better. My legs didn't ache so much and my head was becoming clearer. It occurred to me that there were practical things which needed to be done. My cheque should be paid into the bank. But would it be wise to put my money into Nigel's and my joint account, if he was intending to leave me? Depending upon how soon I managed to get another job, I could well need that money to live on.

Where did one stand in matters like this? I needed advice from a solicitor. Or should I wait until Nigel returned before rushing off to a solicitor? On the other hand, did it matter what Nigel was thinking of doing? The real questions I should be asking myself were: did I want to try and save our marriage or did I want a new beginning?

I did not think about Tobin at all. That doesn't mean to say I had forgotten him. He was there, all the time, in the secret regions of my heart. But his image was fuzzy and I couldn't focus on him. He was like my father and the Princess and Filomena. It wasn't that they weren't important – they just didn't have a place in my present circumstances. They belonged to a whole different existence, to another world even.

If Tobin had appeared in front of me over the breast of a hill, I would not have known what to say to him. In fact, I would probably have run away in the opposite direction. He was separate from all of this – from Nigel and Miles.

When I had found out how I stood with Nigel and obtained a new job – yes, after that – when all the confusion was out of the way and the fog in my head had dispersed, then I would be able to consider Tobin for himself alone. Now, it was still too soon.

On my final day at Biddicombe I walked in a completely different direction, not over the open moors, but alongside the stream, through the woods. They weren't closed in, claustrophobic sort of woods, like those surrounding the Villa Lontana, but spacious and speckled with light, filled with foxgloves. There were even sheep grazing among the trees and sleeping on boulders.

Eventually, the footpath separated from the stream and climbed steeply up a hillside, then the wood ended and open moorland began. I climbed on until I reached the top of the hill and, ahead of me, on the far horizon, was the sea.

The air was salt on my lips. Greedily, I breathed in deep lungfuls of it, feeling almost as though I had just been released from prison and this were my first taste of liberty.

I turned, gazing across the valley and, at that instant, a couple of buzzards glided over my head, hovered above the wood, then soared away down the valley. 'From now on,' I said aloud, 'that's how I'm going to be – free as a bird . . .'

When I went back to Brook Cottage that evening, I told Veronica and Paul that I would be returning to London the next day. 'Do you feel refreshed for your break?' Veronica enquired kindly.

'Infinitely,' I assured her.

'You understand why we are so happy here?'

'Yes.'

'Of course, this sort of existence wouldn't suit everyone,' Paul said. 'A lot of our friends in London thought we were daft when we told them what we were going to do. But it depends what you want from life, doesn't it?'

In my letter box, when I returned to Linden Mansions, was a note from Sherry.

Please let me know as soon as you get back. The whole world seems to have been looking for you. Sherry. XXX

I went upstairs to the flat. It no longer seemed as oppressive as it had the previous Saturday. In fact, it didn't seem anything any more. It was just a suite of furnished rooms – furniture that I didn't much like and pictures on the walls that I didn't like either. Less than ever did it feel like my home.

After going through what was becoming a familiar routine of unpacking, opening windows and switching on the immersion heater, I rang Sherry.

'It's me. I'm back.'

'Are you all right?'

'Better than when I went away.'

'Where have you been?'

'To Exmoor, to a village called Biddicombe.'

'Thank God you left a note before you went, otherwise I'd have been worried sick. As it was, I was beginning to get very concerned.'

'Sorry, I didn't mean to worry you. But I wasn't in a fit state to talk to anyone.'

'Can I come up?'

'Of course.'

We sat in the roof garden drinking tea. 'We've had some girl called Tracey on the phone,' Sherry said. 'If she rang once, she must have rung a dozen times. Apart from her, we've had your Aunt Biddie, Miranda, Juliette from the office – and Tobin.'

'Oh, my God,' I groaned. 'I am sorry.'

'There's no need to apologize. It's brightened up our lives no end. Roly and Tracey are becoming great buddies. I think he's going to invite her out for a drink soon. No, but seriously, Cara, you should have told us that you'd been made redundant. It's a horrible thing to happen. No wonder you were in a state.'

'Did Juliette tell you?'

'Yes, she was terribly upset on your behalf. Tobin knew as well. He said something about having read an item in the newspaper and then ringing you at the office to be told by Juliette that you weren't there.'

'You didn't say anything to Aunt Biddie and Miranda?'

'Good Lord, no. I just repeated what you'd said in your note – that you'd gone away for a few days. They were fine about it.'

I hesitated, then asked, 'What about Tracey?'

'Well, it took us a while to discover who Tracey was and how she had managed to come by our number. Then Roly wheedled out of her that she was Nigel's secretary and was entrusted with the task of enquiring after your well-being. When she couldn't get hold of you at the office or at home, Nigel had apparently given her our number.'

'You haven't spoken to him at all?'

'No, only Tracey.'

I nodded.

'Cara, come clean. It isn't just your job. Something's up with Nigel as well, isn't it?'

She had to know some time. 'Yes, he's having an affair with Bo. I rang him in Kenya after I'd been made redundant and disturbed them in bed together. He says he's in love with her. That's why I went away. I couldn't cope with the double blow. It was just too much.'

Her cornflower eyes blazed. 'What a bastard. I'm sorry, Cara, but he is. Does he know you've lost your job?'

'That's why I rang him. I'd just started to tell him, when Bo said something and I realized what was going on. He rang me back the next morning and told me that she was very special and he loved her and that our marriage was doomed anyway. I don't know. I've been walking for four days, thinking and thinking, and I'm still not clear in my mind.'

'Well, I'm clear in mine,' she stated. Then she clamped her mouth shut.

'Go on,' I said. 'Finish what you were going to say.'

'No. He isn't my husband and it isn't my marriage.

'Still, say it, please. I shan't be upset.'

She looked at me assessingly, then shrugged. 'OK. In my opinion, Nigel is a prize shit. And, if you take him back after this, you are a prize idiot.'

Sherry broke the silence which followed. 'Where does Tobin fit into all this?'

'He doesn't. As I told you before, we were only friends.'

'Having stuck my neck out so far, I may as well go the whole hog. You may be "just friends" with him – but he's in love with you.'

I frowned. 'How do you know? He didn't tell you, did he?'

'He didn't need to. It was absolutely obvious at your birthday dinner party. Why else do you think he gave you that painting?'

'Yes, you're right. He is in love with me – or at least he was. How he'll feel now, I don't know.'

'And how do you feel about him?'

I felt the blood rushing to my cheeks and bit my lip. Then I burst out, 'Oh, what do you think? I adore him. That's half the problem.'

She let out a long slow of exasperation. 'For someone who is basically so intelligent, how can you be so thick on occasions?'

I made to speak but she raised her hand to stop me. 'It's all right. I know. I've been there. I'll say just one thing more and then I'll shut up. You only have one life, Cara. Don't waste any more of it.' She paused. 'And now I'd better leave you to phone some of these people back and put their minds at rest.'

'Before you go,' I said. 'Do you or Roly know a good solicitor?'

A slow smile spread over her face. 'It so happens that we do. His name's David Rinder. He handled my divorce.'

'I think I should talk to him.'

After Sherry had made me see things straight, I was as fine as I could be under the circumstances. I rang Aunt Biddie and told her about having been made redundant, but because I was sounding positive and in control, she assumed that I was.

'It must have come as a shock,' she said. 'I think you were very sensible to go away and get a change of scene. Fancy a village called Biddicombe . . . Well, you know what they say: every cloud has a silver lining. You may find this is a blessing in disguise.'

She asked if I had let Nigel know and I said, yes, I had, and left it at that. There was no point in worrying her by going into detail at this stage.

'You know that if you want to come and stay, you'll be very welcome,' she went on. 'But I should warn you that my friend Jessie will be here this weekend. And you know what the two of us are like when we get together.'

'It's all right,' I assured her. 'I'll take you up on your offer a little later on. Meanwhile, I've got lots of things to get on with.'

I had just put down the phone from her, when Sherry rang through with David Rinder's telephone number and address. Then Tracey rang. 'At last, I've got hold of you! Are you OK?'

'Yes, thanks. And you?'

'Really busy, but fine. Nigel's just been on the phone again and says to let you know that he's coming back on Sunday evening. His flight arrives at five, so he should be with you at about seven.'

'I see.'

'I hope your neighbour didn't mind me keep ringing up. But Nigel was worried about you.'

'I simply went away for a few days.'

'Yes, your neighbour explained. I think it's awfully sweet that Nigel should be concerned about you. I can't imagine my boyfriend being so thoughtful.'

'Hmm,' I grunted.

'Oh, well, he'll be home soon.'

My next call was to David Rinder, who rather took me aback by having a free slot in his diary for eleven o'clock the next morning.

After that, I lifted the phone to ring Tobin – then put it down again – and decided to write to him instead. It wasn't much of a letter. I simply thanked him for his concern and said that the past few days had been pretty horrid but I was starting to get over the shock. I said that I needed to talk to him but I wasn't ready quite yet. I signed it, 'Love, Cara'.

Finally, I went into the study, where I had put Nigel's photograph face down on the desk next to the box containing the glass Lamborghini. For a long time, I studied his face and the message on the back, before taking the photograph out of its frame and ripping into tiny pieces. Then I took the boxed model down to the charity shop on the nearby parade of shops and handed it over the counter, explaining, 'This is an unwanted gift.'

David Rinder's office was in Bedford Street, just off the Strand, near Covent Garden. He reminded me vaguely of a younger version of Miles. There was the same shrewd look in his eye, the same Jewish nose, the same determined jut to his chin.

'You'd better start by telling me the state of play,' he said, after his secretary had brought us both coffee.

I described, as unemotionally as possible, how I had been made redundant and phoned Nigel in the middle of the night and the substance of his call the following morning.

'Charming,' he said. 'Exactly the sort of reaction one needs in a crisis. And since then you haven't spoken to him at all?'

'No.'

'Do you want him back? Would you be prepared to give him a second chance?'

'I don't think so. Not really.'

'Is there anyone else in your life?'

'Sort of,' I admitted. 'But we haven't been having an affair.'

'And is he married?'

'Divorced.'

'Do he and your husband know each other?'

'No. My husband doesn't even know he exists.'

'Hardly surprising if he's never home. Well, now I need to ask you a few questions about yourself.'

Half an hour later, my life and marriage had been condensed on to a couple sheets of A4 paper and David Rinder looked at me commiseratingly across his desk. 'So, basically, nothing is in joint names, except your current account at the bank? The flat is in your husband's name, and any savings and building society accounts are in his name also. How many times have I heard this story? Why don't you women stick up for your own rights?'

'Does it mean I'm not entitled to anything?'

'No, you're protected under the Matrimonial Homes Act. And under the Matrimonial Proceedings and Property Act, each party's contribution to the family welfare is not determined merely by payment in money but also in terms of looking after the home and caring for the family. However, since there are no children involved in this case, if your husband should decide to turn greedy, we could end up with a bit of a battle on our hands.'

'Oh, I don't think he will be,' I said. 'Nigel's never been mean.'

David Rinder raised a sceptical eyebrow. 'Do you have any idea how much the flat is worth and how much is left on the mortgage?'

I shook my head, feeling increasingly foolish.

'It doesn't matter. We'll have to obtain a valuation and your husband's solicitor will supply the rest of the information we need.'

I hesitated, then asked, 'Without wishing to sound greedy myself, what is my legal entitlement?'

'It isn't greedy, it's realistic. There are no hard and fast rules. Every case is different. But I would expect everything to be split straight down the middle. Would you want to remain in the flat?'

'I don't know. Probably not. Apart from anything else, I couldn't afford it on my own. Certainly not while I don't have a job. Which reminds me. What should I do with my redundancy cheque?'

'Open an account in your own name, preferably at a different bank.'

'And what should I say to Nigel when I see him on Sunday?'

'What you say on an personal level is obviously up to you. But I recommend you don't mention your friend. There's no point in handing your husband ammunition. Don't be flustered into making any agreement which you may later regret. If there is a nasty row, try not to walk out. And, if he should get violent, call the police.'

I stared at him in horror, wondering what sort of marriages other people had.

He gave a wry smile and quoted, 'Heaven has no rage, like love to hatred turned.' Then he handed me his card. 'I'll wait to hear from you.'

Nigel arrived on Sunday evening at exactly seven o'clock – the first time I could remember him being punctual in the whole thirteen years of our marriage and all the more extraordinary considering the distance he had travelled.

He looked drawn and had a sheepish, almost hangdog look about him beneath his broad-brimmed hat. We stood for a moment staring at each other, then both sat down, awkwardly, as though we were strangers meeting in a strange environment.

'How are you?' he asked.

I shrugged.

He cleared his throat. 'Listen, I want to explain my side of things.'

'You don't have to. I've been aware for a long time that things weren't right between us. As you said on the phone, we've been growing further and further apart.'

'I have tried to make it work, Cara.'

'So have I, but—'

He ignored my interruption. Obviously, he had his speech rehearsed and was determined to deliver it. 'It's very important to me that you don't blame Bo. She didn't come between us: she wasn't responsible for splitting us up. In fact, she's very concerned about you and the effect all this will have on you.'

'How civil of her.'

'However, even if I hadn't met Bo, we would probably still be having this conversation today, because to go on as we were wasn't fair on either of us. It wasn't fair on you and it wasn't fair on me. Basically, you and I have nothing in common any more. We want totally different things out of life.

'Looking back, I think the problems really started after you lost the baby. I think it might have helped matters if we'd had a family. You would actually have made a very good mother and having a child would have fulfilled you as a woman, as well as giving you a direction and purpose in life. As it is, you've stagnated – and, frankly, as a result, you've become a bit of a bore.

'Now, my work hasn't helped. I recognize that. If I had a nine-to-five-job and didn't travel so much, we'd have seen more of each other and I suppose it's possible that we might be closer now. I doubt it though. And I would certainly have been a damn sight more miserable. I need lots of outside stimulus and the challenge of my career.'

Enough was enough. 'Fine!' I said. 'You've made your point and now can we get to the matter in hand? Would I be right in assuming that, in Bo, you believe you've finally met the perfect match?'

Our eyes met momentarily, then he dropped his gaze. 'Bo and I complement each other. We work in the same profession. We want the same things out of life. It may sound odd to you, but it's like she's my *alter ego*.'

'In which case, it doesn't seem to me that there's a lot more to be said, other than deciding what happens next. Do you want a divorce?'

'That's what I'd like. I hope you won't stand in my way.'

'I've already been to see a solicitor and obtained advice.'

His mouth gaped open.

'Obviously what I need to know now is what you are proposing to do.'

He struggled to get the wind back in his sails. 'Well, I, er, I think it would be best to make a clean break straight away. Apart from anything else, it wouldn't fair on you if I went on living here.'

'Where will you go?'

'To Bo's. Her apartment's huge. Not that we'll be spending much time there in the immediate future. We've still got the rest of the commercials to complete.'

I nodded.

'What about you? Are you planning on staying here?'

'For the time being it would be helpful, because I don't have anywhere else to go, other than to Avonford, which I'd prefer not to do.'

'That night when you rang me, did you say you'd been made redundant?'

'Yes, that's the reason I rang.'

'So you're out of work?'

'Yes.'

'Well, I'll make sure the mortgage is paid each month, at least until we come to a proper legal settlement. What about long-term? Do you think you'll want to stay here?'

'I don't know. I shouldn't think so.'

'There's no need for you to rush into any decisions. I have no intention of selling the roof over your head. I hope that goes without saying.'

'Thank you. Obviously I shall get another job as soon as possible. I'd prefer to be self-sufficient.'

He glanced at his watch. 'While I'm here, I may as well take some of my clothes and other bits and pieces. There's a limit to how much I'll be able to fit in the Porsche, but I should be able to clear quite a lot.'

I stood up and heard myself asking, just as though he were going away on location and not leaving the house for ever, 'Would you like some help?'

'Thanks, but I'll manage.'

'Do you want a coffee?'

'I wouldn't mind actually.'

'Milk and sugar?'

He winced.

After he had gone off to pack, I looked at *Inspiration* and, with a grim smile, removed it from the wall. Lowrie, Hockney and Warhol came down, too. I carried them into the hall and then put the kettle on.

An hour or so later, after several trips up and down stairs, Nigel's car was packed. He stood awkwardly just inside the front door. 'You'll be all right, won't you?'

'I've no doubt I'll survive.'

He reached in his pocket. 'This is Bo's address and telephone number. If you wouldn't mind forwarding any post.'

'Of course not. And this is my solicitor's name and address. He'll be in touch with you.'

'Cara, I'm sorry that it had to end like this.'

He made to kiss me, but I turned my head away.

Without another word, he got into the Porsche, switched on the engine, revved it, then pulled out on to the tarmac. I stood in the doorway and watched him go up the drive, until he reached the main road and disappeared from sight.

I went back up the stairs and rang Sherry's bell. 'I've come to reclaim the portrait of Filomena.'

She clutched my arm. 'You mean . . . ?'

'Yes, he's gone.'

'Oh, you poor darling. Was it dreadful?'

I shrugged. 'Not really. It wasn't anything. I thought I'd feel more, but—'

'Come in and have a drink.'

'No, thanks. If you don't mind, I'd rather be on my own for a bit.'

'Sure. If you change your mind, you know where we are. I'll go and get the painting.'

When she came back with it, I said, 'One good thing, though. There's a parking space free now. Tell Roly, won't you?'

We both laughed weakly.

I moved through the next few days in a stupor, as though I were somehow removed from the world around me and nothing that happened there had anything really to do with me. Certain incidents stand out, but the rest is a blank. I remember going to the bank at the nearby parade of shops to open a new account and it all being incredibly complicated for such a theoretically simple matter, especially since I was trying to pay money in. It was so much effort that I sank down in a chair and burst into tears, whereupon I was rushed into a little office to recover and somehow the account was opened.

I kept bursting into tears.

I remember also ringing David Rinder and telling him the outcome of my conversation with Nigel and him saying sceptically, 'Let's give him the benefit of the doubt, but my guess is he'll start feeling less generous after he's talked to his solicitor. What exactly did he take with him?'

'I don't know. Clothes, personal papers and some pictures . . .'

'Pictures? Were they valuable?'

'I don't care if they were. I hated them.'

'I would suggest you change your front door lock.'

'Why?'

'You don't want him in the flat in your absence, do you – or coming in unannounced in the middle of the night?'

I remember answering, faintly, 'No,' wishing he were not so cynical and suspicious. I didn't get the lock changed.

I remember too buying a copy of *The Times* and going through the appointments pages and finding nothing that I wanted to do. I remember phoning a couple of employment agencies and being informed that jobs for multi-lingual secretaries didn't come up very often.

A girl called Debbie at one of them said she had a lovely job, just come in, at an insurance company, which had a subsidized staff canteen and was two minutes' from Fenchurch Street Station. The hours were only 9.30 to 5.30, with three weeks' holiday and there was an excellent pension scheme. Or, if that didn't appeal to me, what about this one, at a Japanese cosmetics company – did I speak Japanese? No, well, what about this one, working for the fund-raising executive of a charity for disabled children, based in Wimbledon? The salary wasn't so good but the work would be really interesting.

I lacked the energy even to explain that Wimbledon was on the opposite side of London from Highgate. I simply said that, yes, I would come in some time and register. Some time. Not now.

I remember taking off my wedding and engagement rings and putting them in a Dr Barnardo's collecting box.

I remember putting all Nigel's personal belongings – his clothes and books and magazines – into the study and trying to rearrange the rest of the flat to make it more homely. I bought lots of flowers and kept the radio on all the time. But they didn't stop me crying, suddenly, for no apparent reason.

Eventually, I summoned up the courage to tell Miranda what had happened. It seemed easier to tell her than Aunt Biddie. I remember her saying, 'You must come straight up here,' and me saying, 'No, I don't want to. That won't help . . .'

I remember Aunt Biddie ringing and saying, 'Cara, darling, Miranda's just told me. I'm so sorry. Please come up here. I don't like the thought of you in that flat all on your own at a time like this. You don't have to see anyone else.'

And I remember her saying, too, 'I wouldn't have dreamt of saying anything before, but now this has happened I feel free to speak my mind. Nigel took you for granted – he treated you as if you were a part of the furniture.'

In the end, I did go to Avonford. After all, it was home.

When the weather allowed, we sat in the garden, with Tiger lying in the shade of my deckchair and Reynard on a lead at our feet, Gordon parading 'his' goslings up and down the lawn and Chukwa routing round the lettuce patch.

Once I was there, I was glad I had gone, for in the garden of my childhood, I opened my heart to Aunt Biddie. It all spilled out – all the mental clutter I had been accumulating since childhood, all my insecurities, all my good intentions, all my aspirations, all my inhibitions. I explained how I had always wanted to live up to her and Uncle Stephen's example, how I hadn't wanted to let them down, how – especially in recent months – I hadn't wanted to appear to take after my father and the Princess.

In reply, she said, 'If Nigel had been my husband, my patience would have run out long ago. I wouldn't have put up with everything you've put up with. You have absolutely nothing with which to reproach yourself.'

I told her, too, about Tobin, my pledge on the balcony at San Fortunato and how he had told me, after my return from Italy, that he loved me.

And she asked, as Sherry had, whether I loved him.

But the fuzziness was still there. If anything, Tobin's image was even more blurred and he seemed to be receding ever further away. I could recall every word Nigel had said to me at our last encounter but Tobin's declaration of love was like something which had happened in a dream.

'Yes,' I said, 'or rather I believe so. I just can't think clearly at the moment.'

'That's hardly surprising,' she said. 'In any case, it wouldn't be wise to rush into another relationship on the rebound. You did that once before, remember.'

After that, we talked about work and what I should do with the rest of my life. She didn't chide me for my sudden lack of faith in my own abilities. She understood how I felt as though the ground had been taken away from beneath me and that I didn't trust myself to take the next step forward. Instead of taking another permanent job straight away, she suggested I did temporary work – less as a means of earning money, than to get me out of the flat and recover my self-confidence.

One day, we went to Bredon Hill. The Vale of Evesham below us was lush and green and larks sang in the sky above us. I gazed across Housman's 'coloured counties' and peace seemed to settle upon me.

I recalled how, the last time we were up here, after Oliver Lyon's programme, I had felt a contraction of my heart, and a sharp pang of something almost akin to fear, as though I were about to go away somewhere and would never look upon this scene again. In the interim I had indeed travelled far – but I had still returned to Bredon Hill.

Impulsively, I put my arm round Aunt Biddie's waist. She turned and smiled at me, putting her arm round my waist, too. 'It will be all right,' she assured me.

And, to my surprise, I found myself thinking that, yes, maybe it would.

Chapter 22

Back in London again, I registered with Debbie at the secretarial agency, where I suffered the indignity of doing a shorthand and typing test, smiled wanly when Debbie congratulated me on my speeds, and was duly despatched on my first temping assignment.

Little remains in my memory of that first job. I remember it was in Holborn at the head office of an electronics company, that I was working for the head of the marketing department, that the people were nice, going out of their way to show me where things were and how the photocopier worked and similar things. But of what my work actually consisted I have absolutely no recollection, except of my boss being surprised at the speed with which I got through it. The mind, thank heavens, has reserves on which to fall back, when its main operating system fails.

Because I didn't remain long enough at that, or any of the other offices at which I temped, for my colleagues to get to know me well, I felt mantled in a comforting cloak of anonymity, which enabled my inner wounds to start to heal. Gradually, as Aunt Biddie had predicted, my confidence in myself as a secretary came back and, with it, some of my self-esteem.

Of course, I had some bad moments, like the time I came home and turned on the television to find myself confronted with Nigel's first commercial. There was an earth-mover in the desert, with a Jeep bouncing across the sand towards it, to the familiar background music of 'Wheels of Fire'. The copy line flashed up on the screen and a man's voice said, 'Macintyre for when the going gets tough.'

I switched off the television and started to shake again. But I didn't cry, which was one huge step forward.

David Rinder's letters didn't do a lot for me either. Not that they contained bad news, as such. Contrary to his dire prognostications, Nigel did indeed seem to want our separation to be as fair and amicable as possible. But the legal terminology made our divorce seem even sadder, reducing it to the level of a sordid business transaction, and making me feel grasping.

I couldn't help thinking of the Princess – and of Tobin's ex-wife, Dawn, for that matter. I hated the idea of Nigel, at some future time, saying of me, 'She took me for everything she could get.'

Many times, I wished that I could simply walk out of Linden Mansions, renouncing all claim on the marital home. But Sherry prevented me, urging me not to react emotionally, reminding me that Nigel was earning far more than I was, and that I was only taking what was rightfully mine.

Sherry was so good to me – and for me – just as she had been after I lost the baby. That was the advantage of her having been divorced herself. She knew what I was going through – emotionally and in real, everyday terms.

I was, in fact, earning considerably less than I had at Goodchild and struggling to make ends meet, even though Nigel was paying the mortgage. Temping was a useful stop-gap but not a long-term solution. Very soon, if I wasn't careful, I would be eating into my redundancy money. There was no doubt about it, I couldn't afford to stay at the flat, even if I wanted to. It would have to be sold – and very soon.

I had heard nothing from Nigel. All our communications took place through our respective solicitors. It wasn't so much that I wanted to see him or talk to him, I simply couldn't understand how he could make so final a break.

Neither did I hear anything from Juliette. Apart from that one call while I was in Biddicombe, she had not contacted me. And I could not bring myself to ring her. We had been friends – not as close as Sherry and I – but more than just colleagues. I didn't hold what had happened against her or blame her for staying at Goodchild, but neither did I want to know what was going on there. I didn't want to know what my successor was like and what changes Craig Vidler had made. That part of my life was over. A curtain had come down between it and me – Juliette was on one side and I was on the other.

Perhaps, I decided, Nigel felt the same about him and me. Perhaps his sense of shock had been as great as mine at the swiftness of the end of marriage. Perhaps our separation had hurt him more than I gave him credit for. Perhaps he did care more than I realized. And that was why he stayed away.

Nor did I hear anything from Tobin.

And his absence was beginning to hurt. As the fog in my head started to clear, I knew that I loved him. I wasn't sure how much I loved him or what form any future relationship between us should take, because I didn't allow myself to think more than a day ahead. But I was certain that I wanted to see him again.

Did he want to see me, though? If so, surely he would have replied by now to my note? Had he regretted his impetuous words after my return from San Fortunato? Or had he misinterpreted my silence and, because he didn't know Nigel had left me, was he now assuming we were living happily together? Had I been, yet again, my own worst enemy and driven him away?

I reminded myself that, after our dinner in Hampstead, he had said he would leave it for me to get in touch. I reminded myself that in my note to him I had said that I wasn't quite ready yet to talk to him. It was up to me to make the first move and quickly, before it was too late. All I had to do was pick up the phone.

Or was it already too late? Had somebody else slipped in during my absence? Penny, maybe – lovely, bubbly Penny – Penny, who had been going through a rough patch. Penny, for whom he had felt sorry . . .

To telephone Tobin and receive no answer would be bad enough. But to telephone him and learn that he was with someone else – to hear Penny's voice in the background, like I had heard Bo's – that would be more than I could bear.

So I kept putting that moment off. And the longer I left it, the more afraid I became. As the weeks went by, I forced myself bleakly to face up to the fact that Tobin – like Nigel and Goodchild, belonged to the past.

On the Saturday of August bank holiday weekend, the postman delivered a large manila envelope. Inside was a note from Tobin, a Christie's catalogue and two photocopies.

Tobin's note read:

Dear Cara,

I have respected your wishes and not intruded upon you.

But now something has happened of which I think you

ought to be aware. The enclosed two letters are self-explanatory. Needless to say, Oliver and I will be at Christie's on the morning of the 28th August. If you would like to join our little party, you will be most welcome. If there is a possibility of speaking to you – or better still seeing you – before then, it would be even better. I do hope that I am not causing you any embarrassment by sending this note and the contents to your home address.

As ever,

Tobin.

In my heart, a little singing bird, which had long been silent, fluttered its wings within its cage and let forth a few, cautious melodic notes.

The letters were typed on a manual typewriter, the ribbon of which had been wearing out. There were several typing mistakes, which had either been over-typed or crossed out. Both were unsigned. The first, according to the rubber stamp at the top of the page, had been received on 4 of August, the second on the 21st.

Dear Mr Lyon,

I saw your interview earlier this year with the Princess Hélène Shuiska.

On page 30 of the Christie's catalogue for the sale of Russian Works of Art and Icons due to take place in South Kensington on 28th of August, you will see an icon, which is described as having been the property of the Princess.

According to the catalogue, this icon belonged to the Shuiska family in St Petersburg. This is not true. The icon belonged to my mother's family.

This was one of many lies Hélène told and deceits she practised. Others were more serious. I am sure the Princess's heir, the present Earl of Winster, is an honourable gentleman, who is unaware of the shameful secrets in Hélène's life and would not wish to perpetuate them.

If you are the seeker of truth whom I believe you to be, you will be interested in information I have concerning her. Please signify your interest by placing an announcement in the Personal Column of The Times on August 9th, stating: ''La belle dame sans merci.''

Dear Mr Lyon,
I shall be at Christie's on the morning of Thursday, August 28th, to look again at my family heirloom. If I do not see you at the sale I shall know you do not care about making sure that ancient wrongs are rectified.

Before I could invent any excuses for myself and without allowing myself time to consider what I was going to say, I phoned Tobin. He answered on the second ring.

'It's Cara,' I said.

He let out a long sigh. 'How are you?'

'I haven't been very good, but I'm much better now.'

'I've been worried about you.'

'Thank you. And thank you for sending me the letters and the catalogue.'

'We'll talk about them in a minute. First, tell me, have you found another job?'

'Sort of. I'm temping.' I paused. 'Something else happened after I was made redundant. Nigel and I have split up.'

'You've what?'

'We've split up. We're getting a divorce.'

'Christ Almighty! What happened? Or don't you want to talk about it?'

'No, I don't mind. It was a shock at the time but I'm getting over it now.'

'I *am* sorry.'

'You needn't be. It hadn't been a very happy marriage for a long time. But you know how it is. You just go on, hoping it will get better. But it didn't. He said he was going to leave me anyway, even if he hadn't met Bo.'

'Who's Bo?'

'Bo Eriksson. She owns the production company that he's working with on the Macintyre commercials.' I paused again, then decided to get it over and done with, so that he was aware from the beginning of exactly how I stood. 'I rang him in Kenya the night I left Goodchild. They were in bed together. When he came back, he told me that he was moving in with her. That's it really. Now the lawyers are sorting out the divorce arrangements.'

'You poor thing . . .'

It's an indication of the progress I was making that I was able to reply, 'Mmm, it hasn't been much fun. It was the shock of it really, particularly coming on top of getting the sack.'

Tobin was silent for a few moments, then he asked, 'Do you want to meet again or is it still too soon?'

'Do you still want to see me?'

'Any more stupid questions?'

I gave a rueful laugh. 'I'm sorry, but I don't know. I'm not sure of anything any more. It's a long time since we've seen each other.'

'I'll tell you exactly how long it is. The last time I saw you was on the first of June. That makes it two months and twenty-three days.'

The little bird in my heart flapped its wings with extreme vigour.

Half an hour later, the door bell rang and there he was. We stood for a moment, just looking at each other, then he gathered me in his arms. For a long time, we stood there on the landing, our arms round each other, my head against his shoulder, his cheek against my hair.

Eventually, he relaxed his embrace, tipped my face up towards him and kissed me. But it was not the kiss his embrace had led me to anticipate. It was warm, affectionate, but somehow restrained and without passion. Part of me was disappointed. Another part of me was relieved.

I offered him a cup of coffee but he refused, asking, 'Do you have anything planned for the rest of the day?'

'No.'

'In that case, shall we drive somewhere? We could go down to the coast and look at the sea.'

'Yes, that would be nice. I'd like that.'

'It's chilly out there. You'd better bring a jacket or an anorak.'

In the car, there was an understandable awkwardness between us, questions we both wanted to ask of each other but were too important to launch straight into. So, during the drive, we talked mainly about the subject which had brought us together in the first place – the Princess and the anonymous letters.

'Who do you think wrote them?' Tobin asked.

'I don't know,' I said, my mind more on us than on them.

He glanced at me. 'Do you still want to get to the bottom of the mystery? Or would you prefer to stop?'

Yet again my moonlit sojourn at San Fortunato came back to haunt me. But fate had made a mockery of my other pledges that night, and, in any case, the icon and the Princess's Russian past had nothing to do with Filomena.

'I'd like to continue,' I said.

'I think those letters could have come from the blackmailer,' he went on. 'Those we found in the Princess's escritoire were written on the same sort of typewriter.'

It seemed such a long time since my visit to Beadle Walk back in February. 'Did you ever learn any more about the old, aristocratic Russian lady Consuela told me about?' I asked.

'Not a thing.'

'Has your brother seen these letters?'

'Yes, I sent him copies too. His first reaction was that we should notify the police, but I managed to persuade him against that. The writer of those letters isn't actually making any demands – just dropping very big hints. And it could be a coincidence. I'm sure the Princess made more than one enemy during her lifetime.

'In the end, he agreed that our anonymous letter writer must be given the benefit of the doubt – innocent until proved guilty, so to speak. If he or she is not only the moral but the legal owner of the icon, then they'll have to prove that the Princess didn't come by it lawfully. In that case, Harvey may have to withdraw the icon from the sale and end up a few thousand pounds less well off than he thought he was going to be. So what? Judging by the estimates in the Christie's catalogue, he stands to do quite well out of the auction and he's hardly destitute to start with. No, the most important thing is what this could mean for you.

'You remember the paragraph where the writer mentions lies and deceits? That could mean that he or she knows about you. Would you be able to take time off on Thursday?'

'I don't see why not, so long as I let people know in advance. One of the advantages of temping is that you're a free agent. If you don't work, you're not paid.'

'Well, hopefully it will prove worthwhile.'

As we approached Eastbourne, I thought fleetingly of Nigel's parents in nearby Bexhill, from whom I had heard nothing since Nigel had left, not even a note to say they were sorry.

On the outskirts of the town, we stopped at a shop and bought a French stick, butter, cheese, tomatoes, fruit and a bottle of wine. Then we drove up to the headland above Beachy Head lighthouse, where we left the car and, taking our picnic with us, set off along the cliffs.

'What have you been doing since I last saw you?' I asked, hastily adding, 'I mean, workwise.'

'I've been very busy. I believe I told you that my old friend, Penny, had a new series of children's natural history books in the offing? Well, the first of those has materialized. It's an animal book – animals of the wayside and woodland – everything from moles and shrews to deer. Oh, and bunny rabbits, of course.' He laughed.

I laughed, too, though rather hollowly.

'What about you?' he asked. 'After having worked at Goodchild for so long, how are you finding moving from job to job? It must be rather unsettling?'

'Now I've got used to it, I'm actually quite enjoying working in different companies and seeing how they function. In that respect, you could almost say that temping broadens the mind. Or it would, if some of the work I have to do wasn't so utterly tedious. I had one job – which thankfully only lasted three days – when I was typing accounts all day long. And there was another where I was just catching up on the filing for them. But the place I'm at now is a bit better. I'm doing a two-week holiday replacement in the personnel department at an engineering firm.'

It was our picnic which broke the ice. As we unpacked our carrier bag in the shelter of a copse, we realized that we had no plates or glasses and the only knife was Tobin's penknife, which fortunately had a corkscrew attachment.

After we had both apologized to each other for our thoughtlessness, we burst out laughing and from then on, the barrier was down. I can't remember a meal which tasted better, or wine more delicious than that from the bottle which we passed backwards and forwards, each fastidiously wiping the neck clean on a tissue after we had drunk from it, yet aware that our lips were going where the other's had been. Yes, there was an intimacy about that picnic which no candle-lit restaurant could ever have provided.

When we walked on, it was arm in arm. The rolling Downland countryside reminded me in a way of Exmoor and I told him about Biddicombe and my long hikes – not my state of my mind – but about the sheep, ponies, buzzards, Brook Cottage, Veronica and Paul.

At Birling Gap, we went down the rickety stairs to the beach and skimmed stones across the waves, until the unseasonably chill wind drove us back up on to the cliffs and we returned to where we had left the car.

On the way back to London, we stopped for dinner at a country pub and Tobin asked, 'Do you have anything arranged for tomorrow?'

'No, nothing.'

'I wondered if you might be going to Avonford.'

'No, I was up there a couple of weeks ago. Aunt Biddie's friend Jessie is staying with her this weekend.'

'In that case, how do you fancy going for a cycle ride?'

'A cycle ride?'

'You can ride a bike?'

'I used to be able to.'

'Well, I have a bike and my neighbour has a spare one, which I'm sure she'll lend us. We could go along the towpath to Richmond or Teddington Lock.'

I sat back in my chair, still not knowing how I stood and therefore unsure how to respond.

'Or we could do something else,' he said. 'It doesn't have to be a cycle ride. That was just the first thing that came into my head.' He paused. 'Or don't you want to see me again?'

'Yes, but—'

He pushed his knife and fork together, then ran his fingers through his hair. 'It's all right, you needn't say any more. I really am the biggest fool who ever lived, aren't I? I've been taking it for granted that today has been as happy for you as it has for me.'

'It has. I've enjoyed every minute of it.'

'But you don't want to take things any further?'

I bit my lip.

He took out his cigarettes. 'Come on, have a cigarette. We'll order some coffee, then I'll take you home.'

I shook my head. 'You know that evening, after I came back from San Fortunato and we went out to dinner?'

'Yes, I remember it extremely well.'

'You said then that we should have no misunderstandings.'

'I seem to remember that I said a lot of other things as well. And I may as well admit, here and now, that nothing has changed. I still love you as much as ever. But I'm not going to make a nuisance of myself.'

'Maybe I will have a cigarette after all.'

He lit it for me.

Then I asked hesitantly, 'What about Penny?'

'Penny? Where does she come into this?'

'Well, I thought maybe . . . You see, one evening after you saw me you had dinner with her and—'

'Oh, dear. Yes, I think I see which way your mind's going. But you couldn't be more wrong. Penny and I did indeed have an affair many, many years ago. However, after that, she got married and she and her husband Michael are one of the most happily married couples to exist anywhere in the world.'

'But you said that she was going through a rough patch.'

Tobin nodded. 'She still is. She's being treated for breast cancer.'

A cold shiver of shame ran through me. 'Oh, my God. I am sorry.'

'Fortunately, the cancer was diagnosed early and the treatment seems to be working. But it hasn't been easy for her, coping with that on top of running a home and holding down a demanding job. Michael and the children have been excellent and, since she confessed the truth to me, I've been doing what I can to offer moral support if nothing else. At least she knows she doesn't have to worry about the illustrations for this new series of books. And Freddie, my agent, has introduced her to a couple of other very good artists who work in a similar style.'

I tapped the ash from my cigarette, feeling dreadful that my suspicions should have been so totally misfounded.

A waitress took away our unfinished plates and Tobin ordered coffee.

'Well, having cleared the air on that one,' he said, 'what else is there?'

'Nothing, except . . .'

'Come on, spit it out.'

'Except that I don't really know what I want or how I feel about anything. I'd like us to be friends again. I've missed you a lot. But I need time to sort myself out.'

He swirled the wine round in his glass. 'Sometime, I'd like you to tell me about Nigel. I don't know what he looks like, how old he is, what kind of person he is – all I know is that he's in advertising.'

'I'd rather not talk about him tonight.'

'Fair enough. But one day. Yes?'

'Yes, one day.'

The waitress brought our coffees.

When she was gone, Tobin said, 'Let's make a pact to be truthful with each other. If you feel I'm crowding you – or if I inadvertently upset you in any other way – I'd rather you told me straight out than made up excuses not to see me. We've both suffered from other people's deceit, don't let's do it to each other.'

I nodded.

'In addition to that, may I suggest that we take each day as it comes and enjoy it – like we have enjoyed today? For what it's worth, I do know what you're going through and the very last thing I want is to force you into doing something you may later regret.'

'Thank you.'

'And thank *you* for ringing me this morning. Now, let's talk about something else.'

'Let's talk about going for a bike ride,' I said. 'I think that sounds rather fun.'

When we reached Linden Mansions, he said, 'As regards tomorrow, would you mind meeting me at my place?'

'Of course not.'

'Then I'd better tell you how to get there.'

He kissed me again before we parted – a kiss that was warm, affectionate, but not overpowering. As I got out of the car, he said, 'I am glad you're back.'

The road in which Tobin lived was like thousands of other suburban roads in London and his house looked identical to all the others in the road – the same coloured brickwork, the same shaped windows, the same grey slate roof, the same wrought-iron gate leading into the same minute front-garden.

Then he opened the front door and his house became unique. 'Welcome to my home, sweet home,' he said, ushering me. 'And now, first things first. Allow me to introduce you to Bandito, so called because he looks like a mafioso.'

Bandito was a black and white cat, who had been sleeping on a chair in the hall, until he heard his name, whereupon he roused himself, arched his back, looked me up and down, yawned, then sat upright, looking very dapper and dignified.

I crouched down and stroked him. 'Hello, Bandito. Aren't you handsome?'

'Don't be deceived by his expression,' Tobin said. 'If you feel like making a fuss of him, he won't be at all offended. Quite the contrary. There's nothing he likes better than to be cuddled by a pretty girl.'

As if in confirmation, Bandito purred loudly and I picked him up. He settled himself over my shoulder and nuzzled his head against my cheek.

'You see,' Tobin stated. 'He and I have quite a lot in common.' He rubbed the back of Bandito's head, then leaned forward and kissed me on my other cheek. 'It's so good to see you here. I've often imagined it. Would you like to see round?'

'I'd love to,' I said and could hear my voice sounding a little too animated. To be in Tobin's home was quite different from having him in mine. This was uncharted foreign territory, full of potential traps and dangers for my vulnerable heart.

In that, I wasn't mistaken. His house was the complete opposite to my flat. His personality was evident everywhere: in the books which overspilled from shelves onto tables, chairs and floor; in the furniture, most of which he had apparently bought from second-hand shops and sanded down and repainted or re-varnished himself; and, most of all, in the pictures on the walls . . .

Those pictures were sheer magic. They gave me the same sort of feeling as did Amadore Angelini's paintings, although they were quite different in content and style. These were landscapes, with an almost photographic quality to them, and conveying an incredible sense of atmosphere.

'Did *you* paint these?' I asked.

'I'm afraid so. I did them for myself – they weren't commissioned. A couple of years ago, I took a sort of sabbatical and drove round the country, painting views. To have them on display is a bit of an ego trip, I realize, but I like them because they remind me of places I love.

'That's Derbyshire,' he said, pointing to one, where black storm clouds were gathering over bleak hills. 'And that's Morthoe on the north Devon coast, not far from where you were at Biddicombe. The rollers were incredible that day. And this one's Norfolk, of course. I know poppies are a bit of a cliché, but I love 'em. And now, come with me . . .'

He led me upstairs and there, on the landing, was a view very familiar to me. 'It's from the top of Bredon Hill,' I gasped.

He grinned and opened a door. 'Come and see where I work.'

It wasn't a large room and, compared to the rest of the house and bearing in mind that it was a studio, remarkably orderly. 'Not ideal,' he said, 'but it serves its purpose. And this is the sort of thing I spend my days doing.'

On an easel was a detailed painting of harvest mice among ears of corn, in which you could see every hair and every whisker. 'That's lovely, too,' I said. 'I had no idea . . .'

He grinned at me. 'Come on, own up, what did you think my work was going to be like?'

That question was like being asked, after you've met somebody, how you had imagined them beforehand. You have a vague image in your mind but, once you've encountered the reality, that imprecise impression fades and you can only remember them as they are.

'Well, I didn't have much to go on, really,' I prevaricated. 'But I must admit that when you were talking about Easter bunnies, I did rather assume . . .'

'Ah! Let me show you some of my family of bunnies. I have one of the finished products here, though I regret to say that I've eaten the contents.'

He reached up on a shelf and took down a chocolate box, beautifully decorated with lifelike rabbits and spring flowers.

'Oliver Lyon was right,' I said. 'You are wasting your talent. You should be exhibiting in the Royal Academy.'

'Oliver didn't really say that, did he?'

'He didn't actually mention the Royal Academy, but he did say your talent was wasted.'

'Well I never.'

We were about to leave the room when he pointed to a picture with its face to the wall. 'Incidentally, that's Angelini's portrait of the Princess. To be quite honest, I don't know where to put it. It's not something I want to look at every day. So let me ask you again. Would you like it to match the one of Filomena?'

'Thank you, but I really don't want it.'

He paused. 'Do you have Filomena's portrait back now?'

'Yes. It's hanging in the living room.'

'Good.'

I felt I ought to say something more in way of explanation but I didn't know what or how. So, instead, I suggested, 'Why don't you put that into the auction with the rest of the Princess's stuff?'

'It's a bit late for that. But I could always let Ludo Zakharin have it.'

'Well, whatever you decide, I don't want it,' I repeated firmly.

He nodded. 'It's all right. I understand.'

Out on the landing again, I caught a glimpse through another door, slightly ajar, of the end of a bed. Tobin, however, pointed to a third door. 'There's the bathroom, should you need it.' Then we went back downstairs.

'Would you like a coffee before we go out?' he asked, 'or shall we get moving?'

It may sound crazy, but, as well as being unsure of myself, I was jealous of his house. 'Let's go,' I said.

Tobin's bicycle was in a small room beyond the kitchen. 'The outside loo in days of yore,' Tobin explained, 'and now a glory-hole, as your Aunt Biddie would say.'

He wheeled his bicycle out into the street, then asked me to hold it while he locked the house and went next door for mine. His neighbour – a young woman, followed by a small child – brought it to the door and smiled at me.

I thanked her for the loan and promised to try and bring it back in one piece.

'Don't worry about it,' she laughed. 'You're welcome. Have fun, both of you.'

Then we were setting off towards the river, me wobbling a bit to start with and Tobin laughing. I felt better out there in the open. Once we reached the towpath on the opposite bank of the river, he set a gentle pace and most of the time we managed to ride abreast and chat as we rode.

It occurred to me that, during the course of my entire marriage, Nigel and I had never gone for a cycle ride together. After that first, one and only, walk up Bredon Hill, we had never even walked together. Come to that, I couldn't recall when we had last spent two whole days together.

At lunchtime, we stopped at a pub, then made our way leisurely back again. It had been a perfect day, simple and uncomplicated.

'Will you stay to dinner?' he asked, when we were back in Fulham, my bike returned to its rightful owner.

An alarm bell sounded in my head. It wasn't that I didn't trust Tobin, more that I didn't trust myself not to parade my insecurity and spoil everything.

'Or we can eat out if you prefer,' he said.

I continued to dither and he laughed. 'Come on, let's eat here. I'll try not to poison you.'

And I had to laugh back.

While he prepared our meal, I sat at the kitchen table, sipping wine, watching him coat turkey cutlets with breadcrumbs, and chop aubergines, courgettes and tomatoes to make ratatouille. Bandito sat at his feet, waiting expectantly for any chance titbits that might fall his way, and the scene was so reminiscent of 'The Willows' and such a stark contrast again to my marriage with Nigel, that my heart cried for all the things which been missing from my life for so long.

We ate in the kitchen – like I always did with Aunt Biddie at The Willows – and another habit Nigel had detested.

While we were eating, Tobin asked, 'Are you planning on staying at Linden Mansions?'

I shook my head and he nodded. 'It's best to make a clean break and a fresh start, although I know that's easier said than done. Moving isn't fun at the best of times and, when a marriage ends, it's particularly difficult. You can't help having memories . . .'

Suddenly, I realized that he believed I had still been in love with Nigel at the time he had walked out on me. He knew nothing about my home-coming from Paris. He thought I was suffering from a broken heart.

When I didn't respond, Tobin continued, 'In an ideal world, if money were no object, where would you like to live?'

I visualized The Willows and Holly Hill Farm and Veronica and Paul at Brook Cottage. 'In the country,' I replied without any hesitation.

'Anywhere in particular?'

'Not really. It would just be so nice to have a proper garden and fields around and maybe a dog and a cat.'

'There's nothing to stop you going anywhere you like.'

'Oh, it's only a pipe dream. For one thing, my friends are in London. And, for another, I'd still have to earn a living.'

He nodded, then said, 'Have some more ratatouille.'

After our meal, we chatted until about ten o'clock. Then I said, 'I ought to be going.'

He didn't try to dissuade me. All he said was, 'Do you want to meet again tomorrow?'

Chapter 23

Tobin and I spent Bank Holiday Monday in Kew Gardens, after which we didn't see each other again until the following Thursday. On the day of the auction, we met for breakfast in a restaurant on the Old Brompton Road, facing the main entrance to Christie's. On an impulse, I wore the Princess's pendant.

Viewing was from nine o'clock and the auction itself commenced at eleven. We sat at a window table, drinking coffee and nibbling croissants, observing the street outside. A steady stream of people made their way into the auction house, but there was no old lady fitting Consuela's vague description.

A taxi drew up and Oliver Lyon stepped out. 'Well, we may as well wend our way over there,' Tobin said. He signalled to the waitress and asked for our bill.

I seized the opportunity to go to the ladies. There was only one toilet and when I emerged from it, I found myself confronted by a most unconventional figure, studying her appearance in the mirror. I had a fleeting glimpse of a very old and overly made-up face, before she let fall a black, spotted veil, attached to a black, pill-box type hat over a few skimpy curls, bleached an ash blonde. She was very short, reaching scarcely to my shoulder, and wearing a knee-length black cloak.

'Good morning,' she said, in high-pitched voice, like a young girl's, with a strong French accent.

The air reeked of Chanel No. 5.

I returned her greeting, smiling effusively, as one does under such circumstances, to counteract any possibly insulting, initial impression of shocked astonishment. She entered the cubicle and I hurriedly washed my hands, then went back downstairs to rejoin Tobin. 'Did you see the woman who followed me up to the ladies?'

He laughed. 'I'm sorry, not being a voyeur, I tend to keep my eyes discreetly averted from that direction.'

'She was extraordinary! I don't know how you could have missed her.'

We waited a few moments but my veiled lady did not reappear, so we left the restaurant. Inside Christie's, we went through double doors into the Hanger Gallery, where the lots for that day's auction were on view. A large, glass-roofed room, packed with people, it contained a number of bays, in one of which ceramics were displayed, in another glass, in another silver, and so on. Pictures were hanging on the walls as in any normal gallery.

'Ah, I can see Oliver up at the far end of the room,' Tobin said, 'so presumably that's where the icon is. It looks as though he's on his own.'

We made our way slowly in his direction, glancing at the sale objects as we went. Suddenly, my eyes lighted on a familiar object. 'Look, Tobin. Isn't that the Princess's samovar?'

'Yes, poor thing. It seems a rather sad fate, doesn't it?'

We continued towards the icon and again I was struck by the tender expression on the Madonna's face. Other memories came back, too, of the little shrines in the Villa Lontana and Filomena crying, *'I wanted you. I wanted to bring you up as my own daughter . . .'*

Oliver Lyon sauntered over to us. 'Surprise, surprise! Come to take a last look at the Princess's treasures?' he asked Tobin, acting out the pretence they had agreed, in case the anonymous letter-writer should be in the near vicinity.

He shook my hand and said, 'Nice to see you again, Cara. I gather you've made quite a lot of progress since we met.'

I glanced at him sharply, wondering if his statement contained a double meaning, but, if so, nothing in his expression indicated anything other than an urbane affability.

Moments later, there was a stir among the viewers and heads turned inquisitively towards the entrance to the gallery. Through the room, her cloak drawn round her, clutching a be-jewelled evening purse in black-gloved hands, came my veiled lady, tottering on black, high-heeled shoes, above which were pathetically spindly legs, clad in sheer black stockings.

'It's the woman I met in the loo,' I whispered to Tobin.

'I think I'll be getting back to the icon,' Oliver Lyon murmured.

She paused for a moment in front of the samovar, then continued straight past us, yet something told me that she was aware of my presence.

At the icon, she came to halt. We followed unobtrusively in her wake – and in the slipstream of her perfume – stopping in front of another painting.

Oliver Lyon consulted his catalogue, then turned and said something to her, his eyelashes fluttering, whereupon she glanced up at him with a birdlike tilt of her head. He continued to talk, glancing frequently at the icon, while she gazed up at him through her veil.

The gallery was growing ever more packed. The sale was obviously of great interest to dealers and collectors of Russian art and artefacts. The icon especially was attracting a lot of attention and a number of people peered closely at it, several taking it from the wall to inspect it more thoroughly. Occasional curious glances were also thrown in the direction of Oliver Lyon and his companion.

Suddenly, Oliver Lyon was behind us, saying in a low voice, 'It's OK, you can stop the charade. I've explained why you're here and I have a feeling that she knows who Cara is. But go gently with her. She's worked herself up into a bit of state.'

She was looking straight at me as we approached.

Oliver Lyon said, 'Madame, allow me to introduce my friend, Mr Tobin Touchstone, who is the brother of the present Earl of Winster. And this is Mrs Cara Sinclair. Tobin, Cara, meet Madame Sophie Ledoux.'

Tobin inclined his head and I gave a hesitant smile, not liking to refer to our earlier encounter.

'The icon won't be coming up for auction until late afternoon, so may I suggest that, meanwhile, we go somewhere quieter to talk?' Oliver said. Putting his hand under Sophie Ledoux's elbow, he led us through the crowd, which parted to allow our small procession through. I heard the odd mutter of, 'That's Oliver Lyon,' and 'I wonder who she is?'

Outside the building, Oliver did not cross the road to the restaurant we had recently vacated but continued along the pavement a short way until we reached a small hotel. The lounge was conveniently empty.

After a waiter had served us with coffee and lemon tea for Sophie Ledoux, Oliver said, 'Cara, would you mind starting the ball rolling by explaining how you came to meet Tobin and me?'

'No, of course not,' I said, wishing Sophie Ledoux would raise her veil, finding it most disconcerting to be addressing an expressionless head.

Nevertheless, I embarked yet again upon my story, keeping it as simple as possible, explaining first what I had known about my parents before watching Oliver's interview and the shock I had received when I learned the Princess had been married to my father at the time of my birth.

Madame Ledoux's shoulders jerked and I thought she might be about to say something, but she didn't.

'After seeing the television programme, Cara telephoned me and I put her in touch with Tobin,' Oliver said. 'And, through Tobin, I believe I'm right in thinking that she managed to get in contact with Prince Dmitri's son, Ludo Zakharin. That's right, isn't it?'

Tobin explained about the portraits and how Mr Ffolkes had recommended him to Ludo Zakharin as an expert in art of that period. 'Since Cara already knew that her father had been a friend of the Angelini family in Paris before the war, she went to Paris and met Ludo Zakharin.'

The gloved fingers twitched nervously.

I took up the tale again. 'Because Ludo Zakharin was born in America and is only a little older than myself, he wasn't able to help me all that much. Most of what he knew about his father and the Princess concerned their lives after the war. However, a few weeks after my visit, he wrote to Tobin, saying that he had managed to track down the daughter of Amadore Angelini.

'In May, I went to see her in Italy. Unfortunately, she is an invalid and was unable to give me much information, but she confirmed that my father and the Princess had spent the war years at their villa overlooking the village of San Fortunato. And she told me enough to make me believe that the Princess was my mother.'

Sophie Ledoux spoke for the first time, in her high-pitched voice, but with a harsh tone. 'It is possible that Hélène had a child. And if that was the case, it does not surprise me that she abandoned you. That would have been typical of her. She was entirely without conscience. Her existence was founded upon a lie.'

'A lie? How do you mean?'

Instead of replying, she reached down to her tea-cup, then, presumably recognizing the impracticability of drinking without lifting her veil, withdrew her hand. I sensed her eyes moving restlessly behind the spotted net, finally resting on Tobin.

He smiled reassuringly at her and asked, 'May I ask where you first met the Princess?'

'In Paris, after the First World War.'

'And did your – er – acquaintanceship continue in London?'

She leaned back in her chair, drawing her cloak protectively around her.

'The reason I ask,' Tobin explained, 'is because after her death, her housekeeper said that the Princess had one constant friend who came to the house at Beadle Walk, whom she would see even though she turned everyone else away. It was evident to Consuela – the housekeeper – that this visitor was very close to the Princess, for the Princess often gave her little gifts. Consuela had the impression that this friend must have fallen on hard times and that, because the Princess was fond of her, she tried to help her out. I wondered if you might be able to throw any light on the identity of this mysterious friend.'

Sophie Ledoux looked down at her hands. Finally, she asked, 'You don't know the name of this visitor or how she looked?'

'Unfortunately, Consuela was not very observant. And she spoke very little English. She described the visitor as a very aristocratic lady. That is all we know.'

She shook her head firmly. 'If you believe I was a friend of Hélène you are much mistaken. Our friendship, such as it was, stopped many years ago.'

I could feel those eyes gazing at me, searchingly, through the veil. I looked back unflinchingly, willing her to trust me. In the end, she said, 'I recognized you the moment I first set eyes on you. You are without any doubt your father's daughter.'

'So you knew my father?'

'I did not know him well, but our paths crossed in Paris.'

We waited for her to elaborate on this statement but when she did not, Oliver said, 'Would you mind if we returned to the original purpose of our meeting? In your first letter to me, you said that the icon that is being auctioned today belonged to your mother's family and you implied that the Princess had acquired it by, er, dishonourable means.'

The gloved fingers fluttered to her mouth, giving the impression of a butterfly trapped in a net. I couldn't help but feel sorry for her. 'Please trust us,' I begged. 'You needn't tell us anything you don't want to.'

She shrugged, almost in resignation, and raised her veil, placing it on top of her hat, revealing the overly made-up features I had briefly glimpsed earlier: powder densely coated in an attempt to conceal deep wrinkles, with patches of rouge on her cheeks, smudged blue eye shadow on her lids, mascara thickly applied around deep-set, dark eyes, and crimson lipstick made to form a cupid's bow where there were scarcely any lips any more. The effect, combined with the peroxide curls and outlandish clothes, would have been grotesque if it wasn't so tragic.

She picked up her cup, crooking her little finger as she sipped the cold tea. Then she announced, '*Eh bien*, I will trust you . . . But where to begin . . . ?'

'With your mother's family?' Oliver suggested.

'Yes, perhaps. Do you remember, in your television interview, Hélène showed some photographs of a man and a woman, whom she claimed to be her parents? Well, those people were not her parents. They were relations of mine.'

'Of yours? But how – why?

'She preferred their images to her own parents.' She gave a little sigh. 'Yes, I have to start at the very beginning and beg your patience if my story seems long . . .

'*Alors*, my mother was born in St Petersburg, the youngest daughter of the Prince and Princess Trubetskoy. Her name was Natasha Petrovna Trubetskaya. Like all Russian noble families of that time, my Russian grandparents and their family travelled a lot in Europe. One is talking about the period before the Great War and the Revolution, when one could travel the whole of the continent by train with great ease and comfort.

'It was during a visit to France, when my mother was eighteen, that she met my father. He was the eldest son of the Comte de Chatelard-Beaumont. They fell in love and, in due course, they married. After their marriage, my mother brought all her favourite possessions to France – including the icon.

'That icon has a very special significance for me. It had been in my mother's family for centuries and had hung in her bedroom ever since she was a baby. When I was a baby, it used to hang in my bedroom, too. When I looked at it, I used to imagine that the Madonna was my mother and I was the child in her arms.'

Tobin frowned. 'But that was what the Princess . . .'

Sophie Ledoux nodded but did not respond. Instead she turned to me. 'You see, Madame Sinclair, like you, I never knew my mother. She died giving birth to me. I never knew my father either. He was so distraught at her death that he could not bear to remain in France but went to join the staff of the *Gouverneur général* in Dakar in the Sénégal. When I was about five years old, news came that he had perished of a fever. It is extraordinary, is it not, madame, the similarity in our lives?'

I nodded bemusedly, not doubting that she was telling the truth and wondering exactly where she was leading us.

'I was brought up by my French grandparents at their château at le Plessis-St Jacques, which is a small village in Normandy. I had a fortunate childhood. My grandparents – especially my grandmother – were very cultivated people. From them, I learned all about literature, music and art. I was very spoiled. I had only to snap my fingers and I was given all that ever I wanted. I had beautiful playthings, clothes, a pony, a dog.

'But often I was bored, for there were no children of my own age to play with – my grandparents were old and my father's younger brother, my Oncle Louis, was occupied with looking after the estate and farms. Apart from that there were only the servants and the animals – mainly cows. Yes, sometimes it was boring.

'However, every year, in the early summer, I was taken by my governess to St Petersburg to visit my Russian family. That was the great excitement of my life. I looked forward to that above everything else. I loved to go to Russia, for there I felt part of a big family. I had many cousins and there was always much to do with them and their friends. We would go to the theatre, concerts, the ballet and the opera. There would be dinner parties and, when I was old enough, balls.

'My grandfather and a couple of my uncles held court positions and sometimes our family was invited to the palace at Tsarskoe Selo. My cousins were very friendly with the young grand duchesses.'

We all leaned forward very slightly in our seats.

'It was in St Petersburg that I first met Prince Dmitri Nikolaevitch Zakharin. The Zakharins were close friends and neighbours of my family. There were three sons – Vladimir, Dmitri and Ivan – wild, high-spirited boys, always up to some mischief. With them, it was impossible ever to be bored. Their father, Prince Nikolai Zakharin, was an officer in the Guards and, when they were old enough, all three boys entered the military. So, too, did their friend, Count Konstantin Fedorovitch Makarov. I will tell you more about Konstantin later.

'As well as their palace in St Petersburg and their mansion outside the gates of the Imperial Palace at Tsarskoe Selo, my Russian grandparents had two large country estates: one, Pavlovskoe, in southern Russia on the Don River, and the other in Finland.'

She paused and glanced at the pendant round my neck.

'The Finnish estate was called Teisko and was situated on a lake, surrounded by forest, in the district of Karelia, not all that far from St Petersburg. If you look on a map, it was between Viipuri and Kotka. Often, while I was staying with my Russian family, we would make the excursion to Teisko, if only for a few days and, frequently, the Zakharins would accompany us, so that we were a large party.

'Our villa there was very spacious and very simple. Life there was very informal, very natural. We young people would swim and sail, while my grandfather and uncles went hunting in the forest. The estate was taken care of by a Finnish couple, who had two young children, a boy and a girl.'

She stopped again and sipped some more tea.

'On one occasion when we were at Teisko, Dmitri Nikolaevitch kissed me and declared that he had fallen in love with me. We were only fourteen, but Dmitri Nikolaevitch was already very grown up and mature, tall, handsome, debonair and charming. Yes, even at fourteen, he was already *très galant*. I believed his words and, for a long time, my dreams consisted of the sole idea of marrying him.

'Then, back in France, I met Marcel de Prideaux, who really did fall in love with me. Ah, Marcel . . . How can I describe him? He was like a young god. In comparison to him, Dmitri Nikolaevitch seemed a mere *divertissement* – an amusement . . .

'My grandmother liked Marcel a lot. He came from a good family and was in possession of an allowance from his parents which enabled him to pursue his profession as a writer. He was handsome, cultivated and very talented. There was nothing he could not do. He could write, he could paint, he could play the piano. Had he lived, I am sure he would have surpassed Cocteau for the versatility of his accomplishments. He was a brilliant conversationalist. You could talk to him on any subject and he knew about it. But he was never boastful or affected.

'Marcel and I were married in 1910, when I was seventeen and he was twenty-five. My grandmother was pleased with the match – my grandfather was already dead by then. We lived in Paris and were very happy for as long as our marriage lasted. We were young and in love. We had no cares. My grandmother made sure I lacked for nothing. Marcel was planning a book, which, *hélas*, was never written. But he wrote articles for magazines on the arts, which were highly respected and brought the works of many artists to the public attention. Yes, his influence was great.

'Then, in 1914, the Great War began and Marcel, like thousands of others, was called up. This was the beginning of a period of great tragedy in my life. Two years later, Marcel was dead. Broken-hearted, I returned to le Plessis-St Jacques, where I remained with my grandmother for the rest of the war. A year after the war ended, my grandmother died. The estate in Normandy all went to my Oncle Louis, but my grandmother left me well provided for. I inherited a fine mansion in Paris in the rue de Varennes and I was in possession of a good income. In truth, I was extremely wealthy. But money is not everything. I was alone in the world . . .

'I set up home again in Paris, taking with me from le Plessis-St Jacques all my personal belongings, including the items which had belonged to my mother – such as the icon and her jewels. Again, the icon hung in my bedroom, reminding me of her.

'Naturally, during the war, it had been impossible to travel to Russia and then the Revolution broke out. I had lost touch with my Russian family and did not know what had happened to them. You can imagine my excitement when I met with Russian *émigrés* in Paris, who had fled from the Revolution, and my sadness when I learned, all too often, of the death or disappearance of relatives and friends.

'Among the *émigrés*, to my great joy, was Count Konstantin Fedorovitch Makarov. To see him again revived memories of the happiest times of my youth in St Petersburg. *Hélas*, he also brought with him tragic news. My Trubetskoy grandparents, I learned, had fled to Pavlovskoe – believing they would safe – but their house had been sacked and they had perished at the hands of the Bolsheviks. Many of my uncles, aunts and cousins were also dead or vanished. Prince Nikolai Zakharin, Vladimir Nikolaevitch and Ivan Nikolaevitch had all been killed in battle. Dmitri Nikolaevitch himself had been missing so long that it was believed he must be dead.

'Konstantin had been very brave, fighting to the last with the White Army in southern Russia and escaping by sea from the Crimea to Constantinople and eventually reaching Paris. Imagine, he owned nothing, except the clothes he stood in. Yet he laughed. That was the most remarkable thing about him, so far as I was concerned. I had everything and I was miserable. He had nothing and he laughed. "I am alive," he said. "Is that not reason to laugh?"

'He was alive but the dangers were not over for him. The situation in France with regard to Russian *émigrés* was rather confused. For the most part, they were treated with respect as fallen aristocracy, certainly by the upper middle classes. But the government regarded them as refugees, who had no rights and could be thrown out of the country without any warning. To become naturalized, one had to fulfil strict conditions – not least, one had to be employed and able to prove that one could support oneself and a family.

'If they were ejected from France, where could they go? If France did not accept them, England and the United States were unlikely to take them either. That left only the possibility of returning to Russia and almost certain death at the hands of the Bolsheviks, unless one became a communist – which a man like Konstantin was not prepared to do.

'Naturally, those *émigrés* who possessed the financial means to support themselves were made more welcome in France than those who did not. Konstantin, as I have said, had nothing. His family's estates in Russia had been seized by the Bolsheviks and, unlike Dmitri Nikolaevitch, his family did not have property in Paris or foreign bank accounts. Neither did he have any profession, save that of a soldier.

'We consulted with the lawyer who administered my affairs and he informed us that there was an underground commerce in naturalization papers. It would have been a relatively simple matter for Konstantin to obtain papers showing him to be a French citizen – at a price, of course.

'On the other hand, there was I, a Frenchwoman, a young widow, living all alone in a big house – and very lonely. Nobody could ever replace Marcel in my heart – but Marcel was dead and would never return. And Konstantin was a courageous, handsome, virile young man, who reminded me of the people and places which had been most dear to me and were now lost.

'So, we were married and Konstantin obtained his citizenship. To begin with, he expressed his gratitude by proving himself a passionate lover and an attentive husband. Then, a few months later, Dmitri Nikolaevitch arrived in Paris. Konstantin met him in town and naturally brought him back to the rue de Varennes. What a reunion that was! Dmitri was still the same charming, debonair figure I remembered from my youth. We sat up all night, talking and catching up on the years . . .'

Sophie Ledoux stopped and turned to Oliver Lyon. 'Would it be possible to have some more tea? My throat is very dry. I am not used to talking so much. I live alone now and usually go for days on end without talking to anybody.'

'Of course!' Oliver leaped to his feet and went in search of a waiter.

While he was gone, she asked me, 'That pendant. Where did it come from?'

'Tobin gave it to me. It used to belong to Princess.'

She nodded slowly.

Oliver returned with a waiter in tow, carrying a tray of coffees and tea. Sophie Ledoux sipped her tea, then said, '*Alors*, where was I? Ah, yes . . . Dmitri Nikolaevitch . . . Well, he explained that during the war, he had been an aide to a general in the White Army, General Yudenitch, who had held St Petersburg until the arrival of Trotsky. The general had then moved his headquarters to Helsinki in Finland. But Finland, too, soon found itself in the throes of civil war and the Finnish communists occupied Helsinki. Eventually, after many narrow escapes from death, Dmitri Nikolaevitch had tried to get back to St Petersburg, but in vain. So he had followed the example of other *émigrés* and made his way to France instead.

'A day or two after his arrival in Paris, Dmitri Nikolaevitch came again to my house. On this occasion, he had with him a young woman, whom I did not recognize. He introduced her as his cousin, the Princess Hélène Romanovna Shuiska, and explained that he had found her, fleeing from the Bolsheviks, after losing her family in the revolution – the same explanation as Hélène gave in her television interview.

'Her name was as unfamiliar to me as her face. St Petersburg was like a village, where everyone knew the business of everyone else. The existence of a cousin – particularly such a pretty cousin – could not have passed unremarked.

'Dmitri explained that, because she had suffered from poor health as a child, Hélène had spent most of her life in the country, which was why I was unaware of her existence. That seemed plausible. It also provided a reason for her French not being very good. The Russian nobility always spoke French among themselves but Russian with the peasants. Living in the country, Hélène would have spoken Russian more than French. I could not speak Russian at all, so I had no means of assessing her fluency in that language.

'Despite this, however, she held herself well and had a look of haughty grandeur, befitting a young woman of noble blood. Yet there was also a certain humility about her. She seemed shy and timid, which attracted me. She regarded me from big eyes with what I believed to be an appeal for help and understanding.

'Dmitri went on to explain that in her panic to escape the Red terror, his cousin had brought no papers with her and therefore had no proof of her identity. Having learned from Konstantin that I knew a good lawyer, he was hoping that I might be prepared to use my influence to help Hélène obtain a *carnet d'authenticité*.'

Sophie Ledoux's face sagged behind the mask of make-up. 'My initial suspicions vanished when Dmitri said that it was not suitable for a young girl to live alone with a man, even if she was his cousin, and asked if I would, therefore, be prepared to have her to stay with me at the rue de Varennes.

'And, while she was staying with me, could I take her under my wing and prepare her to be received into Parisian high society? Because of her upbringing, she was ignorant of city ways and lacking in refinement. Could I school her in the social graces, teach her to speak and dress, introduce her to literature, music and art?

'It would have required a heart of iron to refuse him. So, for Dmitri's sake, Hélène came to live at the rue de Varennes with myself and Konstantin. Furthermore, I asked my lawyer to recommend a notary, who would be prepared to take the necessary depositions from her that would enable her to apply to the police for the issue of a *carnet*. What was more, I perjured myself by signing a declaration, stating that I had known her in Russia before the war and that she was, indeed, the Princess Hélène Romanovna Shuiska.

'Pah! What a fool I was! But as the old proverb goes, *L'amour est aveugle; l'amitié ferme les yeux*. You understand?' she asked me.

I nodded. 'Love is blind; friendship closes its eyes.'

'*Oui, exactement*. Either way, one elects not to see something which is staring one in the face. And the greatest irony is that I had, indeed, known Hélène before the war, but, in the ten years during which I had not been to Russia, she had changed from child to woman and so I did not recognize her any more.'

She paused. In the process of telling her story, she had grown warm and beads of perspiration were breaking through the powder on her forehead and upper lip. She thrust aside her cloak to reveal a little black dress with cap sleeves. Around her neck was a gold choker, sparkling with diamonds.

'So I played Professor Higgins to Hélène's Eliza. I gave her books to read – the classical and the fashionable. I took her to the Louvre, the

Comédie Française, the Opéra Garnier. I enjoyed our excursions. Konstantin was not interested in culture. He preferred the Moulin Rouge, the Lapin Agile or the Boeuf sur le Toit to the ballet or the opera. Also, if I am honest, the exercise appealed to my vanity. I regarded the education of Hélène as a challenge. It gave me a feeling of power and purpose to fashion another person's character.

'I was also flattered by interest she showed in me. Always she was asking about my family, my childhood, my experiences in St Petersburg. Particularly, she loved to look at my old photograph albums. She used to say how much she regretted the lack of personal souvenirs to remind her of the family she had lost. In the end, I allowed her to keep some photographs of members of my family who she said resembled her own family.'

She stopped and glanced at Oliver. 'Those were the ones she showed in your television programme, Mr Lyon. They were not her parents but an aunt and uncle of my own, whom she had never even met.'

'Then, why—?'

'You will understand in a few moments. First let me finish what I was saying . . .'

'Yes, of course. I'm sorry. I didn't mean to interrupt.'

'Hélène was not lazy. She had a good brain and a curious mind. She was hungry for knowledge and experience, and learned very quickly, observing everything I did and copying me exactly. Above all, she was a good mimic, picking up the words and expressions, which differentiate an upper-class person from someone from the *classe ouvrière*. She would have made a successful actress.

'Most essential for any Parisienne, she acquired poise and chic. That is what she did not have when I first met her. Poise and chic. The art of making good conversation is not to impress one's own point of view upon other people but to ask the right questions and appear interested in the answers. This art she learned very quickly. She also learned to make an entrance, to summon a waiter or a taxi with a wave of the finger, to spend money without counting out the coins. Oh, yes, she learned to be very good at spending money. My money.

'She assured me that she did not take for granted everything I was doing for her. She promised that, one day, she would repay me for my kindness and my generosity. And she did, though not in the way she might have intended.

'I paid for dresses designed specially for her by Poiret and Chanel, for furs from Heim, for jewellery from Cartier. She had a good figure, which suited the fashions of that time, and she moved with a natural grace – like a cat. Yes, she was very like a cat – like a tiger or a leopard – and in the end, when I had taught her everything I could, she bit the hand that fed her . . .'

Her eyes glittered behind their spiky black lashes. 'She seduced Konstantin. I found them in bed together. Imagine! They were not even in her bed, but in the bed I shared with Konstantin.'

With a shaking hand, she reached for her tea.

'She tried to blame Konstantin, pleading that she was an innocent girl, of whom he had taken unfair advantage. Pah! There is a very simple response, I informed her, to situations like that. One employs the word, "*Non.*" And, if the man does not heed that word, one slaps him round the face and runs screaming from the room.

'She left of her own accord – together with all the clothes and jewels I had bought her – of course! After she had gone, I discovered the truth about her. Konstantin told me. He was afraid that I would throw him out and hoped to insinuate himself again into my good graces.

'How they must have been laughing at me behind my back. How they must have mocked themselves of me. For Konstantin had known all the time who she was – the so-called Princess Hélène Romanovna Shuiska.

'She was nothing but an adventuress, he said, as if that excused his behaviour. She was not Dmitri's cousin. She was certainly not a princess. She was merely a peasant girl, the daughter of the *concièrge* at Teisko, the Finnish estate which had belonged to my grandparents Trubetskoy.'

On this dramatic note, Sophie Ledoux stopped and looked from Oliver to Tobin and, finally, to myself. Then she said, 'What this means for you, Madame Sinclair, is that, even if Hélène was your mother, you are not the daughter of a Russian princess.'

There was triumph in her voice, as though, in taking away any illusions of grandeur I might have been enjoying, she had scored a final victory over her hated rival.

'So what exactly had happened?' Oliver asked.

She shrugged. 'Apparently, on his way back from Helsinki to St Petersburg, Dmitri had stopped at Teisko. You remember that I told you earlier that the couple who looked after the estate had two young children, a boy and a girl? Well, the girl was called Helena – Helena Suomela. She had been ten when I last saw her. Now she was twenty and hungry to see the world. She convinced Dmitri to take her with him to Paris and during their journey, she persuaded him to try and pass her off for a Russian princess.

'When I confronted Dmitri, he made no attempt to deny the story. The idea had amused him, he said. And it had been so easy. When I had not only been taken in but agreed to act as his unwitting accomplice, he had decided to keep up the farce.

'He was totally impenitent about the effects of his actions on me, the fact that I had committed a perjury, that I given her in good faith so many presents, that she had rewarded my generosity by seducing my husband. He laughed these things off as though they counted for nothing. And when I asked what he was going to do about Hélène now, he said, "She must look after herself. She was already beginning to bore me by the time we arrived in Paris."

'At that moment, I hated him almost as much as I hated her. But it was not possible to bear a grudge against Dmitri for very long. His charm was such that one soon forgot the less estimable aspects of his personality. He made one feel as if one was making an elephant out of a fly and laughed one out of one's ill-humour. So I forgave him – as I forgave Konstantin his peccadillo. What else could I do? It had been my fault as much as Konstantin's for putting temptation in his way. I should have realized that he would not be able to resist.'

She paused to take breath and, fingering the pendant, I asked, 'Did she bring this from Finland?'

'Yes, that was her only jewellery when she arrived in Paris. Due to the time I had spent in Finland, I recognized it, of course, and found it curious that she should be wearing jewellery so typically Finnish. When I asked her, she said it had been given to her by a friend. If she kept it to the end, perhaps that means there was sentiment in her, after all. But I don't believe it. I think it is more likely that she kept it as an incentive – to remind her in moments of weakness of the life she had left behind, to which she had no intention of returning. It is a very primitive object – the opposite of everything that she was striving towards.'

I rubbed the two-headed horse between my fingers – the sole link to my mother's real past.

'What did she do after she left the rue de Varennes?' I asked.

'She worked as an artist's model, posing for artists like El Toro. She posed for him in the nude. Probably she gave him other services as well.

Toro was an apt name for him. He was a bull where women were concerned. Many young girls were so mesmerized by him that they did everything he asked. The painting of Hélène, which you mentioned earlier, was made at that time. There is a painting, too, in the Tate Gallery – a huge canvas. The model in that is Hélène.'

'Did she also pose in the nude for Angelini?'

'Quite possibly. She saw no shame in exposing her body. However, the difference between Angelini and Toro is that he would have kept his pictures private, whereas Toro would have shown them to everyone. Angelini was a *bon père de famille.* I never heard any scandal about him, whereas Toro was infamous.'

'Do you have any suggestion as to why those portraits should have been so important to Prince Dmitri that, shortly before his death, he tried to win them from Hélène in a game of cards?'

Her surprise was evident.

'Apparently she asked him to lend her some money, which he refused to give her. Instead, he pledged the sum she needed against those two paintings.'

She squirmed uneasily. 'I don't understand. Unless it was to tease her, by reminding her that he was aware of how she had earned her living.'

'But the Angelini portrait is quite different and painted much later.'

'Yes, but, you see, that portrait was like the old photographs – it was another *carnet d'authenticité* – a proof that she was a princess in her tiara and jewels. Since Angelini is not as famous as Toro, I doubt that his paintings have great value, but to her it was worth much.'

'Were people in Paris aware of how she was earning her living, at the time when she was modelling for El Toro?'

'Some must have known. There was certainly much gossip about her. But there are always rumours about the aristocracy, like there are about the very rich. What it did was to lend an air of mystery to her, which added to her prestige. She played her role with such accomplishment that nobody ever suspected she was not a princess. Oh, yes, they were sure that she was a princess, but they were not sure about the other scandals concerning her. As a result, she became a myth, a legend in her own time – a trendsetter, one would say nowadays. All the women wanted to copy *la belle Hélène* – her clothes, her hair, her manner – because she represented an ideal – like a film star. And, among the men, she had many admirers.

'As you know, she eventually married the Baron Léon de St-Léon, who was much older than her, a widower, with two children from his first marriage. By profession, *monsieur le baron* was a civil servant in the *Ministère des Affaires étrangères* – a powerful political figure. He was also very rich. Hélène became a celebrated society hostess. On the side, she conducted her little intrigues, making *le baron* sick with jealousy. Finally, she went too far.'

After another sip of tea, she continued, 'As for me, I distanced myself from her. Konstantin loved to travel and we spent much time away from Paris – in Italy, in Switzerland, in the Midi, at Biarritz. Often, we would spend the winter months in Egypt at Alexandria. We always stayed in the best hotels and afforded ourselves every luxury. My grandmother, as I have said, had left me well provided for, so it did not occur to me that I should have to count the *sous* or that we might be living beyond our means. In the evenings, we would go to the casino and play the tables. Konstantin seemed to have been born under a lucky star. He always seemed to win. Or so I thought.

'Then, in 1929, Konstantin disappeared. Literally, he disappeared. We were in Monte Carlo and, that evening, I had a headache and went to bed early. Konstantin, I remember, was particularly solicitous of my health. When I assured him I would recover after some sleep, he said he was going to the casino.

'He never came back. In the morning, when I awoke and found he was not there, I sent his valet to make enquiries at the casino and at the other hotels, but there was no sign of Konstantin anywhere. In the end, I had no alternative but to advise the police. To begin with, they were not very interested. I think they assumed he had found a girl somewhere and would return. When I heard from the casino of the gambling debts he had run up and then my nightmare began. The police checked with the border police and learned that Konstantin had crossed into Italy the night he had disappeared.

'That was that. I never saw or heard from him again. What happened to him I have no idea. I assume he took a ship from Genoa to some distant part of the world, to South America maybe.

'I settled his debts at the casino and returned to Paris. Then all his other creditors began to demand their dues and the true magnitude of his debts became apparent. He owed everyone money from his barber and his tailor to his friends, men like Dmitri Nikolaevitch, with whom he had gambled and issued promissory notes. It was terrible. His debts amounted to millions and millions of francs.

'Dmitri Nikolaevitch was generous and cancelled the debt. Others were less so, which is understandable. I had no alternative than to sell my house in the rue de Varennes and most of my possessions. It was then that Hélène bought my mother's icon from me. Yes, she bought it. She paid money for it. She did not steal it.

'But when she took it away, together with my mother's jewellery and – oh, things of sentimental value, like my samovar – she gloated over my misfortune. She did not even send her maid or her butler to collect the items, she came herself, pretending to commiserate with me, yet inwardly laughing. Finally, she possessed Russian objects which gave her true *authenticité.*

'*Moi-même*, I was left with nothing – except my pride. I was thirty-seven years old and had never worked in my life. Yet, to my surprise, I discovered I still had a few true friends. For example, my Oncle Louis invited me to come back to le Plessis-St Jacques and live with him and his family. But my pride forbade me. I had no intention of being a charge on his family for the rest of my life.

'To make matters worse, this was the beginning of the Depression. The Wall Street stock market had collapsed and, all over Europe, people were suffering financial hardship as banks collected in their loans. There could have been no worse time to try and borrow money or to look for a job.

'It was Dmitri Nikolaevitch who came to my succour. Out of the economic *débâcle* he was emerging, as always, with a smile on his face. In a bet, he had won a collection of paintings from a fellow gambler, an American who had been living in Paris. He proposed to open a gallery and suggested that I should run it. Above the gallery was a small apartment, where I could live.

'That was the original Galerie Zakharin in the rue du Faubourg St Honoré. Although I say it myself, I earned my keep. I proved a good *négotiante* – perhaps because I had come, very recently, to learn the value of money and because I was aware that it was not my money I was handling. Also, I enjoyed my work and liked the artists whom I met. Many of them, like El Toro, I had already known from the time of my marriage with Marcel. Now I met more, because one artist would introduce me to another. Through Toro, for instance, I met Amadore Angelini.

'And through Angelini, I met your father, Madame Sinclair. I regret for your sake that I did not know him well. We were acquainted only *en passant* and it did not occur to me that he might later prove more important than he appeared then. In any case, I was preoccupied with another writer – Bastien Ledoux.'

'Bastien Ledoux!' Oliver interjected. 'It should have occurred to me before, when you told me your name, but I didn't make the connection. Were you—?'

She nodded happily. 'Yes. When finally I succeeded in obtaining a divorce from Konstantin – which was not easy, that I can tell you – I married Bastien Ledoux. I had known him from before the First War, when he was a friend of Marcel. But after the war, Bastien had retired to the Haûte Savoie and I, of course, had married Konstantin. So we had lost touch. Then, Bastien's marriage broke up and he returned to Paris, which is when we met again.'

'You know who Bastien Ledoux was, don't you?' Oliver asked Tobin and me.

I shook my head regretfully and was relieved when I saw Tobin doing the same.

'Then you've missed something, which I'll have to remedy. I have a copy of his most famous book, *The Falling Star,* at home, which I'll lend to you. It's a wonderful children's story, every bit as good, to my mind, as *The Little Prince*. But, for some reason, it's been neglected. Rather like Connor Moran, in fact, Bastien Ledoux did not deserve to fall into obscurity.'

He turned again to Sophie Ledoux. 'Pardon me for interrupting, madame.'

'It does not matter. On the contrary, it pleases me that Bastien is not completely forgotten.'

'Not by me, I can assure you. But, please, continue. You were telling us about the Galerie Zakharin and the artists you met.'

'Ah, yes . . . I was saying how much I preferred the company of artists and writers to the rich *beau monde* which was my clientèle. Most of these were such snobs, looking down their nose at me, treating me like the last of the last, when not long before they had been enjoying my hospitality. Pah! It amused me to charge them higher prices than a picture was worth.

'There were exceptions among them. The Baron Léon de St-Léon, for example, he was always very courteous. I think maybe he realized how much it had pained me to part with my mother's possessions to Hélène and tried to make up.

'One of my best clients, however, was the American woman, Imogen Humboldt, with whom Dmitri Nikolaevitch eloped to America. What a wasp's nest he disturbed! For me, it meant that I had no job, because in the same way that Dmitri Nikolaevitch had won the gallery in a game of cards, so now he had lost it in another one. The new owner gave me the sack. However, it was not so grave. At that time, I was granted a divorce by the courts on the grounds of desertion and married Bastien, who was able to support me.

'But for Hélène . . . Hah! I shall never forget her fury!' She gave a little cackle of glee, then her face clouded over again. 'But I should not laugh. It was not really funny.

'You have a saying in English: "hell hath no fury like a woman scorned". It is my belief that Hélène was in love with Dmitri Nikolaevitch. I believe that she fell in love with him when she was a little girl and went on loving him throughout her life. Perhaps I am wrong, but I don't think so. In a way, it was the attraction of the inaccessible. She must always have known he would never marry her, but still she loved him.

'When Dmitri Nikolaevitch went with Imogen Humboldt to America, she made everybody suffer in her vicinity. It was revenge for the hurt he had done her. She became blatant in her infidelities. A man only had to come near her and she took him for her lover. She made herself *renommée* throughout the city.

'Then Rüdiger von Herrnstadt entered on the scene. That was, let me see, it was about the same time that German troops invaded the Rhineland.'

She glanced at Oliver, who supplied the date: 'Nineteen thirty-six.'

'Yes, that is probably right. I was never very good with dates of political events. It is only because of Bastien that I remember what was happening. That threat from Germany happened at the same time as Franco started the events which led to the Spanish Civil War. Bastien hated the fascists and he hated the communists. Or perhaps it would be more correct to say that he was a true Frenchman, who believed in *Liberté*, *Égalité*, *Fatemité*.

'Rüdiger von Herrnstadt was an attaché at the German Embassy. He was a very distinguished, handsome gentleman. Once he bought a painting from me and I remember being surprised at his good taste and his good manners. He spoke fluent French and was accepted by the élite of Parisian society, so I assume he must have come from an old-established German family and was not an upstart Nazi, although, as Bastien pointed out, he must have sympathized with the Nazis otherwise he would not have been sent abroad in their service.

'One was always seeing his name in the gossip columns of the newspapers. He was at all the fashionable gatherings, at the races, at the opening nights of plays and opera performances, at dinners and dances. I no longer frequented that society, but even I could not help but be aware of the activities of Rüdiger von Herrnstadt. Neither could I help but notice that his name was frequently mentioned in association with the Baron de St-Léon and *la Princesse* Hélène Shuiska.

'Always, she called herself *la Princesse* Hélène Shuiska – never *la Baronne* de St-Léon. Myself I have always adopted my husband's names, as a wife should. Now I am plain Madame Ledoux. But Hélène gave herself away – it always had to be *la Princesse, la Principessa*, the Princess . . .

'When the war started in September nineteen thirty-nine – that date I do remember – Rüdiger von Herrnstadt was recalled to Germany, along with all the other German Embassy staff. Very soon after that, rumours started to spread that the friendship of the Baron de St-Léon with Rüdiger von Herrnstadt had been closer than was realized and that the baron was a secret Nazi sympathizer who had been passing privileged information to the Germans. There must have been some special incident which occurred that implicated him, but I have no idea any more what it was.

'Under French law, one is guilty until proved innocent. Although *le baron* denied the accusations, he resigned his post at the Ministry and, very soon after that, he died in a car crash. His death was interpreted as suicide and considered to be proof of his guilt.

'Then new rumours began. People started to say that it was not the Baron but Hélène who had enjoyed the special friendship with Rüdiger von Herrnstadt. For two or three years, they had been having an affair, of which Léon de St-Léon had been in ignorance. When the charges were made against Léon, Hélène had admitted the truth to him, which was when he had resigned from the Ministry and, in order to prove his honour and to protect his wife's reputation, had committed suicide.

'There was no proof that this was what had happened, but, suddenly, all Paris knew and Hélène took few pains to deny her guilt. Then came the shocks for her. It transpired that, before his death, the baron had changed his will. Instead of leaving his estate to her, he had left it to the children of his first marriage. Hélène was not as destitute as when she had first arrived in France nor as poor as I had been when Konstantin disappeared, but she was no longer rolling in money. She had her clothes, her jewels, "her" Russian souvenirs – but that was all.

'To make matters worse, her Russian ancestry became a mixed blessing. Daladier, the Prime Minister at that time, began a campaign against the communist and the fascist underground groups. You had the same in England. Communism had originated in Russia, the Germans had signed a Friendship Pact with the Soviet Union. All people of Russian birth became suspect. Some were interned as enemy aliens. Hélène was in double danger and she no longer had the Baron de St-Léon to protect her.'

I glanced at Oliver Lyon, who was nodding sagely.

'Furthermore, the same as had happened to me, her former friends drifted away after the death of the baron. Nobody likes to be associated with failure. And the higher you have risen, the further you have to fall. Hélène moved into the Ritz Hotel and dined alone. Then Connor Moran returned to Paris and, within a fortnight of his return, she was married to him.

'But why she married him and why he married her, I regret I do not know, Madame Sinclair. Perhaps Madame Angelini can tell you more. Myself, I had more important things on my mind at that time than what was happening to Hélène.

'When war threatened, Bastien was called back to the military and given a staff position at High Command. I should perhaps explain that Bastien was an old comrade of le Général de Gaulle. They were the same age and had served in the same regiment during the First World War under Colonel Pétain. De Gaulle had remained in the military, while Bastien returned to civilian life, having received the *Croix de Guerre*. He was always very modest about his achievements, perhaps out of consideration for me, because Marcel had died and he had survived.

'After the Germans broke through the French defences, Bastien and I left Paris along with the French government. For all their talk of miracles and believing in France, the politicians ran away like frightened rabbits, leaving Paris to her fate. We went first to Tours and then to Bordeaux. There were many arguments among the politicians and the generals – you do not need me to tell you about them – they are well recorded in the history books.

'The most terrible thing was the decision of the Marshal Pétain – as he had become – not to fight back against the Germans, but to seek an armistice and to declare Paris an open city, so that the Germans could march through it unchallenged. To Bastien – as to le Général de Gaulle – this was treason.

'It was decided to continue the fight from London. Bastien and I sailed from Bordeaux to England on a cargo ship. Very dirty, very uncomfortable. *Mais tant pis*, it did not matter. In London, we helped form the "Free French", working at the *Bureau Central de Renseignements et d'Action* set up by le Général de Gaulle in Duke Street. Our responsibility was liaison with the resistance. Several times Bastien was flown to Normandy and dropped by parachute into the middle of enemy territory. It was very foolhardy but, as an older man, he was less open to suspicion. On one occasion, he did not return.'

She took a handkerchief from her purse and wiped her eyes.

'When the war ended, I remained in London. The heart had gone out of me and I had no desire to return to Paris. I led a very quiet existence here. I received a small pension and, for a while, royalties from Bastien's books. Then, when his books lost in popularity and were not reprinted, the royalties ran out. Naturally, I was sad, but more for his sake than my own. I was not greedy. I moved into a smaller apartment and made do with what I had.

'And so my life would have continued and we would not be sitting here today, if Hélène had not arrived in London. I remember seeing in a magazine a photograph of her and the caption: "Princess Hélène Shuiska and her good friend, the Earl of Winster". Then came the news of her marriage.'

She slumped back in her chair, suddenly appearing very tiny, almost like a broken doll.

Tobin leaned across to her and placed his hand over hers. 'Madame Ledoux,' he said gently, 'whatever happened after that, none of us will blame you. Oliver and I both knew her when she was married to the Earl of Winster. We know what she was like. And Cara has few illusions about her. Finish your story and then, I think, you will find it is all over at last.'

She looked at him from tired eyes, then gave a resigned little shrug. '*Eh, bien*, she became an obsession with me. Every day, I went to the library, to go through all the newspapers and magazines, finding out about her. Always, she seemed to be in the newspapers and the magazines, in the William Hickey column, in the *Tatler*.

'I discovered where she lived and went and stood outside her house, just watching it, waiting to catch a glimpse of her. Then, one day, she came along the pavement on her own. I said, "Hélène." She started, not recognizing me. "I am Sophie," I said, "do you not remember me?" She looked at me as if I was dirt. "Sophie who?" she asked.

'"Now I am Sophie Ledoux," I said, "but, when you lived at my house in Paris, I was Sophie Makarova, the wife of Konstantin Fedorovitch." The change in her was extraordinary. I saw hatred and I saw fear in her eyes. "What do you want?" she demanded. Until then, I had not been sure what I wanted. Had she been sympathetic and invited me for a coffee and conversation, I would probably have refused and gone away and never troubled her again. But, as it was, suddenly I wanted revenge.

'I knew why she was afraid. If I exposed the truth about her, revealing her as a charlatan, she would lose her reputation, she would be ridiculed in society. She could not be sure that it would not amuse Dmitri Nikolaevitch to back up my story, that he would not take my side against her.

'She hustled me into the house, into her salon. What a shock I had there. It was like going back to St Petersburg. There was my mother's icon on the wall, together with the paintings by El Toro and Angelini.

'Hélène went to a cabinet and took some bibelots – some ornaments by Fabergé – and thrust them into my hand. "Is this enough?" she demanded. "Will this help you to forget?"

'In French, we have the expression, *faire chanter quelqu'un*. It means to make someone sing. It was so easy. I did not have to make demands. I had simply to arrive at her door and she gave me something else. Even between ourselves, we maintained the fiction that she was repaying me for my past help and assisting me in my own hour of need. That may be true, but it does not excuse me.'

The old lady's speech became more flurried and idiomatic, her accent growing stronger. 'The more my hunger for revenge was nourished, the more it increased, until it became my entire *raison d'être*. The most crazy thing was that I could do nothing with my gains. This necklace I am wearing was hers. I didn't want it. I wanted my mother's jewellery back. Once I tried to sell it to raise some money and the assistant in the shop called the manager, who asked me questions about the object, where and when I had acquired it and so on. I was afraid. I thought maybe he would have a way of verifying my story. So I excused myself and took it away. After that, Hélène gave me money.'

'So you were the mysterious visitor to Beadle Walk?' Tobin said.

She looked down at her empty cup. 'Yes, but I was no friend of Hélène. I was the enemy of whom she spoke in her last sentence.'

I poured her some more tea.

She thanked me and turned to Oliver. 'Then she died . . . I watched your television programme, Mr Lyon, and saw the photographs of my family and heard part of my own childhood being repeated. I felt as if she had stolen my very soul.'

Into the silence which ensued, Oliver asked, 'Do you have any idea why she agreed to that interview?'

'No. I don't know. Perhaps it had something to do with the death of Dmitri Nikolaevitch. Maybe that frightened her, making her aware of her own mortality.'

'The ironic thing is that if she had told the truth about herself, it would have been more interesting than the fiction. For sixty years, she had successfully carried off a role. What a triumph it would have been if she had personally exposed – to a national audience of television viewers – the deception she had practised. What a wonderful opportunity she missed for a swan song.'

Sophie Ledoux shook her head vigorously. 'No, Mr Lyon, that might have been a triumph for you, but not for her. You still do not understand. She would have liked to have been born a princess. Failing that, she wanted to die and pass into eternity as a princess.'

'What finally decided you to write to me? Why did you leave it so long?'

'After her death, I felt as if I had lost all reason to live. My days were empty. There was nothing to wake up for in the morning. Yet the anger in me was as intense as ever. When I learned that Hélène's belongings were being sold, I bought a catalogue and there was my mother's icon. It was just too much.'

Tobin asked gently, 'Would you like the icon back? If you would, it can be withdrawn from the sale.'

She spread her hands, emptily. 'Thank you. You are very kind. But now Hélène is dead, I am free to sell the things she gave me. I have sufficient money myself to buy back everything. And yet, I don't really want them. I went to the auction house on Wednesday, to the first day of the viewing, and sat for a long time looking at the icon. In the image of the Madonna, I did not see my mother. I simply saw a very old religious painting. And the samovar was merely a samovar. Do you understand? Now Hélène is dead, they do not seem so important any more.'

'Then why did you make the veiled threats in your letter?' Oliver asked.

'I'm not sure any more. I suppose I didn't expect you to be so kind. I didn't think you would believe me.'

'I think we all believe you,' I said. 'I certainly do. And I am deeply grateful that you found the courage to tell us the truth.'

'Pff. Courage – I have no sense of courage. Only of shame.'

'We all do things which we later regret.'

'Yes, perhaps, but . . .'

With that she lifted her head with a semblance of her former pride and gathered her cloak around her. 'Now I must not detain you longer.'

'There is no hurry.'

But she rose to her feet with a decisive movement.

Oliver said, 'Allow me to call you a taxi.'

'Thank you, but that is not necessary. I do not live far away.'

We all stood up. Tobin and Oliver shook hands with her, but I could not resist the impulse to bend down and kiss her cheek.

She took my hand in hers and gazed up into my eyes. 'If I have upset you, I am sorry. There must have been other sides to Hélène's character of which I was unaware. She was not completely bad, any more than I am completely bad. Everybody must have some good in them.' Then she let fall my hand and walked through the lounge, teetering on her high heels.

Oliver hurried after her. The waiter came to clear away our cups. Oliver returned and said, 'I don't know about you two, but I feel in need of a drink.'

We ordered drinks, then Tobin and Oliver began discussing Sophie Ledoux's revelations, while I sat quietly, trying to come to terms with these further revelations about my mother's character. Sophie Ledoux's parting words could not mitigate the feeling that, wherever my mother went, she had engendered the hatred of everyone she had met.

Chapter 24

We did not return to the auction. Oliver took his departure and Tobin and I wandered, arm in arm, up Exhibition Road to Hyde Park, where we walked in silence until we reached the Serpentine.

There we sat down on the grass and I hugged my knees to my chest, looking across the lake, where people were swimming and sailing and rowing.

'That all came as a bit of a shocker, didn't it?' Tobin said. 'How terrible to be old and alone and consumed by hatred. To be old and alone is sad enough.'

I thought of another lake hundreds of miles away, overlooked by a villa high up on a wooded hillside, and heard a voice cry, 'Oh, why have I had to go on living? I can only believe my life is a form of divine retribution. God is punishing me by keeping me alive.'

There were so many unhappy people in the world and so much tragedy – real tragedy, like the accident which had confined Filomena to a wheelchair.

And death could come so quickly. *'Two years later, Marcel was dead . . . Konstantin disappeared . . . I never saw or heard from him again. What happened to him I have no idea . . . Several times Bastien was flown to Normandy and dropped by parachute into the middle of enemy territory. On one occasion, he did not return . . .'*

'Rosso never came back . . . He never returned to this house. I never saw him again . . .'

There was my father on a cross-Channel ferry, blown up by a mine after the war had ended . . .

There was Uncle Stephen, alive one moment and dead the next from a heart attack . . .

There was my baby, who never even experienced life . . .

There was the Princess – my mother – who had experienced the deaths of four husbands before her own death.

But I was alive and young and sound of limb. Compared to Filomena's suffering and everything Sophie Ledoux had undergone, my own troubles – the loss of my job and Nigel going off with Bo – seemed trivial. Essentially they were, as Tobin had described the effect upon him of Dawn going off with Mark – merely a blow to my pride. I hadn't understood at the time what he had meant.

Life suddenly seemed immensely precious.

'Do you regret not having the blood of the Tsars in your veins?' Tobin asked.

'No, that's one good thing to come out of today. I can cope better with the idea of being the daughter of a Finnish peasant girl than the daughter of a Russian princess.'

'Would you like to go to Finland and see if you can find out more about her?'

'No,' I said slowly. 'One has to call a halt somewhere and I think this is it.'

He lit us both cigarettes. 'You know, as a result of what we learned today, I'm starting to feel rather sorry for her. My guess is that she ran away from Finland because she was in love with Dmitri. When he dumped her after they arrived in Paris, that must have hurt badly. For God's sake, she was twenty and alone in a foreign land. The rest of her life was basically revenge. She was saying to him, "Sit up and take notice of me." And all he felt was amusement.

'Actually, in my opinion, Dmitri comes out worst in all of this. He teased the Princess – I'm sorry, I'm going to have to go on calling her that – right up to the end. I'm not even sure that, if Sophie Ledoux had carried out her threat to expose her, Dmitri wouldn't have taken Sophie's side. I'm glad I never met him. I think he might have been one of the very few people in this world I hated.

'Admittedly, the Princess made a lot of other people unhappy, but she didn't make herself happy as a result. In fact, in view of everything we've found out, I take back some of the things I said to you originally about her relationship with Howard.'

I turned to him and reached out my hand. 'Thank you. But it's all right. Knowing what I now know about her character and background makes it easier to understand why she didn't want me. It's like I originally assumed after Oliver's interview – I was a mistake. These things happen. I'm not unique in that respect. There are thousands of adopted children in the world. I'm not bitter about it.'

We sat in silence for a while, then I said, 'I'd like you to meet Aunt Biddie.'

'I'd very much like to meet her too. And Miranda, Jonathan and especially Stevie. After all, she was indirectly responsible for us meeting.'

'Would you really like to come with me to Avonford?'

'Of course I would.'

'I have to warn you that they may consider you as . . .' I didn't quite know how to continue.

'You mean they'll be giving me the once-over as a potential husband?'

'Well, yes, I'm afraid they probably will.'

'I think I might manage to cope with that situation. If Jonathan takes me aside and asks my intentions, I shall assure him they are strictly honourable.'

'Oh, they're not like that. They're terribly well-behaved.'

Tobin lit us both cigarettes. 'Once, in my far-off, misbegotten youth, I had a girl-friend called Janet from a – without meaning to sound snobbish – working-class background, whom I had dated only a few times, when she said she'd like to introduce me to her family. We met them at a pub. There must have been thirty of them. Janet and I were sat at a table in the middle of the bar, as though we were on display, and questions were thrown at me from all sides. I was put through the third degree about my job, my prospects, my politics, my views on sport, my religion, my family of course – she'd told them about Howard and so I was considered a real nob – and, finally, at the end of the evening, her grandmother announced, "I think you'll be very good for her." Whereupon, her grandfather said, "No, get it right. She'll be very good for him." And her sister asked Janet, "What sort of ring are you going to buy?"'

I smiled. 'What did you do?'

'What do you think? I showed a clean pair of heels. Poor Janet.'

'It must be extraordinary to come from a very large family. I can't imagine it. It must be great fun at times like Christmas.'

'Very expensive.'

'Yes, I suppose there's a downside to everything.'

We finished our cigarettes, then he said, 'Shall we walk on a bit?' Standing up, he pulled me to my feet and, hand in hand, we strolled on until, as if fate had directed our footsteps, we found ourselves at the statue of Peter Pan.

I heard Filomena saying, 'He had the gift to enter a child's world. In fact, I don't think he ever really grew up. He was like Peter Pan. He used to tell the most wonderful stories.'

In that uncanny way Tobin had of following my thoughts, he said, 'Will you write to Filomena and let her know about the Princess not being a princess?'

I shook my head. 'I don't think so.'

'It would seem a great pity if you lost touch with her completely – for both your sakes. You obviously meant a lot to her.'

'Maybe. But I still think I've done harm enough already, without raising any more ghosts or uncovering any more skeletons in cupboards.'

Tobin didn't attempt to sway me.

We left Peter Pan and walked back along the Serpentine, stopping at a café for a coffee and a sandwich, before returning to South Kensington. 'Try not to brood,' Tobin said as we parted.

'No, I won't. Don't worry.'

He kissed me lightly on the lips.

Back at Linden Mansions, I wrote down all Sophie Ledoux had told us and my own personal thoughts which had resulted from the meeting.

That day marked a turning point in my own life. From then on, I became steadily stronger. Matters which had been defeating me, which I hadn't possessed the energy and mental courage even to contemplate, suddenly no longer appeared insuperable.

Next morning, I spoke to David Rinder about selling the flat and he rang me back shortly to say that he had conferred with Nigel's solicitor, who raised no objections, and that I was therefore free to place it on the market.

He was also able to give me a rough idea of the sort of money I would have available for a deposit on a new property. By the time the balance on the outstanding mortgage was deducted from the sale price of Linden Mansions, along with the all the legal costs, and the remainder divided equally between Nigel and me, I should find myself with around five thousand pounds, which doesn't sound much nowadays, but was quite a lot then. Together with my redundancy pay, I would have sufficient to put down a deposit and raise a mortgage on the sort of house Tobin lived in, for instance.

The next thing was to ring a local estate agent and arrange to meet him at the flat on Saturday morning. Like so many other things in life, it was all far easier than I had feared.

That same afternoon, after the estate agent had assured me that selling the flat should present no problem whatsoever, measured all the rooms and taken away my solicitor's details, Tobin and I went house-hunting.

We started by doing a round of estate agents roughly between Highgate and Fulham, coming away with great sheaves of particulars, which kept us occupied all evening. Next day, having discarded half the properties, we went viewing.

Had I been on my own, it would have been rather depressing, for nothing we saw matched the cosy, idyllic image I was carrying in my head. But Tobin made it fun. At most of the houses we went to, the occupants assumed us to be husband and wife, and, far from being embarrassed, Tobin hammed up the part of my husband to the full, including calling me 'dear' and saying things like, 'Now what do you think, my dear? Wouldn't you find that kitchen rather small?' Or, 'The lack of storage space worries me. There's nowhere to store one's golf clubs.'

In the privacy of the street, he said, 'I love nosing round other people's homes. It gives you such an insight to their minds. Now, would you have imagined, if you had met those people at the last house we went to on the street, that their bathroom would be painted purple and have stars on the ceiling? And the place before that – a room full of empty whisky bottles on shelves. That puts a whole new complexion on collecting. It's a hobby I could be tempted to take up myself.'

I laughed but, within me, alarm was mounting.

Back at his own house in Fulham, I asked, 'What am I going to do if Linden Mansions is sold before I find anywhere?'

'You could always do what I did and rent somewhere for a while.'

'I don't think I could cope with a temporary job and temporary accommodation.'

'Of course you could. I'm not suggesting you move into a bedsit. But a little studio flat, while you decide where you really want to go.'

'It's an idea,' I allowed unenthusiastically.

'Picking up your mention of your job, are you going to continue temping or look for something permanent?'

'I can't decide. Debbie keeps ringing me up to tell me about some wonderful job or other that has just come in, but I can't summon up enthusiasm for any of them. The truth is that I don't really want to go on being a secretary. If I'm honest, I was starting to feel that before I was made redundant. I believe I'm capable of doing more than just taking down other people's words and pounding a typewriter.'

'Then find a job that isn't secretarial.'

'That's easier said than done. Once a secretary always a secretary, so far as most employers are concerned. In any case, not being negative, I don't possess any specialist knowledge which would enable me to make the switch to management. I'd have to re-train and there's nothing I really want to re-train as.'

It's extraordinary the way things sometimes work out. The very week following that conversation, Debbie asked if I would consider taking on a long-term assignment to cover a maternity leave. The job, working for a senior partner at a firm of head-hunters, sounded infinitely more interesting than anything I had done to date. It also carried more responsibility, requiring someone who not only had good shorthand and typing speeds, but was used to dealing with people at director level and could be relied upon to keep confidential information to herself. Furthermore, the rate would be one pound an hour higher than I was currently being paid.

I didn't hesitate. Next day in my lunch hour, I went for an informal interview with the Personnel Manager at Grosvenor Management Consultants and was introduced to Douglas Curtis-Hooper, a man in his late forties, who was impressed by the fact that I had worked for Miles and my length of service at Goodchild.

'It's a tough old world,' he commented. 'Well, so far as I'm concerned, I'd be delighted for you to take over from Yvonne while she's away. If you can start next Monday, she'll hand over to you, which will make your life easier. Or, put it this way, it'll make mine easier.'

I settled in relatively quickly at Grosvenor Management Consultants. A very pregnant Yvonne did an efficient job of handing over to me and, although my brain was reeling at the end of the day, next morning, when I got up, I found myself looking forward to the day ahead in a way that I hadn't since I left Goodchild. I might still be a secretary, but at last I was being given something to get my teeth into, instead of copy typing, audio typing and photocopying.

Douglas was a dynamic individual, with the encyclopaedic kind of memory needed for his work. I soon came to realize that he was the driving force behind Grosvenor Management Consultants and enjoyed tremendous respect in the international business world. His client list was most impressive, including many blue chip companies and some civil service departments.

Like Miles, he did not tolerate fools gladly and I was grateful both for my years at Goodchild and my experience temping, which had given me a much broader insight into the workings of commerce and industry, so that I wasn't constantly having to ask questions liable to incur if not Douglas's wrath then certainly his impatience.

Soon, the offices were starting to feel like home and my colleagues more like friends than friendly strangers.

Meanwhile, an offer had been made on 9 Linden Mansions, which was acceptable to both mine and Nigel's solicitors, by a couple with a small child, who were keen to include many of the fixtures and fittings in their purchase price. They had been living abroad and were returning to England because their little boy was due to start school. I was glad that the flat was at last going to be lived in by a proper family.

However, that increased the pressure on me to find somewhere to move to. I looked at several small houses, not dissimilar to Tobin's, in good structural condition and a reasonable state of decoration, but although I could afford them, I found it impossible to commit myself. The idea appealed tremendously of furnishing a house according to my own taste but, at the back of my head, I was aware that a house was not a home.

In the middle of October, Tobin and I went to Avonford. I did the driving, in my car: Tobin had done more than enough for me – the time had come for me to stop relying on him and make a few contributions of my own.

It made such a difference having a passenger during that long journey. The miles simply sped by and, what's more, Tobin said, 'You're a very good driver. I suppose I should have guessed.'

It's funny how much a little compliment like that can set you up. Nigel had never let me drive when we were out together.

Then we were crossing the bridge over the Avon, passing the river meadows, going up Bridge Street and into the High Street, slowing down at Priest's Lane and turning right into the tall gates, which Aunt Biddie had, bless her, opened in readiness.

And there was Aunt Biddie herself, emerging from the conservatory as I drove into the courtyard, any apprehension she might be feeling concealed behind a bright smile. 'How lovely to see you here so early,' she exclaimed. 'I wasn't expecting you for hours yet.'

She kissed me quickly and turned to Tobin, as he got out of the passenger door, giving him a quick, searching look. I introduced them and he took her hand between both of his, saying, 'I am extremely pleased to meet you, Mrs Trowbridge. I've heard so much about you that I feel I know you already.'

'Cara, what have you been saying?'

Tobin laughed. 'Only good things, I assure you.'

She smiled. 'Well, in that case, there's no need to call me Mrs Trowbridge. I should prefer Biddie. And now, come along in both of you. Not being sure what time you'd get here, I've made a casserole.'

There's no need for me to describe every detail of that weekend. Suffice it to say that Tobin and Aunt Biddie hit it off from the word go and that he fell in love with the house on sight. He also made instant friends with Tiger, Joey and Reynard. He admired Gordon and her now grown-up goslings, who had been named Michael, Simon and Timothy. He made just the right sort of 'Chch-chch' noises to Nutkin and, before the weekend was over, had constructed a special hibernation box for Chukwa.

So far as Aunt Biddie was concerned, he didn't need to make any special effort to say the right things to please her: the words came naturally to his lips. Long before dinner was over that first evening, he and she could indeed have been old friends and I was finding it hard to get a word in edgewise.

However, I do have to mention a couple of little incidents. The first happened after supper, when Tobin was out of the room obeying a call of nature, and Aunt Biddie said to me, 'I wasn't sure what you'd be expecting in the way of sleeping arrangements, so I've made up the double bed in the Blue Room and your own bed as well.'

The blood rushed to my face. 'That's very thoughtful, but we'll be sleeping in separate rooms.'

Aunt Biddie gave me a funny look – the same sort of look as she used to give me in the past when I mentioned Nigel, or even when I was a little girl and, instead of rushing off to play as soon as I was given permission to get down from table, lingered with the adults – the sort of look which implied, 'What's the matter with you?'

It did not escape my notice that she had even put Tobin in a different room from the one Nigel and I had used to sleep in.

However, Tobin slept alone in the double bed and I in my little room, with Tiger on the hot-water bottle at my tummy, and Teddy, Big and Little regarding me solemnly from the windowsill. And that was how it had to be. Even if Tobin and I had already slept together, I couldn't have shared a bed with him at The Willows. It had always felt strange enough sleeping with Nigel there. To have slept with a man who wasn't my husband would have seemed like a betrayal – though of what I'm not quite sure – my childhood innocence, I suppose.

The other incident took place on Saturday morning. After showing Tobin all round the house and garden, including the stable where Phoebus resided and Old Harry had used to weave his baskets, Aunt Biddie went off to prepare lunch, while Tobin and I took the punt on to the river – Tobin poling and me baling out the water which gushed through the rotting hull.

'Next time we come here – assuming there is a next time – I'll have a go at mending this,' he said. Then he went on, 'Weren't you lucky to grow up in a place like this? No wonder you're finding it hard to decide upon a house. After this and Linden Mansions, everything else must seem a come-down.'

I didn't reply, but went on baling water.

'Which reminds me of something I've kept meaning to ask you for a long time. What happened to The Book? I suppose you haven't been in the mood to continue with it recently?'

'I'm afraid I have rather ground to a halt.'

'A pity. But I'd still like to read it.'

'As I told you before, it isn't very good. It sort of fell to pieces along the way and doesn't say what I meant to say.'

'I could always try reading between the lines.'

Again, I didn't respond.

Over lunch, Aunt Biddie told Tobin about the abbey clock and fulminated against the pedestrian precinct, which – alas! – seemed likely to go ahead. In the afternoon, we went over to Honey Hill Farm, where Tobin made an equally instant hit with Miranda, Jonathan and Stevie. And, on Sunday, we climbed Bredon Hill.

When the time came to leave, Aunt Biddie reached up and kissed Tobin on the cheek, wherewith he took her in his arms and gave her a big hug. 'You're smashing, Biddie,' he declared.

She turned pink with pleasure. Then she gave me an extra affectionate hug and kiss and said, 'I do hope you'll both come and see me again soon.'

During the drive back to London, we neither of us said much. There was nothing awkward in our silence, no underlying tension, no sense of needing to talk for the sake of it. That was part of the magic of being with Tobin.

What he was thinking I don't know. For my part, I was carrying out a serious reappraisal of my situation. That weekend had clarified something in my mind. It was not that I was nursing extravagant dreams about the kind of house I wanted. It was quite simply that I didn't want to live on my own anywhere, even if it was furnished according to my tastes. I wanted to live with Tobin.

Back at Linden Mansions, I took The Book from its folder and read through it from the beginning. I had written more than I realized: my account went up to Nigel joining Massey Gault & Lucasz.

The last paragraph went:

> *He had discovered his aim in life. The dizzy heights of professional success were calling to him. His career had became all-important. And against such a rival, I had no defence.*

It was discomfiting to be confronted by my own descriptions of myself, especially in the context of all the events which had taken place during the past months. I didn't much like the me that emerged. All too often, I appeared to myself weak, rather silly and very stupid, lacking in gumption, always taking the line of least resistance, afraid almost of my own shadow. To think that I was the daughter of a princess – Russian or otherwise – seemed quite ridiculous. That I was my father's daughter was improbable enough.

No wonder Nigel had preferred Patti Roscoe and Bo Eriksson.

The following Sunday, I took The Book and my diary with me to Fulham and, with a palpitating heart, handed them over to Tobin. He thanked me gravely and said he would wait until the evening, when he was alone, before starting to read them.

We did not go house-hunting that day, but drove into Kent, parking the car up on the North Downs. There was a nip in the air and the leaves were changing colour as we set off briskly along the Pilgrims' Way. Below us the Weald stretched away into the hazy distance. Blackberries were plump and juicy on brambles in the hedgerow and, every so often, Tobin stopped to pick one and pop it in my mouth.

They were bittersweet on my tongue and I savoured each one of them, as I savoured every minute of that autumn day, terrified in case it would turn out to be the last Tobin and I ever spent together.

When I left work the following evening, he was waiting outside, leaning against the railings, a serious expression on his face, which filled me with foreboding, tempting me to run back into my office and hide until his patience gave out and he went away. Then he saw me and his expression changed. Tenderness glowed in his eyes and the corners of his lips twitched upwards in a smile. Hope – tentative, fragile, not daring quite to trust – reasserted itself in my heart.

Without saying a word, he took my hand and, holding it very tightly, led me down the road to where his car was parked. Still not speaking, he drove to Fulham, parked and, taking my hand again, led me into the house.

On the coffee table in the living room lay the folder containing The Book and my diary. Tobin's glance lingered on them for a moment, before resting on me. 'You are a fool,' he said gently. 'Why didn't you tell me before? Why did you let me assume—?'

I shook my head.

Then he wasn't saying anything any more but folding me in his arms and kissing me in a way that I had never known kissing could be. And my arms were around him and I was responding to his kiss, trying to convey to him through it all the things I was unable to express verbally, all my love and gratitude, my devotion, my longings, my hopes and desires.

As we were kissing, I became aware of tears on my cheeks, the salt of them reaching our lips. And then I realized that they were Tobin's tears – and I knew them to be tears of happiness – and then I, too, was crying and our tears intermingled with our kiss . . .

We drew slightly apart, crying and laughing simultaneously. And Tobin said, 'Oh, my darling, darling Cara, I love you so much.'

And I replied, not afraid any more, 'I love you, too, Tobin. Oh, Tobin.'

And that little bird, which had been so long captive in my heart, burst into full-throated song.

We kissed again and again, abandoning ourselves to the sheer, intoxicating delirium of our two mouths each on each as though we had both been starving and sustenance had come.

Eventually, Tobin drew away again and led me upstairs. In the bedroom he picked me up and lay me on the bed, sitting beside me, gazing down at me. My lips tingled from our kisses, my limbs were trembling and my heart was pounding.

He rested his hand over my heart and my whole being quickened and quivered and rose yieldingly to his touch. I lifted my arms and put them round his neck and drew his head down to me, giving him my answer with the soft fullness of my lips.

I did not return to Linden Mansions that night, but slept wrapped in his arms. From time to time, I awoke and Tobin stirred in his sleep, drawing me closer to him. Then I lay very still, not daring to trust my happiness, believing I must be in a dream and that, when morning came, my dream would end.

The dream did not end. I was still lying in Tobin's arms when the morning light flooded through the windows. More wonderful still, we slipped into love again, a different kind of love, gentle and warm, an effortless melting of bodies, perfectly attuned, dissolving each into each.

Then we showered and ate breakfast together, Tobin wrapped in a towel and me in his towelling robe.

Shortly after I reached work – hoping nobody would remember I was wearing the same clothes as yesterday, then suddenly not caring if they did – Tobin rang.

'I love you,' he said.

Fortunately, the door connecting Douglas's office to mine was shut.

'I love you too,' I whispered.

'I had a strange dream last night.'

'Was it a happy one?'

'Very. I dreamt I was sleeping with an angel.'

'That's funny. I dreamt I was sleeping with one too.'

'Can I see you at lunchtime?'

'Don't you have work to do?'

'Yes. But I don't want to do it. I want to see that angel again. One o'clock outside your office?'

'That would be wonderful.'

'Tell me again that you love me.'

'I do, I do. I love you. Oh, Tobin, I love you so much.'

'And I love you for ever and ever.'

We bought sandwiches and ate them on a bench in Hyde Park, sitting very close together, our legs and shoulders touching. And Tobin said, 'Now I want to talk to you seriously about a couple of things. Firstly, The Book and your diary.'

Fearing questions I did not want to answer, I threw some crumbs to the pigeons flocking round our feet.

'I don't want to talk about Nigel,' he went on. 'Another day perhaps. That's up to you. But not now. There is something far more important.'

He paused and I continued to watch the pigeons pecking at the crumbs.

He took my hand in his. 'You do yourself many injustices. But one of the greatest injustices you have done yourself was when you told me that The Book wasn't very good. That is untrue. I read through everything you had written in it – and your diary – three times at least. And, even if I hadn't known you, it would have been impossible for me to put those pages down.

'I don't care whether you won the English prize at school or if you came bottom of the class. And I don't care whether your father was the greatest poet who ever lived – or simply a sponger, hiding under the mask of a poet. I am convinced that you, yourself, are going to become a great writer. You possess wonderful powers of description and an amazing understanding of your fellow human beings. Through the medium of your words, people and scenes spring to life from the page. It is a great gift you have, Cara. Please, I beg you, from the bottom of my heart, don't waste it.'

Tears welled at the back of my eyes and I tried to squeeze them back behind my lids. Then a teardrop trickled out of my eye and splashed on to Tobin's hand. I lifted his hand to my lips and kissed the damp spot. 'Thank you,' I gulped. 'Oh, thank you.'

'And now to the other thing,' he said. 'Will you stop snivelling, please.'

He got up from the bench, scattering the pigeons, and knelt on one knee in front of me. Then he asked, 'Will you marry me?'

Chapter 25

I wish I could say that, from that moment on – after Tobin and I confessed our love for each other and he proposed to me and I said yes – all my troubles disappeared and we lived happily together ever after, like people do in films and novels. The truth is that it takes longer to accustom yourself to happiness than it does to unhappiness. When you've been badly hurt, like I had been by Nigel, you are extremely wary of making the same mistakes again. First, you must learn to trust and that takes time.

So, although Tobin asked me to move in with him straight away, I didn't. In fact, right from the beginning, I was hesitant about moving into his house. I loved him and wanted to live with him, but I wanted to make a clean break with the past and begin our life together in surroundings that were new to both us of.

This was how Nigel and I had started off. I had moved into his flat in Islington and, from then on, he had maintained the upper hand. Sure, Tobin wasn't Nigel and his house in Fulham wasn't Nigel's flat in Islington. But the situation was the same.

Indeed, it was almost identical, for just as I had brought very few possessions of my own when I had moved in with Nigel, so I would be taking very few with me when I left Linden Mansions. Nigel's solicitor informed David Rinder that Nigel would like any furniture from Linden Mansions that I didn't need and I had said he was welcome to every stick of it. It had not been my choice in the first place and, wherever I finished up living, I didn't want it.

All this doesn't mean to say that Tobin and I didn't discuss the situation. Far from it. We were both open with each other. I explained my apprehensions and he admitted to some on his part as well. After all, he had been living alone for seven years and had adapted his house to his needs. For instance, there was no spare bedroom. When guests came, they slept on a sofa-bed in the sitting room. Yes, he too needed time to adjust.

However, it made sense to take things one step at a time. First I had to leave Linden Mansions. Contracts were exchanged in the middle of November and the new owners were keen to move in before Christmas. With Christmas rapidly approaching, few people were thinking of moving unless they absolutely had to. So we decided it would be best to wait until the property market picked up again in the new year before we started looking for a place of our own. By then, our financial situation would also be clearer and we would have a better idea of what we could afford.

That was another thing – money. I didn't suddenly become mercenary as a result of my divorce and David Rinder's advice. I wasn't adopting the attitude of what's mine's my own. Quite the opposite. I was determined to pay my own way as far as possible.

In fact, to David Rinder's disgust, I insisted that Nigel should be reimbursed from the divorce settlement for the mortgage payments he had made while I was still living at Linden Mansions. David Rinder might think me mad, but so what? I hated the thought of being beholden to Nigel in any way.

My determination to remain financially independent led to the nearest thing Tobin and I had to an argument. That happened after Yvonne rang the office to let us all know she had had a baby boy and hinted to me, during her call, that she was in two minds about returning to work when her pregnancy leave was up. Naturally, I mentioned this to Tobin and asked whether he thought I should take the job with Douglas on a permanent basis if it was offered to me.

He was against the idea. 'If you really want my opinion, I think you should work your term out and then stop temping altogether. I honestly believe you have a career as a writer. I'd like you to try your hand at writing a proper book.'

'And if it's not any good and nobody wants to publish it?'

'If that should turn out to be the case, which I very much doubt, then at least you'll have tried.'

'And what am I supposed to do for money while I'm writing it?'

'I'm fully prepared to back you.'

'But I'm not prepared to be kept.'

'Then use your redundancy pay. After all, that's the purpose for which it was intended.'

'But we may well need it when we move. I can't throw away five thousand pounds on a sort of gamble. No, it's very sweet of you to have such confidence in me but I don't share your faith.'

Fortunately, he didn't persist and we agreed to discuss the subject of whether or not I remained at Grosvenor Management Consultants again later, when and if Yvonne decided not to return. Meanwhile, my redundancy money would stay where it was.

So, against this background, the gradual transition from my old life to the new was made. During the week, Tobin and I lived separately. Unless we were going out somewhere – to the theatre, a concert or an art exhibition – I went home from the office to Linden Mansions. And, at weekends, I went to Tobin's and stayed the night.

One way and another, I was actually very busy, which was a good thing, meaning I didn't have too much time to worry and brood. While Nigel and I might not have amassed anywhere near the same amount of clutter as Aunt Biddie had at The Willows, we had still accumulated a surprising number of belongings over the years, all of which had to be sorted through, some thrown away and the rest packed into boxes – most for Nigel and some for me. The kitchen alone took me a week of evenings to go through. Furthermore, because I wanted the flat to be welcoming for its new owners, as I cleared cupboards and rooms, I gave them a thorough clean, shocked at the amount of dirt, dust and cobwebs I uncovered.

On top of that, there was Christmas shopping and sending Christmas cards, the latter presenting their own little problem. Not that I had a large number of cards to write, because most of those I had used to send in the past had been to Nigel's friends, acquaintances and family. However, I did still have friends of my own, who should be advised that Nigel and I had split up.

In the end I opted for the easy way out and added a note saying that a lot had happened during the past year, that I was moving from Linden Mansions on 20 December and would be in touch soon.

My weekends with Tobin were somehow unreal. We didn't do all the usual weekend chores, like supermarket shopping, washing and cleaning, because Tobin had already done them during the week. As a result, our weekends were rather like holidays and I felt more like a guest at Fulham than the future mistress of the house.

To add to the sense of unreality, we were invited out a lot, for Tobin wanted to introduce me to his friends and they were eager to meet me.

They were all extremely nice, welcoming me to their homes, not talking over me like Nigel's friends had done, but making me feel interesting and even important. They all demonstrably cared for Tobin, making obvious their joy that he had found happiness.

I particularly remember Penny's reaction, when we went to dinner with her and Michael. Clasping my hands, she said, 'I've heard so much about you since Oliver's interview with the Princess, but I was beginning to wonder if we would ever meet. I'm sorry for all the troubles you've been going through, but I'm glad they're over now and you and Tobin can start afresh.'

She was so sweet and kind that, face to face with her, I couldn't imagine how I could ever have considered her a rival. Unsure how much I was supposed to know about her own troubles, I said hesitantly, 'I believe you've been unwell. Are you better now?'

'Much, much better,' she assured me. 'The advances they're making in medical science are quite miraculous.'

Just to bring Penny's story up-to-date, she did recover fully. At the time that I am writing, she retired not long ago from Rambler Books. She and Michael recently spent the weekend with us . . .

During that time, I also met Tobin's children, who proved rather harder to win over – or at least, Pamela did. Joss was never really a problem. On his twentieth birthday at the beginning of December, we went to Canterbury, where he was reading law at the university, and took him out to dinner. In appearance, he bore an uncanny resemblance to Tobin and had the same outgoing personality. Joss was no tongue-tied youth, shy when away from his peers. Upon being asked a question, he replied at length and remarkably sensibly, I must admit. To my amusement, he treated Tobin with tolerant affection, almost as though their situations were reversed and he was the father and Tobin the son.

On the drive back to London, Tobin laughed. 'Talk about a chip off the old block. He's so like my father and Harvey, it's not true. But at least he isn't pompous with it – well, not yet anyway . . . There's no doubt where his future lies. When he becomes a barrister – as I assume he will – he'll twist juries round his little finger.'

Joss might be going to twist juries round his little finger in due course, but his sister was already twisting men round hers. She was small and very pretty, with blonde hair and big blue eyes. She too was very pleased with the sound of her own voice but, unlike Joss, who could converse interestingly on a wide variety of topics, Pamela always brought attention back to herself. In this, she was assisted by her current boyfriend, Benjamin, who was tall, dark and handsome, but with a moody, introverted look about him. He kept his arm round her shoulders or his hand on her thigh throughout the meal we took them to at a restaurant in Covent Garden, and cannot have spoken more a couple of dozen words during the entire evening.

Pamela more than made up for his silence. We heard about her progress at ballet school, her problems with keeping down her weight (if she weighed seven stone, I'd have been surprised) and a nasty spot she had on her chin (almost invisible). She contrived to introduce her mother and Mark into the conversation with amazing frequency. When she mentioned her mother, it was in tones of endearment, obviously intended to let me know that I couldn't possibly hope to replace her. When she spoke of Mark, the message came through loud and clear that she felt Tobin had deserted her, leaving her to suffer under a cruel stepfather.

On the assumption that she took after her mother, no wonder Tobin had had problems with Dawn.

To my relief, Tobin wasn't taken in. Back in Fulham, he said, 'I'm sorry about that. I should have warned you beforehand, but I didn't realize she was going to be quite so bad. Just to put the record straight, she and Dawn are always squabbling, trying to out-vie each other, while she and Mark actually get along very well. That was mainly an act put on for your benefit.'

Maybe, but I would naturally have preferred a girl more like Stevie as a future step-daughter. However, in consolation, at least I wasn't being confronted by the prospect of having to share my home with her.

When next I met Pamela, it was after Christmas, by which time I had moved in with Tobin. She came to see us at Fulham – on her own – for Benjamin had become a thing of the past by then. 'He was so possessive,' she complained. 'If I so much as spoke to another man, he was jealous. I mean, he was even jealous of Daddy.' She gazed coyly at her father and raised a challengingly little eyebrow towards me.

No, Pamela was not exactly sugar and spice and all things nice. But, unknown to her, she taught me a lesson. From that day on, I ceased feeling any sort of jealousy towards Dawn and merely felt sorry for Tobin, for all he must have suffered during his marriage.

Meanwhile, the sale of 9 Linden Mansions was completed. The evening before I moved out, Sherry and Roly invited Tobin and me to a farewell dinner – although we were all at pains to stress that we weren't so much commemorating an end as celebrating a beginning. Yet I couldn't help but be aware that Sherry's and my friendship must suffer as a result. Sure, Fulham wasn't far from Highgate, but it was far enough not to allow the informality of neighbourly visits.

I drank rather too much or possibly the wine just went to my head quicker than usual and suddenly found myself making a sentimental speech about how much Sherry meant to me, how grateful I was for everything she had done for me over the years and how she really was the best of all possible best friends. And then, realizing my words might be upsetting Tobin, I started explaining that I didn't mean anything against him, whom I loved with all my heart and soul, but that I loved Sherry, too, in a different but equally important way. At this point, Roly – very wisely and unequivocally – told me to shut up and made us all coffee.

Next day witnessed the final rites. Nigel sent a removals van to take away the furniture and the rest of his belongings. I wondered if he would come himself, but he didn't. I told the removals men to take our bed as well, even though he had specifically said he didn't want it.

My own things – my clothes, books, records, some pots and pans, Miranda's pottery, Aunt Biddie's wine glasses, Angelini's portrait of Filomena and the few other objects of mainly sentimental value I had collected over the years – fitted into the Fiesta with the back seat down. I know material possessions shouldn't assume undue importance: nevertheless, mine seemed pathetically few to show for thirty-five years.

I hadn't believed that I would be upset to leave the flat, yet, when the moment came, I did feel sad in a funny sort of way. After all, it represented seven years of my life and a lot had happened to me while I lived there, even if little of it was happy.

And, when I reached Fulham, I was glad to find Tobin waiting there for me. During my absence he had cleared space for my clothes – or at least some of them – in a wardrobe and, on Sunday, he put new shelves up for my books. Angelini's portrait of Filomena went up in the sitting room over the fireplace.

Yet, despite Tobin's efforts, I couldn't help experiencing a moment of sheer panic at the sense of history repeating itself. This was it. The die was cast. And I was doing the very thing I had least wanted to do. I should be feeling happy. Instead of which, I had a terrible feeling of déja-vu.

However, almost immediately, Christmas was upon us.

On Christmas Eve, we went to Avonford, arriving in time for lunch, after which we decorated the tree with all the old familiar decorations from my childhood, and listened to the carols from King's College, Cambridge, on the radio. Tobin put up paper chains and holly along the tops of all the pictures and hung a sprig of mistletoe in the hall, under which he kissed Aunt Biddie and me.

After tea, we took turns to read poetry aloud – something I hadn't done since I was married to Nigel – all the old favourites, like 'The Lady of Shalott' and 'The Village Blacksmith' and 'Lochinvar'. Then Aunt Biddie read 'The Tailor of Gloucester', like she used to do when I was a small girl, and when she came to the end, to the bit about the stitches being so small that they looked as if they had been made by little mice, I was sniffing.

Last of all, Tobin read 'A Visit from St. Nicholas':

> '*Twas the night before Christmas, when all through the house*
> *Not a creature was stirring, not even a mouse;*
> *The stockings were hung by the chimney with care . . .*'

Next morning, when I woke up in my little room, it was to find a stocking at the end of my bed. I went downstairs and made tea for all of us. I took Aunt Biddie's tea in first and found she had a stocking as well. Then I woke Tobin up and he laughed. 'Do you mean to say you don't believe in Santa Claus? Shame on you.'

He and I sat on the edge of Aunt Biddie's bed, while the two of us unpacked our stockings. Everything was there – a lump of coal, an orange, an apple, an old sixpenny piece – even a sugar mouse.

Miranda, Jonathan and Stevie came over just after breakfast, bringing their presents to put round the tree. Leaving Aunt Biddie and Miranda to get lunch, the rest of us went for a walk. Jonathan and Tobin went ahead, having men's conversation, while Stevie and I followed behind.

'I knew you were in love with him when we were San Fortunato,' Stevie informed me.

'You're making that up,' I accused her.

'No, I'm not. You're just not very good at subterfuge.'

'Well, and . . . ?'

'Oh, I already approve,' she said airily. 'I could never understand what you saw in Nigel. He was such a prat.'

After lunch, we followed the time-honoured Willows tradition and the cooks went off to change, while the rest of us washed up. Then we gathered in front of the television and watched the Queen's Speech, raised our glasses in a toast, after which we opened our presents. Tobin had presents for everyone and they all had presents for him. He gave Aunt Biddie *The Country Diary of an Edwardian Lady* and me a painting.

It was a view of the Villa Lontana and the Abbazia e Convento della Madonna della Misericordia looking up from the lake, copied from one of Stevie's photographs. It captured the mood of San Fortunato absolutely, as if he had been with us in our rowing boat. I could almost feel the sunshine on me and hear the cuckoos in the woods . . .

After tea, Aunt Biddie played the piano and we all sang carols, just like we used to do when I was a child.

On Boxing Day, we went to Holly Hill Farm for the day and Miranda said, 'You and Tobin deserve each other.'

We stayed at Avonford until New Year's Day. Tobin discovered a mass of little jobs around the place that needed doing, from door hinges that squeaked and light bulbs that needed replacing, to the punt that he set about repairing. Aunt Biddie insisted that he didn't have to do any of these things, but he said, 'I can't sit around all day doing nothing. No, you two girls catch up with each other and leave me to get on. I'm more than happy pottering about, so don't worry about me.'

In fact, Aunt Biddie and I didn't have all that much time for sitting around doing nothing either. Apart from the usual household tasks and looking after her menagerie, we received a constant stream of visitors, from neighbours who just popped in for a cup of coffee to the select few who were invited to tea. Word of Nigel's and my separation had obviously spread like wildfire amongst Aunt Biddie's cronies, and they were all eager to inspect my new boyfriend.

I lost count of the number of times I heard, 'So sorry to hear about you and your husband, Cara, dear. But these things happen, I'm afraid. Still, I gather you've already found someone else?'

At which point, Aunt Biddie would give a smug little smile and say, 'Yes, Tobin is such a nice man. He's been very kind to Cara. And he's extremely handy about the house. You know I've been complaining for ages about not being able to shut the larder door? I asked Tom to try and sort it for me when he was decorating the house in the spring, but he never got round to it. Well, Tobin fixed it in about half an hour and now it shuts perfectly.'

In this way, she scored one up on her friends, I was saved the necessity of answering searching questions about my future and Tobin emerged with flying colours without having to undergo personal scrutiny.

Nevertheless, Aunt Biddie and I still managed to find some time on our own, during which I described my reservations in respect to moving in with Tobin. I also told her about Tobin's reaction to my efforts at writing and that he wanted me to try and write a proper book.

Very wisely, she didn't venture any opinions of her own, but merely nodded sympathetically and said, 'Yes, I do understand.'

It was on New Year's Eve that we first saw Dingle's Gate. Tobin had completed his jobs and we had gone for a drive out towards Malvern, meandering round the country lanes, when we suddenly came upon the house, right in the middle of nowhere. Tobin stopped the car and we all sat and gazed.

A mixture of gate house and Victorian folly, it was situated about a quarter of a mile up a tree-lined drive and was constructed in the form of an archway, with two storeys to either side and a room spanning the space between them where the drive had presumably continued in the past but now stopped at the front of the house. Obviously, it had once stood at the entrance to a country mansion, but now it was a property in its own right. Each of the side portions had a little pointed tower on top, with a crenellated balcony and the roof across the archway bit was crenellated too.

'Now that's exactly the sort of place you two need,' Aunt Biddie declared. 'Cara could write in one half and you could paint in the other, Tobin. And when you wanted to meet there's the hall or corridor in the middle.'

It was lovely. No, it was more than that. It was my dream house. Without even seeing its interior, I knew that everything about it was right: its size, its location, its garden, its proximity to Avonford and Holly Hill. I sat there in the car at the end of its drive and lusted after it like I had never lusted after any material object before.

'I'm sorry, darling,' Tobin said, rightly interpreting my expression, 'but it has a very lived-in appearance.'

'It could be for sale,' Aunt Biddie said. 'People don't always have boards outside.'

I shook my head. 'Even if it was, I'm sure we couldn't afford it.'

When we returned to The Willows, we sat round the drawing room fire, drinking tea and eating hot buttered toast with honey. I drifted off into a daydream about Dingle's Gate, imagining Tobin's half fitted out with his furniture from Fulham and my half decorated according to my own taste.

How many rooms were there? I wondered. Say there were four on each side. The kitchen and dining room must be next to each other, and presumably the bathroom was above the kitchen, which meant there would be one bedroom on that side. In the other half would be two reception rooms and, above them, two more bedrooms, while in the middle was the connecting hall. That must be a wonderful room, with windows to front and back. And finally there were those little turrets. Oh, I could have one of those all for myself, furnished and decorated exactly how I wanted.

I could sit in my little tower and write books. I could have a desk beneath a window looking out towards the Malverns and write.

At this point, my thoughts tailed off, as I had a sudden image of my father scorning Patricia's generosity and telling Imogen Humboldt that, only if he could escape from London would he be able to compose incomparable poetry. And now, here was I, indulging in the same fantasies, with even less to back them up than my father. At least he had known he possessed some talent, whereas all I had was Tobin's assurances on the strength of The Book and my diary.

Then I realized that Tobin and Aunt Biddie were discussing me.

'I do understand and respect her desire to remain independent,' Tobin was saying. 'But it seems such a waste of ability.'

'Yes, I know,' Aunt Biddie agreed. 'However, I do sympathise with her point-of-view. What sort of book do you think she should write?'

'An historical novel, I think, with fictitious characters set against a factual background.'

'She's certainly met enough interesting people in the past year to give her a starting point. And, with her knowledge of France and Italy, she could set it one or other of those countries. That would make it more interesting. I always like books which teach me something at the same time as entertaining me.'

'But you made a very good point when we were out today,' Tobin went on. 'She does need a room of her own. I think what I'm going to do, when we get back to Fulham, is turn the dining room into a study for her.'

'Am I allowed any say in this matter?' I enquired.

'Yes, of course, dear,' Aunt Biddie said.

'Well, your faith in me is very touching, but I'm still not going to give up work in order to write a book for which there is no guarantee that it will ever be published.'

'Neither of us are suggesting that you should,' Aunt Biddie assured me. 'But, as Tobin has just been telling me, you apparently achieved a lot of writing during your evenings and weekends. You could, at least, start planning a novel.'

'And if we have people to dinner?'

Tobin laughed. 'They'll just have to eat off trays on their laps.'

In the evening Miranda, Jonathan and Stevie came over. At midnight we stood at the front door and listened to the abbey bells pealing in the new year. I couldn't help thinking of a year ago and that ghastly party at Liam Massey's. Little had I then imagined how much my life was about to change.

After Miranda, Jonathan and Stevie had left and Aunt Biddie had gone to bed, Tobin and I remained in the drawing room in front of the dying embers of the fire. He raised his glass to me. 'Here's to our future.'

I clinked my glass against his. 'Thank you for everything.'

'I hope you didn't feel that we were ganging up on you this afternoon. It must have seemed like it, but we do actually both care for you a lot.'

I smiled. 'Yes, I know you do. And I am grateful. My fear is that I won't live up to your expectations.'

When he had put out the fire according to Aunt Biddie's instructions and placed the guard round it, he took me in his arms and held me very close to him. 'I understand why you don't want to sleep with me here before we're married, but my bed is so big and comfortable. Couldn't I possibly tempt you to come and share it for a little while? You're looking so beautiful tonight. And I love you so much.'

I went to the Blue Room with him and somehow it did not seem like a betrayal of anything. In the early hours of the morning, Tiger jumped on the bed and woke us, at which point I crept back to my own little room. Who says animals don't have a sixth sense? And who says old ladies don't either? When Aunt Biddie brought my cup of tea, she didn't ask how I'd slept like she normally did. She just said, 'It's a lovely bright day out there,' and gave a satisfied little smile.

In fact, most of my forebodings about living with Tobin proved unnecessary, although I would be lying if I pretended that I ever settled in properly at Fulham. However, like so many other things, the prospect turned out to be worse than the reality. Sure, some of my belongings remained in their boxes and some of my clothes in a suitcase, which gave me a weird sense of dislocation to begin with, but since they were all items I didn't immediately need, that feeling wore off after a while.

Because we were both aware of the potential pitfalls, we took care to avoid them. Above all, we respected each other's privacy. I took care not to interrupt Tobin at his work unless absolutely necessary and always to knock before entering his studio. And, once the dining room became my room, he showed the same courtesy to me. Mind you, I didn't actually take over the dining room. After all, I didn't require a lot of space – just somewhere to put my portable typewriter, paper and the books I started to accumulate once I began planning my first novel. All of those were easily cleared to the sideboard, enabling us to entertain if not in great style, at least in comfort.

You see, I did take heed of Tobin's and Aunt Biddie's words of encouragement and decided that my novel should be about White Russians in Paris in the twenties and thirties. Talking about the characters and plot kept Tobin and me amused while we were cooking or eating, and I used my tube journeys to work to read more books on the period.

In the middle of January, Yvonne announced that she was not returning to work. Douglas duly offered me her job at a considerably better salary than I had been receiving as a temp and I accepted, with the proviso that he understood I was not intending to spend the rest of my life working for Grosvenor Management Consultants.

'I should hope not,' he replied. 'We're in the manpower business, remember. If a better offer comes along, I would expect you to take it.'

I left it at that.

When I told Tobin what I'd done, he merely said, 'Now you've started thinking about writing a book, that's all that matters. I just wanted to get you started.'

The first dinner party we gave was on Tobin's forty-sixth birthday on 23 of January, which coincided with a judge somewhere granting Nigel and me a decree *nisi*, meaning that in six weeks and one day's time my marriage would be finally over. So, in effect, it was a double celebration.

Our guests were Penny and Michael, Oliver and his wife, Tobin's agent Freddie and his girlfriend, and Sherry and Roly. At the end of the meal, Oliver made a short speech. 'Cara and Tobin represent my first and only attempt at match-making,' he stated. 'However, I must admit that, when I initially told Tobin about Cara, I didn't actually expect it ever to come to anything. They were obviously ideally suited, but there were rather a lot of obstacles in the way. At times, watching from the sidelines, I couldn't help wishing that they could be a little less – er – shall I say virtuous? But, in the end, love conquered.'

Astounded, I turned to Tobin and asked, 'What did he say to you about me?'

'Well, he did paint you in quite glowing colours. He described your hair of burnished gold and said you were extremely intelligent – as well as various other things which I quickly worked out for myself anyway, once I met you.'

'You're forgetting something,' Oliver said. 'I also told you that Cara didn't appear to be happily married.'

'How on earth did you work that out?' I demanded. 'I don't think I even mentioned Nigel to you. In fact, I'm sure I didn't.'

'You had a habit of nervously twiddling your wedding ring,' Oliver informed me blandly. 'Women who do that are usually trying to get a message across, even if it's only subconscious. Sometimes it's a warning to say, "Keep off. I'm not available." In your case, it was obviously a sign of insecurity and nervousness. Of course, it could have been that you were nervous about meeting me. But though that would have been flattering, it seemed unlikely, since you were so self-possessed in every other respect.'

'I could just have been uptight as a result of finding out about the Princess.'

'Oh, yes, I realized that, of course. But when we were talking about her, you didn't fiddle with your wedding ring.'

I gave a rueful laugh. 'Well, all I can say is that, whatever the reasons, I'm extremely glad you did introduce us.'

Events like that dinner party helped considerably in making me feel part of Tobin's life. And I must admit that, at the end of the working day, it was wonderful to come home to him.

During that time, we also started house-hunting again but my heart was no more in it than it had been before. For one thing, I couldn't forget Dingle's Gate. For another, until the decree absolute came through and my marriage was finally over, I couldn't bring myself to consider any firm plans for the future. Although there was no reason for there to be any hitches at this final stage, I suppose it seemed like tempting providence. Until those precious papers were in my hand, there was always lurking fear that something might go wrong at the last moment.

On 14 March, 1981, the decree absolute was granted and it was as if a huge weight had been lifted from my shoulders. Nigel was gone for ever. I was free.

Tobin took me out to dinner to celebrate and, when he raised the subject of getting married, I suddenly found I was able to consider our future in a far more positive light.

Unfortunately, our ideas differed as to the form our wedding should take. Since we were both divorced, a church wedding was out of the question, so a registry office it had to be. On that we were fully agreed. Where we didn't agree was on the location and the number of guests.

Tobin wanted a very quiet ceremony at somewhere like Chelsea Town Hall with just a couple of witnesses – Sherry and Oliver, he suggested.

'But I can't get married and not invite Aunt Biddie, Miranda, Jonathan and Stevie,' I objected.

'No, I suppose not,' he allowed. 'But if we invite them, we'll have to invite my kids and Harvey and Gwendolen as well.'

'And why not?' I asked. 'It's only right that Joss and Pamela should be present and, as for Harvey and Gwendolen, I haven't even met them yet.'

'That's because I've had your best interests at heart.'

'What does that mean?'

'They are rather overwhelming to say the least.'

'Are you trying to say that they would look down on me?'

'No, not exactly, but—'

'As the daughter of the Princess Hélène Romanovna Shuiska, I hope I can hold my own with the Earl and Countess of Winster,' I retorted.

He gave a dry laugh. 'OK. *Touché*. Well, after we're married, maybe I'll take you up to Kingston Kirkby Hall.'

'But why can't they come to the wedding? Are you ashamed of me?'

'Good Lord, no! It's just that I would like our wedding to be as quiet as possible. After all, it's a private matter between you and me.'

I nodded, fighting back my disappointment.

'Listen, darling, when Dawn and I were married, we went into the full act – the church wedding, the bridesmaids and a reception with a hundred guests. I don't want a repetition of all that.'

I nodded again and toyed with my food.

There was silence between us for a while, then he said, 'I'm sorry, I am being rather selfish. Why don't you tell me what you have in mind?'

I looked up. 'Well, I too would like our wedding to be different from when I married Nigel. I'm not saying I want lots of people there. I don't want it to be an excuse for a big party. But I don't really want to be married at a London registry office. That's what Nigel and I did.'

'So what do you have in mind? Gretna Green?'

I hesitated then decided to come straight out with it. 'What I'd really like is to be married in Avonford.'

'If that's all, I haven't the slightest objection.'

'And then we could have a small reception afterwards. I wouldn't want to put Aunt Biddie to any trouble, so maybe at an hotel.'

He leaned back in his chair and grinned. 'So where's the problem? Why are we arguing? We'll get married at Avonford. That's agreed. Now, the next question. When shall we do it? What about your birthday in May?'

'I don't know what day my birthday falls on. Hold on, I've got a diary in my bag. Oh, it's a Friday. That's not very good. It means people will be at work. Why don't we have the wedding on the Saturday before and then we'll be away on our honeymoon for my birthday. That is – I assume we will be having a honeymoon?'

'I should jolly well hope so! I had thought we might go to Italy. Unless you have any better ideas?' he added hastily.

I shook my head. 'I'd love to go to Italy with you.'

'You could show me San Fortunato. In fact, if we planned it right, we could be in San Fortunato on your birthday. How about that?'

'That sounds wonderful.'

'And now, in return for all the concessions I've made, will you do something for me?'

'Anything,' I promised rashly.

'Will you write to Filomena Angelini and tell her that you're getting married and that we'll be coming to Italy on our honeymoon?'

'Why?'

'For the same reason that I gave you before. Because you obviously mean a lot to her. I understand that. You're extremely precious to me, too.'

So, not without certain misgivings, I wrote to her and, to my surprise, she replied, wishing me happiness on my wedding day and asking me please to come and see her – and bring my new husband with me – while we were in Italy.

At Easter, we went to Avonford and announced our plans. Aunt Biddie was thrilled. 'But if you think you're having your reception in an hotel, you have another think coming,' she stated. 'We'll hold it here. Mrs Tilsley's daughter is a caterer. She's very good and her prices are very reasonable.'

On Easter Saturday, the miracle occurred.

We couldn't resist going to look at Dingle's Gate and when we got there, to our astonishment, there was a FOR SALE notice outside. What was more, while we stood there gawping, the owner actually came out and next thing we knew we were being shown round.

Inside, it was almost exactly how I had visualized it, with four rooms to either side and a hallway spanning them. 'I'm afraid it needs rather a lot of work done on it,' the owner said apologetically. His name was Mr Simpson and he was elderly, about the same age as Aunt Biddie probably, but nowhere near as fit. Rather bent and supporting himself with a stick, he explained that he suffered badly from arthritis, which wasn't helped by the lack of central heating at Dingle's Gate.

It was, indeed, in dire need of redecoration and a certain amount of refurbishment. The little towers, in particular, were in a sorry state. The tiles obviously leaked quite badly, for there were water stains down the walls and some of the floor boards were rotting.

'How long have you lived here?' I asked.

'I've only been here since the war,' he said. 'But my wife grew up here. Her grandfather was the gatekeeper, at the time when this was the gate house to Hartley Manor. His name was Dingle, so it became known as Dingle's Gate. What happened was that the Esmonds, who own Hartley Manor, suffered the same as many other gentry from high taxation and death duties. They were forced to sell off a lot of their land and property. Because they knew my wife, they sold us Dingle's Gate at a very reasonable price. Ah, we've been happy here and I must confess it's a wrench to have to part with it. But that's life, isn't it?'

We all nodded sympathetically and, encouraged, he continued, 'My wife died last year, you see, and ever since then my eldest son's been pestering me to go and live with him. He's done well from himself, he has. He's a foreman up at the Jaguar works in Coventry and has a big, modern house. Now his girls have married and left home, it's too big for him and his wife, like this place is too big for me. So it makes sense for us to live together. And this last winter was almost too much for me, I have to admit. I went down with the 'flu something terrible.'

'Yes, I'm afraid old age creeps up on us all,' Aunt Biddie said. 'I think you're being very wise. In your position, I'd do exactly the same thing.'

'Have you had many people looking at the house?' Tobin enquired.

'Only a few and I don't think any of them were really interested. It's too far off the beaten track for most people and it's got a big garden.'

'How much land does it have?'

'About an acre. And, as you can see, it's badly overgrown. I used to be a keen gardener in my younger days but I just can't do it now.'

We stayed for about an hour, while Mr Simpson chatted on, obviously glad of our company. When we eventually left and made our way back up the drive to the car, Aunt Biddie remarked, 'You could always keep donkeys. They'd keep the grass down.'

I looked at Tobin and he looked at me. 'I can work from anywhere,' he said. 'But would you be prepared to give up Grosvenor Management Consultants?'

'We don't even know how much he wants for it,' I objected.

'Then let's go to the estate agent and find out.'

The estate agency was in Malvern and, more importantly, it was open. Furthermore, the agent responsible for Dingle's Gate was actually on duty that morning. 'Ah, yes, Dingle's Gate, beautifully situated in the heart of the countryside. In need of a little modernization but, umm . . .'

'Mr Simpson has already shown us round it,' Tobin stated. 'All we need to know is the price.'

'Tut, tut, most irregular, but he is a rather quaint gentleman. Well, the asking price is forty-nine thousand, five hundred, which, bearing in mind the number of rooms and the amount of land, is extremely reasonable.'

It was less than I had feared, but I was still unsure whether we could afford it.

I looked at Tobin and he looked at me. Then he grinned. 'We'd like to put in an offer,' he told the estate agent.

'At the asking price, sir?' the estate agent asked, trying to conceal his astonishment.

'As you said, it seems very reasonable.'

'I should point out that there's a preservation order on the property, in case you were thinking of developing it any way.'

'I'm delighted to hear of the preservation order. Any changes we make will be merely to preserve, not to alter its character.'

'Will you be requiring a mortgage?'

'Yes, I'm afraid so.'

'In that case I should point out that, in view of the age of the building and its rather, er, run-down condition, most building societies will probably be rather conservative in the amount they are prepared to lend against it.'

'That doesn't surprise me. But it shouldn't prove a problem.'

'In that case, sir, if I could take a few details?'

Out on the street again, I threw my arms round Tobin's neck and kissed him. 'Oh, thank you. It's the most wonderful, wonderful thing ever to happen to me – well, after meeting you, of course.'

'I'm glad you added that.'

'But are you sure we can afford it?'

'Where there's a will there's a way. Don't worry, we'll find the money from somewhere.'

'You could keep sheep as well,' Aunt Biddie said.

Back in London, on Tuesday, I summoned up my courage and told Douglas that I was getting married and probably moving out of London. He looked slightly aggrieved for a moment, then shrugged. 'Well, you did warn me. And thank you for giving me advance notice. When do you want to leave?'

'Not until we move, which will be in three months or so, I assume, depending on how quickly my fiancé can sell his house. However, I would be grateful if I could take time off for a honeymoon. Naturally, I wouldn't expect to be paid.'

'For God's sake!' he exclaimed. 'Who do you think I am? Miles Goodchild? Of course, you'll get paid while you're on your honeymoon. Just organize a good temp for while you're away. You don't have a twin sister by any chance, do you?'

That evening, when I arrived home, Tobin greeted me with a huge smile. 'Three guesses who I've been talking to today.'

'An estate agent.'

'Yes, I have been talking to an estate agent – several of them, in fact. And I've put this house on the market. I've also talked to our friend up in Malvern and Mr Simpson has accepted our offer with great pleasure. He said he was hoping we would buy Dingle's Gate, because we seemed the right kind of people. But that isn't the answer to my question. You'll have to try again.'

'Umm, the building society.'

'Yes, I've done that, too. And, subject to a satisfactory survey, it doesn't look as if there should be any problems. But that's not it, either. Go on, guess again.'

'I don't know. Aunt Biddie?'

'No. She's about the only person I haven't spoken to today. Well, I suppose I'll have to tell you. I've been talking to Ludo Zakharin, who sends you his kindest regards, incidentally, and is delighted to hear of our approaching nuptials.'

'Why were you talking to *him*?'

'If you recall, we still have Angelini's portrait of the Princess. Obviously, I didn't agree to any deal with him before talking to you, but he is prepared to offer about ten thousand pounds for that portrait, which should pay for most, if not all of the work which will need to be done on Dingle's Gate.'

'Ten thousand pounds,' I breathed. 'Why didn't you just say yes?'

'Because it's your decision as well as mine. She was your mother.'

'Huh! I'm sorry, but given a choice between her and Dingle's Gate – well, there is no decision to be made.'

'In that case, I suggest that we drive to Italy and stop off in Paris on the way to deliver the portrait. We could see your friend Ginette while we're there. I'd like to meet her. She sounds rather fun.'

Even though we weren't getting married in church, a certain amount of tradition was still brought into play for our wedding, mainly due to Stevie, backed up by Aunt Biddie. For a start, Tobin and I weren't allowed to spend the previous night in the same house, so he stayed at Holly Hill Farm, while I slept at The Willows.

We had full house at The Willows. For the first time in decades, every room was occupied, because Aunt Biddie refused to allow people to stay in an hotel when she had space enough and to spare. The other bedrooms – not including the glory-hole – were occupied by Sherry and Roly, Oliver, Freddie, Penny and Michael, and Joss. Pamela – dear little thing

– had made the excuse that she was too busy preparing for exams to be able to attend. Neither Tobin nor I were altogether sorry.

Far from being perturbed at this sudden influx of guests, Aunt Biddie was in her element, especially at having so famous a television personality as Oliver Lyon sleeping under her roof. She cooked an enormous joint of beef, with all the trimmings, and followed it up with Fairy Pudding, regaling the company with the story of how it had been Connor's favourite dessert and how she and I had found the recipe again when we were searching for his book of poetry. Because it was such a merry evening, I scarcely had chance to feel nervous.

When we all went up to bed, Sherry came to my room with me and perched on the window seat next to Big and Little, while I sat on the bed, stroking Tiger, who was already snuggled up against the hot-water bottle. 'Happy?' she asked.

'Very.'

'So am I – on your behalf.' She paused. 'I don't know whether I ought to tell you this tonight, but I'm going to. I bumped into Nigel the other day in Camden. He enquired about you. His manner was so – oh, so smooth and condescending – and he had such a pitying sort of tone to his voice when he mentioned your name – that I'm afraid I couldn't resist telling him that you were about to get married. I hope you don't mind?'

'Not at all. What did he say?'

Sherry's face broke into a huge smile. 'Oh, I do wish you could have been there to see his expression. He was shocked rigid. "Getting married?" he asked. "Who to?" "A man, of course," I replied. "But *what* man?" he asked. "The sort of man I'd marry like a shot at if I wasn't already married to Roly," I informed him. "He's tall, good-looking, extremely kind – and he's an aristocrat." Well, I know that isn't really true, but I couldn't resist it.'

I couldn't help laughing. 'Did he say anything about Bo?'

'Oh, yes. I asked him, very sweetly, of course, how he and his girlfriend were getting along, and he said that, umm, er, she was actually away at the moment, shooting a commercial in the States – although she was due back very soon.'

'So the biter has been bit,' I murmured. 'Now he's the grass widower.'

'You're not cross with me, are you?' Sherry asked.

'Of course I'm not.'

'Well, now I'm going to leave you to get your beauty sleep.' She stood up, crossed the room and gave me a little kiss. 'Forget Nigel and dream of Tobin.'

When we left for the registry office in the morning, a dozen or so people were gathered outside the house, among them several faces I recognized.

We went in two cars – Aunt Biddie, Oliver and me with Sherry and Roly in his Volvo – and the other four in Freddie's car. Aunt Biddie, dressed in a turquoise ensemble with a matching, turban-like hat, reminded me of the Queen Mother, as she waved a white gloved hand to the spectators through the car window.

As for me, I was wearing – at Stevie's insistence – something old, something new, something borrowed and something blue, though I did rather cheat. The something new was my outfit: a classically simple cream dress and jacket. The something old, something borrowed and something blue all took the form of a brooch of Aunt Biddie's, which had belonged to her mother. It was a lovely little thing, shaped like a dragonfly, and inset with tiny sapphires.

More onlookers were waiting outside the registry office. Aunt Biddie had certainly spread the word.

The party from Holly Hill Farm had already arrived and were also standing in the sunshine: Tobin and Jonathan very smart in dark grey lounge suits; Miranda in a loose-fitting, Indian smock; and Stevie looking absolutely stunning in a pale yellow pinafore dress, with her shining, dark brown hair down to her waist.

Tobin hurried across as we drew up. He gave me a kiss and laughed. 'I thought we were having a quiet, private ceremony.' Then there was an excited murmuring among the spectators and he murmured, 'Oh, my God . . . Well, don't say I didn't warn you.'

Drawing up behind our little cavalcade, was a gleaming, chauffeur-driven Rolls Royce. The uniformed chauffeur got out and, casting a supercilious glance at all of us, opened the passenger doors.

From one emerged a lady in a navy blue suit, which reminded me of that worn by Ludo Zakharin's assistant – so, presumably, it was Chanel – with a fur cape draped round her shoulders and a 'wedding hat' perched at an angle on her immaculately groomed hair. She was considerably larger than Ludo Zakharin's petite assistant, but that did not detract from her elegance.

The gentleman, who bore a slight facial resemblance to Tobin but was rounder of face, shorter in stature and fuller of figure, was wearing a pearl grey morning suit and a top hat.

Tobin took my arm. 'Come and meet Harvey and Gwendolen.'

Fortunately, time did not allow for a prolonged introduction and conversation. The registry office doors opened and we all trooped in. However, I couldn't help overhearing Aunt Biddie informing her acquaintances, in a loud whisper, as she passed them, 'That's the Earl and Countess of Winster. He's the bridegroom's brother.'

So stunned was I by Harvey and Gwendolen's appearance, that I almost forgot I was nervous about getting married.

The registry office was beautifully decorated with flowers and the registrar a charming woman, who made the brief formal ceremony as personal as possible and sounded as if she really meant it when she wished us both happiness at the end. Then Tobin was taking me in his arms, kissing me and saying, 'I love you, Mrs Touchstone.'

When we emerged, it was to find a photographer waiting for us. Mistaking Harvey for the bridegroom, he approached him and said, 'Dick Smith, of the *Avonford Gazette*. Allow me to congratulate yourself and your new wife.'

'Mr Smith!' Aunt Biddie's voice called. 'That's the wrong gentleman. This is the bridegroom, here, with my niece.'

'How come the local press has arrived?' Tobin demanded of her.

Aunt Biddie opened her eyes innocently wide. 'I've absolutely no idea. But now Mr Smith is here, let's allow him to take some photographs. He's very good, you know. He took some excellent pictures during our campaign to save the abbey clock.'

We all arranged ourselves in a group and the photographer clicked away. Then he did some shots of Tobin and me on our own, followed by some with Oliver and Tobin's brother and sister-in-law. Glancing at Harvey, I sensed that he was not amused.

The photography over, the band of well-wishers pushed forward. Tobin and I had our hands seized and shaken and I found myself being kissed by a number of elderly ladies. Several people approached Oliver with autograph albums, while Harvey and Gwendolen were gazed upon in awe.

When we eventually arrived back at The Willows, a waitress greeted us with a tray of glasses of champagne as we came in through the front door and another waitress ushered us into the dining room, where a magnificent buffet had been laid out.

The next quarter of an hour passed in introductions among those guests who didn't know each other and congratulations to Tobin and myself, after which the two waitresses handed round plates and dishes of food and the party divided itself into little groups.

By the window, Joss was talking to Stevie with an adoring look in his eyes, while she gazed up at him with the same captivating expression which had stolen poor Giuseppe's heart in San Fortunato. Those were two people at least about whom I did not have to worry, I thought to myself.

Roly had joined Freddie, Penny and Michael, and they seemed to have discovered some topic of conversation in common, for they appeared happy enough. Sherry was with Miranda and Jonathan, laughing to them about something. And, in the centre of the room, Harvey and Oliver were renewing old acquaintance, while Tobin and Gwendolen chatted nearby. Aunt Biddie was generally scurrying around, urging everyone to have some more to eat and asking if anyone would like to go out into the garden, where there were tables and chairs set out?

Tobin beckoned to me and I joined him and Gwendolen. He put his arm round my shoulder and Gwendolen said, in a terribly county accent, 'Tobin has just been explaining to me who you are. I didn't realize your connection to the Princess. Harvey never told me. It must have slipped his mind. You must come up and stay with us during the summer.'

Next to us, Harvey was saying, making no attempt to keep his voice low, 'We felt we ought to put in an appearance. Didn't realize it was going to be such an informal affair. Knowing Tobin, I suppose I should have guessed, though.'

Glancing at Tobin and taking another sip of champagne, I wished I had heeded his warning.

Sherry must have been watching me and caught my anxious expression, for she came over, followed by Miranda and Jonathan. Somehow, without me quite knowing how it had happened, she had succeed in getting Gwendolen and Jonathan into a discussion about horses.

I drew back and Miranda linked her arm through mine. 'Don't look so worried. Everyone's enjoying themselves.'

'I hope so,' I murmured doubtfully.

'Of course they are.'

But I felt sure they would all be enjoying themselves far more if Harvey and Gwendolen weren't there.

Tobin and I continued to circulate but, the whole time, I was aware of Harvey's and Gwendolen's voices, louder than all the others. Gwendolen was still on horses and Harvey was still talking to Oliver, whom he obviously considered the only person in the room worthy of his attention.

Suddenly, I heard a strange noise coming from the hall and a patter of feet on the mosaic tiles. Aunt Biddie must have heard the sound at the same time, for she spun round and exclaimed urgently, 'Nanny! What are you doing in here?'

Everything happened at high speed after that. Naturally those who heard Aunt Biddie, turned, expecting to see an old nurse. Instead, trotting in through the doorway – with a collar round its neck, from which trailed a ragged piece of rope – was a nanny goat.

Ignoring Aunt Biddie's admonition, Nanny made a bee-line towards the table, whereupon Aunt Biddie launched herself upon her, her turban falling off in the process. She failed to catch the goat who, startled, picked up speed, lowered her head and butted Harvey in the rear, causing him to stagger forward and throw the contents of his glass and chocolate mousse all over Oliver.

Aunt Biddie made another vain attempt to catch the animal, calling, 'Nanny, come here at once, you naughty girl.'

Jonathan rushed to her assistance, grabbed hold of the goat's collar and, after giving her a reassuring stroke, led her firmly back towards the door. As if to show how totally unrepentant she was, Nanny picked up Aunt Biddie's hat from the floor and left the room with it firmly clasped in her jaws.

'Oh, dear, I am so sorry,' Aunt Biddie cried. 'She was tied up at the bottom of the garden but she must have chewed through her rope. Oh, I do apologize, I really do. Lord Winster, Mr Lyon – are you all right?'

Harvey was clearly feeling far from all right. His face was red with indignation and his lips were forming soundless words.

At that moment, Joey piped up, 'Who's a pretty boy then? Ark. Ark.'

Oliver, with champagne dripping from one shoulder and chocolate mousse splattered over the other, raised his hand to his mouth to conceal a smile. At which point a great chortle of laughter rang through the room, followed by another and then another. 'Oh, that's the funniest thing I've ever seen in my life!' Gwendolen whooped. 'Harvey, you presented such a wonderful target!' She was shaken by another spasm of laughter. 'I'm going to dine out on this for years to come.'

Oliver removed his hand from his mouth and laughed too. So did Tobin. And so, at the window, did Joss and Stevie. Their laughter was contagious and the rest of us were struggling to keep straight faces. Meanwhile, Aunt Biddie was dabbing anxiously at Oliver's jacket with a napkin, while Harvey's expression became even more affronted.

Tears were running down Gwendolen's cheeks and she was clutching her chest. 'Harvey, stop looking like that, you're making it worse. If only you could have seen yourself, standing there holding forth to Oliver, and that goat coming up behind up and butting you in the rump. And that budgerigar. Who's a pretty boy then? Oh, I can't remember when anything last made me laugh so much.'

It was touch and go. Harvey sucked in his breath. 'I'm glad to have afforded you such amusement, Gwendolen.'

'It wasn't you,' she explained, 'it was the goat. It was the way it lowered its head and went for you. That's what was so funny. Oh, come on, Harvey, where's your sense of humour?'

Harvey forced his features into a smile and we all started to relax.

'Let me re-fill your glass, old boy,' Tobin said, still laughing himself. 'And be thankful it wasn't your hat Nanny went off with.'

Jonathan returned to the room, grinning broadly. 'That's Nanny safely tethered again, with a length of chain this time. And, incidentally, Biddie, Gordon has a decidedly broody look. I think you're due for some more goslings soon.'

Aunt Biddie perked up. 'Wonderful! Tobin and Cara can have them at Dingle's Gate. Which reminds me, both of you, I've ordered two Jacob's sheep as a wedding present.'

Gwendolen wiped her eyes and said, 'First a goat, now a gander having goslings, and I've never heard of anyone giving sheep as a wedding present before. Tobin, I'm not yet sure what sort of family you have married into but I'm starting to like them more and more.'

Aunt Biddie spun round to beam at her and sent Harvey's refilled glass of champagne flying out of his hand and all over Oliver's shoes . . .

This time, we all burst out laughing – even Harvey.

By six o'clock, when Tobin and I left, all the barriers between our guests had been broken down and the party looked set to continue for a good many hours yet. It may have been our wedding, but Aunt Biddie was the real star turn. Several times I noticed Oliver take out his notebook to jot down a few words and it did not seem beyond the realms of possibility that, at some future date, we might be seeing Aunt Biddie featuring as the guest in one of his interviews. Meanwhile, Gwendolen had issued her with a standing invitation to Kingston Kirkby Hall, and Joss had been invited back to Holly Hill Farm for the rest of the weekend.

Tobin and I said goodbye to everyone and went out to the car, only to find it plastered with JUST MARRIED signs and the mandatory trail of tin cans trailing behind. 'Who's responsible for this?' Tobin asked laughingly.

The response was handfuls of confetti and rice from Stevie and Joss.

That evening – after stopping beyond the bridge to remove the JUST MARRIED signs and the tin cans – we drove as far as a little village outside Oxford, where we spent the night. When we went to bed, we were still laughing about the afternoon's events, which can't be a bad to start married life.

Next morning, we continued to Dover, crossed the Channel and made our way leisurely to Paris, stopping overnight at a converted château. On Monday evening, we met Ginette for dinner.

'So I was right, after all,' she said, with a knowing smile. 'But why did you have to spoil it by *marrying* him?'

I enquired after Jean-Pierre and she shrugged, 'He is spending the night with his parents-in-law. Today is their golden wedding anniversary. But he has just bought me a car, so who am I to complain?'

The following morning, we reported to the Galerie Zakharin. Ludo Zakharin greeted us with urbane suavity, seating us at the art deco table, with birds instead of legs, in the centre of the room, while he went off to examine the painting. When he returned, he said, 'I'm glad to say that my offer stands, Mr Touchstone. I have a banker's draft prepared for you.'

Then he turned to me. 'How did your quest progress? Did you ever go to see the Signora Angelini?'

I could not lie but neither was I prepared to tell him the whole truth. 'Yes, I did, but she was an invalid and unable to be of very much help, I'm afraid.'

'A pity.'

At that moment, his assistant emerged from one of the doors at the far end of the room. 'If you will excuse one moment,' he said.

He returned and explained, 'I regret that I must leave you. I have an important client on the telephone. Our conversation may take some time.'

So we took our departure and left the Princess back on Zakharin territory again – and Ludo Zakharin none the wiser about her true origins.

From Paris, we drove to Switzerland, where the weather was cold and the clouds so low that the mountains were invisible. In the Bernese Oberland, it was snowing and people were skiing. So we continued down to the Ticino and crossed the border into Italy, where we entered what could have been another world.

When we reached the Hotel del Lago in San Fortunato, it was to step out of the car into warm, welcoming sunshine.

Chapter 26

The afternoon was very still and a blue haze hung over Lake Lugano as Tobin drove slowly up the narrow, twisting road from Varone to Granburrone. From time to time through the clearings in the trees we could see the Abbazia e Convento della Madonna della Misericordia on the far side of the valley. We passed through Granburrone and there, round the next corner was the Villa Lontana and, beyond that, the craggy ridge of the mountains.

Tobin parked, where I had the year before, next to Cesare's Fiat. We got out of the car and stood for a moment, looking down onto the red-tiled roofs of San Fortunato and the blue, misty lake far below, breathing in the fresh mountain air and listening to that evocative sound of the cuckoos.

Then we went to the front door and I tugged on the bell pull. Almost immediately, the door opened and Lucia appeared. I held out my hand to her and, after a moment's hesitation, she shook it. I could read concern in her eyes and sensed that she had been against our visit. Still, she wished me good day and, nodding at Tobin, said, '*Entrate, per favore, Signore.*'

'How is the Signora?' I asked.

'*Molto agitata*. But she insists that she is well enough to see you.'

'I shall try not to excite her.'

She shrugged, as though resigned to the fact that my visit could have no other outcome.

We went down the marble hall and through the door, beside the statuette of the Virgin Mary with a flickering candle before it, into that room of white and golden light. Filomena was in exactly the same position as on the occasion of my first visit, staring out across the balcony.

She turned her wheelchair and I crossed the room, crouching down beside her and taking her two frail, cool hands in mine. They were trembling slightly and I could feel the agitation in her which Lucia had mentioned.

'I was so pleased to receive your letter,' I said 'And it's very good to see you again.'

'I am happy to see you, too, again – Cara.' She looked past me to where Tobin was still standing with Lucia. 'And this is your new husband?'

I beckoned Tobin over and introduced them. Filomena kept his hand in hers while she gazed up at him, her eyes searching his face. Then she nodded and let go his hand.

Behind me, Lucia asked, 'Would the *Signore* like coffee?'

I looked questioningly at Filomena, who shook her head. 'Not for me. But, please, you have some.'

When Lucia had gone and we were seated, Filomena said, 'It is your birthday today. Many congratulations. It is kind of you to come on your special day.'

Wary of distressing her, I fought back the impulse to say that it seemed an appropriate place to be on my birthday and contented myself with smiling.

'Please, tell me now about yourself. I did not know that you were divorced, when you were here last year.'

'I wasn't. In June, after I saw you, I went through a bad time. I lost my job and my husband left me for another woman.'

She shook her head sadly.

'Please don't disquiet yourself,' I begged. 'It had not been a happy marriage for a long while. Naturally, I was shocked when it ended in such a way, but when I recovered from the shock I realized it was for the best.'

'And then you met Signor Touchstone?'

'We were already acquainted. After that, we became closer. He has been extremely kind and understanding.'

She glanced at Tobin. 'Yes, I can believe that. He has a good face. He is an artist, you said. What kind of pictures does he paint?'

'Mostly landscapes.' I reached in my bag. 'This is a photograph of one of his paintings. You may recognize it.'

'*Bontà de cielo!* Was he in San Fortunato before?'

'No, he painted it from a photograph Stevie took last year.'

She shook her head wonderingly, then said to Tobin, '*È bellissimo.*'

'Would you like to keep this photograph?' I asked.

'That would be very kind.' She gazed at it in silent reverie. 'How strange that you should marry an artist and one whose style is not unlike my father's. Or, put it this way, they both paint what they see.'

She pointed at the portrait of the artist on the wall. 'I don't know if I showed you last time. That is my father – a self-portrait. And the woman over there is my mother.'

I translated for Tobin's benefit and he walked across to study them.

'And you, Cara,' Filomena asked, 'you do not paint?'

'I'm afraid not.'

She looked down at her thin hands, with their raised blue veins, then, from beneath the blanket covering her legs, she withdrew her rosary. Fingering the beads, she said, 'I feel sure you have some creative talent.'

I hesitated, then admitted, 'Tobin and my aunt have convinced me that I have an ability to write. I am planning to write a novel.'

At that moment, Lucia brought our coffee and a glass of water for Filomena. She looked apprehensively from one to the other of us, then, with a warning glance at myself, went away again.

'But you are still working?' Filomena asked. 'You found another job?'

'Oh, yes. That wasn't difficult.'

I went on to explain that we were in the process of buying a new home in the country – not far from where I spent my childhood and, after that, we chatted for about an hour – or rather, she asked questions about my life in England, about Stevie and the rest of my family and the new house we were planning to buy.

Her interest in my replies was not feigned. Yet, all the time – possibly because it was a characteristic I recognized in myself – I couldn't help feeling that she was really waiting to broach some other topic, that she was poised on the brink of something, but holding back, putting off some evil moment.

However, I did not need Lucia's warning to be wary of re-evoking old ghosts . . . I had only to look across the balcony towards the cuckoo wood and recall my headlong flight to the edge of the ravine – and hear again in my head Filomena's anguished voice crying, '*Rosso wanted you. Rosso adored you. And I wanted you. I wanted to bring you up as my own daughter. But he wouldn't let me . . .*' – to appreciate the inherent perils in re-awakening old memories, especially on such a sensitive day as this, my birthday.

Then the sun began to sink, the bells pealed from the Abbazia, summoning the faithful to vespers. Lucia reappeared and I knew it was time to make our departure.

'We had better be going,' I said reluctantly.

Filomena nodded. 'How long are staying San Fortunato?'

'We haven't decided. A few days certainly.'

'I have something for you, something of your father's. I should have given them to you last time you were here, but I was so disturbed that I did not remember. In view of what you have told me this afternoon, however, it seems especially apt.'

'Something of my father's?'

'You will see. I have kept them all these years, but I can do nothing with them. It is much better that you should have them.'

'Whatever they are, thank you.'

'I hope you will not be disappointed.'

I went over to her and crouched beside her again. Letting her rosary fall onto her lap, she reached out her arms and drew my head down onto her shoulder. 'Happy birthday, Cara *mia*,' she murmured.

In the hall, Lucia handed me a carrier bag, inside which was a parcel, wrapped in brown paper and tied with string. 'This time it was better,' she said approvingly, in a low voice. 'I will tell you now, Signora, last year, it was over a month after your visit before she recovered.'

'I'm sorry,' I assured her. 'The last thing I want to do is distress her.'

She shrugged, resignedly, as though to say, 'You cannot help it.'

Out in the road, Tobin took the bag from me and put it in the car. 'There's still an hour at least before dusk. Shall we walk?'

Hand in hand, we went up the road, away from Granburrone, until we came to a footpath leading off on our right into the woods. 'Is this the path that leads to the abbey?' he asked.

'I think it must be.'

It was just wide enough for us to go side by side.

'I managed to get the gist of some of what you were saying,' Tobin said, 'enough to gain the impression that you were basically making polite conversation.'

'What did you think of her?'

He didn't answer my question directly. Instead, he said, 'Underneath the calm exterior, she was very nervous. Did you notice the way she kept fidgeting with her rosary and looking beyond us, as though waiting for somebody to appear?'

'I didn't notice that particularly. But I was aware of her holding back.'

'I think my presence acted as a bar. I shouldn't have come with you.'

'I don't agree. She wanted to see you. It was important for her to know what you were like, just as she did really want to know about our life in England.'

'Mmm, if you say so.'

He lapsed into silence. After a while, the trees thinned out and we found ourselves on the side of the ravine, going along the path Stevie and I had seen from the Abbazia, heading towards the bridge over the waterfall.

We went as far as the bridge, leaning against the wooden balustrade, looking down at the turbulent cascade beneath us, as the sun started to dip behind the Villa Lontana. I shivered, but not from the cold, and Tobin put his arm round my shoulders. 'Yes, there's something eerie about this spot. Let's get back to the car.'

At the Hotel del Lago again, we sat on the balcony and Tobin opened a bottle of wine while I undid the string of my parcel. I unwrapped the brown paper and inside were two thick folders, inside which were—

'Oh, my God, Tobin, look!'

Confronting me were two thick wodges of manuscript in my father's handwriting. On the front sheet of the first folder was written:

The Wishing Cap
A novel by
Connor Moran

The title page in the second folder read:

Italian Nights
Random Sketches
by Connor Moran

A cursory glance at the manuscripts themselves was sufficient to show that they were not going to make easy reading. My father's writing constantly changed in style, from being large and flamboyant – as in his letters to Aunt Biddie – to minute scribbles in which the individual characters were barely decipherable. The pages had obviously been worked over many times, with words crossed out and new ones added. Whole sentences straggled down the margins, circled and affixed to the point where they belonged with arrows. There were whole paragraphs – whole sections even – which were marked as belonging elsewhere. One thing was immediately obvious: my father had not possessed an orderly mind.

Reading a dead man's unpublished novel and memoirs can be few people's notion of the ideal way to spend a honeymoon, but that is what Tobin and I did for most of the next three days. Each morning after breakfast, we went for a stroll or a row, then we sat on the balcony and I started on *The Wishing Cap*, while Tobin read *Italian Nights*. Then we swapped, not giving away anything to the other about the contents of what we had read.

Here is not the place to describe in detail the contents of *The Wishing Cap*. Suffice it to say that the hero was a rumbustious, lusty, bucolic peasant called Fortunatus who is given a magic wishing cap, and that the tale was a fantasy, inspired by the legend of San Fortunato Rocca and an Italian fairy story written in the mid-1500s. It was beautifully written, the style poetic without being flowery. There was only one thing the matter with it: the story finished in mid-paragraph.

Italian Nights was a very different kind of book. It was what it purported to be – a collection of sketches describing incidents which had occurred to my father or others – in a way not dissimilar to my own diary.

There were various references among its pages to Amadore, Bettina and Filomena. Amadore's mother also made appearances; sometimes my father called her *la nonna* – the grandmother – but usually it was *la strega* – the witch. Benedetto and Emilio, however, received only one mention – and the Princess none at all.

My father's greatest friend and companion in San Fortunato seemed to have been a man to whom he referred simply as *il dottore*, with whom he spent many evenings playing chess and indulging in philosophical discussion.

There were vignettes of other local personages, including Don Giovanni, the owner of the Albergo del Lago – as it was then, yet to be promoted to hotel status; a fisherman aptly called Pietro; a rascally poacher named, of all things, Archangelo; Don Matteo, the pious priest at the Church of San Fortunato Rocca; and Suora Serafina, a tender-hearted and hard-working Sister of Charity at the Abbazia e Convent della Madonna della Misericordia.

As the book progressed, the contents changed from rather whimsical anecdotes to more serious accounts of the war, including fulminations against Mussolini, King Victor Emmanuel, Marshal Badoglio, Hitler and the Nazis.

It was after the Italians had changed sides in 1943 and northern Italy was occupied by the Germans, that *Italian Nights* became truly gripping reading. Then it was that Mussolini had set up new headquarters, under the protection of the Nazis, at Dongo on Lake Como. At that same time, the Conte di Montefiore had arrived at his villa also on Lake Como. And at that same time too Emilio Angelini had been killed in combat and Benedetto Angelini sent to a labour camp in Germany. My father shed no tears for either brother.

From the summer of 1943 onwards, my father took an active role in the hostilities. He and *il dottore* formed the *Brigata Cucola* – the Cuckoo Brigade – one of many partisan groups working under the auspices of the underground National Liberation Committee in Turin. The signal between members of the *Brigata Cucola* was the call of the cuckoo. Its task – as my father put it – was to lay exploding eggs in the enemy's nest.

The *Brigata Cucola*'s headquarters was the Villa Lontana and its weapons were stored in the cave where, according to legend, San Fortunato had lived after renouncing all his worldly goods. A veritable arsenal was amassed – revolvers, rifles, submachine guns, mortars and cases of ammunition, some dropped by the Allies, others seized in raids from the Germans and the *Brigata Nera*, as well as canisters of petrol and a walkie-talkie radio.

Often, reading the book, I could not help but be reminded of a gang of schoolboys playing war games – cowboys and Indians, armed with real guns. And the biggest schoolboy of them all was my father – Rosso – the leader of the gang.

Yet the danger they faced was very real. Their principal enemy was the *Brigata Nera*, the Black Brigade – Mussolini's fascist guerrillas, who sought to destroy the resistance movement while the German armies tried to fight back the encroaching Allies. A number of their members were wounded and even killed during sabotage missions, and my father narrowly escaped death on several occasions. If they were captured, they faced being sent to a German concentration camp, or, more probably, summary execution.

There was potential danger, too, from another source – from informers – for there were still fervent supporters of Mussolini in those mountain regions. For instance, while the Abbot and the Mother Superior at the Abbazia gave medical aid and refuge to partisans, escaping prisoners-of-war and Jews, Don Matteo upheld the fascist cause.

Political ideology, however, tended to rank second to personal animosities – to private feuds and vendettas, disputes over property, wives and girlfriends. Recent events had proved to the Italian people, yet again, that today's enemy on the battlefield could be tomorrow's ally. However, turning in a long-standing personal enemy suspected of partisan activities was an excellent way of setting an old score.

Members of the *Brigata Cucola* usually reached the Villa Lontana by means of the Via San Fortunato Rocca – the path to the Abbazia, marked by the saint's fourteen stations of the cross – for this route took them past no human habitation except the abbey and the only perilous moment was when crossing the footbridge. San Fortunato's cave was also safe, for it was hidden deep in the woods belonging to the Villa Lontana and although many people knew of its existence, few – even then – were aware of its exact location.

It was on that bridge – where Tobin and I had stood three evenings previously – that my father nearly lost his life during the very last months of the war. He was bringing two escaped RAF pilots across from the abbey to the Villa Lontana, where the poacher Archangelo – dressed in the captured uniform of an SS officer – was due to meet them and smuggle them over the mountains and across the border in Switzerland.

The two British pilots had fortunately reached the other side but my father was still crossing it, when the bridge blew up – presumably due to a bomb left by the *Brigata Nera.* My father dropped into the icy mountain torrent, where he was thrown downstream and only by a miracle managed to grab hold of a boulder and drag himself to the shore. He caught a chill, which settled on his lungs, already severely weakened by the injury he had sustained in the Spanish Civil War, and turned into double pneumonia.

In *Italian Nights,* he gives credit to Filomena for nursing him through this near fatal illness. Then he writes, 'I must be a cat. If so, and if my tally is right, I have lost eight of my nine lives. But I still have the ninth, which is more than many poor blighters have.'

When Tobin and I had read both manuscripts, we packed them carefully away and, by unspoken mutual consent, left the hotel and set off up the steep Via San Fortunato Rocca towards the Abbazia.

We did not go all the way to the top of the Sacro Monte, but stopped at the eighth station of the cross, where a bench in a sunny clearing gave a view across the ravine to the cuckoo wood.

'Do you feel any better about your father now?' Tobin asked

'Yes, I do and, at the same time, I also feel even more confused. Do you think he saw himself as Fortunatus?'

'Doesn't every novelist put aspects of his own personality into his characters?'

'I don't know. I've never written a novel.'

'Not yet. But you will.' He paused, then went on, 'I have no idea whether either of those books are likely to have public appeal nowadays. It's possible that there have been so many war memoirs written, that no publisher will be interested in *Italian Nights*, although they are memoirs with a difference. But *The Wishing Cap* is another matter. That story is as relevant today as it was when your father wrote it. I'd love to illustrate it.'

He sighed longingly. 'Can't you just see Fortunatus staggering home from the pub lavishly distributing his wealth, riding in his grand carriage – travelling to foreign lands and, all the time, wearing his amazing cap?'

'I didn't know you drew people.'

'I don't know that I can. But I'd love to have a go.'

'Then why don't you? If I typed up the manuscript – which I'd like to do anyway . . .'

'It's going to need more than just typing up. It needs proper editing and it also needs an ending. But you're perfectly capable of doing that.'

'I'm not so sure that I am.'

'Of course you are.' He paused, then went on, 'I have a suggestion to make. Thanks to Ludo Zakharin, we shan't need your redundancy pay for the deposit on Dingle's Gate or any work which needs doing on it. So instead of getting another job once we move, will you please use that money to finance your new career? As I've said before, that's what it was intended for.'

'And if I fail?'

'You could say the same for my illustrations.'

I gazed across to the woods where somewhere was concealed the cave where San Fortunatus had lived as a hermit and the *Brigata Cucola* had concealed their arms during the war.

And then, in a blinding flash, I was struck by the true importance of *The Wishing Cap*, over and above its literary excellence and what it might mean to Tobin's and my personal careers.

There were more than two hundred pages of intensively worked manuscript, the result of months – if not years – of effort. The book stopped in mid-paragraph. It had no ending.

If my father had not been intending to return to San Fortunato after taking me to Avonford, surely he would also have taken his memoirs and his unfinished novel with him? But he hadn't. He had left them at the Villa Lontana.

CHAPTER 27

My letter to Filomena, thanking her for the manuscripts, resulted, two days later, in a telephone call from Lucia, requesting my presence again at the Villa Lontana. From her tone, I knew that she had resisted her mistress every inch of the way.

This time, I went on my own, leaving Tobin on our balcony, with a sketch pad and pencil, drawing fantastical images of Fortunatus.

Lucia again greeted me with pursed lips but saved her admonitions, merely leading me through the white and golden room down to the courtyard garden where Filomena was already waiting in her chair.

She was very pale and her cheek, when I kissed it, cold as marble.

'What was written in Rosso's papers?' she asked.

'You don't know?'

'Rosso didn't tell me – and I cannot read English.'

'One is a story about a man called Fortunatus.' I gave her the gist of the plot and added, 'It was unfinished. And the other was about my father's experiences here at the Villa Lontana during the war – about the *Brigata Cucola*.'

She nodded. 'Tell me exactly what Rosso said.'

I did my best to remember all the details.

'He didn't mention the Princess?'

'No, not once.'

'And where did he finish?'

I described the incident at the bridge but said nothing about his nine lives.

'And, after that, there was nothing more?'

'No, that was the end.'

She shook her head. 'No, that was not the end either.'

For a long time she was silent, then she said, 'I cannot let you go away, yet again, without telling you the truth. Each time I have wanted to before, my courage has failed me. I have not told you lies, but I have allowed you to rest under a great misapprehension. Now, I am still afraid, but, knowing you better, I dare to hope that you will understand. I beg you to listen quietly and, if possible, with compassion.'

I laid my hand on hers. 'Nothing you may tell me will change my affection for you.'

'Wait before you make such a rash promise.'

She fell silent again. I left my hand on hers and looked down towards the cuckoo wood.

Eventually, she continued, 'I described to you how we left Paris in the summer in 1940 and came here to the Villa Lontana. I told you that your father and the Princess were with us. And I told you how the Princess renewed her friendship with the Conte di Montefiore and how, in her absence, your father and I became closer. I told you that I was always in love with your father. All of that was true. But other things happened as well. Many other things.

'To begin with, the war did not really affect us, apart from the fact that Emilio and Benedetto were away fighting in it. From time to time, my parents received letters from them and passed the message to us that our two brave soldiers were well. For ourselves, there were no bombs and no fighting up here in the mountains, so I could not imagine the horrors of war. Remember, there was no television, we never went to the cinema, and I was too young to take in the implications of radio reports. I could not visualize what I could not see. In any case, so much of the news was propaganda. We were told what Mussolini wanted us to believe – that Italy was on the road to victory.

'Sometimes, Rosso would return, very angry, from *il dottore*'s house in the village with accounts of the terrible things that were happening elsewhere in the world. He used to say that *il dottore* was the only cultivated man in the district, the only person with whom he could have a civilized conversation.

'No, for ourselves, our troubles were purely domestic. The Princess was always complaining and my grandmother was always jibing at her and at me. Rosso kept the peace between us. So long as I was with Rosso, I felt secure and happy. I regulated my life around his, so that we did as many things together as was possible. The Princess used to liken me to a puppy dog which follows everywhere in its master's footsteps. She took every opportunity to belittle me and poke fun at me.

'When Rosso worked in the garden, I would find reasons to go and see him – to pick vegetables or take him a glass of water. We would go down to the village together to buy provisions. After he began to work on his book, I would sit with him when he wrote, finding a simple pleasure in watching his face furrowed in thought and his pen forming words on paper.

'I don't believe the Princess was jealous or suspicious of our friendship, so much as resentful that nobody was paying attention to her. And she was very bored with her existence here. Compared to her life in Paris, the Villa Lontana and San Fortunato offered few entertainments. I think she attempted the occasional flirtation but the local men were wary of offending Rosso. He was a big man, with a temper that could flare up. And, although the Princess made herself up to look youthful, she was not. The young men preferred girls of their own age. Most were more interested in me than they were in her, which did not improve her disposition.

'My grandmother was more perspicacious. She made a habit of telling me moral stories about fallen women – from the Bible and from real life. She seldom left the house, but her cronies kept her in touch with everything that happened in Granburrone and San Fortunato. So I heard about this girl or that who had had an affair with a married man or had a baby without being married – and whose father had thrown her out of home as a result. Yes, my grandmother made sure that I was in no doubt about the wages of sin.

'But I had nothing then with which to reproach myself, apart from my growing hatred of the Princess. I tried to overcome this and, every week, when I went to confession, I confessed my feelings about her and Don Matteo made me perform a penance, making me say prayers to the Madonna, asking for her mercy and forgiveness. My love for Rosso, however, was still that of a child for a favourite uncle and I saw no necessity to tell the priest about such an innocent feeling.

'Such was our life, then, until the course of the war changed in the summer of 1943. That was the real beginning of the war for us. After the Germans occupied northern Italy, Rosso and *il dottore* formed the *Brigata Cucola*.

'Sometimes, I helped the *Brigata Cucola* by taking messages to the headquarters of other partisan groups, information that had been received on the *radiotelèfono* or from the Allies, about the progress of the war and German troop movements, as well as instructions about enemy targets.

'Because I was a girl, I could go where I wanted, whereas the men – certainly the younger ones – had to keep themselves concealed. If they were caught by the Germans, they would be sent – like Benedetto – to labour camps in Germany. Nevertheless I still found it frightening. There was no law and the mountains were full of guerrilla fighters, bandits and smugglers.

'On a couple of occasions, we were visited by American and British soldiers, who had been dropped by parachute. Then there would be a fine dinner, with much wine and much laughter. I remember finding it strange to hear Rosso talking in English. With the Princess, he always spoke French, with my grandmother Italian, and with myself either French or Italian. Never before had I heard him speaking in English. It made him seem like a different person, like a stranger.

'My grandmother was very angry about all this and so, too, was the Princess. They blamed Rosso for placing us in great peril. If the *Brigata Nera* or, worse still, the Germans discovered for what purpose our house was being used, we might all be arrested or, worse still, killed. Guards from the *Brigata Cucola* used to patrol the woods and the road outside, but they were amateurs compared to the trained soldiers of the *Brigata Nera* and the German army.

'You did not know who to trust. To many of the people of San Fortunato and Granburrone, Rosso, the Princess and myself were all foreigners and they regarded us with suspicion. There were many incidents when members of the *Brigata Cucola* were ambushed and it was evident that somebody had betrayed them.

'Then a pattern evolved. Every time an attack was made on the *Brigata Cucola*, it happened after the Princess had been on a visit to the Conte di Montefiore. There was a huge argument between Rosso and the Princess, at the end of which she left the Villa Lontana in a furious temper.'

Filomena stopped and raised her eyes to the sky, where the first graceful swallows were swooping and gliding. Then she lowered her head again.

'It was after the Princess had gone to live with the Conte di Montefiore that Rosso and I became lovers. It happened very simply, very easily, as such things do between a man and a woman who have been friends for a long time and trust each other implicitly. My head told me that what we were doing was wrong, but my heart and my body told me that it was right and natural.

'When, the following Sunday, I went to confession, I did not tell Don

Matteo what had happened between Rosso and myself. Perhaps, if we had been in Paris, I would have confessed to a stranger, but Don Matteo was too close an acquaintance and the village too small for me to trust anyone with such a precious secret.

'Possibly my grandmother suspected, but we took every precaution that she should not find out. I would wait until I was sure she was asleep and then I would go to Rosso's room and spend the night with him. That is to say, those nights when he was not away on missions. On such nights, I would stay awake, waiting for the sound of the gate and his footsteps coming through the garden.

'We lived like husband and wife, except that we were not married. But he promised that, when the war was over, he would obtain a divorce from the Princess and marry me. "But first we must win the war," he said. "That is the most important thing. Freedom is more important than anything else in the world."

'To begin with, he was always careful that I should not become with child. But I was only human. I longed to have his baby. That seemed to me the ultimate expression of love. And, also, to be the mother of his child would put me above the Princess, who was incapable of having children. You see, there was something the matter with her that made it impossible.'

For a moment, my heart seemed to stop beating. My grasp on her hand tightened and she glanced at me with mute appeal.

'At Christmas 1944, I became certain that I was with child. To my great relief, Rosso was not angry – indeed, he was very happy – although he was afraid on my account, because of the stigma attached to having an illegitimate baby. On the other hand, both my parents were dead by then, so they could not be upset. As for my grandmother, what could she do, except to say angry words? That left only the Princess and she was living most of the time by then with the Conte di Montefiore.

'For many months, there was no outward sign of my condition. Because I led such an active life, I was very slender and could conceal the bulge of my stomach under my thick winter clothes. But, as my time approached, the secret could be kept no longer. My grandmother was furious, calling me all sorts of names. In no time at all, the news was all round the village. Everyone knew that I was expecting, and they all knew who the father was.

'At the end of April 1945, the fighting stopped. The Germans surrendered. Mussolini and his mistress were seized and hanged. A few days later, my labour pangs began. Rosso took me across the bridge to the nuns at the Convento.

'It was there, on the eighth of May, 1945, that you entered the world as Cara Angelini. We chose to call you Cara because it meant "dear girl" in Italian and because it was also an Irish name, meaning you would go through life, knowing you were held in deep affection, as well as being linked to both your parents.'

She stopped, but only to take a sip of water and regain her breath. I said nothing but looked out across the valley to the Abbazia e Convento della Madonna della Misericordia – to my birthplace . . .

'When I was recovered, Rosso came to bring us home. He carried you in his arms, a look of wonderment and adoration on his face. Never have I known a man react in such a way to becoming a father. He worshipped you from the first moment he set eyes on you. You became the most important thing in his life. If you cried in the night, he would be awake and at your cradle before I was.'

She crossed her hands against her chest. 'To my great shame, I had little milk and so I was unable to feed you for very long. *Il dottore* recommended a wet nurse but Rosso refused to allow any other woman near his daughter. Instead, he paid a fortune for baby milk and food on the black market. He would tell me when it was time for you to be fed and often would give you the bottle himself. He would have liked to have bathed you and changed your napkins as well, but this I would not permit. Such things were not suitable for a man to do.

'In the meantime, he went to the Princess and told her he wanted a divorce. I remember that she came to the Villa Lontana, to take away such of her belongings as were still here. Never had I encountered such malevolence. I had heard speak before of the evil eye, but never had I experienced it.

'But then she was gone from our lives and I believed our troubles were over. Because she wanted to marry the Conte di Montefiore, she had agreed to divorce Rosso and I believed that, in due course, he and I and you would be able to form a proper family. Of course, our marriage would not be recognized by the Church – but I was so much in love with him that I did not care about that.

'For four months, we lived happily and peacefully together. My grandmother was gradually accustoming herself to our situation. Rosso went on with his book and working in the garden. As the result of my father's death, we had a small income, enough to enable us to live in modest comfort. And then Benedetto returned.'

Her voice cracked and she withdrew her hand from mine, letting it flop over the edge of her chair.

Eventually, in a dull, dead tone, she continued, 'Yes, Benedetto came back. How can I describe his return? For three years, he had fought in the war. For two years, he had been a prisoner in East Prussia, working for the Germans in miserable conditions in a munitions factory.

'He had been liberated by the Russians, but the Russians were not in a hurry to send the victims of war back to their homes. Benedetto had gone from a prisoner-of-war camp to one camp after another for refugees and displaced persons. He was in rags. He was tired. He was hungry. And he was angry.

'He was angry about everything. He was angry about the wasted years of his life, about his treatment by the Germans and the Russians, about the volte-face of the King and Badoglio when they turned from being allies of the Germans to being their enemies, about the outcome of the war, about the Russians being among the victors. He was angry about Emilio's death and about the death of our parents. He was angry at the role of the partisans, who had, he claimed, contributed to Mussolini's defeat.

'But his anger at all these things was as nothing compared to his anger at discovering that I had become an unmarried mother. Then his rage exploded. He had known Rosso before the war and, although they had not been such good friends as my father and Rosso, Benedetto had liked him well enough.

'Now you would have thought Rosso was the devil incarnate. He accused Rosso of being a coward, because he had not fought in the war, and a fornicator for having taken advantage of a young girl. It became even worse when he found out about the *Brigata Cucola.*

'It made no difference that the Princess had left Rosso. In Benedetto's eyes, that merely made Rosso less of a man. A real man would have fought back to defend his honour. However, since the Conte di Montefiore had been a staunch supporter of Mussolini – even though he had turned coat when it was obvious that defeat was imminent – in Benedetto's opinion, the Princess was to be forgiven in preferring him to Rosso.

'Not that Benedetto expressed all these feelings coherently and at one time. So consumed was he by his anger, that he was incapable of rational thought. He needed action. He needed to hit out at something. And Rosso and I represented the easiest target. He was encouraged by my grandmother, who was frightened that he might hold her responsible.

'Upon his return, Benedetto became the official head of the household. And, because I was still under age, only twenty, he was my legal guardian. He would not let me keep you. He said you must be sent to an orphanage and that I must go into a convent. He even spoke to Don Matteo and the Mother Superior at the Abbazia.

'Rosso refused to allow you to be sent away. He and Benedetto had a terrible fight. Rosso was the bigger man of the two, but he was also the older, and he had been much weakened by his pneumonia. Benedetto drew a knife – I thought he was going to kill Rosso. But something stopped him. I cannot believe it was conscience, so perhaps it was the fear that, if he killed Rosso, the *Brigata Cucola* would avenge the murder by killing him.

'So Benedetto adopted new tactics. Instead of fighting Rosso, he directed his violence against myself and you. He threatened that if we left the Villa Lontana, he would follow us wherever we went. From then on, the three of us slept together in the same room at night, with the door locked and the windows closed.

'One day, we had left you momentarily unattended and you began to cry. I heard you from the distance and hurried back to you. You were screaming by then. I arrived just as Benedetto was holding you over the edge of the balcony about to fling you down here into the garden. Your screams and my own screams brought Rosso running just in time launch himself upon Benedetto and bring him to the ground, while I snatched you from his hands and saved your life.

'After that, we knew we could no longer remain in the same house as Benedetto. All night, we stayed awake, discussing what we should do. It was not easy. We had little money. Now Benedetto was back my father's money went to him. If we ran away, it would be easy for Benedetto to find us again. He had the law on his side. Rosso was a foreigner. He was easily recognizable. The obvious solution was to go abroad, but I had no passport. When we had come to Italy from Paris, I had travelled on my parents' documents.

'In the end, after great heart-searching, we decided that your safety was supreme. If you were safe, we could better look after ourselves. We had a car and there was still petrol in the cave of San Fortunato. We agreed that, the following night, Rosso would take you in the car across the border into Switzerland and from there on the train to his sister in England.

'In two or three days, he could be back again. He would collect the car from where he had left it and return to Italy. Then he would send me a message telling me where to meet him and he would take me somewhere. For two adults to hide would be easier than with a baby. We would obtain a passport for me and go to join you. Should I fail to receive such a message, I should go each evening at six o'clock to the footbridge over the river.

'Meanwhile, I would pretend to Benedetto that Rosso had deserted me, that he had run away with you without my knowledge. If Benedetto believed that I had been deserted by my lover we thought he would be unlikely to do me any harm.

'So we arranged all our plans. Rosso moved the car and left it in such a position that it would roll down the hill without needing to be started, so that the noise of the engine would not wake Benedetto.

'That night, Rosso left with you. I watched the car roll slowly down the hillside and eventually heard the engine start as he reached Granburrone. Through the trees, I saw the headlights. And then there was nothing. You were gone. I felt as though my heart were breaking but at least I knew you would be safe.

'In the morning, I had to face Benedetto. Instead of triumph at having frightened Rosso away, he felt thwarted at being defeated. First there was a silence, like the silence before a storm. Then the storm broke. He seized hold of me and started to hit me, to punch me on the body and the face. He was like a madman. I succeeded in breaking away and ran out of the house, down the garden and into the woods. He followed me. I didn't think where I was going. I simply ran. And suddenly, I found myself on the edge of the ravine. He caught up with me and in seeking to escape him I fell down the ravine.

'He went away and I remember lying there in terrible pain, my legs crumpled beneath me, thinking he had left me there to die. But eventually he returned with some men from Granburrone. They came down the side of the ravine and managed somehow to lift me out. After that, I do not remember any more until I regained consciousness in a bed in the convent, being tended to by the nursing sisters.

'The story Benedetto had given them was the story I had given him, that Rosso had run away with my baby. In my distress, I had gone into the woods and thrown myself over the edge of the ravine.

'I remained in the convent hospital for many weeks, hovering between life and death. Whenever I regained consciousness, I asked the sisters if they had seen Rosso on the path between the abbey and the Villa Lontana.

'Eventually, my fever left me and I began to regain my strength, only to learn that my accident had left me crippled for life. Nowadays, with modern medicine and techniques of surgery, it is possible that I could have walked again. But, in those months immediately following the war, such surgeons and such operating techniques were not available.

'Every day, I would sit by the window, looking down onto the little footbridge, hoping against hope that, one day, I would see Rosso waiting there for me. The sisters were very kind but it was clear they believed my mind to have become deranged in my misfortune.

'Sometimes, Don Matteo came to visit me. He said that it was solely due to the Madonna della Misericordia that my life had been saved, that she had taken pity upon a poor sinner. He did not realize that without Rosso – and without you – life had lost all meaning for me.

'When I was finally released from the hospital and returned here, to the Villa Lontana, it was to discover that Benedetto had gone to Saronno to work in the silk factory. There was only my grandmother and Lucia, whom Benedetto had hired to keep house for us. Lucia came from Domodossola, which was far enough away for her to be unaware of the scandals which had taken place in our family, and she naturally attributed my state of mind to my accident. Like the sisters, she was very kind and very protective, but she did not understand.

'All Rosso's papers were where he had left them, but nowhere could I find the address of his sister in England. I knew she was married but I did not know her surname or where she lived. Had I been able to walk, I could have come to England and maybe found you, but, as it was, I was a prisoner in my own house. There was nothing I could do.

'It must have been two or three years later, that *il dottore* came to see me, bringing with him a newspaper report of the marriage between the Princess and the Conte di Montefiore. It was stated there that the Princess's former husband had been drowned in 1945 in the English Channel.

Her voice sank to a whisper. 'I assumed that you had died with him, that you were together when his ship sank. All I could do after that was to pray to the Madonna della Misericordia for your two souls. It was like a miracle when the letter arrived from Ludo Zakharin telling me that you were still alive and an even greater miracle when I heard your voice on the telephone – when I heard you say, "I am Cara." And then you were suddenly here with me – looking so like Rosso.'

Her voice trailed off. I knelt beside her, burying my face in her lap, and felt her hands caress my hair.

'Can you forgive me?' she murmured.

'There is nothing to forgive. You could not have acted any differently.'

'I should have told you the truth last year. I was going to, but my nerve failed. You were so certain that the Princess was your mother. And you yourself appeared so poised, so self-assured, so worldly, that it began to seem almost possible to me that you were indeed her daughter. I was so frightened of losing you again and I thought perhaps it was better that you should continue to believe that she was your mother. I hated her, but still she was an aristocrat, related to the Tsar of Russia. Of such a mother you could be proud, whereas of me. . .'

The thought crossed my mind of repeating Sophie Ledoux's story, but I knew it would be wrong. Perhaps, on another future occasion, I would tell her that the Princess had never been a princess, but not now. Now, she needed to hear not another woman's reputation destroyed but to be reassured of her own value.

'I, too, have been afraid,' I said, looking up at her. 'From the first moment I saw you, I hoped that you were my mother. But I dared not let myself hope too much, for fear of being disappointed.'

'Do you mean that?'

'Yes. I could never have loved the Princess. But I have felt a deep, deep affection for you from the beginning.'

'And now?'

'I feel only love.'

At that moment, Lucia came out of the door under the loggia and stood regarding us apprehensively.

'It's all right, Lucia,' I said with quiet authority. 'The Signora is fine.'

Filomena turned her head. 'Yes, Lucia, all is well now. And all will be well from now on. You see—' She paused and then her face broke into a smile – a smile that was dazzling in its radiance. 'You see, I have my daughter back.'

When I left the Villa Lontana, the sun was low in a sky splashed with crimson, amethyst and burnished gold. The bells of the Abbazia e Convento della Madonna della Misericordia were calling the faithful to vespers and the air resounded with the evening song of birds, loudest among them the cuckoos.

I got into the car and drove back down to San Fortunato, where Tobin was waiting for me and, with him, the beginning of the rest of my life.

Author's Note

The Wishing Cap was published in English in 1983, with my father shown as author, and I as editor. Oliver Lyon wrote a foreword and Tobin did the illustrations. A year later, the novel appeared in Italian translation. *Italian Nights* followed in 1985. Both have been reprinted several times and Connor Moran has eventually achieved his rightful place in the literary hierarchy. My own first novel, *A Russian Soul*, was published in 1987, since when I have completed four more historical novels.

Every year in May, we went to stay with Filomena at the Villa Lontana until, in May 1996, our visit had a sadder purpose – to see her laid to rest in the Chiostro del Paradiso at the Abbazia e Convento della Madonna della Misericordia.

Upon our return home, I took The Book and my diary from the drawer where they had been lying dormant and re-read my inexperienced scribblings of long ago. Now Filomena could no longer be hurt, it was a story which could finally be told.

But in writing *The Cuckoo Wood* I had a deeper purpose than merely to inform and entertain. By means of it, I have been trying to say thank you to all the people I love, including Filomena – but most of all to Tobin and to you, dear, darling Aunt Biddie. From the bottom of my heart, thank you for being you.

C.T.
Dingle's Gate
September 1997